The
Last Devil
to Die

ALSO BY RICHARD OSMAN

The Thursday Murder Club

The Man Who Died Twice

The Bullet That Missed

The
Last Devil
to Die

A Thursday Murder Club Mystery

RICHARD OSMAN

PAMELA DORMAN BOOKS / VIKING

VIKING
An imprint of Penguin Random House LLC
penguinrandomhouse.com

First published in hardcover in Great Britain by Viking, an imprint of Penguin Random House Ltd,
London, in 2023

First United States edition published by Viking, 2023

A Pamela Dorman Book/Viking

ISBN 9780593299425 (hardcover)
ISBN 9780593299432 (ebook)

Library of Congress Control Number: 2023939947

Printed in the United States of America
1st Printing

Set in Adobe Jenson Pro
Designed by Cassandra Garruzzo Mueller

To Fred and Jessie Wright, with love and thanks.
You will always be the start of my story.

The
Last Devil
to Die

K uldesh Sharma hopes he's in the right place. He parks up at the end of the dirt track, hemmed in on all sides by trees, ghoulish in the darkness.

He had finally made up his mind at about four this afternoon, sitting in the back room of his shop. The box was sitting on the table in front of him, and "Mistletoe and Wine" was playing on the radio.

He made two phone calls, and now here he is.

He switches off his headlights and sits in total darkness.

It's a hell of a risk, that's for sure. But he's nearly eighty years old, so when better to take that risk? What's the worst that can happen? They find him and kill him?

They would surely do both, but would that be so bad?

Kuldesh thinks about his friend Stephen. How he looks now. How lost, how quiet, how reduced. Is that the future for him too? What fun they used to have, the whole lot of them. The noise they would make.

The world is becoming a whisper to Kuldesh. Wife gone, friends falling. He misses the roar of life.

And then in walked the man with the box.

Somewhere in the distance a faint haze of light plays through the trees. There is engine noise in the cold silence. It is starting to snow, and he hopes the drive back to Brighton won't be too treacherous.

A sweep of light crosses his back windscreen, as another car approaches.

Boom, boom, boom. There's that old heart of his. He'd almost forgotten it was there.

Kuldesh doesn't have the box with him now. It is quite safe though, and that will keep him safe for the time being. That is his insurance. He still needs to buy a bit of time. And if he can, then, well . . .

The headlights of the approaching car dazzle his mirrors, and then switch off. The wheels crunch to a halt, the engine idles, and all is darkness and silence once again.

Here we go, then. Should he get out? He hears a car door close, and footsteps start their approach.

The snow is heavier now. How long will this take? He'll have to explain about the box, of course. A bit of reassurance, but then, he hopes, he'll be on his way before the snow turns to ice. The roads will be deadly. He wonders if—

Kuldesh Sharma sees the flash of the gunshot, but is dead before he can hear the noise.

PART ONE

So What Are You Waiting For?

1.

once married a woman from Swansea," says Mervyn Collins. "Red hair, the lot."

"I see," says Elizabeth. "Sounds like there's quite a story there?"

"A story?" Mervyn shakes his head. "No, we split up. You know women."

"We do know them, Mervyn," says Joyce, cutting into a Yorkshire pudding. "We do."

Silence. Not, Elizabeth notes, the first silence during this meal.

It is Boxing Day, and the gang, plus Mervyn, are at the Coopers Chase restaurant. They are all wearing colorful paper crowns from the crackers Joyce has brought along. Joyce's crown is too big and is threatening to become a blindfold at any moment. Ron's is too small, the pink crêpe paper straining at his temples.

"Are you sure I can't tempt you to a drop of wine, Mervyn?" asks Elizabeth.

"Alcohol at lunchtime? No," says Mervyn.

The gang had spent Christmas Day separately. It had been a difficult one for Elizabeth, she would have to admit that. She had hoped that the day might spark something, give her husband, Stephen, a burst of life, some clarity, memories of Christmas past fueling him. But no. Christmas was like any other day for Stephen now. A blank page at the end of an old book. She shudders to think about the year ahead.

They had all arranged to meet for a Boxing Day lunch in the restaurant. At the last minute, Joyce had asked if it might be polite to invite Mervyn to join them. He has been at Coopers Chase a few months and has, thus far, struggled to make friends.

"He's all alone this Christmas," Joyce had said, and they had agreed that they should ask him. "Nice touch," Ron had said, and Ibrahim had added that if Coopers Chase was about anything, it was about ensuring that no one should feel lonely at Christmas.

Elizabeth, for her part, applauded Joyce's generosity of spirit, while noting that Mervyn, in certain lights, had the type of handsome looks that so often left Joyce helpless. The gruff Welshness of his voice, the darkness of his eyebrows, the mustache and that silver hair. Elizabeth more and more is getting the hang of Joyce's type, and "anyone plausibly handsome" seems to cover it. "He looks like a soap-opera villain," was Ron's take, and Elizabeth was happy to accept his word on the matter.

Thus far they have tried to speak to Mervyn about politics ("not my area"), television ("no use for it") and marriage ("I once married a woman from Swansea," etc.).

Mervyn's food arrives. He had resisted the turkey, and the kitchen agreed to make him scampi and boiled potatoes instead.

"Scampi fan, I see," says Ron, pointing to Mervyn's plate. Elizabeth has to hand it to him, he's trying to help things along.

"Wednesdays I have the scampi," agrees Mervyn.

"Is it a Wednesday?" says Joyce. "I always lose track around Christmas. Never know what day it is."

"It's Wednesday," confirms Mervyn. "Wednesday, the twenty-sixth of December."

"Did you know that 'scampi' is the plural?" says Ibrahim, his paper crown fashionably askew. "Each individual piece is a 'scampo.'"

"I did know that, yes," says Mervyn.

Elizabeth has cracked harder nuts than Mervyn over the years. She once had to question a Soviet general who had not uttered a single word in more than three months of captivity, and within the hour he was singing Noël Coward songs with her. Joyce has been working on Mervyn for a few weeks now, since the end of the Bethany Waites case. She has so far gleaned that he has been a head teacher, he has been married, he is on his third dog, and he likes Elton John, but this does not amount to all that much.

Elizabeth decides to take the conversation by the scruff of the neck. Sometimes you have to shock the patient into life.

"So, our mysterious friend from Swansea aside, Mervyn, how's your romantic life?"

"I have a sweetheart," says Mervyn.

Elizabeth sees Joyce raise the most subtle of eyebrows.

"Good for you," says Ron. "What's her name?"

"Tatiana," says Mervyn.

"Beautiful name," says Joyce. "First I've heard of her though?"

"Where's she spending Christmas?" asks Ron.

"Lithuania," says Mervyn.

"The Jewel of the Baltic," says Ibrahim.

"I'm not sure we've seen her at Coopers Chase, have we?" asks Elizabeth. "Since you've moved in?"

"They've taken her passport," says Mervyn.

"Goodness," says Elizabeth. "That sounds unfortunate. Who has?"

"The authorities," says Mervyn.

"Sounds about right," says Ron, shaking his head. "Bloody authorities."

"You must miss her terribly," says Ibrahim. "When did you last see her?"

"We haven't, just as yet, met," says Mervyn, scraping tartar sauce off a scampo.

"You haven't met?" asks Joyce. "That seems unusual?"

"Just been unlucky," says Mervyn. "She had a flight canceled, then she had some cash stolen, and now there's the passport thing. The course of true love never did run smooth."

"Indeed," agrees Elizabeth. "Never did it."

"But," says Ron, "once she's got her passport back, she'll be over?"

"That's the plan," says Mervyn. "It's all under control. I've sent her brother some money."

The gang nod and look at each other as Mervyn eats his scampi.

"Apropos of nothing, Mervyn," says Elizabeth, adjusting her paper crown just a jot, "how much did you send him? The brother?"

"Five thousand," says Mervyn. "All in all. Terrible corruption in Lithuania. Everyone bribing everyone."

"I wasn't aware of that," says Elizabeth. "I have had many good times in Lithuania. Poor Tatiana. And the cash she had stolen? Was that from you too?"

Mervyn nods. "I sent it, and the customs people nicked it."

Elizabeth fills up the glasses of her friends. "Well, we shall look forward to meeting her."

"Very much," agrees Ibrahim.

"Though, I wonder, Mervyn," says Elizabeth, "next time she gets in touch asking for money, perhaps you might let me know? I have contacts and may be able to help?"

"Really?" asks Mervyn.

"Certainly," says Elizabeth. "Run it past me. Before you have any more bad luck."

"Thank you," says Mervyn. "She means a great deal to me. Been a long time since someone paid me any attention."

"Although I've baked you a lot of cakes in the last few weeks," says Joyce.

"I know, I know," says Mervyn. "But I meant romantic attention."

"My mistake," says Joyce, and Ron drinks to stifle a laugh.

Mervyn is an unconventional guest, but Elizabeth is learning to float on the tides of life these days.

Turkey and stuffing, balloons and streamers, crackers and hats. A nice bottle of red, and what Elizabeth assumes are Christmas pop songs playing in the background. Friendship, and Joyce flirting unsuccessfully with a Welshman who appears to be the subject of a fairly serious international fraud. Elizabeth could think of worse ways to spend the holidays.

"Well, Happy Boxing Day, everyone," says Ron, raising his glass.

They all join in the toast.

"And a Happy Wednesday, twenty-sixth of December, to you, Mervyn," adds Ibrahim.

2.

Mitch Maxwell would normally be a million miles away when a consignment was unloaded. Why take the risk of being in the warehouse when the drugs were present? But, for obvious reasons, this is no ordinary consignment. And the fewer people involved, the better, given his current circumstances. The only time he has stopped drumming his fingers is to bite his nails. He is not used to being nervous.

Also it's Boxing Day, and Mitch wanted to be out of the house. Needed to be out, really. The kids were playing up, and he and his father-in-law had got into a fistfight about where they'd seen one of the actors on the *Call the Midwife: Christmas Special* before. His father-in-law is currently in Hemel Hempstead Hospital with a fractured jaw. His wife and his mother-in-law are both blaming Mitch, for reasons he can't fathom, and so he thought discretion might be the better part of valor, and driving the hundred miles to East Sussex to oversee things himself turned out to be very convenient.

Mitch is here to ensure one simple box containing a hundred thousand pounds' worth of heroin is unloaded from a truck straight off the ferry. Not a lot of money, but that wasn't the point.

The shipment had made it through customs. *That* was the point.

The warehouse is on an industrial estate, haphazardly constructed on old farmland about five miles from the South Coast. There were probably barns and stables here hundreds of years ago, corn and barley and clover, horses' hooves clattering, and now there are corrugated-iron warehouses, old Volvos and cracked windows on the same footprint. The old creaking bones of Britain.

A high metal fence surrounds the whole plot to keep out petty thieves, while, inside the perimeter, the real villains go about their business. Mitch's warehouse bears the aluminum sign SUSSEX LOGISTICS SYSTEMS. Next door, in another echoing hangar, you'll find FUTURE TRANSPORT SOLUTIONS LTD, a front for stolen high-performance cars. To the left is a Portakabin with no sign on the door, which is run by a woman Mitch has yet to meet, but who apparently churns out MDMA and passports. In the far corner of the lot is the winery and storage warehouse of BRAMBER—THE FINEST ENGLISH SPARKLING WINE, which Mitch recently discovered is actually a genuine business. The brother and sister who run it could not be more charming, and had given everyone a crate of their wine for Christmas. It was better than Champagne, and had led, in no small part, to the fistfight with his father-in-law.

Whether the brother and sister at Bramber Sparkling Wine had their suspicions that they were the only legitimate company in the whole compound, Mitch couldn't guess, but they had certainly once seen him buying a crossbow from Future Transport Solutions Ltd and hadn't batted an eyelid, so they were sound enough. Mitch suspected there was good money to be made in English sparkling wine, and had thought about investing. In the end he hadn't taken the plunge, because there was also good money to be made in heroin, and sometimes you should stick to what you know. He's beginning to revise that opinion now, however, as his troubles keep piling up.

The warehouse doors are shut, and the back door of the lorry is open. Two men—well, a man and a boy, really—are unloading plant pots. The minimum crew. Again, because of the current situation, Mitch has already had to tell them to be careful. Sure, the little box hidden deep among the pallets is the most important cargo, but that doesn't mean they can't make a few quid off the plant pots too. Mitch sells them to garden centers around the South East, a nice legitimate business. And no one is going to pay for a cracked plant pot.

The heroin is in a small terra-cotta box, made to look old, like a tatty piece of garden junk, in case anyone comes snooping. A boring ornament. It's their regular trick. Somewhere in a farmhouse in Helmand, the heroin has been placed in the box, and the box has been wedged shut. Someone from Mitch's organization—Lenny had drawn the short straw—had been in Afghanistan to oversee it, to make sure the heroin was pure and no one was trying to pull a fast one. The terra-cotta box had then made its way in Lenny's care to Moldova, to a town that knew how to mind its own business, and there it had been carefully concealed among hundreds of plant pots and driven across Europe, by a man called Garry with a prison record and not much to lose.

Mitch is in the office, on a makeshift mezzanine level at the far end of the warehouse, scratching the "God Loves a Trier" tattoo on his arm. Everton are losing 2–0 to Man City, which is inevitable but still annoying. Someone had once asked Mitch to join a consortium to buy Everton Football Club. Tempting, to own a piece of his boyhood club, his lifelong passion, but the more Mitch looked into the business of football, the more he thought, once again, that he should probably stick to heroin.

Mitch gets a text from his wife, Kellie.

Dad's out of the hospital. He says he's going to kill you.

This would be a figure of speech to some, but Mitch's father-in-law is the head of one of Manchester's largest gangs, and once bought Mitch a police-issue Taser as a Christmas present. So you had to be careful with him. But doesn't everyone have to be careful with their in-laws? Mitch is sure it'll be fine—his marriage to Kellie had been the love that conquered all, the Romeo and Juliet who had united Liverpool and Manchester. Mitch texts back.

Tell him I've bought him a Range Rover.

There is a hollow knock at the flimsy office door, and his second-in-command, Dom Holt, comes in.

"All good," says Dom. "Pots unloaded, box in the safe."

"Thanks, Dom."

"You wanna see it? Ugly-looking thing."

"No thanks, mate," says Mitch. "This is as close as I ever want to get."

"I'll send you a picture," says Dom. "Just so you've seen it."

"When's it heading out?" Mitch is aware that they are not yet home and dry. But his big worry had been customs. Surely it was safe now? What else could go wrong?

"Nine in the morning," says Dom. "The shop opens at ten. I'll send the boy over with it."

"Good lad," says Mitch. "Where's it going? Brighton?"

Dom nods. "Antiques shop. Geezer called Kuldesh Sharma. Not our usual, but the only one we could find open. Shouldn't be a problem."

Man City score a third goal, and Mitch winces. He switches off his iPad—no need for any further misery.

"I'll leave you to it. Better head home," says Mitch. "Could your lad nick the Range Rover parked outside the Sparkling Wine place and drive it up to Hertfordshire for me?"

"No problem, boss," says Dom. "He's fifteen, but those things drive themselves. I can drop the box off myself."

Mitch leaves the warehouse through a fire exit. No one but Dom and the young lad has seen him, and he and Dom had been at school together, been expelled together, in fact, so no worries there.

Dom had moved to the South Coast ten years ago after setting fire to the wrong warehouse, and he looks after all the logistics out of Newhaven. Very useful. Good schools down here too, so Dom is happy. His son just got into the Royal Ballet. All turned out nicely. Until the last few months. But they're across it. So long as nothing goes wrong with this one. And, so far, so good.

Mitch rolls his shoulders, getting ready for the journey home. His father-in-law won't be happy, but they'll have a pint and watch a *Fast & Furious* and all will be well. He might get a black eye for his troubles—he's got to give the guy a free punch after what he did—but the Range Rover should placate him.

One little box, a hundred grand in profit. Nice work for a Boxing Day.

What happens after tomorrow is not Mitch's business. His business is to get the box from Afghanistan to a small antiques shop in Brighton. As soon as someone picks it up, Mitch's job is done. A man, maybe a woman, who knows, will walk into the shop the next morning, buy the box and walk out. The contents will be verified, and the payment will hit Mitch's account immediately.

And, more importantly, he'll know that his organization is secure again. It's been quite a few months. Seizures at the ports, arrests of drivers, arrests of errand boys. That's why he's kept this one so quiet, talking just to the people he can trust. Testing the waters.

From tomorrow, he hopes he will never have to think about the ugly terra-cotta box again. That he can just bank the money and move on to the next one.

Had Mitch looked over the road to his left as he was leaving the business park, he would have seen a motorcycle courier parked up in a lay-by. And the thought might then have occurred to him that this was an unusual place at an unusual time on an unusual day for the man to be parked there. But Mitch doesn't see the man, so this thought does not occur, and he drives merrily on his way back home.

The motorcyclist stays where he is.

3.

Joyce

Hello again!

I didn't write in my diary yesterday because it was Christmas Day, and it all caught up with me. It does, doesn't it? Baileys and mince pies and television. The flat was a bit too hot, according to Joanna, and then, once I'd done something about it, a bit too cold. Joanna has underfloor heating throughout, as she isn't shy of reminding you.

The decorations are up all around me, making me smile. Reds and golds and silvers glinting off the lightbulbs, cards on the walls from friends old and new. On top of my tree (it's not real, don't tell anyone, it's John Lewis and you wouldn't honestly know the difference), an angel Joanna made at primary school. It's a toilet roll, some aluminum foil, lace and a face drawn on a wooden spoon. It's been on top of the tree for forty-one years now. Half a lifetime!

For the first four or five years Joanna was so proud and excited to see her angel on top of the tree, then there were two or three years of increasing embarrassment, leading to, I'd say, thirty years of outright hostility toward the poor angel. In the last few years, though, I've noticed there has been a thawing, and this year I came back into the room with Jaffa cakes on a plate to find Joanna touching the angel, tears in the corners of her eyes.

Which took me by surprise, but, then, I suppose it's been there almost a whole lifetime for her.

Joanna came down with her beau, Scott, the football chairman. I had been expecting to go to theirs—Joanna's house looks so lovely and Christmassy on Instagram. Flowers and bows, and a real tree. Candles too close to the curtains for my liking, but she's her own woman.

Joanna left it until December 20th to announce they would be spending Christmas at mine, and told me not to worry about food, as they'd be bringing everything down, all precooked, from some restaurant in London. "No need for you to cook a thing, Mum," she had said, which was a shame, as I would have looked forward to cooking.

Why were they at mine? Well, they were flying out to St. Lucia on Christmas evening and, at the last minute, their flight had been changed from Heathrow, near them, to Gatwick, near me.

So I was convenient. Which is the best you can ask for sometimes, isn't it?

Let me tell you something else, while it's on my mind. We had goose for Christmas dinner. Goose! I said I had a turkey and I could put it on, but Joanna told me that goose is actually more traditional than turkey, and I said, My foot is goose more traditional than turkey, and she said, Mum, Christmas wasn't invented by Charles Dickens, you know, and I said, I knew that very well (I wasn't really sure what she meant, but I sensed the argument was slipping away from me, and I needed a foothold), and she said, Well, then, goose it is, and I said, I'll get the crackers, and she said, No crackers, Mum, it's not the eighties. Other than that it was a nice Christmas, and we watched the King's speech even though I knew Joanna didn't want to. In truth I didn't really want to either, but we both knew I was due a victory. I thought Charles did a good job—I remember my first Christmas without my mum.

Joanna bought me a lovely present: it's a flask they use in space, and it has *Merry Christmas, Mum! Here's to no murders next year* engraved onto it. I wonder what they made of that in the shop? She brought flowers too, and the football chairman bought me a bracelet that I would describe as a nice thought.

It's lovely to open presents though. I bought Joanna the new Kate Atkinson book, and some perfume she had emailed me the name of, and I bought the football chairman some cufflinks, which I suspect he would also describe as a nice thought. I always put the receipts in with things. My mother used to do the same. But I don't imagine he'll be taking them back, as they were from the M&S in Brighton, and he always seems to be either in London or Dubai.

Lunch with the gang today, so I finally managed to have my turkey and crackers. I insisted. You could see Elizabeth beginning to object to both, but she thought better of it, so I must have looked determined. However, I made what I suspect was an error by inviting Mervyn to join us. I keep thinking he's going to melt, but I fear I might be barking up the wrong tree with this one. I just hope I can bark up the right tree one of these days. Before I run out of trees. Or before I stop barking altogether.

We retired to Ibrahim's flat afterward, and Mervyn headed home. He revealed he has an online girlfriend, Tatiana, who he has never met but seems to be funding nonetheless. Ibrahim says Mervyn is a victim of "romance fraud" and is going to speak to Donna and Chris about it. When do the police start work again after Christmas? Gerry used to go back somewhere around the 4th of January, but the police are probably different to West Sussex County Council.

I will detail the presents we all bought each other.

Elizabeth to Joyce—A foot spa. The one they advertise on TV. I am in it now. My feet anyway.
Joyce to Elizabeth—M&S vouchers.

Elizabeth to Ron—Whisky.

Ibrahim to Ron—An autobiography of a footballer I hadn't heard of. Not David Beckham or Gary Lineker.

Ron to Elizabeth—Whisky.

Joyce to Ron—M&S vouchers.

Ibrahim to Elizabeth—A book called *The Psychopath Test*.

Elizabeth to Ibrahim—A painting of Cairo, which made Ibrahim cry, so they have obviously had a conversation at some point that I wasn't party to.

Joyce to Ibrahim—M&S vouchers. And this was after Elizabeth's present, so I felt I could have done better.

Ibrahim to Joyce—M&S vouchers. Phew!

Ron to Joyce—*The Kama Sutra*. Very funny, Ron.

Ibrahim to Alan—A telephone that squeaks.

Alan to Ibrahim—A clay tablet with Alan's paw print on it. Ibrahim cried again. Yes!

Ron to Ibrahim—A fake Oscar statue with *My Best Mate* on it. Which set us all off.

We drank, we had a little singalong—Elizabeth doesn't know the words to "Last Christmas," if you can believe that? But then I suppose I don't know the words to "In the Bleak Midwinter." We listened to Ron rail against the monarchy for about twenty-five minutes, and then we went our separate ways.

When I got back I unwrapped a present that Donna had sent me, which was lovely of her, as I don't really know how much police constables earn. It was a little brass dog, which, if you squint, looks a bit like Alan. She bought it at Kemptown Curios in Brighton. It's run by Stephen's friend Kuldesh, who helped us in our last case. Sounds like my type of place. Perhaps I'll visit, because now I have to buy Donna something in return. I do like having people to buy for.

So, all in all, I've had a lovely Boxing Day, and am going to fall asleep in front of a Judi Dench film. All that's missing is Gerry working his way through a tin of Quality Street and leaving the wrappers in the tin. Irritating at the time, but I'd give everything I own to have him back. Gerry liked the Strawberry Delights and Orange Crèmes, and I liked the Toffee Pennies, and if you want to know the recipe for a happy marriage it is that.

Joanna gave me a big hug when she left and told me she loved me. She may be wrong about turkey and crackers, but she still has a few tricks up her sleeve. What is it about Christmas? Everything that's wrong seems worse, and everything that's right seems better.

My lovely friends, my lovely daughter. My husband gone, his silly smile gone.

I feel like I should drink to something, so I suppose let's drink to "No murders next year."

4.

Kuldesh Sharma is glad that Christmas is over. Glad to be back in his shop. Lots of the other small businesses in the area were shut for the duration, but Kuldesh was opening Kemptown Curios bright and early on December 27th.

He is dressed up for the shop, as always. Purple suit, cream silk shirt. Yellow brogues. Running a shop is theater. Kuldesh looks at himself in an antique mirror, nods his approval and takes a small bow.

Would anyone come in? Probably not. Who needed an Art Deco porcelain figurine or a silver letter opener two days after Christmas? No one. But Kuldesh could have a little spruce-up, rearrange some bits and bobs, trawl the online auctions. Basically, he could keep himself busy. Christmas Day and Boxing Day pass very slowly when you are by yourself. There is only so much reading you can do, so many cups of tea you can make, before the loneliness crowds in around you. You breathe it in, you cry it out, and the clock ticks slowly, slowly, until you are allowed to sleep. He hadn't even dressed up on Christmas Day. Who was there to dress up for?

The hardware store opposite is open. Big Dave who runs it lost his wife to cancer in October. The coffee shop further down the hill is also open. It is run by a young widow.

Kuldesh sips his cappuccino in the back office of his shop. He only opened up a matter of minutes ago, and he is taken by surprise when he hears the jingle of the shop bell.

Who has come calling, at such an hour, on such a day?

He pushes himself out of his chair, his arms doing the work his knees used to, walks through the office door into the shop and sees a well-dressed, powerfully built man in his forties. Kuldesh nods, then looks away, finding something he can pretend to be busy with.

You must only ever *glance* at new customers. Some people want eye contact, but most do not. You must treat customers like cats, and wait for them to come to you. Look too needy and you'll scare them off. If you do it right, the customers end up thinking you are doing them some sort of favor, allowing them to buy something in your shop.

Kuldesh doesn't have to worry with this particular customer though. He's not a buyer, he's a seller. Close-cropped hair, expensive tan, teeth too bright for his face, as seems the fashion these days. And in his hand a leather holdall that looks more expensive than anything in the shop.

"You the guy who owns this place?" A Scouse accent. Unafraid. Threatening? A touch perhaps, but nothing that scares Kuldesh. Whatever is in that expensive bag will be interesting, Kuldesh knows that. Illegal, but interesting. See what he would have missed if he'd stayed at home?

"Kuldesh," Kuldesh says. "I trust you had an enjoyable Christmas?"

"Idyllic," says the man. "I'm selling. Got a box for you. Very decorative."

Kuldesh nods; he knows the score. Not really his racket, this, but perhaps all the regular places are shut until New Year. Still, no need to give in without a fight.

"I'm not buying, I'm afraid," he says. "No room for anything—got to clear some stock out first. Perhaps you'd like to buy a Victorian card table?"

But the man isn't listening. He places the bag, carefully, on the counter and half unzips it. "Ugly box, terra-cotta, all yours."

"Traveled a long way, has it?" Kuldesh asks, taking a peek inside at the box. Dark and dull, some carving hidden by a layer of grime.

The man shrugs. "Haven't we all. Give me fifty quid, and a lad'll be in early tomorrow morning and buy it off you for five hundred."

Is there a point in discussing it? In arguing with this man? Attempting to send him on his way? There is not. They have chosen Kuldesh's shop, and that is all there is to it. Give the man his fifty, keep the bag under the counter, hand it over in the morning and don't lose any sleep thinking about what's in the box. This is just how things are done sometimes, and it's best to play nice.

Either that or you'll get a petrol bomb through your front window.

Kuldesh takes three tens and a twenty from the till and hands them to the man, who quickly buries them deep in his overcoat. "You don't look like you need fifty pounds?"

The man laughs. "You don't look like you need five hundred, but here we both are."

"Your overcoat is exquisite," says Kuldesh.

"Thank you," says the man. "It's Thom Sweeney. I'm sure you know this already, but if that bag goes missing someone will kill you."

"I understand," says Kuldesh. "What is in the box, by the way? Between you and me?"

"Nothing," says the man. "It's just an old box."

The man laughs again, and this time Kuldesh joins him.

"God speed, young man," says Kuldesh. "There's a homeless woman on the corner of Blaker Street who might appreciate that fifty pounds."

The man nods, says, "Don't touch the bag," and disappears through the door.

"Thank you for calling," says Kuldesh, noting that the man is heading down the hill in the direction of Blaker Street. A motorcycle courier passes in the opposite direction.

An interesting start to the morning, but many interesting things happen in this business. Kuldesh had recently been involved in tracking down some rare books and catching a murderer with his friend Stephen and Stephen's wife, Elizabeth. Elizabeth runs a "Murder Club," of all things.

This box will be in new hands tomorrow, and the whole episode will be forgotten, just one of those things that happens in a trade that is not always beyond reproach.

Trinkets and trouble, that was the antiques business.

Kuldesh lifts the bag onto the counter and unzips it again. The box has a sort of squat charm, but is not the sort of thing he could sell. He shakes it. It is certainly full of something. Cocaine or heroin is his best guess. Kuldesh scrapes some dirt from the lid. What is this worthless box now worth? More than five hundred pounds, that is for certain.

Kuldesh zips the bag up and puts it under his desk in the back room. He will Google the street price of heroin and cocaine. That will make the day go a little quicker. He will then lock the bag in his safe. It would be a very bad day for a burglary.

5.

ervyn, there isn't an easy way to say this. Tatiana isn't real." Donna holds out a comforting hand for Mervyn to take, but it remains untaken, as Ibrahim could have told her. Mervyn is not one of life's hand-takers. He lives life at a safe distance.

They have asked Donna to visit Mervyn's flat, to have a chat about his apparent new love, Tatiana. Joyce felt that a police officer might make more of an impact on him, though something in Mervyn's eyes at the Boxing Day lunch had told Ibrahim that very little ever had an impact on Mervyn.

Mervyn gives a little smile. "I'm afraid I have photographs and emails to suggest otherwise."

"I wonder if we might take a look at those photographs, Mervyn?" Elizabeth asks.

"I wonder if I might look at your personal emails?" Mervyn replies.

"I wouldn't recommend it," says Elizabeth.

"I know it's difficult," says Donna. "And I know it might feel embarrassing—"

"Not embarrassing in the slightest," says Mervyn. "You couldn't be further from the truth there. You're miles from the truth, my love."

"But perhaps a misunderstanding?" says Joyce.

"A crossing of wires? Simply that," says Ibrahim.

Mervyn shakes his head in amusement. "It might be unfashionable, but I have a little thing called faith, which, I venture, is undervalued these days. In the police force, and elsewhere."

Mervyn looks at the whole gang as he says this.

"I know that the four of you are very much the 'cool kids' around here, I get that . . ."

Ibrahim notes that Joyce looks thrilled.

". . . but you don't always know everything."

"I keep telling them that, Merv," says Ron.

"You're the worst of them," says Mervyn. "If it wasn't for Joyce, I wouldn't put up with any of you. I gave up Boxing Day lunch to keep you lot company, don't forget that."

"It was greatly appreciated, Mervyn," says Elizabeth. "And, I agree, we are flawed, as individuals, and as a group, and, in my view, you are probably right to single out Ron as the worst of us. But I believe Donna would like to show you a few things that might sway you."

"I will not sway," says Mervyn.

Donna turns on a laptop and starts the business of opening some windows.

"It is very kind of you to visit us on your day off," says Joyce.

"Not at all," says Donna.

"Do you know Donna arrested someone on Christmas Day?" Joyce tells Mervyn. "I didn't know you could do that."

"What was it?" asks Ron. "Reindeer rustling?"

"Soliciting a sexual act," says Donna.

"At Christmas," says Joyce, shaking her head. "You'd think people would be too full."

Donna has found what she is looking for, and she angles the screen toward Mervyn. "Now, Mervyn, Joyce forwarded me a photograph of Tatiana that you sent her—"

"Did she indeed?"

"I did," says Joyce. "Don't act irked. You only sent it to me to show off."

"Male vanity," agrees Ibrahim, glad to have something to add.

"She's a cracker," says Ron. "Whoever she is."

"She is Tatiana," says Mervyn. "And your opinions are unwelcome."

"Well, that's just it," says Donna. She shows Mervyn his photograph on her computer screen, next to another identical photograph. Same woman, same photograph. "You can do a reverse-image search of any photograph on the internet, so I did that with your photograph of Tatiana, and you'll see that, far from being a photograph of somebody named Tatiana, the photograph is actually of a woman named Larissa Bleidelis, a Lithuanian singer."

"So Tatiana is a singer?" says Mervyn.

"No, Tatiana isn't real," says Donna.

They can all see that this is as clear as day, but Mervyn is having none of it.

As Ibrahim listens, he thinks this is like trying to talk to Ron about football. Or about politics. Or about anything else. Mervyn calls this new theory "preposterous." He even calls it "poppycock," which, Ibrahim judges, is as close to swearing as Mervyn would ever go. Mervyn fights, says he has plenty more photographs, private messages, proclamations of love. The lot. He even keeps them in a file, which makes Ibrahim warm to him slightly more.

Joyce takes the baton now. "Have you ever heard of something called 'romance fraud'?"

"No, but I've heard of love," says Mervyn.

"There's a television program all about it," continues Joyce. "It's on after *BBC Breakfast.*"

"I don't watch television," says Mervyn. "I call it the gogglebox."

"Yes, I think lots of people do," says Elizabeth. "You didn't invent that expression."

"This is a tangent," says Ibrahim. "And I mean nothing by it, but a surprising number of serial killers don't own a television."

Joyce's dog, Alan, is licking Ibrahim's hand, a favorite hobby of his. The others see it as a bond between the two of them, without realizing that Ibrahim always keeps a Polo mint in his pocket, after discovering Alan has a fondness for them.

Donna opens another window on the laptop, and more photos appear. "The fraudsters use the same photos over and over again. There's a Canadian pilot, there's a lawyer from New York, there's Larissa, and plenty of others like her. The romance-fraud gangs just pass them around. The look they like is beautiful but unthreatening."

"That's the look *I* like," says Joyce.

Donna shows Ibrahim the pilot and Ibrahim could see the appeal. Very steadfast.

Mervyn is still unmoved, and protests that he has been speaking to Tatiana for five or six months. Many times a day.

"Speaking?"

"You know, writing, same thing," says Mervyn.

Ibrahim can imagine the lonely man filling his hours. No one calling, no one needing him.

Joyce then points out to Mervyn that he has also sent Tatiana five thousand pounds, and he blusters that of course he has, and that if someone you love needs a new car, say, or a visa, you help out. That this is simply manners.

"You'll all see," he adds. "She's coming over on January the nineteenth and, when she does, there will be plenty of humble pie eaten in Coopers Chase. Apologies will be expected."

Everyone feels it is best to leave it there for now, and they gather up their things and start the walk back to Joyce's with a quandary to consider. Elizabeth heads home to Stephen, so Joyce takes the opportunity to ask Donna about her Christmas with Bogdan.

"And is he tattooed everywhere?"

"Pretty much, yes," confirms Donna.

"Even . . . ?"

"No, not there," says Donna. "Joyce, has anyone ever called you a pervert?"

"Don't be such a prude," says Joyce.

Ibrahim wonders what they should do about Mervyn. He was a difficult man, that much was certain, and he had come into their orbit only because Joyce couldn't resist a deep voice and a sense of mystery. But he was a lonely man, and he was being taken advantage of. And, besides, it might be nice for the Thursday Murder Club to have a new project that moved at a gentler pace than usual. Something a bit less *murdery* would be quite a novelty.

6.

Samantha Barnes is drinking a late-night gin and tonic and adding Picasso's signature and an edition number to some pencil drawings of a dove. Samantha has signed Picasso's name so often over the years that once, by accident, she signed it instead of her own on a mortgage-application form.

Her mind is wandering. This is the fun part of the job. This, and the money.

Forging a Picasso is a lot easier than you'd think. Not the big paintings, sure, that takes a skill Samantha doesn't have, but the sketches, the lithographs, the stuff people will buy online without looking too closely—that's a breeze.

There is money in real antiques, of course there is, but there is a lot more money in fake antiques. In fake furniture, in fake coins, in fake sketches.

Let's say Samantha buys a mid-century Arne Vodder desk for £3,200, and sells it for £7,000; her profit is £3,800, very nice, thank you.

However, if Samantha pays £500 to a man called Norman, who works out of an old dairy shed in Singleton, to knock up an exact replica of an Arne Vodder desk, and then sells it for £7,000, her profit is £6,500. You, as her Garth insists on saying, do the maths.

Equally, if Samantha spends her evening forging limited-edition Picasso lithographs, as she has been doing this evening, after coming home from Bridge Club, her cost of materials might be £200 or so, but, by the time she's sold them all online to people from London who like the idea of having

Picasso's signature on their wall, and aren't too fussy about the provenance, her profit will be about £16,000.

All of which goes to explain why Samantha Barnes no longer has a mortgage.

She starts taking photographs of the Picassos for her online store. She'll advertise them for £2,500, and she'll happily take £1,800.

Samantha used to be legit, she really did. Back when it was her and William. Their little shop in Petworth, their trips around the country building their stock, their loyal customers, the haggling, all good fun, all mildly profitable. But, as they got older, the shop grew too familiar, it closed in on them. What was once cozy and safe became constraining, like a childhood home. The trips around the country became chores, the same faces selling the same porcelain cats.

So they started to play little games, Samantha and William. Sam and Billy. Purely for fun, nothing else. One must get through the day, mustn't one? And one particular game led her to exactly where she is now. And where is she now? Pretending to be Picasso while listening to the *Shipping Forecast*, in the finest house in West Sussex.

She often thinks back to how it all started.

William brought home an inkwell, a duff, dull runt among a haul of goods he'd picked up on Merseyside. They were about to throw it away when William suggested a bet. William bet that he could sell the worthless inkwell for £50 before Samantha could. Not to any of their regulars of course, and not to anyone who looked like they couldn't afford it, but just as a bit of sport between the two of them. They shook on their bet and continued unpacking the real antiques.

The next day William had put the inkwell in its own locked glass display case, and with a tag saying, *Ink stand, possibly Bohemian, possibly eighteenth century, please inquire about price. Serious offers only.*

Was this naughty? Yes, a bit. Should they have done it? No, they shouldn't have, but they were bored, and in love, and they were looking to entertain each other. It's not one of the worst crimes you could commit in the antiques business. As Samantha knows well, having now committed them all.

Regulars would come in, take a look at the case and ask what was special about the ordinary-looking inkwell. Samantha and William would give a little shrug—"Probably nothing, just a hunch"—but all parties soon forgot about it. Until three weeks later when a large Canadian man, who had parked in the accessible space outside the shop, bought it for £750. "He haggled me down from a thousand," William had confided.

Samantha signs another Picasso and lights a cigarette. Two things there, smoking and wide-scale forgery, that she didn't do before Garth. But the cigarette smoke is actually rather good for aging the paper.

They repeated the "inkwell" trick a few times. A broken clock, a vintage-style plate, a one-armed teddy bear. The "antiques" went to grateful homes, and the money, most of it anyway, to charity. They would eagerly riffle through job lots of antiques to pick out the new challenge: the next occupant of the glass display case with the lock. A secret game between the two of them.

And then William died.

They were on holiday, in Crete. He went out swimming after lunch, and was carried away by the tide. Samantha returned to England with the coffin in the hold, and was dragged away by a tide of her own.

She spent her next few years too sad to live but too scared to die, reeling through a haze of grief and madness, always quick with a cup of tea and a smile for her customers, accepting their well-meaning sympathies, playing bridge, tending the shop, reciting from memory the pleasantries and the platitudes, while hoping every day might be her last.

Then one morning, three years or so after William had died, the large Canadian man who had bought the inkwell came back into her shop, with a gun.

And everything changed again.

She hears Garth coming through the door now. Even though he is able to be quiet, he chooses not to be.

It's the middle of the night, and she wonders where he has been, but it doesn't really do to ask sometimes. You must let Garth be Garth. He has never let her down yet.

He will see that her studio light is on, and he will be up with a whisky and a kiss for her before long.

A couple more Picassos and she will call it a night.

7.

Joyce

OK, I have a riddle for you.

How can you celebrate New Year's Eve with your friends, and still get to bed early?

Because I have done just that this evening.

We've had the most wonderful New Year's Eve bash. We drank, we counted down to midnight and watched the fireworks on TV. We sang "Auld Lang Syne," Ron fell over a coffee table, and we all went home.

So a very happy New Year to one and all and, best of all, it is still only ten p.m., so I can get into bed at a reasonable hour.

And here's how.

There is a lovely man called Bob Whittaker from Wordsworth Court—not my type, before you get ideas—and he was something in computers, before everyone was something in computers. He eats lunch by himself, but is very approachable. Last year he built a drone and flew it over Coopers Chase and invited us all into the lounge to watch the film. It was wonderful—he'd even put music on it. You could see the llamas and the lakes, and you could see that the Ocado delivery vans had OCADO written on their roofs—they really have thought of everything. I think that was in the summer, before the first murder, but you lose track, don't you? After the film he gave a talk about drones, which was less well attended but, according to Ibrahim, very good.

So this was Bob's idea. He hired out the lounge, and the big screen, and everyone was invited. In the end there must have been about fifty of us. Sometimes when you're in a group like that you really see how old you are, like walking through a hall of mirrors.

We all brought along food and, mainly, drink, and watched some episodes of *Only Fools and Horses* that Bob had illegally downloaded.

Then, at about 8:50, Bob switched the screen to a Turkish television channel, where they were counting down to the New Year three hours ahead of us. I don't know where he found it, on the internet, I imagine. They would have Turkish television there, wouldn't they?

They had music, dancers, and a host who we couldn't understand, but you absolutely knew the type, so you had a rough idea of the sort of thing he'd be saying. A countdown clock appeared on the screen—Turkish numbers are the same as ours—and a brass band started playing the Turkish national anthem or something similar. When it reached "10" we all joined in counting down; and, as it hit nine p.m. here it hit midnight in Turkey and they set off the fireworks and we all hugged and cheered and wished each other a Happy New Year. A rock band started playing on the TV so Bob turned it down, and Ron started "Auld Lang Syne" and we linked arms and thought of old acquaintances, and thanked our lucky stars for seeing another New Year. Ten minutes or so later, we drifted home, New Year celebrated and ready for an early night.

To look at Bob in the restaurant, or wandering through the village, you might dismiss him as boring. He is quiet and shy, and is always in a gray jumper over a stiff white shirt. But this man had the wherewithal to give us all a wonderful evening. To be able to get Turkish TV on an English telly, and also to have the kindness to understand how much everyone would enjoy it, well, that takes quite a man.

And I know what you're thinking, but, again, he's not my type. I wish that he was.

I texted "Happy New Year" to Joanna, and she texted back "HNY," as if the effort of spelling out the words was a bit too much. I texted "Happy New Year" to Viktor too, and he texted back "May you be granted health and wealth and wisdom, and may you see your beauty reflected in those around you," which was much more like it. I then raised a glass to Gerry, as I always do.

I also raised a glass to Bernard, here last New Year, and gone now. We won't all be here this time next year, that's just the facts of the matter. Those at the back of the line will fall, and no one will tell you where you are in the line. Though at my age I have a rough idea. As Ibrahim always says, "The numbers don't look good."

There are plenty of things to look forward to though, and that's the key. What's the point of another year if you don't fill it? I am looking forward to Donna's scheme to help Mervyn, even if I've rather given up on Mervyn himself. Why can't Bob from Wordsworth Court have Mervyn's eyebrows and his deep voice, and why can't Mervyn have Bob's kindness and cleverness? I'm so shallow, I wish I wasn't.

When I think about it, Gerry had kindness and cleverness *and* eyebrows, so perhaps you are only gifted one of those men in a lifetime?

I can hear Alan's tail thumping against the leg of my desk, even though the man himself is fast asleep.

A very Happy New Year to you. May you see many more.

8.

The victim is a man called Kuldesh Sharma, and the body has been here for some days. An antiques dealer from Brighton. The car had been found at around six thirty this morning, by a local man walking his dog. Walking his dog in the dark on New Year's Day? I mean, sure, mate, whatever you say. Not Chris's problem though—he has a corpse to deal with.

And so here they are. It's so nearly a lovely view, thinks Chris, his breath frosty in the early-morning air.

A narrow, deeply pitted track cuts through the Kent woods, ridged with frost, ending at a wooden fence, penning in winter sheep. A scene from across the centuries, unbroken for generations. Silver-white branches reach out overhead, latticing a brilliant blue sky.

It might be a Christmas postcard, but for the extreme violence.

Chris has had a few days off over Christmas. Patrice had come down from London, and Chris had cooked her a turkey, which was much too big and had taken far too long to cook, but which seemed to be greatly appreciated. Briefly, possibly during *The Sound of Music*, with Patrice in tears, Chris had been tempted to propose, but bottled it at the last moment. What if she thought it ridiculous? Too soon? The ring remains in his jacket pocket at home. There for when the courage strikes.

Donna had been at work. Christmas at the station is often quite good fun though. Mince pies, the odd arrest, double pay. She had joined them in the evening, with Bogdan. Chris had suddenly panicked that Bogdan might have proposed. And with a nicer ring? But that really would be too soon.

The frost crunches underfoot.

If the birds had been disturbed by the gunshot, their disturbance was long forgotten, and their happy noise echoes above. Even the sheep are back about their business. It is serene and peaceful, and the pure-white overalls of the forensic officers shine in the low winter sun. Chris and Donna duck under the police tape and walk toward the small car, plump and berry-red in this Christmas grotto.

The track is off a lane, which is off a hedge-canyoned road, which meanders slowly and peacefully from a Kent village. The village itself was so beautiful that Chris had been surfing Rightmove up to the moment they finally reached the scene. £1.8m for a farmhouse. The village was described as "tranquil."

Even the finest estate agent in Kent would be hard-pressed to describe it as that today.

"Mum said you had no Quality Street?" says Donna. "The whole Christmas?"

"No Quality Street, no Terry's Chocolate Orange, no Baileys," says Chris. The foods of Christmas Past. Ghosts to him. On the plus side, he almost has abs now.

"I can't believe you didn't propose though," says Donna.

"Early days," says Chris. "And I'd have to buy a ring first."

The smell hits them before anything else. The best estimate was the body had been here since late on the 27th. Five days ago now. Chris and Donna reach the car. A forensic officer named Amy Peach greets them.

"Happy New Year," says Amy, carefully placing a bloodied headrest into a plastic container.

"Glad tidings," says Chris. "This is Mr. Sharma?"

"According to his heavily embossed business card," says Amy. "And his monogrammed handkerchief."

The bullet had passed straight through the driver's-side window, and then straight through the skull of poor Kuldesh Sharma. The blood spattered on the passenger-side window had long since formed into rosé ice crystals in the brutal cold.

Chris can see by the frozen tire marks that there had been two cars here. Two cars had pulled up down this quiet track, leading to nowhere, a few days after Christmas. For what reason? Business? Pleasure? Whichever it was, it had ended in death.

Judging by the tire marks, Chris concludes one car had reversed back out, business over, back to life. The other had reached its final destination.

He surveys the scene. Fantastically secluded. No one for miles around. No CCTV en route—you couldn't pick a better spot for a murder. He looks at the car window. The single gunshot.

"Looks professional," he says. Donna is staring at the body. Has she spotted something that Amy Peach has missed?

Chris and Amy Peach had once shared a drunken night together after a colleague's leaving party, and neither of them had been at their brilliant best. Amy had been sick on Chris's sofa, but only because Chris had fallen asleep on the bathroom floor, wedging the door shut. They have been quietly awkward around each other ever since. No one would ever know, but their mortified dance would no doubt continue until one of them retired, or died. Better that than ever mentioning it.

"That's your job, not mine," says Amy. "But you're right that it's very clean."

Amy is now married to a solicitor from Wadhurst. Chris eventually had to get rid of the sofa altogether.

Further back up the lane, casts of the tire tracks, preserved in the ice, are being taken as pattern evidence. If this was a professional job, these would lead to nothing. A stolen car wiped of prints would eventually surface somewhere. Left in a car park with no security cameras. Or crushed by the local friendly wrecker's yard. Chris had learned a long time ago never to assume, but this has all the hallmarks of a falling-out between drug dealers.

Actually, not all the hallmarks. Drug dealers important enough to be killed would usually be driving a black Range Rover, not a red Nissan Almera. So perhaps there was more to this than met the eye.

"I met him," says Donna.

"Kuldesh Sharma?"

"When we were investigating the Viking," says Donna.

"Jesus," he says. "So recently?"

Donna nods. "Met him with Stephen. Elizabeth's husband."

"Of course you did," says Chris. "Maybe we can keep Elizabeth and the gang out of this one?"

"Ah," says Donna. "The impossible dream. He was a nice guy. Did you really buy my mum gardening gloves for Christmas?"

"That's what she said she wanted," says Chris.

Donna shakes her head. "Every time I think I've got you trained up, I realize how far we've got to go."

They walk back along the track together. Donna is deep in thought.

"You thinking about Kuldesh?" Chris asks. "I'm sorry."

"No," says Donna. "I'm thinking, what's the deal between you and the forensic officer?"

"The deal? Nothing," says Chris. "We're colleagues."

Donna waves this away. "Sure, to be discussed."

"Not a word of this to Bogdan, by the way," says Chris. "He'll only tell Elizabeth."

"I promise," says Donna. "If you promise me there was never anything between you and the forensic officer."

9.

They shot him in the head," says Bogdan, hunched over the chessboard. "A single bullet." Today is a good day. Stephen remembers him, and Stephen remembers chess. A nice start to the year.

"Awful," says Stephen. "Poor Kuldesh."

"Awful," agrees Elizabeth, walking into the room with two teas. "Bogdan, I've given you only five sugars, you should cut down. New Year's resolution. Any suspects?"

"Donna says was professional," says Bogdan. "A hit."

"Hmm," says Elizabeth, and turns to her husband, happy to see the spark in his eyes, so often missing now. "Kuldesh the type to get mixed up in things?"

Stephen nods. "Oh, absolutely. Kuldesh? Absolutely. I saw him the other day, you know?"

"We saw him together, Stephen," says Bogdan. "He was very helpful. Very nice gentleman."

"Whatever you say, old chap," says Stephen. "Always up to something though."

"And they'd broken into his shop too?" says Elizabeth. "Did I hear that correctly? Before or after they'd killed him?"

"After they killed him, says Donna."

"Didn't find what they were looking for," says Elizabeth. "Still, strange to kill him. What else did Donna have to say for herself?"

"I'm not allowed to tell you," says Bogdan. "Is police business."

"Nonsense," says Elizabeth. "Won't do any harm to have another brain on the job. Any witnesses at the shop? CCTV?"

Bogdan holds up a finger. "Wait!" He takes out his phone, scrolls to a voice note and presses play. Donna's voice fills the room.

"Elizabeth, hello, it's Donna here. I know that Kuldesh was a friend of Stephen's, hello, Stephen by the way—"

"Absolute cracker, that one," says Stephen.

"Bogdan is under the strictest instructions not to share details of this case with you, so please don't play your usual tricks—"

"Tricks . . ." says Elizabeth, offended.

"He is aware of the consequences for him if he chooses to tell you details of the case. You are a woman of the world, Elizabeth, and you can probably guess what those consequences are . . ."

Stephen raises an eyebrow at Bogdan, and Bogdan nods in confirmation.

". . . so I would be enormously grateful if you could just let us get on with our job. Love to everyone, bye for now!"

Bogdan puts down the phone and gives Elizabeth an apologetic shrug.

"Bogdan, she's bluffing. If I were having sex with you, I would be shooting myself in the foot to withdraw it, look at you. No offense, Stephen."

"Oh, none taken," says Stephen. "Look at the man."

"I gave my word," says Bogdan. "Is my bond."

"God, men can be so noble when it suits them," huffs Elizabeth. "Bogdan, will you be here for the next couple of hours?"

"I can be," says Bogdan. "Where are you going?"

"I'm going to pick up Joyce, and pay a visit to Kuldesh's shop. I don't see that I have an alternative."

"You could just leave it to Donna and Chris?"

"Honestly," says Elizabeth, pulling on her coat. "What a perfect waste of everyone's time."

"Darling, you will enjoy it," says Stephen.

"That is beside the point," says Elizabeth.

"Give Kuldesh my love," says Stephen. "Tell him he's an old dog from me."

Elizabeth walks over to her husband and kisses him on the top of the head. "I will, my darling."

10.

Kuldesh's shop is unrecognizable. Ransacked, smashed to pieces. Someone was looking for something, and hadn't been in a good mood about it. Donna doesn't want to think too much about everything that must have been lost here. She wants to think happier thoughts.

"Any resolutions?" she asks Chris. Donna's New Year's resolution is to pretend to learn Polish, putting in just enough effort for Bogdan to understand when she eventually gives up.

"I'm going to go sea-swimming every day," says Chris. "Unbelievably good for you. Circulation, joints, the lot."

"You'll never do that every day," says Donna.

"You underestimate me," says Chris. "Big mistake."

"You're going to go sea-swimming today?"

"Well, no, not today," says Chris. "We're working, aren't we?"

"Did you go yesterday?"

"We were uncovering a murder scene, Donna," says Chris. "So no. But every other day I will."

They walk through to the back office, also upended: they find drawers pulled out, papers strewn across the floor and a large, green floor safe forced open.

"Jesus," says Donna. In her mind she can still see the corpse of Kuldesh Sharma, in his suit, silk shirt unbuttoned rakishly low. In truth she had recognized him from behind, that shiny head still intact. Last time Donna had seen him—and indeed the first time—had been in this very shop, with

Bogdan and Stephen, asking for his help in tracking down some rare books. Was Kuldesh dodgy? Certainly. Involved in drugs? Donna couldn't see it. But here they were, in a smashed-up shop, investigating his very professional murder.

Subtle signs that perhaps he was involved in *something*.

"Someone was looking for something, eh?" says Chris.

"And after they killed him too," says Donna. The local police had been called to the shop at around noon on December 28th—hours after someone had put a bullet through Kuldesh's head. Donna thinks about the statue Bogdan had bought for her. The statue Kuldesh had ended up giving him for a pound in the name of love. Does that make the statue bad luck? Donna hopes not.

Christmas with Bogdan had been everything she could have hoped for and more. Well, maybe not everything: his present to her had been quad-bike lessons.

"So someone arranges to meet Kuldesh," says Chris.

"Kuldesh has something for them, they have something for Kuldesh. Money, let's assume." Donna is now flicking through a book of receipts.

"The cars drive down the lane, pull up. Our killer walks out of their car, one bullet through the window, then picks up whatever Kuldesh has for them?"

"Except he doesn't have it, it's not in his car. He's kept it back here. For insurance."

The receipts show that Kuldesh's shop was very quiet on the 27th. Three sales. A lantern, seventy-five pounds in cash; an "unsigned seascape," ninety-five pounds on the credit card of a "Terence Brown"; and "assorted spoons" for a fiver.

Donna spots a mobile phone wedged behind a radiator. She wonders why Kuldesh hadn't taken it with him, then remembers he is eighty. Either way, he has gone to the trouble of hiding it, so perhaps it contains something of interest. She eases it out and places it in an evidence bag.

Of course Kuldesh might have sold any number of things off the books. CCTV would give them a better idea. Though if that CCTV was linked to Kuldesh's hard drive, they are out of luck, as it lies smashed to pieces next to the empty safe.

"So the question is, what were they looking for? What did Kuldesh have?"

"And," says Donna, looking at the empty safe again, "did they find it?"

As they walk out of the office, Donna looks at the cameras rigged up inside the shop. They seem serious, and she hopes they are backed up somewhere other than on the shattered computer in the office.

She hears familiar voices outside. Chris has heard them too.

"Shall we?" Donna asks.

"I suppose we'll have to," says Chris.

11.

Elizabeth and Joyce have been unable to get inside Kuldesh's shop. The police tape was still wrapped across the front, and large boards had been nailed across the broken windows. This being Brighton, the boards had already been graffitied with the words WATCH CAPITALISM BURN and plastered with flyers for the seafront nightclubs. Elizabeth tries to get some purchase under one of the boards, but no luck.

"You should have brought an ax," says Joyce. "I could just see you with an ax."

"Don't be facetious, Joyce," says Elizabeth.

Joyce looks up and sees CCTV cameras.

"CCTV cameras!"

"Contain your excitement," says Elizabeth. "Anyone professional enough to kill a man with a single bullet through a car window is professional enough to disable a CCTV camera. We're not dealing with children."

Donna and Chris emerge from a side alley.

"Can I help you, ladies?" asks Donna. "We're from the police, we investigate crime for a living, how lovely to meet you."

"Window shopping," explains Elizabeth.

"Happy New Year!" says Joyce. "Thank you for my brass dog, Donna."

"My pleasure," says Donna, then turns to Elizabeth. "I thought I was quite polite when I asked you to leave it to us? Polite for me at least?"

"Impeccably polite," agrees Elizabeth. "I was very proud of you."

"And yet"—Chris gestures to the two women, and to the ransacked shop—"here we all are."

"I realized I had never been to Kuldesh's shop," says Elizabeth. "I thought I should put that right. Donna, you have been recently, of course, with Bogdan and Stephen. That was an unauthorized little adventure, so I thought I might have one of my own."

"I don't think Stephen needs you to authorize his adventures," says Donna.

"I meant you and Bogdan, dear," says Elizabeth.

"I don't think I need—"

"And I do like antiques," says Joyce. "Gerry collected horseshoes. He had seven or eight of them by the end."

"Well, as ever, you seem to attract corpses," says Chris.

"Always have," says Elizabeth. "They seem drawn to me. Any luck with the CCTV?"

"Too early to tell," says Chris. "Also none of your business. Choose whichever answer you prefer."

"My view," says Joyce, "is that anyone professional enough to kill Kuldesh with a single gunshot in a country lane is also professional enough to disable the CCTV."

"That's your view, is it, Joyce?" asks Elizabeth.

Joyce is now staring at a colorful nightclub flyer pasted onto the wooden boards. "I wonder what 'Ket Donk' is?"

"I think there's a café further down the road," says Chris. "You might like that."

"Ooh, a café," says Joyce.

"We're working, Chris," says Elizabeth. "Stephen's friend has been murdered. You think you can palm us off with a café?"

"We're working too," says Chris. "It's our actual job. I'm sure you understand."

"I understand perfectly," says Elizabeth. "We shall let you get on. Will you let us know if you find anything?"

"I don't work for you, Elizabeth," says Chris.

"Sorry," says Donna. "He finds you quite emasculating. Even I do—I don't know how that works. Perhaps just let us deal with this one."

"As you wish," says Elizabeth. "We don't always have to share."

Elizabeth slips her arm through Joyce's and leads her down toward the café.

"You took that lying down," says Joyce. "I thought you'd kick up more of a fuss."

"I noticed the café on the way up," says Elizabeth. "Cakes in the window . . ."

"Wonderful," says Joyce. "I haven't eaten since elevenses."

". . . and a CCTV camera outside."

Joyce smiles at her friend. "Something for us both, then?"

"Quite so," says Elizabeth. "And we've just agreed that we don't always have to share."

12.

Connie Johnson unwraps her Christmas present from Ibrahim. It is a small, black leather-bound notebook.

"You often see it on television, don't you?" says Ibrahim. "Drug dealers like to keep notebooks. Numbers and transactions and so on. You can't trust computers, because of law enforcement. So when I saw it I thought of you."

"Thank you, Ibrahim," says Connie. "I would have bought you something, but all you can buy in prison is Ecstasy and SIM cards."

"Not at all," says Ibrahim. "Besides, you are not supposed to buy presents for your therapist."

"And are therapists supposed to buy notebooks for drug dealers?"

"Well, it was Christmas," says Ibrahim. "Although if you really wanted to give me a present, there are a couple of questions I might ask you?"

"I'm guessing not questions about my childhood?"

"Questions about a murder. Elizabeth made me write them down." Yesterday's meeting of the Thursday Murder Club had been an absolute barnstormer. In Ibrahim's view it had really done exactly what it said on the tin. "I promise we will get to your childhood in time."

"Go on," says Connie Johnson.

"Let me describe a scenario," says Ibrahim. "We are at the end of a remote country lane, in deep woodland. It is late at night. There are two cars."

"Dogging," says Connie.

"Not dogging, I think," says Ibrahim. "The driver of Car A, an antiques dealer . . ."

"The worst," says Connie.

". . . remains in his seat, while somebody from Car B walks up to the window and fires a bullet through his head."

"One shot?" asks Connie. "Kill shot?"

"Kill shot," confirms Ibrahim. He enjoys saying it.

"This is good," says Connie. "Let's talk about my childhood another time."

"Car B disappears, back whence it came . . ."

"No one else I know says 'whence,'" says Connie.

"Then you must widen your social circle," says Ibrahim. "Some hours later, the shop belonging to the antiques dealer is burgled."

Connie nods. "OK, OK."

"No useful prints, either at the scene or at the shop."

"There wouldn't be," says Connie, making a note in her new book.

"Oh, I'm so happy to see it's already useful," says Ibrahim.

"CCTV though?"

"None at the shop, but at a café down the hill, at which Joyce says there were excellent macaroons, CCTV captures a man in an expensive overcoat. We know about this, but the police, as yet, don't."

"Big surprise there," says Connie.

"He comes in to eat and has a conversation with the lady who runs the café. Louise, if you need her name."

"I don't," says Connie. "When I need information I'll ask."

"The good news is that Louise said she prefers not to speak to the police because Covid was a hoax," says Ibrahim. "Words to that effect. Now, while we don't know for certain that he had been to the antiques shop, that *is* the direction he came from, and he had fifty pounds or so in cash in his pocket, which he took out when he paid, so Louise surmised that he might have done. I'm led to believe that people rarely pay in cash these days."

"It's a nightmare," says Connie. "Even I have to take Apple Pay now. Did he have an accent, the man?"

"Liverpudlian," says Ibrahim. "From Liverpool."

Connie nods again. "You know you overexplain sometimes?"

"Thank you," says Ibrahim. "The prevailing wisdom, which one must not always follow, but occasionally it prevails for good reason, is that this murder carried the hallmarks of a professional execution, and I was wondering if that was something on which you might have a view?"

"I do have a view, yes," says Connie. "You came to the right woman. Country lane, one shot, professional hit. Antiques dealer, perfect fence for stolen goods if nothing else is available. You promise the police don't have this information yet?"

"They remain clueless," says Ibrahim.

"OK, then well-dressed Scouser suggests a man called Dominic Holt, runs heroin through Newhaven. Lives down here now, house by the sea. They'll have used the shop as a drop-off: 'Look after our heroin for twenty-four hours,' that sort of thing. Dom Holt wouldn't normally do a delivery himself, but we all get careless."

"Does he have a boss?" Ibrahim asks.

"Another Scouser, Mitch Maxwell."

"And are they the type to murder someone?"

"Oh, God, absolutely," says Connie. "Or the type to hire someone else to murder someone."

"Same thing," says Ibrahim.

"Uh, not really," says Connie. "Killing someone and hiring a hitman to kill someone are completely different."

"OK, well, we will cover this in our session," says Ibrahim. "Because it is very much the same thing."

"Let's agree to disagree," says Connie.

"Do you know where I might find them, this Dominic Holt and Mitch Maxwell?"

"Yes," says Connie.

"Would you care to elaborate?"

"No, I think I can leave the rest up to you," says Connie. "You tell me an antiques dealer is murdered on the day he gives cash to a sharp dresser from Liverpool. I tell you heroin, and the names Dominic Holt and Mitch Maxwell. Anything further is grassing, Ibrahim. You're not the only one who swears an oath."

"I don't think you swear an actual oath," says Ibrahim. "And Dom Holt is not a rival of yours?"

"No, he's a heroin dealer; I'm a cocaine dealer."

"Do the worlds not intersect from time to time?"

Connie looks at Ibrahim as if he is mad. "Why on earth would they? Christmas drinks maybe. Not this year of course."

Ibrahim nods. "But if I find out more information, would you like to be kept informed?"

"Very much," says Connie. "Shall we get on with the session? I've been thinking about my dad, like you asked."

Ibrahim nods again. "And are you angry?"

"Very," says Connie.

"Splendid," says Ibrahim.

13.

Joyce

In the Coopers Chase newsletter, *Cut to the Chase*, they often have the names of new residents moving in. They have permission from the people of course, and it can be a nice way of introducing yourself to the community before you turn up with the removal van. It gives us a chance to be nosy too.

Anyway, there is a man moving in next week called Edwin Mayhem.

Edwin Mayhem!

It must be a stage name, mustn't it? Perhaps he was a magician or a stuntman? Or a sixties popstar? Either way he would be a good subject for my "Joyce's Choices" column. This month I interviewed a woman who swam the Channel, but they forgot to time her so she had to do it again a month later. She still swims now, in the pool.

I shall certainly be beating a path to Edwin Mayhem's door. I'll give him a couple of days to settle in, get his furniture how he likes it, and I'll be round with a lemon meringue and a notepad.

It is late, and I'm looking out of the window at the lights going off in random windows. There are a few of us still awake though. Coopers Chase looks like an advent calendar.

I had a Cadbury's advent calendar this year, and I sent one to Joanna too, at the end of November. Joanna says that Cadbury's have changed the way they make their chocolate and she won't eat it, but I can't taste any difference. She used to love a Dairy Milk, she really did, but you'd wait a long time to hear that from her now. Perhaps next year I'll get her an advent calendar full of diamonds or hummus.

I am looking at my flask now. *Here's to no murders next year.* That would have been nice. Or would it? I'm beginning to forget what I did before all the murders started happening. I remember I was going to learn to play bridge, but that's gone on the back burner. I've also got more episodes of *Morse* backed up on my Sky Plus than I know what to do with. Poor Kuldesh though.

There are so many ways to die when you're almost eighty, it seems unfair to add murder to the list. They shot him, so he'd obviously upset someone. I asked Elizabeth how she knew all the details, and she said she's on a WhatsApp group that gets to hear things. I have only recently discovered WhatsApp groups. I'm in the "Dog Walkers" group and the "Local Celebrities Seen in Kent" group. I have had to mute the "Things My Grandchildren Say" group, because I think it is mainly showing off. An eight-year-old saying, "Granny, you look like a princess"? I'm sorry, I don't believe it. I know I shouldn't be so cynical.

Our first line of inquiry in the murder is a man named Dominic Holt. He runs a company called Sussex Logistics on an industrial estate conveniently near to all the big ports, so the day after the funeral Ibrahim is going to drive us down there and we shall see what there is to see. Like a stakeout. Elizabeth will be the brains, Ibrahim will be the driver, and I'll be in charge of snacks. Ron complained that he wouldn't have anything to do, but Elizabeth says he's there to add color, and that seemed to placate him.

Ron has been grumpy, or grumpier, for the last week or so. He had a row with Pauline at Christmas. He won't tell me what it was about, but Ibrahim says it was to do with when you're supposed to open presents.

Ron said it's straight after breakfast, but Pauline said not till after lunch, and the whole thing got heated. When Ibrahim went round there on Christmas evening they wouldn't even play charades with him, and Ron knows that Ibrahim loves to play charades, so it must have been serious. I remember Ibrahim once mimed *Fifty Shades of Grey* for Elizabeth, and you've never seen anything like it.

Ibrahim had Christmas dinner alone, which he says is how he likes it. I had invited him to mine—there was more than enough goose to go around—but he said he doesn't really buy into Christmas. It's too sentimental. It's worth noting, though, that when he came over to take Alan for a walk, he was wearing a Santa hat.

Elizabeth had stayed in with Stephen, of course. I got very little out of her, except that she gave some turkey to the little fox that has taken to visiting them. They call him "Snowy" because he has white tips to his ears. When he lies on the ground he thinks he is camouflaged, but his little ears always give him away. He comes a bit nearer to their patio every day. He'll be out there now, somewhere in the dark.

I will see them all at Kuldesh's funeral tomorrow. We didn't really know him, but he had no family left, so you want to fill the pews out a bit, don't you? You'd want someone to do it for you.

So much for "no murders," Joanna, although I will be using my flask tomorrow. Crematoriums are often very drafty.

14.

It's eight thirty a.m., January 4th, and the troops have been told to gather in the Incident Room at Fairhaven police station to discuss their progress on the murder of Kuldesh Sharma.

Chris should be out front, giving orders, discussing theories, in charge of the marker pens and the whiteboard, but this morning had brought a surprise.

A surprise in the form of Senior Investigating Officer Jill Regan of the National Crime Agency, who, it has become clear, is now in charge of the murder inquiry—for reasons none of them have yet been able to fathom.

An antiques dealer from Brighton has been murdered in Kent. What has that got to do with the National Crime Agency, and with SIO Jill Regan?

She is currently writing on Chris's whiteboard, with Chris's pens. Donna can feel Chris bristle.

"So what do we have?" says Jill Regan. "We have the square root of absolutely nothing. Just over a week since the murder, and we have no clues, certainly no evidence, and we have"—Jill looks slowly around the squad assembled in the room—"no intelligence."

"She's a charmer," Donna whispers to Chris.

Jill continues. "We've no CCTV from the shop—no use crying over it. The track marks from the lane led us nowhere—when do they ever? No fingerprints, no useful DNA, no eyewitnesses, and I'm in a room full of coppers sitting on their arses."

"You told us to sit down?" says Donna.

"I'm being metaphorical, if you've ever heard of it," says Jill. "Four days, no progress. That stops now. At midday, I have a team arriving from the NCA, and you will be relieved of duty. This room will be out of bounds. My office—Chris, I have authority to use your office—will also be out of bounds. Any questions?"

Chris starts to raise his hand. "Yeah, just—"

"I'm joking," says Jill. "No questions. Thank you all for coming in early. Please find some other crime to solve, if you have any down here."

The team begin to disperse, some glad of the opportunity for a quiet day. Chris hangs back, so Donna also chooses to.

"What's going on?" Chris asks Jill.

"Nothing," says Jill. "That's just the problem."

Chris shakes his head. "Nope. Something's up. A murder in Kent, and they call in the NCA?"

"I don't know what to tell you, Chris," says Jill.

"Do you need a briefing from me? Everything we know so far?"

"No, thank you," says Jill. "We're fine. A bit of peace and quiet is all we need. Give us the chance to do our job. Did you find his phone?"

"Whose phone?" says Chris. "Kuldesh's?"

"Wow," says Jill. "What a razor-sharp mind. Yes, Kuldesh's."

"Didn't have it on him," says Chris.

"Didn't find it in the shop?"

"If we'd found it in the shop, it would have been logged into evidence, ma'am," says Donna. She was supposed to log it in yesterday, but the evidence store was unmanned. Donna is thankful for police underfunding for once.

"Is it an organized crime thing?" guesses Chris. "Crosses over with an international drugs case you're already investigating?"

"If that were the case, I wouldn't tell you, would I?" says Jill. "Now, I'm sure you've got things to be getting on with."

"Not really," says Donna. "Someone near Benenden has had a horse stolen."

"Then investigate that," says Jill. "I don't want to see either of you anywhere near this Incident Room. DCI Hudson, they've found a temporary office for you in the Portakabin in the car park. Off you toddle."

"And we just stop our investigation of Kuldesh Sharma's murder?" says Chris.

"Leave it to the professionals," says Jill. "You track down that poor horse."

Sensing this might be a battle best left for another day, Donna ushers Chris out, and follows him down the main stairwell of the station.

"What do we make of that?" he says.

"Surely no one's that obnoxious in real life?" says Donna.

"Just what I was thinking," says Chris. "That's someone who really, really wants to be left alone. But why?"

"There's something about the murder she doesn't want us to know?"

Chris nods. "Feels like that's something we should investigate, doesn't it?"

"First things first," says Donna. "I'll head down to my locker and get Kuldesh's mobile phone."

Chris nods again. "We'll just put a quick trace on his calls. And then we can get straight on that horse theft in Benenden."

15.

There are only two rows of seats filled at the funeral. Kuldesh had not been a practicing Hindu, or indeed a practicing anything, and the only instructions he had left were that he would like a simple cremation, presided over by the local vicar his late wife had once met, and very much liked, on a Speed Awareness course ("John something, from Hove, I'm sure you can look him up").

In the front row sit Joyce, Elizabeth, Ron and Ibrahim. In the row behind them are Chris, Donna, Bogdan and a man in a hat who has thus far only introduced himself as Big Dave. The vicar, surprised to be there at all, is trying his best.

"Kuldesh was a shopkeeper, a man who loved antiques. He was from Brighton, so he must have loved the sea . . ."

Elizabeth decides she can probably skip this bit and turns to the row behind to address Chris.

"Let's share information," she whispers.

"We're at a funeral," Chris whispers back.

"He lived in a bungalow in Ovingdean," the vicar continues. "Kuldesh was clearly not a man who enjoyed stairs—"

"OK," says Chris, nodding to Elizabeth. "You go first."

"I think our information is better than your information," says Elizabeth. "So, with respect, you go first."

"Thank you for your respect," says Donna.

"She is right, in this instance," says Ibrahim, turning to join the conversation. "We have a big piece of the puzzle that you don't have."

"Is that right?" says Chris. "I'll take my chances. We're progressing quite nicely."

"If you could all join me now in prayer," says the vicar. "If Kuldesh was a man of faith, he kept that faith quietly, but you never know. Our Father . . ."

As the vicar continues his prayer, Elizabeth and Chris continue their whispered conversation, heads now bowed.

"CCTV come good?" asks Elizabeth. "You know who visited Kuldesh on the day he died?"

"Not yet," says Chris.

"Interesting, because we do."

"No, you don't," says Donna, eyes still closed and hands clasped together. "They're bluffing, Chris."

"Amen," says everyone together as the prayer finishes.

"And now," continues the vicar, "do please join me in a moment of silence as we remember our friend Kuldesh Sharma. Or just keep whispering away to each other. You knew him better than I did, though I did like his wife when we met."

Chris gives it a couple of beats, then gets back to business.

"Honestly," says Chris. "We've got this one. It's only been five days. We've got a team on it, a good team, all with decent intelligence, and we've got forensics going over everything. Whatever's happened here, we'll solve it. Not by magic but by hard work."

"So you spoke to Louise at the café?" asks Joyce, finally joining in. "That's good."

"To . . . who?" says Chris, momentarily off guard.

"Louise," says Elizabeth. "The lady who runs the café down the road? The one where you sent us to get us out of the way? You spoke with her?"

"Yes," says Donna. "I did speak with her. That's what the police do."

"That's the trouble though, isn't it," says Elizabeth. "Not everyone trusts you, heaven knows why. I think you do a terrific job, few bad apples of course, but not everyone holds the same view. So perhaps she might have been more forthcoming to a couple of older women enjoying a cup of tea and a slice of cake?"

"A macaroon, actually," says Joyce. "Details, Elizabeth."

"And now," says the vicar, "I believe a friend of Kuldesh's would like to say a few words. Bogdan Jankowski."

Joyce claps her delight as Bogdan walks to the front. No whispering from anyone now. Bogdan tests the microphone with his index finger. He is satisfied with the acoustics.

"Kuldesh was a good man," says Bogdan. "And not everyone is a good man."

"Hear, hear," says Ron.

"He was kind to me, and kind to Donna, and he was good friends with Stephen," says Bogdan. "I asked Stephen to tell me about him. Stephen says he was kind and loyal. That he would be called names in the street and keep on walking. Stephen says he was a piece of work, but in a good way. Always laughing, always helping. So I want to say this, in front of God . . ."

Bogdan looks at the tiny congregation before him.

"Kuldesh, you were a friend of Stephen's, and that means you are a friend of ours. And I promise we will find the person who shot you. We will hunt them down and kill them—"

"Or arrest them, babe?" suggests Donna.

Bogdan shrugs. "Kill them or arrest them. Thank you, Kuldesh. Please rest now." Bogdan crosses himself.

As he returns to his seat, Big Dave gives a whoop, and that leads everyone into a round of applause.

The ceremony continues with a little more reverence, even tears from Joyce, Bogdan and Ron.

As it ends, the vicar has a few final words. "I feel I've been a little surplus to requirements today. But I wish you all luck, and I do wish I had met him. Farewell, Kuldesh."

The mourners start to file out.

"What did this Louise tell you?" Chris asks Elizabeth.

"Forgive me," says Elizabeth. "I thought we weren't sharing information? Here are the facts of the matter. We have an eyewitness description of a man who visited Kuldesh Sharma on the day he died. Do you?"

Chris and Donna look at each other, then shake their heads.

"Furthermore, we have been given a name fitting that precise description, and that name was given to Ibrahim by one of the leading drug importers on the South Coast—"

"Whom I am unable to identify," says Ibrahim.

"Do you have a named suspect?" asks Elizabeth.

Chris and Donna look at each other once more, and shake their heads again.

"And, lastly, I am told that the National Crime Agency have taken over your investigation, so this bravado of yours is only for show. Which is perfectly understandable, but does slow things up."

"How do you—" starts Chris, but Elizabeth waves this away.

"Whatever case you are currently working on," she says, "it is not the murder of Kuldesh Sharma."

"Someone stole a horse in Benenden," says Donna.

"Ooh," says Joyce.

"So we have a great deal of information," says Elizabeth. "Do you have anything for us in return?"

Donna pulls a phone out of her bag. "We have his phone, Elizabeth. We shouldn't, but we do."

"Sweet," says Ron.

Elizabeth claps her hands. "Wonderful, Donna, wonderful. Bogdan is very lucky to have you. I'm sorry if I was overbearing. I will work on that. Our assumption is that a shipment of heroin was delivered to Kuldesh's shop by a Dominic Holt, and that Kuldesh, for reasons best known to himself, decided to steal it, and that, furthermore, someone then murdered him. Does that bring you up to speed, Chris?"

"It confirms a lot of things I'd suspected—"

"Nonsense," says Elizabeth. "Now, in return, what do we learn from the phone?"

"He made two calls," says Chris. "At around four p.m. on the day he died."

"One to a woman named Nina Mishra," says Donna. "She's a professor of historical archaeology, in Canterbury."

"A professor, goodness me," says Joyce.

"Professors," says Ron, with a gentle eyeroll.

"Have you been to see her?" asks Ibrahim.

"We only just got the records back this morning," says Donna. "So no."

"Feels like a job for us, perhaps?" says Elizabeth.

"Yes, ma'am," says Chris.

"Splendid," says Joyce. "I was hoping we were going to go to Canterbury."

"And the second phone call?" Ibrahim asks.

"About ten minutes after the call to Nina Mishra," says Donna. "But untraceable, so far."

"Untraceable," says Elizabeth. "No such thing."

"It comes back as 'Code 777,'" says Donna. "We see it from time to time."

"Ah," says Elizabeth.

"Code 777," says Joyce. "What does that mean?"

"Happens with high-end criminals," says Chris. "It's blocking software, highly illegal, very expensive, but means you don't have to keep buying burner phones."

"Probably from the dark web," says Ibrahim, nodding sagely.

"So Kuldesh rings a professor," says Joyce. "And straight afterward rings a high-end criminal?"

"There will be other explanations," says Elizabeth.

"I look forward to hearing them," says Chris.

"There are two key questions," says Elizabeth. "Was Kuldesh trying to sell this heroin? And, if so, to whom?"

"I don't buy any of this," says Ron. "Sorry. Kuldesh gets a stash of heroin and decides to sell it? Nah. He'd be terrified. Someone else has come in and nicked it. I guarantee you. No way has Kuldesh stolen it."

"I'm sorry," says a voice. "Couldn't help overhearing."

They turn to see Big Dave, the stranger from the funeral.

"Only I think I was the last person to see him alive," says Big Dave.

"When was this?" asks Elizabeth.

"Evening of the twenty-seventh," says Big Dave. "About five. I was closing up, not much business that day."

"Did he say anything?" asks Chris. "Tell you where he was going?"

"Nah, he just wished me Merry Christmas," says Big Dave, buttoning up his coat. "And then he bought a spade."

16.

Elizabeth is thinking.

The journey home from the funeral had been full of theories. Rival drugs gangs, blackmailers. Ron, as always, wondering if the Mafia might be involved. But certain interesting questions remained. Why had Kuldesh not simply done as he was told? Why had he rung Nina Mishra? And who was the second call to? The Code 777 call? Elizabeth had brushed off Chris's comment about criminals, but he was right. To have a number that leaves no trace is a very difficult undertaking. And is a tactic used by a very particular type of person.

And, key to it all, of course: where was the heroin now?

Elizabeth yawns, her long day done, and opens her front door.

Instantly she can tell something is wrong. Senses that something very bad has happened. This is a sense she has learned to trust.

The TV is off, that's unusual. Stephen will sit and watch all day now. The History Channel. He used to tell her about what he watched, but not so much these days. Sometimes she will watch with him in the evening. It is mainly Nazis and Ancient Egypt. Not bad.

She slips off her coat and hangs it on one of the hooks in the hall. It is next to Stephen's waxed Barbour jacket. The walks they used to take, the two of them. Yomping for hours, then a pub with a fire and a friendly dog, help Stephen with the crossword. Now they try for an hour a day, through the woods. No country fireplaces. Another thing lost, and so little left. She touches the sleeve of the jacket.

It is quiet, but Stephen must be here. There is a smell she has smelled before. Familiar, but from where?

Has Stephen fallen? Had a heart attack? Is she about to find him on the floor? Gray face and blue lips. Is this how it ends, this beautiful affair? With her strong man slumped on a carpet? With Elizabeth alone. Without a goodbye?

"Elizabeth?" Stephen's voice, from behind the door of his office. Elizabeth nearly buckles in relief. She pushes the door open and there he is. He's fully dressed, shaved, his hair neat, sitting at the desk he has worked at for years. Surrounded by his books—Islamic art, Middle Eastern antiquities, a shelf of Bill Bryson. For hours she would hear him in here, bashing away on an old word processor he refused to upgrade. She always teased him that he typed like an elephant, but she knew the joy behind it. How he loved his work, writing, lecturing, teaching, corresponding. What she would give to hear his galumphing typing again.

"Hello, dear," says Elizabeth. "We don't often find you in here?"

Stephen motions for Elizabeth to sit down. She sees he has a letter on his desk.

"I want . . ." starts Stephen. "If you don't mind, that is, I want to read you a letter I was sent today?"

She sees the envelope on his desk. The post had come after Elizabeth had left. "Please," she says.

Stephen picks up the letter from his desk, but before he starts reading he looks straight at Elizabeth. "And I need you to be honest, if you understand? I need you to love me and be straight with me."

Elizabeth nods. What else is there to do? Who has sent Stephen a letter? And about what? Kuldesh perhaps? A clue to his murder? A plea for help to an old friend?

Stephen begins to read. He used to read to her in bed. Dickens, Trollope. Jackie Collins when he was in the mood.

"*Dear Stephen,*" he begins. "*This is a difficult letter to write, but I know it will be a great deal more difficult to read. I will come straight to it. I believe you are in the early stages of dementia, possibly Alzheimer's."*

Elizabeth can hear her heart beating through her chest. Who on earth has chosen to shatter their privacy this way? Who even knows? Her friends? Has one of them written? They wouldn't dare, not without asking. Not Ibrahim, surely? He might dare.

"I am not an expert, but it is something I have been looking into. You are forgetting things, and you are getting confused. I know full well what you will say—'But I've always forgotten things. I've always been confused!'—and you are right, of course, but this, Stephen, is of a different order. Something is not right with you, and everything I read points in just one direction."

"Stephen," says Elizabeth, but he gently gestures for hush.

"You must also know that dementia points in just one direction. Once you start to descend the slope, and please believe me when I say you have started, there is no return. There may be footholds here and there, there may be ledges on which to rest, and the view may still be beautiful from time to time, but you will not clamber back up."

"Stephen, who wrote you this letter?" Elizabeth asks. Stephen holds up a finger, asking her to be patient a few moments more. Elizabeth's fury is decreasing. The letter is something she should have written to him herself. This should not have been left to a stranger. Stephen starts again.

"Perhaps you know all this already, perhaps you are sitting reading this asking, 'Why is this blasted fool telling me what I already know?' But I have to write, because what if you don't know? What if you are already too far down the slope to know the truth of your slide? If these words seem distant, I hope, at least, that they will ring a bell deep within you, that you will recognize the truth of what I am saying. And you know you can trust me."

"Trust who?" says Elizabeth.

"Does it matter?" Stephen asks her kindly. "I can see in your eyes that it's true. I mean, I knew it was true, but I'm glad, I suppose, to see you confirm it. Let me carry on—it's not a long letter."

"I have to write this letter now, because, Stephen, if that bell is ringing for you, I need you to do two things. I need you to read this letter aloud to Elizabeth, and I need you to make her promise that she will let you read this letter every day, should you forget it. Which, from what I understand, you will."

Elizabeth knows now who wrote the letter, of course she does.

"You wrote the letter to yourself?" she says to Stephen.

"It seems I did, yes," says Stephen. "A year ago to the day."

It's the least Elizabeth should have expected. "What did you do? Send the envelope to your solicitors, and tell them to post it to you in a year's time?"

"I must have done," says Stephen. "I must have done. But, more to the point, I assume it's all true?"

"It's all true," says Elizabeth.

"And it's getting worse?"

"Much worse, Stephen. This is a rare good day. We are clinging on."

Stephen nods. "And what is to be done?"

"That's up to you," says Elizabeth. "That will always be up to you."

Stephen smiles. "What rot. Up to me. It's up to us, and it sounds like we have rather small windows left open to us. Should I be living here? Is it impossible?"

"It is difficult," says Elizabeth. "But not impossible."

"Soon it will be impossible."

"I don't care about soon," says Elizabeth. "I care about now."

"Lovely though that thought is, I feel perhaps I don't have that luxury," says Stephen. "There are places, I am sure, where I could receive care. Where you would be given some respite? I still have some money, I hope? Haven't gambled it away?"

"You do have money," says Elizabeth.

"I sold some books recently," says Stephen. "Expensive ones."

Stephen must have seen something cross her eyes.

"I didn't sell any books?"

"You didn't," says Elizabeth. "Though you helped to solve a murder by tracking some down."

"Did I indeed? I have quite the hinterland."

"Do you want to finish the letter?"

"Yes," says Stephen, "I would like to." He picks up the page again.

"Stephen, what a life you have led. You have filled every unforgiving minute and what a woman you have found in Elizabeth. You have led what they call a charmed life. What luck you have had, what opportunities, what sights you have seen. You are a lucky bugger, and you were probably due a sticky patch. And here it is. You must deal with it however you choose, and this letter is my gift to you, to let you know what you are facing, if everything else has failed. I am reading about dementia every day now, trying to cram while I can, and they say that in time you forget even the people closest to you. I am reading time and again of families where husbands forget wives, where mothers forget children, but, after the names and the faces disappear from your memory, what seems to hold on the longest is love. So whatever position you are in, I hope you know you are loved. Elizabeth will not send you away, we both know that. She will not lock you in a home, however bad you get, and however difficult things become. But you must persuade her that this is the right course of action. She cannot continue to care for you, for her sake or for yours. Elizabeth is not your nurse; she is your lover. Read her this letter, please, and then ignore her objections. I have left a page of suggestions tucked inside The Handbook of the Baghdad Archaeological Museum, *on the third shelf to your right. I hope that something there should fit the bill.*

"Stephen, I am losing my mind—I feel it slipping away daily. I send you my love, dear man, a year into the future. I hope you are able to do something with this letter. I love you and, assuming you have done what you're told and read this to Elizabeth, then, Elizabeth, I love you too. Yours faithfully, Stephen."

Stephen puts down the letter. "So there we have it."

"There we have it," agrees Elizabeth.

"Feels like we both should be crying?"

"I think we both might need cool heads for a moment," says Elizabeth. "Crying can come later."

"And have we had this conversation before?" Stephen asks. "Have we spoken about dementia?"

"From time to time," says Elizabeth. "You certainly know something is up."

"And how long, impossible question I know, but how long until we're not capable of having this discussion? How many windows like this do we have left?"

Elizabeth can fool herself no more, can keep Stephen to herself no longer. The day she knew must arrive is here. She has been losing him a paragraph at a time, but the chapter is done. And the book is close to its end.

Stephen, fully dressed and shaved, stands among his books. The urns and sculptures from his travels, things he found significant and beautiful, gathered over a lifetime. The awards, the photographs, old friends smiling on boats, boys at school dressed like men, Stephen on mountains, on desert digs, raising a glass in a far-off bar, kissing his wife on their wedding day. This room, this cocoon, every inch of it is his brain, his smile, his kindness, his friendships, his lovers, his jokes. His mind, fully on display.

And he knows it is now lost.

"Not many," says Elizabeth. "Your good days are further apart, and your bad days are getting worse."

Stephen puffs out his cheeks as his options dwindle. "You need to send me somewhere, Elizabeth. Somewhere they can care for me properly, twenty-four hours a day. I will look at my list of suggestions."

"I can care for you properly," says Elizabeth.

"No," says Stephen. "I won't have it."

"I hope I might have a say in the matter too."

Stephen reaches across the desk and takes Elizabeth's hand. "I need you to promise me you won't destroy this letter."

"I won't make a promise I can't keep," says Elizabeth. My God, his hand, my hand, she thinks, the way they fit together, the two of them.

"I need you to show me this letter every day," says Stephen. "Do you understand?"

Elizabeth looks at her husband. Then she looks at the letter that this clever man wrote to himself a year ago. What must he have been going through? One of those days of galumphing typing had been this letter. Probably came back into the living room with a big smile on his face. "Cup of tea, old girl?"

To show Stephen this letter every day would be to lose him. But to not show him would be to betray him. And that is no choice at all.

"I promise," she says.

Now the tears come from Stephen. They stand and they embrace. Stephen is shaking and sobbing. He is saying sorry, she is saying sorry, but to whom, and for what, is lost on them both.

Elizabeth realizes what the smell was when she had walked into the flat, fifteen minutes earlier, a whole lifetime ago. She knew she had recognized it.

It was fear. Cold-blooded, sweat-soaked fear.

PART TWO

Whatever You're Looking For, You're Sure to Find It Here!

17.

In theory Ron was all for keeping an eye on a major heroin importation hub, and trying to find a murderer.

However, thus far, in practice, it has largely involved sitting in the back of his Daihatsu, looking through some binoculars he bought from Lidl, at a hangar that no one had entered or exited for an hour, while listening to Ibrahim reading Joyce an article about Ecuador from the *Economist*.

"Is being a spy always this boring?" he asks Elizabeth. She has been unusually quiet today.

"It's ninety percent this, five percent paperwork and five percent killing people," says Elizabeth. "Ibrahim, is this article going to take much longer?"

"I'm enjoying it," says Joyce.

"Joyce is enjoying it," says Ibrahim, and continues with a paragraph about the pressures felt by the tech sector in Quito.

A black Range Rover pulls up in front of them in the lay-by, blocking them in.

"Aye, aye," says Ron, putting down his binoculars. Elizabeth's hand moves instinctively to her bag. In front of them a man steps from the driver's seat of the Range Rover and approaches the Daihatsu. He knocks on Ibrahim's window. Ibrahim winds it down.

The man pokes his head across the threshold, and takes in the four figures, one by one.

"Day out, is it?" A Scouse accent.

"Birdwatching," says Ron, holding up his binoculars.

"That's a lovely overcoat," says Joyce. "Would you like a Percy Pig?"

She holds out a bag of sweets to the man; he takes one, and talks as he chews.

"You've been looking at my warehouse for an hour," he says. "Seen anything?"

"Not a thing, Mr. Holt," says Elizabeth.

Dominic Holt pauses for a moment at the sound of his name.

"Call me Dom," says Dom.

"Not a thing, Dom, not even a hint of heroin," says Elizabeth. "Commendable on your part. Though I suppose shipments are few and far between?"

"Most days it's just admin?" asks Joyce.

"I run a legitimate logistics company," says Dom.

"And I'm a harmless pensioner," says Elizabeth.

"Me too," says Joyce. "Another Percy Pig? I can never have just one."

Dom Holt holds up his hand to decline. "May I ask how you know my name?"

"One doesn't have to scratch very far under the surface of the South Coast heroin trade before your name crops up," says Elizabeth.

"Right," says Dom, contemplating. Ron has seen the effect that the Thursday Murder Club has on people before.

"Don't know what to make of us, do you, son?" says Ron.

Dom gives them another look, and seems to make up his mind.

"I'll tell you what I make of you," says Dom. He points at Ron. "You're Jason Ritchie's old man. Roy?"

"Ron," says Ron.

"Seen you with him before. He's a wrong 'un, so I'm guessing you are too." Dom points at Ibrahim. "I don't know your name, but you're the guy who goes to see Connie Johnson at Darwell Prison. Word is you're a Moroccan cocaine importer. That true?"

"No comment," says Ibrahim. Has Ron ever seen him look so proud?

"You," says Dom, nodding his head toward Elizabeth. "No idea who you are, but you've got a gun in your bag. Badly hidden."

"I'm not hiding it," says Elizabeth.

"Now do me," says Joyce.

Dom looks at Joyce. "You look like you've fallen in with a bad crowd."

Joyce nods. Dom beckons to them all. "Come on, out. All of you."

The gang exit the car. Ron thinks it's nice to be able to stretch his legs. Dom appraises them as a group.

"So I've got a dodgy cockney, a coke dealer, some old bird with a shooter, and . . ." He looks at Joyce again.

"Joyce," says Joyce.

"And Joyce," says Dom. "Staking out my warehouse on a January morning. You see that a reasonable man might have questions?"

"Quite right," says Elizabeth. "And we have questions of our own. So why not invite us in? We can have a good old chinwag, and clear everything up."

"You ever used that gun?" asks Dom, pointing at Elizabeth's handbag.

"This particular one, no, it's clean," says Elizabeth. "I'm not an amateur."

"You work for Connie Johnson, is that it?" asks Dom. "You her gran or something? What does she want?"

"Connie is simply our friend," says Ibrahim.

"Not mine," says Ron. "To be fair."

"She wants to kill Ron," says Joyce.

Dom looks at Ron and nods. "Yeah, I can see that. So what is it? What are you after? Do I need to worry about you, or can I go about my day?"

"You'll be relieved to hear it's very simple," says Elizabeth. "We're looking for the man who murdered our friend."

"OK," says Dom. "Who's your friend?"

"Kuldesh Sharma."

Dom shakes his head now. "Never heard of him."

"But you were in his shop just after Christmas," says Joyce. "Perhaps it slipped your mind? Antiques shop. In Brighton?"

"Nope," says Dom.

"He was murdered late on the twenty-seventh," says Elizabeth. "So you see why we thought you might be involved?"

Dom shakes his head again. "Never heard of him, never been in his shop, didn't kill him. Sorry for your loss though."

"Did you find the heroin?" asks Ibrahim. "When you ransacked his shop? Perhaps you have it in your warehouse this very moment?"

"You've an active imagination," says Dom. "I'll give you that."

"Well, you've certainly heard of Kuldesh," says Elizabeth. "A fool could see that as soon as we mentioned his name. And we have fairly solid proof you've been in his shop."

"Proof?"

"Nothing that would hold up in court," says Elizabeth. "Don't panic."

"So the only question we have left," says Ron, "is did you kill him?"

"And that's why we're here," says Joyce.

"Just to see what we can see," adds Ibrahim. "And a day out also."

"Wait here," says Dom, and returns to his car.

Joyce watches Dom Holt root around in the boot of the Range Rover. "He seems very nice. For a heroin dealer."

"Uh-oh," says Ron, looking past Joyce. Dom Holt has returned with a golf club, and is now pulling a large knife from his perfectly tailored overcoat. He nods to the friends.

"Just checking youse lot have got AA membership?"

"Never bothered," says Ron. "They rip you off."

"Ron, I don't know how you can live on such a tightrope," says Ibrahim, and Ron shrugs. "How on earth do you sleep?"

"Well, look," says Dom. "I'm going to slash your tires and smash your windscreen. So you're going to need some help."

"Perhaps you could consider—" begins Ibrahim, before Dom crouches and slashes the right front tire.

"I can't have you following me all day. There's a garage a mile or so up the road though," says Dom, popping back up. "I'll give you his number and he'll come and bail you out."

"Thank you," says Joyce. "Whatever would we have done without you?"

"If I ever see you again, you'll get worse," says Dom.

"You know all this is making me think you killed Kuldesh Sharma," says Elizabeth.

Dom shrugs. "Couldn't care less. This is my place of work, and I don't like being disturbed. Especially by a cockney West Ham fan who's too cheap to pay for AA membership, a coke dealer who hangs out with Connie Johnson, an old woman too scared to use her gun, and Joyce. I didn't kill your mate, but if you keep poking round where you're not welcome, I'll kill you." He ducks down again.

"An old woman too scared to use her gun?" says Elizabeth, as the car clunks toward the ground again. "We'll see about that."

"I don't suppose you lot know where the heroin is?" Dom asks, hands on hips, catching his breath from the exertion. "If you've got it, best to tell me?"

Silence from the gang.

"You're wrong about AA membership," says Ron. "You save more money by—"

But the rest of Ron's defense is drowned out by the sound of the windscreen being repeatedly smashed by a Liverpudlian with a golf club and a grudge.

Further up the lay-by, a motorcycle courier looks over at the scene, as he buys a burger from a roadside van.

18.

ere's the thing. It is a great deal easier being interviewed by the police than by another criminal. Mitch Maxwell has been interviewed by the police many times, and their resources and opportunities are limited. Everything is on tape, your overpaid solicitor gets to sit next to you shaking her head at the questions, and, by law, they have to make you a cup of tea.

Doesn't matter what you've done—set fire to a factory, kidnapped a business associate, flown a drone full of cannabis into a prison—and it doesn't matter what evidence they have—"You would agree that this CCTV shows you, Mr. Maxwell, running from the scene with a petrol can"—you can just sit there in peace, say, "No comment," every time you notice a silence and wait twenty-four hours until they have to let you go.

A police interview can be an inconvenience, sure. Perhaps you had planned a round of golf with the boys, perhaps you are due to collect a suitcase full of cash from the toilets of a motorway service station. But, so long as you are not a fool, and Mitch Maxwell is no fool, then no one is going to charge you with anything.

So, while, ideally, Mitch would rather not be questioned *at all*, he would always choose to be questioned by the police rather than by, say, the taxman, a journalist or, as the pool cue swings toward his head once more, by his good friend and business partner Luca Buttaci.

"If you're lying to me," screams Luca, as the cue connects with Mitch's skull, "I will kill you." Mitch has been hit many times before. This is OK.

It'll be sore, but he'll live. If Luca was really serious, it would be a base-ball bat.

"Luca, mate," says Mitch.

"A hundred grand's worth of heroin goes missing, and we're mates, are we?" shouts Luca, and throws the cue against a concrete wall. Mitch wonders again where they are. Nice setup Luca's got here. Spacious, pool table in the corner, lots of broken cues, clearly soundproofed. Strictly speaking, Luca is taking a liberty here. Mitch is too senior for this sort of treatment; the two men are equals. Luca's been in the business a bit longer, Mitch will grant the guy that, but their houses have both got a pool, a tennis court and stables. You know? Equals.

Besides, Luca knows the troubles they've been having just as well as Mitch does. It has affected them both.

They usually have a neat division of labor. Mitch does the hard work of importing drugs into the country. Luca does the hard work of distributing them when they're here. Neither needs to know the first thing about how the other goes about his business.

But between the two of them is a very simple but crucial mechanism. The exact details change, but it usually comes down to something like this: somebody Mitch trusts will take a terra-cotta box filled to the brim with heroin into an antiques shop and, the following day, somebody Luca trusts will go into the same shop and buy that box. That is the moment when Mitch's job ends and Luca's job begins.

But, in this instance, there was, let's say, a hiccup. The heroin was delivered to the antiques shop. Tick. But, come the next morning, the shop was shut, and the box was gone. Somewhere, overnight, a hundred grand's worth of heroin had gone missing, and Luca is, understandably, frustrated by this. Especially after all the other problems they've been having, shipments being intercepted, profits collapsing.

"You understand why I have to do this?" says Luca, calming down a little.

"Of course," says Mitch. "I'd be doing the same. Dotting the i's and crossing the t's."

Luca nods. "That box is somewhere, innit? Someone's got it?"

Mitch knows what Luca is thinking. Either Mitch's courier, Dom, stole it; or the antiques guy stole it; or Luca's courier stole it. It should be the simplest of riddles to solve, and, yet, there is still no box.

Therefore Luca must at least also be entertaining the possibility that Mitch himself is behind the theft. Which is why Mitch is currently tied to a chair, bleeding from the temple, while *Celebrity Antiques Road Trip* plays loudly on a big-screen TV on a far wall. No complaints from Mitch.

"For sure, someone's got it," agrees Mitch. On *Celebrity Antiques Road Trip* an eighties pop singer is buying an ill-advised tankard.

Luca nods again. "It's not the hundred grand, you know that. It's the future of the whole business. We're leaking to death."

"I get it," says Mitch. This little arrangement, between Mitch and Luca, has been enormously profitable for them both. There had been bumps in the road, but nothing like this. And, as Luca says, the money is not really the main thing. The whole relationship, this business, is built on the bedrock of trust. If Luca can't trust Mitch, the whole enterprise collapses.

"While I've got you here," says Luca, "there's a guy on a motorbike I've seen hanging around a few times. He one of yours?"

"Nah," says Mitch. "Police?"

"Nah," says Luca. "Not police."

As Luca starts to untie him, Mitch gets a better look around.

"Nice place, Luca," he says. "Where are we?"

"Under an IKEA," says Luca. "If you can believe that?"

Well, that certainly explains why all the guns are on wooden shelving units.

Mitch knows that, although he and Luca are old friends, very old friends, it will all count for nothing if Luca stops trusting him.

Luca helps him to his feet and shakes his hand. But, as Mitch looks into the eyes of his old mate—just plain John-Luke Butterworth when they first met at the Young Offender Institution, Luca Buttaci when he felt he needed something more fearsome—he knows this whole situation could well end up with one of them killing the other. Tensions being high and what have you.

The best thing to do, all around, would be to find that heroin. That'll settle everyone. He and Dom had absolutely taken the shop apart, and found nothing. It must be somewhere. More to the point, some*one* must have it.

It's about four a.m., and he has to take his daughter ice skating at seven a.m. That's when the rink opens for serious practice.

"Are we done?" Mitch asks.

"For now," says Luca. "One of the boys will give you a lift home."

Mitch stretches his shoulders. He needs to take some Nurofen, watch some ice skating, and then find a box full of heroin.

As it happens, he already has an unlikely lead. Dom says a group of pensioners had been hanging around, asking questions. One of them works for Connie Johnson. Mitch will find out where they live, and pay them a little visit.

No rest for the wicked.

19.

I wish I had gone to university," says Joyce, as they wait outside Nina Mishra's office.

Elizabeth knew the effect that Canterbury would have. Medieval walls, cobblestones, tea shops called "tea shoppes." It was absolute catnip to Joyce. She has been in a trance since they got off the train.

"What would you have studied?" Elizabeth asks.

"Oh, I don't know about studying," says Joyce. "I just would have liked to have swanned about on a bicycle, with a scarf. Did you enjoy it?"

"As much as I ever enjoy anything," says Elizabeth.

"Did you have love affairs with older men?"

"Not everything is about sex, Joyce," says Elizabeth. There had been older men, of course, and one or two younger ones. Not so much "love affairs" as "occupational hazards." There had been twelve women at her college, and around two hundred men. Which had very neatly prepared her for the world of espionage. Elizabeth had long told herself that she preferred the company of men, though it has occurred to her more recently that she'd had very little choice in the matter. She was happy, as they'd walked through the University of Kent campus earlier, to see there were as many young women as men.

"I can just see you, in the library," says Joyce. "Opposite a shy boy in glasses."

"Stop projecting, Joyce," says Elizabeth, looking out through the waiting-room window, across the stone buildings under silver skies. Students bunched and hunched against the cold, scurrying toward warmth. But Joyce is not to be stopped.

"You catch his eye, and he blushes, and looks down at his book. His hair falls over his eyes, like Hugh Grant. You ask him what he's reading . . ."

Through the window Elizabeth sees a young woman drop her books. In Joyce's world, a fellow student would stop to pick them up for her, and their eyes would meet.

"And he says, I don't know, 'A book about history,' or something, and you say, 'Forget history, let's talk about our future.'"

"For goodness' sake, Joyce," says Elizabeth. Annoyingly a handsome young man is now helping the woman pick up her books. She is tucking a loose strand of hair behind her ear.

"And you put your hand on the table, and he puts his hand on your hand. Then he slips off his glasses, and he's very handsome, like Colin Firth, and he asks you to dinner." Joyce continues her story as the clumsy girl and the handsome boy go their separate ways. In Joyce's world they would each glance over their shoulder, moments apart. Which is exactly what they do. Typical.

"And you say no. But then you say, 'I shall be here again tomorrow, and again the day after, and one day I shall say yes,' and he says, 'I don't even know your name,' and you say, 'One day you will.'"

Elizabeth looks at her friend. "Have you been reading books again?"

"Yes," admits Joyce.

The door opens and Elizabeth takes in Nina Mishra. Tall, elegant, an unnecessary purple streak in her hair, but she looks fun enough.

Nina smiles. "Elizabeth and Joyce? So sorry to have kept you."

"Not at all," says Elizabeth, standing. The appointment is taking place seven minutes late, and that is absolutely within the realms of acceptability. Twelve minutes is the cut-off for rudeness. Nina ushers them into her office and sits down behind her desk, as Elizabeth and Joyce take seats across from her.

"I love the purple streak in your hair," says Joyce.

"Thank you," says Nina. "I love your earrings."

Elizabeth hadn't noticed that Joyce was wearing earrings. They look fine.

"You want to talk to me about Kuldesh?" says Nina. "What a horrible shock. Were you friends?"

"He was a friend of my husband's," says Elizabeth. "Were you friends?"

"He was a friend of my parents', really," says Nina. "But he would ask for favors from time to time. And, for Kuldesh, I would always say yes. He had that effect on people."

"Favors?"

"Things he had come across," says Nina. "What was my view."

"As a historian?" asks Elizabeth.

"As a wise friend," says Nina. "Kuldesh was not always after my opinion on antiques. Sometimes . . . *morality*."

"So not so much valuations, as—"

"It was more questions concerning"—she is picking a word carefully—"provenance."

"They talk about provenance a lot on *Antiques Roadshow*," says Joyce.

"Meaning, is this stolen?" asks Elizabeth.

"Is it stolen?" says Nina. "Is it too good to be true? What is it doing in England? Any time something didn't seem right, he knew he could call on me. What does the law say? That's one of my areas. And he trusts me. Trusts I would never tell."

"And how often were things not quite right?"

Nina smiles. "My parents were both dealers, Elizabeth. Unsuccessful ones. Far too honest. The world of antiques and antiquities is not always squeaky clean. My parents knew it, I know it, Kuldesh knows it."

"Knew it," says Elizabeth.

"Oh, God, yes," says Nina. "Poor Kuldesh. Sorry."

"What did you speak about on the day he died?"

"How do you know we spoke?"

"We're not always squeaky clean either," says Joyce.

"But I promise we are friends," says Elizabeth. "And I promise we are not the police."

"Then who are you?"

"We're the Thursday Murder Club," says Joyce. "But we don't have time to go into all that now, because we have to get the four fifteen train."

Nina puffs out her cheeks. "Kuldesh asked how I was, we made small talk, I was in a hurry, I wish I hadn't been now, so he got to the point and he said he had a problem I could perhaps help him with."

"A problem?" says Elizabeth. "Those were his words?"

Nina thinks for a moment. "A dilemma, that's what he said. A dilemma. He needed advice."

"Any sense of what the dilemma might have been?"

Nina shakes her head.

"And if you had to guess?"

"Here are the things it would normally be. Someone has brought in a piece Kuldesh knows is stolen. Should he buy it anyway?"

"No," says Joyce.

"Someone has brought in a valuable piece, and has no idea of the value. Should Kuldesh let them know what they have?"

"Yes," says Joyce.

"Or someone has asked Kuldesh to sell something, or to store something, and to keep it off the books."

"Money laundering," says Joyce. "Well, we know all about that."

"Do you now?" says Nina.

"And what did your instincts tell you this time?" asks Elizabeth.

"He'd never sounded quite like this before," says Nina. "So whatever it was, was serious."

"Or valuable," says Elizabeth.

"Or valuable," agrees Nina. "But, if you want my instinct, I would say he was scared and excited."

"Like Alan when he sees a cow," says Joyce.

"I suppose," says Nina. "It was more, 'What have I got myself into?' than 'You'll never guess what I've just bought.'"

"That's very helpful, Nina," says Elizabeth. "Have you ever taken heroin, I wonder?"

"Excuse me?"

"Heroin? Have you ever taken it? I notice you have a purple streak in your hair, perhaps you enjoy an alternative lifestyle?"

"She's charming, your friend," says Nina to Joyce.

"She doesn't understand fashion," says Joyce.

"You think heroin was involved?" Nina asks.

"We think a man called Dominic Holt left a parcel of heroin at Kuldesh's shop on the morning of the day he died," says Elizabeth.

"Oh, Kuldesh," says Nina, and slumps a little in her chair.

"Under sufferance, we think," says Elizabeth. "But, yes, even so."

"The next morning," says Joyce, "another man comes to pick up the parcel, but Kuldesh is nowhere to be seen."

"Kuldesh stole the heroin?" asks Nina. "He wouldn't be so stupid. Impossible, sorry. Impossible."

"And yet he was shot dead," says Elizabeth. "After having spoken to you, and, who knows, perhaps even arranging to meet you? And the missing heroin has yet to be found."

"So it does look a bit suspicious," says Joyce.

"He didn't arrange to meet you?" asks Elizabeth.

"No," says Nina. "Perhaps he said, 'I'll see you soon,' nothing more than that."

"And he didn't mention the heroin to you?" asks Elizabeth.

"Heroin? Of course not," says Nina. "He would have known what my reaction would be."

"You wouldn't have been tempted to make a bit of money?" Joyce asks.

"No one would blame you," says Elizabeth. "You were the first person he rang, so no one else would ever find out?"

"I thought you said you weren't the police?" says Nina.

There is a quiet knock at the door, and Nina tells the visitor to come in. A slightly stooped, balding man who could be anywhere between mid-forties and late sixties enters the room. His entrance, like his knock, carries an air of apology.

"Sorry," he says. "You summoned me, m'lady?"

"This is Professor Mellor," says Nina Mishra. "He's, how would you describe it, Jonjo?"

"Sort of your boss?" suggests Jonjo.

"How lovely to meet you, Professor Mellor," says Joyce, standing. "I'm Joyce, and this is Elizabeth, who is also sort of my boss."

Professor Mellor nods to Elizabeth, who nods back, and takes a seat.

"We have a 'once a week,'" says Nina. "In the department. Share our worries. And, I hope you don't mind, but I shared my worries with Jonjo. He does advisory work with some of the local auction houses."

"Military mainly," says Jonjo.

"So someone else *did* know?" notes Elizabeth.

"I just thought he might be useful," says Nina.

"It's fascinating," says Jonjo. "Murder aside, quite *fascinating*. Is that quite the word? You are friends of the dead gentleman?"

"We are looking into his death," says Elizabeth, wondering whether Jonjo's guileless manner is an act. Good one if it is.

"Nina was the last person to speak to Kuldesh," says Joyce.

"That we know of," says Elizabeth.

"That you *know* of," says Jonjo, taking an orange out of his pocket and starting to peel it. "And there's the rub. We might see a million white swans, and yet we are not able to say that all swans are white. Yet we see just one black swan, and we can say with absolute certainty that not all swans are white."

"A swan chased Alan the other day," says Joyce.

"Orange segment?" says Jonjo, offering one to any takers. Joyce takes one.

"Vitamin C is the most important vitamin after vitamin D," she says.

"Do you know much about the drugs trade, Nina?" asks Elizabeth. "Or you, Professor Mellor? Does one come across such things in your line of work? Boxes full of heroin and what have you?"

"A parcel full of heroin?" says Jonjo. "More intriguing still."

"You hear of companies using antiques as a front," says Nina.

"Importing things that shouldn't be imported," adds Jonjo.

"But that's way above Kuldesh's pay grade," says Nina. "He had a little council lock-up garage somewhere in Fairhaven. Where he would keep a few things 'off the books,' but nothing like this, I'm sure of it."

"Would you happen to know where that lock-up is?" Elizabeth asks.

Nina shakes her head. "Just that he had one."

"If I might ask a final question," says Elizabeth. "We know that Kuldesh rang you at around four p.m., yes? And he didn't ask to meet you?"

"No, he didn't," confirms Nina.

"So you say," says Elizabeth. "You are the only witness to what was said in that call."

"You're very fierce," says Jonjo. "I like it."

"Minutes later, Kuldesh made another phone call," says Elizabeth.

"But we can't trace who to," says Joyce.

"So my question is this," says Elizabeth. "If you were to come into possession of this heroin in the way Kuldesh had, and you decided, for whatever reason, to sell it, who would you ring?"

"Samantha Barnes," says Nina.

"Samantha Barnes," agrees Jonjo, without hesitation.

"I'm afraid you both have me at a loss," says Elizabeth.

"Antiques dealer," says Jonjo. "Lives in a stately home just outside Petworth."

"Do many antiques dealers live in stately homes?" Joyce asks.

"They do not," says Jonjo.

"Unless—" says Elizabeth.

"Well, quite," agrees Nina. "She's very well *connected*. I'm scared of her, but I suspect you two won't be."

"I suspect so too," says Elizabeth. "Is she the sort of person who might have an opinion on heroin?"

"She is the sort of person who would have an opinion on everything," says Nina.

"Not another one," says Joyce.

"And Kuldesh would have known her?"

"Would have known of her, at the very least," says Nina.

"Then I wonder if we might pay Samantha Barnes a visit," says Elizabeth.

"Canterbury, Petworth, what a social whirl," says Joyce.

"Do you have her number?" says Elizabeth.

"I can get it," says Jonjo, finishing his orange. "Please don't tell her we sent you though."

20.

Samantha Barnes always looks forward to her book group. First Tuesday of every month, except for the one time Eileen was in the hospital with her feet, and the one time Samantha herself was being questioned by the Metropolitan Police for defrauding the Victoria & Albert Museum. They were both free in no time.

Garth always leaves them to it. Literature is not for him—"The whole thing is lies, honey, none of it happened." He is a figure of curiosity to her friends, and people often like to turn up a little early to catch a glimpse of him. They will say, "Hello, Garth," and he will say, "I don't know which one you are," or just ignore them completely. His authentic indifference seems to delight them.

Samantha gets that. On the day he'd walked back into the shop—big beard, plaid shirt, woolly hat—and pointed his gun straight at her, Samantha, submerged in grief, had simply started to cry. No fear, no bargaining. Let him shoot her. Garth had waited, very patiently, for her to stop crying before he spoke.

"Why'd you sell me that inkwell?"

"It was fun."

"Wasn't fun for me."

"Sorry, you did park in the accessible space though."

"I'd only just got to England; I didn't know about accessible spaces."

"Are you going to shoot me?"

"Nah, just wanted to ask you a few questions. Where's your husband?"

"He died."

"Sorry for your loss, ma'am. You like fun?"

"I did."

"You wanna buy a stolen painting?"

And she discovered, to her immense surprise, that she did.

Today, as ever, Garth hasn't told Samantha where he is going, but, as he was carrying a cricket bat, she is very much hoping he's gone to play cricket. You just never knew with Garth though.

Her gang of pals are knocking back the wine, and *Wolf Hall* is starting to get better and better reviews. Gill, who works at the vet's on the square, says she would have given Thomas Cromwell a piece of her mind had she been around at the time. Do they know what Samantha does for a living? They must have an idea at least. Bronagh from the deli, for example, once got lost on her way to the loo and walked into a room where a newly painted Jackson Pollock was drying. Also, no one else in Petworth has a Ferrari Testarossa. The clues are there.

Samantha retires to the kitchen to make coffee. She received a phone call just before everyone arrived, and it has been worrying her. Worrying her? Perhaps that's pushing it. Playing on her mind perhaps.

A woman named Elizabeth. Very sure of herself. Sorry to trouble you, I wonder if you might have heard of a man named Kuldesh Sharma? Samantha declined to volunteer this information to Elizabeth. Never volunteer information unless you have to. That's something Samantha has learned in the last few years. Ah, Elizabeth had sighed, that *is* a shame, I felt sure you would have. Something in Elizabeth's manner made Samantha defensive. Like she was being interrogated by a great spymaster. What did Samantha know about heroin dealers, Elizabeth wanted to know next. Well, that was quite a question. Samantha could have given her the long answer but instead chose the short answer of "nothing." Elizabeth paused again, as if she were writing this down. Elizabeth then asked what the parking was like in Petworth, and Samantha, glad finally to have a question she could give a straight answer to, said, It could be the devil's own work, and Elizabeth said, They won't like that, but they'll have to take their chances, I'm afraid. To which Samantha replied, quite naturally, *Who* will have to take *what* chances? Elizabeth had informed her that "they" were Joyce and Ibrahim, that they would be coming to see her very soon, and that they could both be very chatty in different ways, but they both meant well. Samantha said that she wasn't around for the next few days, as she would be at a fair in Arundel, and wasn't that a pity, and to this Elizabeth said, Samantha, never lie to a liar.

She then wished Samantha a very good evening, and rang off.

What to think? Samantha walks back in with the coffees and gets gratified *oohs* in response. Perhaps she should just make herself scarce for the next few days? Keep out of harm's way?

Samantha has a nose for trouble, but she also has a nose for opportunity. It's the same nose, if truth be told.

Elizabeth hadn't sounded like a police officer. Too old, and not nearly polite enough for that. So perhaps she should talk to this Joyce and Ibrahim? What was there to lose? They surely didn't know anything? But perhaps they knew something?

The ladies have moved off the subject of the book and onto the subject of postmenopausal sex. Samantha raises her coffee cup and says she has no complaints. Which is true—her big Canadian bear never does anything by halves.

During the phone call, Elizabeth had dangled some very tempting fruit. Kuldesh Sharma. Heroin. Maybe Samantha would learn something to her advantage? She will talk it over with Garth, but she knows what he will say. What he always says.

"Babe, is there money in it?"

And, on this occasion, there just might be.

21.

The lights are low, the music is low, and, if he is being entirely honest, Chris is low too. Joyce is finishing an anecdote about Dom Holt, the heroin dealer.

"With a golf club, if you can believe that," says Joyce. "And a big knife for the tires. It was like a documentary. I would have taken a photo, but I didn't get the chance to ask, and I didn't want to be rude."

"You don't feel like pressing charges, I suppose?" asks Chris, sipping a lime and slimline tonic.

"Oh, take a day off once in a while," says Elizabeth, and Patrice laughs into her whisky.

Chris is frustrated. He'd love to arrest Dom Holt for a bit of criminal damage. That would throw the cat among the pigeons back at Fairhaven nick. He walked past the Incident Room the other day, just to catch a peek, but all the blinds were drawn. Patrice has taken him and Donna to the pub to cheer them up, and Elizabeth and Joyce have joined them.

Why was the investigation taken from them? He still has no answer to that.

"Dominic Holt's offices are near Newhaven," says Joyce. "Elizabeth says we should break in and have a look around."

"Don't you dare," says Chris. "I'm honestly in the mood to arrest someone, and you'll do."

"Well, somebody has to do something, Chris," says Elizabeth. "Any news from SIO Regan?"

"She asked Chris to move his car so she can park in his space the other day," says Donna. "If that counts as news?"

"The teacher at my old school had her own private cubicle in the toilets," says Patrice. "FOR THE USE OF DOROTHY THOMPSON ONLY was Blu-Tacked to the door."

"I'm guessing you used it?" says Donna.

"Course I did," says Patrice. "We all did. But it reminds me of your SIO Regan. That sort of thing never works in the long run, does it? She had an affair with the head of RE in the end, got caught banging in one of the science labs. You've just got to wait these people out."

"How many whiskies have you had, Mum?" asks Donna.

"Just enough," says Patrice.

"But they have yet to find the heroin?" Elizabeth asks.

"As far as we know," says Chris.

"Good," says Joyce. "I'd far rather we found it."

A waiter brings over their bill, and Chris waves the others away. "I've got this. Still useful for something."

"Any news on Dominic Holt's boss, Mitch Maxwell?" Elizabeth asks. "Are they following him?"

"Wouldn't know," says Chris. "What part of this aren't you getting?"

"To more important business. Do you know if the name Samantha Barnes is on her radar?" Elizabeth asks. "Is it on yours?"

"Never heard of her," says Chris, looking at the bill with a twinge of regret.

"She's like Connie Johnson," says Joyce. "But for antiques."

"Should we be taking an interest?" Chris asks.

"No, no," says Elizabeth. "Entirely unconnected, I'm sure. So what's your plan for Dom Holt?"

"There's nothing we can do," says Chris. "We're not on the case."

"Oh, there's always *something* you can do," says Elizabeth. "If you put your mind to it."

"We're not like you, Elizabeth," says Chris, tapping his contactless card on the waiter's machine. "We're not allowed to break the law."

Elizabeth nods, stands and starts to pull on her coat. "It wouldn't harm you to bend it every now and again though, dear. I think Joyce and I might need to avoid Dom Holt for a while, so it might be time for you to pull your weight. Thank you for the drinks by the way."

"Pleasure," says Chris. "Up to a point."

"Would anyone mind if I took these pork scratchings home for Alan?" asks Joyce.

"And I wonder if I might ask a favor," says Elizabeth, taking out her phone. "Donna, do you think you might be able to check my phone records? To see who I've rung?"

"Don't you know who you've rung?" Donna asks.

"Not an unreasonable question," says Elizabeth. "But all the same I wonder if you might indulge me?"

Donna takes the phone. "Anything I shouldn't see on here?"

"Plenty," says Elizabeth.

"And what are we hoping to find?" Donna asks.

"With any luck, our prime suspect," says Elizabeth. "Thank you, dear."

22.

Ron can't be doing with computers. He has been outlining this view to Bob Whittaker from Wordsworth Court.

His speech was, to his own mind, impassioned but fair. At one point he heard himself use the phrase "Karl Marx must be spinning in his grave," but, in the main, he was concise, reasonable and to the point. Ron has just slumped back into his chair after his final salvo of "And that's before I even get started on Facebook."

Ron tries to decipher Bob's look. Impressed? No, that's not it. Thoughtful? That's not quite it either. Also, where has Ibrahim got to?

As if on cue, Ibrahim walks back into the living room.

"I've been standing in the hallway for eight minutes and forty seconds, Ron," he says. "Waiting for you to finish."

"I was chatting with Bob," says Ron. "About computers."

"Yes, quite the chat," says Ibrahim. "In that entire eight minutes and forty seconds, poor Bob said just four things, and I noted them all down for you. He said, and these are direct quotes, 'I see'—that was after about a minute and a half. At three minutes and seventeen seconds he said, 'Yes, I understand why you might think that.' At just past the five-minute mark, you drew breath long enough for him to say, 'Well, that's certainly a view I have heard before,' and, about ninety seconds ago, Bob's final contribution to the conversation was 'Do we know where Ibrahim has got to?'"

"Yeah, well, he was listening," says Ron. "People like hearing my opinions; they always have done."

"And yet here he sits, looking both bored and frightened."

Ah, yes, Ron realizes, that's the look. Bored and frightened. Ron must admit, and not for the first time, that he can get carried away.

"Sorry, Bob," says Ron. "Wear my heart on my sleeve sometimes."

"Not at all," says Bob. "Plenty of food for thought. And I will certainly pass your feedback on to someone at IBM should that opportunity arise."

"You will learn fairly quickly, Bob, that you don't need to be polite with Ron," says Ibrahim. "It took me around a week to figure that out."

Bob nods.

"Also, he is easy to distract. If you ever feel that Ron has gone off at a tangent, which on occasion he does, then a simple 'Did you see the match?' or 'Did you see the fight?' works as a reset button."

"How Chelsea won that one, I'll never know," says Ron, shaking his head. "Daylight robbery."

"To work, then, gentlemen," says Ibrahim.

Bob's laptop is open on Ibrahim's desk, and the three men gather round. Ron and Ibrahim had paid Mervyn another little visit yesterday and explained what they thought was going on, man to man. Better that it came from them, had been Ron's judgment, Mervyn being one of those men who found information harder to take in when that information came from women.

Mervyn had agreed to go cold turkey for a week, and hand his correspondence with Tatiana over to Ron and Ibrahim. The big idea was to lay a trap, to see who was behind the scam and if they could be brought out into the open, after which, in Ron's view, they should be "given a good hiding" or, in Ibrahim's view, "turned over to the relevant authorities."

And, of course, Mervyn still feels there is a chance that Tatiana is Tatiana, and that his loneliness might come to an end. Ron understands that. He had spent his Christmas Day with Pauline, and it hadn't gone entirely smoothly. She's a smashing bird, really she is, and Ron knows he's punching above his weight, but Ron had wanted to open presents after breakfast, which is the correct way of doing things, while Pauline wanted to wait until after lunch. They had opened them after lunch, of course, but it wasn't the same. Ron is no stranger to compromise, far from it, but that's taking things too far. They are having a little break from each other to allow things to simmer down. Ron is missing her, but is not about to apologize for something when he's so clearly in the right.

Bob Whittaker had been recruited as a tech expert after his blinding work on New Year's Eve. They'd all watched the Turkish New Year together, then toddled off to their beds. Ron and Ibrahim had stayed awake, drinking whisky, and seen in the New Year again, three hours later, raising a toast to Joyce and Elizabeth in their absence.

Joyce had warned them that Bob could be shy, and might say no. But Ibrahim had explained the plan to Bob, and Bob, who had seen the same program as Joyce about "romance fraud," had been only too happy to help. Had jumped at the chance, in fact.

He has just opened Tatiana's last message to Mervyn. After a brief negotiation it is agreed that Ron can read it out, which Ron is pleased about as he senses that neither Ibrahim nor Bob would do it with the accent, and the accent is surely half the fun. Ron reads.

"*My darling, my prince, my strength*—all right love, Christ—*It is just over a week until I see you, until I melt into your arms, until we kiss as lovers*—I'm actually going to stop doing the accent now—*I hope you are as excited as I. I have one problem, my sweet, kind boy*—oh, here we go—*My brother is recently in the hospital for an accident at his work, he fell from a ladder and it will take perhaps two thousand pounds to pay for his bills*—I'll bet it will—*If I cannot pay, I fear I cannot come to see you, as I shall worry with concern for my brother. Darling, what shall I do?*—I've got a couple of ideas—*I cannot ask you for more money, as you have been so generous already. But without the money I fear I shall have to stay and care for my brother. You are always so good with ideas, my Mervyn, perhaps you will know what to do. The thought that I will not see you next week might break my heart. Your ever loving Tatiana.*"

"Poor Mervyn," says Ibrahim.

"So what now?" asks Bob.

"Now we reply," says Ibrahim, and starts typing. *"My darling Tatiana, how I long for your touch . . ."*

Much as he loves romantic poetry, Ron decides to call it a night, and leaves Bob and Ibrahim to it. Ib seems fairly happy. Ron still feels guilty that they didn't play charades at Christmas. But Ibrahim understood the principle of the thing.

As Ron walks through Coopers Chase, a fox scurries across his path. White tips to both of his ears. Ron sees him about a lot, darting in and out of bushes. You know where you are with foxes; they're not trying to kid you they're something they're not.

"Good luck to you, old son," says Ron.

Perhaps Ron won't have Pauline to worry about for too much longer anyway? Presents after lunch, I ask you. A few other rows too, to be honest. She listens to Radio 2 instead of talkSPORT, made him watch a French film, that sort of thing. Though once you're used to Radio 2 it's not bad. And the film was good too, a good murder, even with the subtitles. And, actually, opening presents after lunch was OK, he was just too indignant to appreciate it at the time. Perhaps she is *good* for him? Though, if she is good for him, and Ron's jury is still deliberating on that case, then is he good for her? What does Pauline get from him apart from stubbornness? Though he's only stubborn when he's right, so that's not about to change, no way, no sir.

But Ron wishes, he realizes, that she was here.

Ron looks at his phone. No new messages. Well, that tells its own story. She'll have gone to bed without sending him a goodnight kiss. Should he send her one? He stares at his phone for a while, as if it might somehow have the answer.

In fact, he realizes later, this was probably why he missed the sign that something wasn't right. Missed the fact that the light in his flat was off, when he always leaves it on.

That was why he walked straight into the trap.

23.

Stephen wanders through the living room.

It is late, and he is alone, which doesn't feel quite normal. Feels off. Hard to tell why.

He knows the sofa, and there is safety in that. It's his, of that he is certain. Brown, some sort of velvet, the imprint of his backside in a lighter, golden brown. If he knows the sofa, things can't be too out of kilter. Worse comes to the worst, sit yourself down, wait and see what happens, trust that it will all make sense in the end.

He cannot find his cigarettes, for love nor money. He can't even find an ashtray. No lighter, no nothing. He has opened all the drawers in the kitchen. Stephen can see the sofa from the kitchen, so it stands to reason that it must be his kitchen. There's some blasted business going on. Something is being hidden from him. But what, and why?

The key is not to panic. He feels like he has been through all this before. This confusion, these thought processes. Deep inside, he wants to scream, he wants to cry for help, to cry for his father to come and collect him, but he clings to the positive. The sofa. His sofa.

There is a picture on the kitchen worktop. It is a picture of him, looking much older than he remembers, and he is with an old woman. He knows her, knows her name even. He can't access it right now, but he knows it's there. A cigarette would calm him down though. Where has he put them? Is he forgetting things? Something is spinning, but it's not the room, and it's not his eyes. It's his memory. His memory is spinning. However much he tries to tether it down, it is refusing to hold still.

He decides he will drive to the petrol station on the corner and buy some cigarettes. There is a jacket on the hook in the hallway, so he slips it on and searches for his car keys. Nowhere to be found. Someone has been having a spring clean. Very frustrating—just leave things be, leave things in their place, why does everything have to move around? That spinning again. Time for the sofa.

Stephen takes the weight off. He feels much older than he should, perhaps he ought to go to the doctor. But something tells him no. Something tells him he has a secret that others mustn't know. Sit tight on the sofa, don't raise the alarm. Everything will come back into focus soon enough. The mist is sure to clear.

The outside security light flicks on. Stephen looks out of the window. In a field he doesn't quite recognize, leading to an allotment he can't quite place, though he is sure he walked by it today, there is someone he knows well. A fox.

Every evening the fox comes a little nearer; Stephen remembers this quite clearly. A curving walk, eyes scanning from side to side, a man who understands fear, understands that people wish to do him wrong. And then the fox settles, head on paws, and looks into the window, as he does every night. Stephen looks back, as he does every night. They nod to each other. Stephen knows they don't actually nod to each other—he isn't barmy—but certainly they acknowledge each other's existence. Stephen calls him Snowy, because of the white tip to each of his ears. Snowy lies down and thinks he's camouflaged, but the tips of those ears always betray him. Stephen himself has white hair now; he saw it only this morning and was taken aback. His father has white hair too though, so perhaps he is getting mixed up.

Snowy rolls over on the ground, about twenty feet away from the patio, and Stephen remembers. *Elizabeth*. The woman in the photo. The old woman. Stephen laughs: well, of course she is an old woman, he is an old man. He can just make himself out in the window's reflection. Elizabeth has told him not to encourage Snowy, told him Snowy was a pest. She shoos him away if she sees him. But someone has left a bowl of dog food on their terrace, and it wasn't Stephen.

Elizabeth will be back soon. She will find his car keys and he will go out and buy cigarettes. Perhaps he will visit his dad—there is something he needs to tell him, though he can't for the life of him remember what it is for now. He will have written it down somewhere.

Snowy, the sofa, Elizabeth. Stephen is loved and safe. Whatever else is going on, and something most definitely is, Stephen is loved and Stephen is safe. That's a starting point. A rock on which to stand.

Outside a dog barks and Snowy decides to make his exit. Stephen approves; it pays to be cautious. All very well rolling around on the grass, but you mustn't ignore a barking dog. Until tomorrow, my friend.

Elizabeth lives here—Stephen can tell by the pictures on the wall, and the glasses on the hall table. He is looked after. They are married; perhaps they have children. That's something he should know. Why doesn't he? That's a question he needs to crack.

When Elizabeth arrives, he will go to kiss her, and he will be able to tell for certain if they are married. He is sure they are, but you can't be too careful. It pays to be cautious. Barking dogs and what have you. He will make her a cup of tea. He wanders into the kitchen, his kitchen, though you'd be forgiven for not knowing, and realizes he doesn't quite know how to go about it. There's a knack, he knows that. He begins to worry that he should be at work. There's a job he hasn't done. Is it urgent? Or perhaps he has done it already?

What's the chap's name? His pal? Kuldesh, that's it. The name on everyone's lips. Married to Prisha, Stephen sent his love to her.

He turns on the tap. That's the starting point, he is convinced of it, and it surely isn't beyond the wit of man to work out the next step. He looks for clues. He's in a kitchen, but not his own. He begins to feel small and weak, but tells himself to calm down, to breathe. There will be an explanation. He starts to cry. It is just fear, he knows that. Bloody pull yourself together, old chap. Whatever this is, it will pass; the picture will clear, there will surely be a voice to soothe him?

Back to the sofa is probably the safest option. Back to the sofa and wait for this Elizabeth. Bit of thinking time, try to work out what's missing. Maybe see if Snowy will visit him today. Snowy is a fox with white ears, quite the sight, visits every evening. Elizabeth feeds him in secret, and she thinks Stephen doesn't know.

He sits. There is a key in the lock. Could be anyone. Stephen is scared. Scared but ready. Water is overflowing from the sink and falling onto the kitchen floor.

It is Elizabeth, the woman from the picture. She smiles, and then sees the water pouring onto the kitchen floor, and she sploshes over to turn off the tap. She is very beautiful.

"I was making you a cup of tea," says Stephen. He must have left the tap on.

"Well, I'm here now," says Elizabeth. "Why don't I do the honors?"

She walks to the sofa and kisses Stephen. And what a kiss. Boy, oh boy, oh boy, are they ever married!

"I knew it," he says. But why couldn't he remember? Why wasn't he sure? A bell rings somewhere deep within. Harsh and shrill.

She touches his face and he starts to cry once more. Elizabeth kisses the tears away but more come.

"I've got you," says Elizabeth. "No need for tears."

But the tears keep rolling. Because Stephen has had a flash of memory, of recall. The flash is fuzzy and bent, like a beam of sunlight through a broken stained-glass window. But it is enough. He knows, in that moment, precisely what is happening. He sees the water on the kitchen floor, looks down at his tattered pajama trousers, and holds the pieces of his mind together for long enough to understand what they mean. And what they are going to mean in the future. Oh, Stephen, of all the luck. He looks at his wife, and sees in her eyes that she knows it too.

"I love you," he says. Because what else is there to say?

"And I you," says Elizabeth. "Are you cold?"

"Not with you here," says Stephen.

Elizabeth's landline rings. On the stroke of midnight.

24.

Ron is bundled to the floor the second he opens his front door. A hand over his mouth, a knee in his back. An urgent whisper in his ear.

"You make a sound and I'll kill you? Understand?" A Liverpool accent. Not Dom Holt though. Ron nods his assent. This is the sort of treatment he used to get from the police on the picket lines in the eighties, but he's forty years older now. Let's get the lights on and assess the situation.

The hand is removed from Ron's mouth, and strong arms help him up from the floor. "Upsy-daisy, old fella. No sudden moves, no noise."

"Sudden moves?" says Ron. "I'm nearly eighty, mate. You proud of yourself?"

"Stop moaning," says the man. "I've seen your son box. I was taking no chances."

A light is flicked on, and Ron takes a look at the man. Late forties, polo-neck top under a dark suit, gold chain, thick, dark hair and blue eyes. Handsome bugger. An enforcer for Dom Holt? Looks too rich. The man motions for Ron to take a chair, and then sits opposite him.

"Ron Ritchie?"

Ron nods. "You?"

"Mitch Maxwell. You know why I'm here, Ron?"

Ron shrugs. "You're a psychopath?"

"Worse than that, I'm afraid," says Mitch. "Someone has stolen something from me."

"I don't blame them," says Ron. His hip is beginning to ache. The sort of ache that is not going to disappear by morning. "You work for Dom Holt, is it?"

Mitch laughs. "Do I look like I work for someone?"

"Everybody works for someone," says Ron. "Only a weak man pretends otherwise."

"Mouthy little sod, ain't ya?" says Mitch. "Typical West Ham fan. Dom Holt works for me."

"Does he? Tell him he owes me three grand for the Daihatsu."

"Mr. Ritchie," says Mitch, "on December twenty-seventh a little box, absolutely stuffed with heroin, was delivered to your mate Kuldesh Sharma. By the next day, the box, the heroin and your mate had all disappeared. Now your mate has turned up, bullet through the skull, terrible shame, but my heroin is still nowhere to be seen. We smashed his shop up, and nothing. So maybe you know where it is? Kuldesh had it all day. Maybe he brought it over here, eh? Asked his mates to look after it while he tried to pull a stroke?"

"Not my mate," says Ron. "Heard of him, but never met him."

"You heard he died though? You accused Dom of killing him?"

"Yup," agrees Ron. "Makes sense, doesn't it? Scumbag heroin dealer gets ripped off. Then kills the person who ripped him off. No offense to *your* mate, could have been you too. You look like the type."

The hip is starting to throb now. Ron has no intention of showing his pain.

"People get killed," says Mitch. "But the heroin's still missing. And I need it quick."

"So you broke into my flat?"

"Put yourself in my shoes, Ron," says Mitch. "A perfectly normal consignment of heroin enters the country in a small box in the back of a lorry. It goes missing. A couple of days later you pay my offices a visit. Jason Ritchie's dad, so I'm going to take an interest. Then I hear one of Connie Johnson's buddies is involved, and there's an old woman with a gun. What would you think?"

Ron smiles. "You think Kuldesh gave us the heroin before he died?"

"It's a theory," says Mitch. "Until you prove otherwise."

Ron leans forward, careful not to wince. He rests his chin on his hands. "You free for the next couple of hours?"

Mitch looks at his watch. "My son's got street dance before school, but you've got me till then."

"I'm going to make a couple of calls," says Ron. "Get my friends over here. See if we can't work this out."

"Can I trust them?" says Mitch.

"No," says Ron, picking up his phone and dialing. "Can we trust you?"

"No," says Mitch.

"Well, let's make the best of what we have," says Ron, waiting for his call to be answered.

He is ringing Elizabeth first. He has to. If he rings Ibrahim first, she'll find out and there'll be hell to pay. "Liz, it's Ron, pop your shoes on and come round to mine. You OK? You sure? OK, I believe you, millions wouldn't. You ring Joyce, I'll ring Ib—yeah, I probably would bring a gun."

He ends the call, and dials Ibrahim.

"Whisky?" Ron asks Mitch. "While we wait?"

Mitch nods and stands. "I'll get it. You need something for that hip?"

Ron shakes his head. He obviously wasn't hiding it as well as he thought. Still, he's not going to give Mitch the satisfaction of knowing he's hurt him. "I'll walk it off."

Ron's call connects. "Ib, it's me. Me. Ron. Who do you think's going to ring you at this time of night? Meghan Markle?"

"I can usually get heroin," says Mitch. "If you ever need it."

25.

Mitch would rather be talking to Luca. Rather be fending off blows from a broken pool cue in an underground hangar. You know where you are then. You know the rules. But here he is, in the dead of night, in a comfortable armchair, drinking good whisky with four pensioners.

There's no doubt about it, Mitch is out of his comfort zone.

His plan had been so simple. Scare the living daylights out of this Ron Ritchie guy, then torture him until he told him where the heroin was. But that's not how things were working out. The woman with the gun appears to be their ringleader. Elizabeth, she's called. The gun doesn't scare Mitch, but she does. He's seen that look in the eyes of a few people over the years. Most of them now dead, in prison or in big villas with high fences in Spain.

"Are you proud of the way you make a living?" Elizabeth asks.

"We're not here to talk about me," says Mitch.

"If you break into someone's house at midnight, it's probably polite to answer a few questions. A common courtesy." This was the guy who introduced himself as Ibrahim. The one who works with Connie Johnson. He is taking notes.

"It's a bit grubby, isn't it? Heroin dealing?" This is Elizabeth again, her gun on her lap. What's her story? Mitch knows everyone in the business, but he doesn't know her.

A smaller woman, in a green cardigan, leans forward. "Mr. Maxwell. We didn't ask you to come here. That was your choice."

"Quite so, Joyce," says Elizabeth. "You beat up our friend—"

"He didn't beat me up," says Ron.

"Well, let's see if your GP agrees with that tomorrow," says Elizabeth. "Now, you'll notice, Mr. Maxwell, we don't give two hoots about how tough you are; we've dealt with an awful lot worse than you."

"You are barely top ten," says Ibrahim. "And, believe me, I have a top ten."

"If I might make an observation, it seems we have a common goal, Mr. Maxwell," says Elizabeth. "We want to find out who killed Kuldesh, and you want to find your heroin. Correct?"

"I want my goods back," says Mitch. "*Need* my goods back."

"Oh, God," says Elizabeth. "Spare us the euphemisms; we're not children or police officers. Call heroin heroin."

"I need my heroin back," confirms Mitch. "It's in a little terra-cotta box, it's worth a lot of money, and it's mine."

"Morally you must find heroin dealing unsettling?" says Ibrahim.

"Says the guy who works for Connie Johnson," counters Mitch. "Listen, I have a simple question before we go any further. Who are you?"

"I'm Joyce," says Joyce.

"And we are all friends of Joyce's," adds Ibrahim. "So, with that cleared up, let us ask you a few more questions, just so we can get to know you a little. So we feel we can trust you."

Mitch throws his hands up. "Go on, then."

"Are you proud of being a heroin smuggler?" Elizabeth asks him again.

"I'm proud of my success," says Mitch, realizing he's never really thought about this before. "But, I guess, no. I just fell into it, and then I was good at it."

"You could do something else?" suggests Joyce. "IT?"

"I'm nearly fifty," says Mitch.

How dearly he would love to give all this up. When he finds the heroin, that's it. He's quitting.

"Have you ever been to prison?" asks Ibrahim.

"No," says Mitch.

"Have you ever been arrested?" asks Joyce.

"Many times," says Mitch.

"Have you ever killed anyone?" asks Ron.

"If I went around admitting to killing people, I would have been to prison, wouldn't I?" reasons Mitch.

"Is your hip all right, Ron?" Joyce asks.

"My hip is fine," says Ron.

"And the biggest question of all," says Elizabeth. "Who killed Kuldesh Sharma? You?"

Mitch smiles. "You'll have to try harder than that."

"More whisky?" asks Ibrahim.

Mitch declines. He's got to drive back to Hertfordshire in a bit, and he has a semiautomatic weapon in his boot, so he wouldn't want to get pulled over for drunk driving.

"A simpler question, then," says Elizabeth. "Who else knew about the box with the heroin?"

"A few Afghans," says Mitch. "But no one who'd need to steal it. A middleman who saw the drugs into Moldova—but he's one of my guys."

"His name?" asks Ibrahim, making notes.

"Lenny," says Mitch.

"Someone here has just had a great-grandson called Lenny," says Joyce. "Names come back around, don't they?"

"Where might we find him?" asks Ibrahim.

"Dom will have his number," says Mitch.

"Ah, our friend Dom," says Elizabeth. "He also knows everything of course? You must have asked yourself whether he stole the heroin himself? Whether he set Kuldesh up as the fall guy?"

Mitch shakes his head. "He knows everything, but I trust him with my life."

"But he knew what was in the box. He delivered the box. He met Kuldesh?"

"And it's a lot of money," says Joyce.

"Not in the grand scheme of things," says Mitch.

"You make more money than him though," says Ron. "A hundred grand's still a lot for Dom."

"Is it tax free?" Ibrahim asks. "Yes, it must be. I'm answering my own question. Do you know when you win money on quiz shows, that's all tax free too? Something quiz shows and heroin smuggling have in common."

Everyone waits until they are absolutely sure that Ibrahim has finished.

"Everyone's loyal until they're not," says Ron.

"I don't see it," says Mitch. "Sorry."

"Anyone else you might steer us in the direction of?" asks Elizabeth. "You were selling the heroin, but who was buying it?"

"Nope," says Mitch. "You've got all you're going to get from me."

"For now," says Ibrahim.

"Can I ask a couple of questions?" says Mitch. "Before I go?"

They all seem happy with this prospect. So he turns, first, to Ibrahim.

"Do you really work for Connie Johnson?"

"I do," confirms Ibrahim.

"What do you do for her?"

"I can't tell you," says Ibrahim.

"That bad, eh?" says Mitch. He then addresses Elizabeth. "And you. Why do you have a gun?"

Elizabeth gives a quizzical smile. "Why do I have a gun? To shoot people with."

Jesus. Mitch turns to Ron. "Did I really hurt your hip?"

Ron nods. "Course you did. I'm an old man, you idiot."

"Sorry," says Mitch. "I thought you stole my gear."

"We didn't," says Joyce.

"And to all of you, seriously," says Mitch. "You don't really think Dom would steal from me? Even for a hundred grand, that makes no sense. Why would he think he could get away with it?"

"Well," says Joyce, who has been fairly quiet up to now. Mitch had almost forgotten she was there. "You said you'd trust him with your life. He probably knows that, doesn't he? So who better to steal from?"

She says it with such kindness that Mitch recognizes instantly that she might just be right.

26.

Early morning and the Portakabin is cold, so Donna is still wearing her puffer jacket. Chris has both hands around a cup of vending-machine tea.

"The more I ask around about Dom Holt and Mitch Maxwell, the worse it gets," says Chris. "Kuldesh had no idea who he was dealing with."

"Dom Holt wouldn't steal his own heroin though, would he?" says Donna.

"Perhaps he had a falling-out with his boss?" suggests Chris.

He screws up a ball of paper and throws it in a high arc toward a bin in the corner of the room. It hits the rim and bounces out.

"Yeah, bosses are the worst," says Donna. "Anyway, we could take a look at him without alerting SIO Regan and her merry men? Anyone we could talk to?"

"Jason Ritchie?"

"Ron's son?" says Donna. "He moves in interesting circles."

Chris is now blowing on his hands. "We could see what he knows. I'll talk to Ron."

A blast of January air cannons into the Portakabin as SIO Jill Regan opens the door.

"You forgot to knock," says Chris.

"Is that how you dress on duty?" Jill asks Donna.

"Some idiot put us in a Portakabin," replies Donna, doing up her zip still further. "Ma'am."

Jill takes a seat. "In the habit of calling superior officers idiots, are you, constable?"

"She is," says Chris. "I've got used to it. How can we help you?"

"Something struck me as strange," says Jill.

"You work for the National Crime Agency," says Chris. "That must happen a lot?"

"Where's his phone?" says Jill. "That's what's bothering me."

"Whose phone?" asks Donna.

"Kuldesh Sharma's," says Jill. "Where's his phone, I wonder?"

"Not our case," says Chris.

"Yeah," says Jill. "That's what I thought too. Out chasing horses, aren't you?"

"Doing our best," says Chris. "They're very fast."

"Only . . . Donna was making a request for phone records yesterday," says Jill. She rubs her hands together. "Cold in here, isn't it?"

"Routine inquiry," says Donna.

"So I looked back," says Jill Regan. "And you requested some other phone records previously? I haven't seen the results of that request anywhere?"

"We're police officers," says Chris. "We request a lot of phone records. I don't suppose you've got a spare heater up in the Incident Room?"

"If you have his phone," says Jill, "you'll be off the force, you know that?"

"Lucky we don't, then," says Donna.

Donna, Chris and Jill stare at each other for a while. Chris tries to do a gentle spin on his chair, and one of the wheels falls off. In Donna's view he styles it out fairly well.

"Stay away from this case," says Jill.

"Of course," says Chris. "It's in the safe hands of the National Crime Agency. If you need us, we'll be leaning on a gate, chewing on some straw."

Jill gets up. "If you happen to stumble across that phone?"

"Then we know where you are," says Chris.

"Colleague to colleague," says Jill, "don't get mixed up in this."

"Noted," says Chris. "Make sure you shut the door on the way out."

Jill exits, leaving the door wide open.

As Chris gets up to close it, he makes sure she has gone. "Anything from Elizabeth's phone?"

Donna checks her watch. "Should get something anytime now."

27.

As it is a Thursday, the gang are in the Jigsaw Room. There is a half-demolished Victoria sponge on the jigsaw table.

From time to time they like to invite experts to speak to them, and today Nina Mishra and her boss, Jonjo, have come to give them a lesson in how the antiques business works. You never know what might be helpful. Ibrahim, as always in these situations, has done some light reading in advance, and suspects there is now little he doesn't know.

"If we start with the basics," says Jonjo. "An antique is anything over one hundred years old. Everything else is vintage, or collectible."

"That chimes with what I have read," agrees Ibrahim. "He's right."

"I didn't know that," says Joyce. "We're collectible, Elizabeth."

"And with anything over a hundred years old, every object has a story to tell," says Jonjo. "Who made it and where?"

"Who bought it, and for how much, and when?" says Nina.

"Has it been cared for, played with, dropped, repaired, repainted, left in sunlight," says Jonjo.

"Gerry bought a gravy boat from a car-boot sale once," says Joyce. "He was convinced it was hundreds of years old, but then we saw the same exact one in British Home Stores."

"BHS seventies stuff is actually very fashionable now," says Nina.

"Oh, he'd love to have known that," says Joyce. "I called him all sorts of names at the time."

"But even if things are over a hundred years old," says Jonjo, "almost all of them are pretty much worthless. Mass produced, or low quality, or simply not what people are looking for."

"My parents used to bring home the most wonderful things sometimes," says Nina. "Corkscrews in the shape of peacocks, a Big Ben biscuit tin, and they'd put them in the shop for a tenner."

"Nina is right," says Jonjo. "Almost nothing is worth anything. The easiest way to make a small fortune in antiques is to start with a big fortune and lose it. Which means that the few things that are worth something make the whole antiques business go round. Right now that might mean a Clarice Cliff dinner set or some Bernard Leach pottery. Next year it will be something else."

"So if you just want to make a living," says Nina, "the equation is pretty simple. If you're selling things for a tenner, make sure they only cost you a fiver, and make sure you know what's fashionable."

"What sells," adds Jonjo.

"If you can do that right, year in, year out, you can make a comfortable living," says Nina. "My parents never quite worked that out. They always fell in love with things."

"First rule of the antiques game," says Jonjo. "Never fall in love with things."

"Sound advice for life," says Ibrahim.

"And might that have been the sort of living that Kuldesh made?" Joyce asks.

"I would say so," says Jonjo. "He was at it for fifty years, knew what to look out for, had clients who trusted him and a rent he could afford. I'm sure he had quiet weeks, but that's not a bad recipe for a healthy business."

"And you get the joy of working with unusual, or beautiful, or rare things," says Nina. "You'll never be a millionaire, but you'll also rarely get bored."

"And if you do want to become a millionaire?" Ron asks. "How might you go about that?"

Jonjo holds a finger in the air. "Well, isn't that the question of the day?"

"Have you been to see Samantha Barnes yet?" Nina asks.

"It's next on our to-do list," says Joyce.

"Let me show you something," says Jonjo.

Jonjo delves into a leather briefcase and takes out a small velvet pouch. He then slips on a pair of white gloves, loosens the drawstring of the pouch and tips a silver medal into his hand.

"Ooh," says Joyce.

Jonjo places the medal on the flat of his palm, and shows it to each of them in turn. "Now what you're looking at here—please don't touch—is a DSM, a Distinguished Service Medal, awarded in the Second World War. Been in the same family since then, but they're putting great-grandkids through university, so they brought it in to me and asked for a valuation."

"This would look lovely on Instagram," says Joyce. "I mainly just do pictures of Alan. Would you mind?"

"One moment," says Jonjo. "I asked the family what they expected the medal to be worth, and they said they had read it could be worth up to ten thousand pounds."

"Nah," says Ron.

"I had to tell them they had been misinformed," says Jonjo. "And that actually, given the condition of the medal, and the provenance, having been in the family since it was awarded, it would be worth much nearer thirty thousand pounds."

"Bugger me," says Ron.

"Ron," says Joyce.

"It's beautiful, isn't it?" says Jonjo.

"Very," says Joyce.

Jonjo slips the medal back into the bag and peels off his gloves. "What's beautiful about it, Joyce, would you say?"

"Well, it was very . . . shiny?"

"I'll tell you what was beautiful about it," says Jonjo. "And that will tell you how you become a millionaire in the world of antiques. What was beautiful was the velvet bag, and the white gloves, and the way my voice dropped a tone in reverence."

"I do that sometimes," says Ibrahim.

"What was beautiful was the story," says Jonjo. "The great-grandchildren, the family finally deciding to sell."

"Well, yes," says Joyce. "That was beautiful too."

"But all lies," says Jonjo, tipping the medal unceremoniously onto the table. "It's a piece of tat, knocked up in a workshop about twenty miles from here. There's a gentleman who makes them for a living, and you have to keep a keen eye out for them. This one slipped through the net at a local auction house, and, fortunately, I was on hand to show them the error of their ways. I've kept it ever since to teach the exact lesson I'm teaching you—the lesson being that if you can tell a story, you can sell a five-bob bit of metal for thirty thousand pounds. And that's how you become a millionaire."

"And that's Samantha Barnes's game," says Nina. "Forgeries. Knockoffs. Mainly artwork. Virtually every limited-edition Picasso print you'll see online is one of hers. Most of the Banksys, Damien Hirsts. She does Lowrys, all sorts."

"And I suspect she's involved in worse than that now," says Jonjo. "And Kuldesh would have known her."

"Known her reputation too," agrees Nina.

"I read somewhere that Banksy is really the man from *DIY SOS*," says Joyce. "Nick Knowles? I don't know if that's right."

Ibrahim takes this as his cue to get down to the real business of the day.

"Here is the timeline," he says, handing out laminated sheets. "I am beginning to think that I should start to distribute this sort of information digitally. Hard copies are very wasteful. I would like, if possible, the Thursday Murder Club to become carbon neutral by 2030."

"You could also stop laminating everything," suggests Ron.

"One step at a time, Ron," says Ibrahim. "One step at a time."

He knows, in his heart, that Ron is right, but he doesn't feel able to let go of his laminating machine. This must be how America feels about coal-fired power stations.

"I have to leave at eleven forty-five," says Elizabeth. "Just by the way."

"But the meeting is until twelve," says Ibrahim. "As always."

"I have plans," says Elizabeth.

"What plans?" asks Joyce.

"A drive with Stephen," says Elizabeth. "Some fresh air. Ibrahim, let's get on with the timeline."

"Who's driving?" asks Joyce.

"Bogdan," says Elizabeth. "Ibrahim, please, I'm holding you up."

"Perhaps I might have liked a drive," says Joyce, to no one and everyone.

Ibrahim takes charge again. He wishes he'd known they had only forty-five minutes for the meeting. His life is measured out in hours. No matter— just go with the flow, Ibrahim. He has prepared a preamble of around eight minutes' duration concerning the nature of evil, but he will have to save it for another day and dive straight in. Frustrating.

"To get to the heart of the murder," he begins, "it seems we have two key questions yet to answer. One, where is the heroin now; and, two, who did Kuldesh ring after he rang Nina? Am I missing anything?"

"Why did he buy a spade?" says Ron.

"That is covered under 'Miscellaneous Facts' on your sheet, Ron," says Ibrahim.

"My sincere apologies," says Ron. "So where's the heroin?"

"Nina says that Kuldesh has a lock-up garage in Fairhaven?" says Joyce.

"He did," says Nina. "No idea where."

"Perhaps the heroin's there," says Joyce. "I bet we could track it down."

"Perhaps," continues Ibrahim. "Or perhaps it has already been sold. I believe heroin is much in demand. Certainly it doesn't seem as if Mitch Maxwell has the heroin in his possession. So who does?"

"I wonder," continues Elizabeth, "if Connie Johnson might have something more for us as well, Ibrahim. We still don't know who Mitch was supposed to be selling to."

"I will be seeing her on Monday," says Ibrahim.

"Who's Connie Johnson?" asks Jonjo.

"She's like Samantha Barnes but for drugs," says Joyce. "Perhaps I could bake her some scones, Ibrahim. I don't suppose they have scones in prison."

"Sure," says Ron. "She wants to kill me. Bake her some scones."

"What will you be doing though?" Joyce asks Elizabeth. "While you're out and about?"

"Things to do, people to see," says Elizabeth.

Joyce's phone rings. She looks at the display, then answers.

"Hello, Donna, this is a pleasant surprise, I was just thinking of you yesterday. There was an episode of *Cagney & Lacey* on ITV3 and Cagney, or maybe Lacey, the blonde one anyway, was in a bar and she said . . . oh . . . yes, of course, yes . . ." Joyce, a little crestfallen, hands her phone to Elizabeth. "It's for you."

Elizabeth puts the phone to her ear. "Yes? Mmm hmm . . . Mmm hmm . . . Mmm . . . hmm. Yes . . . yes . . . that's none of your business . . . yes . . . thank you, Donna, I am most grateful."

Elizabeth hands the phone back to Joyce.

"Cagney or Lacey was in a bar, you see, and—"

"Ibrahim," says Elizabeth, "are you free this afternoon?"

"I was hoping to do Zumba," says Ibrahim. "They have a new instructor and he—"

"You're going to Petworth with Joyce," says Elizabeth. "I need you to speak to Samantha Barnes immediately."

"Well, I do like antiquing," says Ibrahim. "And I'm also very interested in heroin smuggling. The transgressive has—"

Elizabeth holds up a hand to stop him. "Donna has been checking my phone records."

"Aye, aye," says Ron.

"At four forty-one p.m. on Tuesday I made a call to Samantha Barnes."

Ibrahim looks up from his notes. "And?"

"And," says Elizabeth, "Samantha Barnes's number showed up in the phone records as Code 777."

28.

They are crawling along in traffic on the A23, just north of Coulsdon, but Stephen, in the front with Bogdan, seems to be enjoying the drive. He hasn't stopped asking Bogdan questions since they left Coopers Chase.

"There's a museum," says Stephen. "In Baghdad. Have you been?"

This is the second time he has asked this question.

"Have I been to Baghdad?" asks Bogdan. "No."

"Oh, you must," says Stephen.

"OK, I will," says Bogdan.

It was bad timing: Elizabeth wishes she hadn't had to cut the meeting short like that. But Viktor has a tight schedule, and she must see him. And Viktor must see Stephen.

Joyce saw them all getting into the car together, and didn't even wave goodbye, so perhaps she suspects something is awry. She hopes Joyce's mission to see Samantha Barnes will distract her. It had been a lucky guess on Elizabeth's part, a hunch, to have Donna check Samantha's number to see if it came back as Code 777. Had Kuldesh really rung Samantha? To ask advice? To sell her the heroin?

Elizabeth tries to put these questions out of her head. She needs to concentrate on far more important matters.

"Things like you wouldn't believe," says Stephen. "Thousands of years old. Puts things into a bit of perspective. You ever touched something six thousand years old?"

"No," says Bogdan. "Ron's car maybe?"

"We must go there, Elizabeth, we must all go. Get on to the old travel agent."

"They don't have travel agents no more," says Bogdan, using a bus lane to bypass a line of traffic.

"No travel agents," says Stephen. "News to me."

"I'll look into it," says Elizabeth. "Baghdad." What she would give for that trip. Stephen with an arm around her waist. Cold vodka in the Middle Eastern sun.

Bogdan now drives onto the hard shoulder to overtake another car.

"You drive terribly," say Elizabeth. "And illegally."

"I know," says Bogdan. "But I promised you we would arrive at one twenty-three."

"We have all the time in the world," says Stephen. "Time swirls about us, laughing at us."

"Tell that to Google maps," says Bogdan.

"Where are we off to?" says Stephen.

He has also asked this before.

"London," says Elizabeth. "To see an old friend."

"Kuldesh?" Stephen asks.

"Not Kuldesh, no," says Elizabeth. She feels guilty. She has been asking Stephen about Kuldesh an awful lot. Known associates, that sort of thing. She even mentioned Samantha Barnes and Petworth, but not a flicker.

"Old friend of mine, or old friend of yours?" Stephen asks. "Can we pop into the Reform Club on the way back? They have a book I'm after in the library."

"A friend of mine, but someone you've met," says Elizabeth. "Someone who can help."

Stephen turns in his seat to look at her. "Who needs help now?"

"We all do," says Bogdan. "If we gonna make it by one twenty-three."

The traffic doesn't let up all the way to Battersea. London is clogged.

Elizabeth barely misses London now. She and Stephen would be up and down here all the time, exhibitions, plays, lunch at the club. They once saw Professor Brian Cox give a lecture at the Albert Hall. The majesty of the cosmos. We all come from the stars, and we all return to the stars. She had enjoyed the lecture, but there were lasers she could have lived without.

Had she really understood then that those were the best of times? That she was in heaven? She thinks she did understand, yes. Understood she had been given a great gift. Doing the crossword in a train carriage, Stephen with a can of beer ("I will only drink beer on trains, nowhere else, don't ask me why"), glasses halfway down his nose, reading out clues. The real secret was that when they looked at each other, they each thought they had the better deal.

But, however much life teaches you that nothing lasts, it is still a shock when it disappears. When the man you love with every fiber starts returning to the stars, an atom at a time.

And London? London is slow, gray and clogged. You have to wade through it now. Is that what life is to become without Stephen? A slow trudge of exhaust fumes and brake lights?

Bogdan tries every move in the book, while Stephen points out landmarks. "The Oval! The Oval, Elizabeth!"

"That's cricket, is it?"

"You know full well it is," says Stephen.

Bogdan drives the wrong way down a narrow, cobbled backstreet.

They arrive at 1:22.

29.

brahim is beginning to despair. They have driven into the very center of Petworth, with no parking spaces yet evident. The town is very beautiful—cobbled streets, flowers in the windows, antiques shops every five yards—but he is unable to enjoy it. What if there is simply nowhere to park? What then? Park illegally? No thanks, a ticket on the windscreen or, worse, the car towed away. Then how would they get home? They would be stuck. In Petworth. Which, charming as the guidebooks have made it sound, is alien to Ibrahim. Wherever he is, and whatever he is doing, the primary thought in Ibrahim's mind is always "How will I get home?" With one's car impounded? Impossible.

He tries to control his breathing. He is about to say, "Well, there are no parking spaces, Joyce, so let's go home and come back another day," when a Volvo reverses out from a parking space directly on their right. Jackpot.

"It's our lucky day," says Joyce. "We should buy a lottery ticket!"

Ibrahim sighs but is glad to have the opportunity to teach Joyce an important lesson. "Joyce, that is precisely the opposite of what we should do. There are no 'lucky days,' just individual parcels of 'luck.'"

"Oh," says Joyce.

The space is wide and open and welcoming. Even the wing mirrors can relax.

"We have just had a single piece of luck: the parking space opening up. Expecting an immediate, second piece of luck is folly. Small bits of good luck, such as this, are actually, in the scheme of things, bad luck."

"Shall we get out of the car?" asks Joyce.

"Now the *reason* they are bad luck," Ibrahim continues, "is that we might logically assume that we are all allocated the same number of moments of random luck in our lives. Forget for a moment the 'luck' we bring upon ourselves through hard work; I am speaking merely of the luck that falls into our laps. Happenstance, as the poets might say."

"I think Alan might need the toilet," says Joyce, and Alan, roaming the backseat, barks in agreement.

"And if we are allocated the same number of these random moments of luck," says Ibrahim, straightening the car for what he hopes will be the final time, "it is better not to waste them on small things. Perhaps you might catch the bus with a second to spare, or find the perfect parking space; but those two bits of luck may mean that you will have no moments of luck left for the big things, for example, winning the lottery or meeting the man of your dreams. You would do a great deal better to choose a day when we *hadn't* found a parking space and then say, 'We should buy a lottery ticket.' Do you see?"

"Of course I do," says Joyce, undoing her seat belt. "Thank you, as always."

Ibrahim is not convinced that she does see. Joyce sometimes does this to humor him. Lots of people do. But he is right. Save your good luck for big things, and your bad luck for small things. Joyce is out of the car and putting Alan's lead on. Ibrahim steps out and takes a look around him. Now that he has parked, he is able to appreciate what a pretty place Petworth is. And, if he has memorized the map correctly, and he has, then Samantha Barnes's antiques shop must be straight up the road ahead of them, second right and first left. And the café where Joyce wants to have lunch is back in the same direction, left, then first right. He downloaded the menu for her, but he has not printed it out, because you have to start somewhere. Ibrahim has stuck a Post-it note on both his printer and his laminator saying *What would Greta Thunberg do?*

Joyce leads the way, with a delighted Alan stopping to smell wondrous new things every few yards. He barks at a postal worker, a constant for Alan wherever he might find himself, and tries to drag Joyce across the road when he spots another dog. They take the second right, and then the first left, and find themselves in front of G&S ANTIQUES—FORMERLY S&W ANTIQUES.

The bell on the door gives a comforting small-town "jingle" as they walk in. Samantha Barnes is waiting for them, prewarned by Elizabeth, with a pot of tea and a Battenberg on the shop counter. Elizabeth will want to know what Samantha Barnes looks like. Ibrahim is very bad at noticing that sort of thing, but he will try. She is wearing black and looks very elegant. Ibrahim feels unqualified to comment any further. Though, if he really concentrates, he can see that she has dark hair and red lipstick. Joyce will be able to fill in the details.

"You must be Joyce and Ibrahim?" says Samantha.

Joyce takes Samantha's hand. "And Alan, yes. You are very kind to be meeting us like this; you must be very busy."

Samantha gestures to the empty shop. "I'm intrigued to hear what you have to ask. There's a bowl of water behind the counter if Alan gets thirsty."

Ibrahim offers his hand now. "Ibrahim. You wouldn't believe where we parked. You simply wouldn't believe it."

"I'm sure I wouldn't," agrees Samantha, shaking Ibrahim's hand. She bids them to sit and pours the tea. "What's all this about heroin, I wonder? It doesn't sound very Petworth."

"Heroin crops up everywhere," says Joyce. "Once you start noticing it. I'll slice the Battenberg while you pour."

"And murder too?"

"Alarmingly common," says Ibrahim. "We are told you have a very fine house, Mrs. Barnes?"

"Call me Samantha," says Samantha. "Who might have told you that?"

"We pick things up," says Joyce. Ibrahim can see that, in Elizabeth's absence, Joyce is channeling her, and enjoying it.

"Well, the rule here is that if you pick things up, you pay for them," says Samantha. "Milk and sugar?"

"Is it normal milk?" Joyce asks.

"Of course," says Samantha.

Joyce nods. "Just milk for both of us. You heard that our friend Kuldesh Sharma was murdered?"

"I read all about it in the *Evening Argus*, yes," says Samantha. "And you think, what? That I killed him? That I know who killed him? That I might be the next victim? Thrilling whichever way, I would say."

"We were just hoping you might have some information," says Ibrahim. "We think somebody used Kuldesh's shop to sell a consignment of heroin. Does that sound far-fetched to you?"

Samantha sips her tea. "Far-fetched? Not at all. I wouldn't say it was an everyday occurrence in the antiques world, but one hears about such things."

"And has anyone ever asked you to do the same?" Joyce asks.

"They have not," says Samantha. "Nor would they dare."

"It then seems that Kuldesh decided to take matters into his own hands and sell the heroin himself," says Ibrahim. "Did they mention that in the *Evening Argus?*"

"They did not," says Samantha. "Do you know who he sold it to?"

"That's why we're here," says Joyce. "This Battenberg is terrific by the way, is it M&S?"

"My husband, Garth, made it," says Samantha.

"He's a whizz," says Joyce. "We're not here to pry into your business, or accuse you of this, that or the other. It just seems that you own a small antiques shop—"

"And yet you make an awful lot of money," says Ibrahim.

"And so it occurred to us," continues Joyce, "admittedly via Elizabeth, that you might be a good person to consult on the subject of where antiques and crime collide. Does that sound a reasonable assumption?"

"I'm sure I don't know what you're driving at," says Samantha. "But I could offer an amateur insight, if you think it might help?"

"Simply that," says Ibrahim. "Another pair of eyes."

"If you were to come into possession of a large amount of heroin—" asks Joyce.

"How large?" interrupts Samantha.

"A hundred thousand pounds' worth, or so," says Joyce. "Who might you think of selling it to? Are there shadowy figures you can call?"

"Not off the top of my head," said Samantha.

"There is a suggestion," says Ibrahim. "And only a suggestion, that if Kuldesh were of a mind to sell the heroin, he might call you."

"Indeed?" says Samantha, sipping her tea. "And where does this suggestion spring from?"

"Kuldesh made a call to an untraceable number," says Ibrahim. "Shortly before he passed away. And, for reasons best known to yourself, perfectly innocent, I'm sure, you yourself have an untraceable number. So, with that in mind, we wondered if you might be the shadowy figure we seek?"

"Mmm," says Samantha. "That's quite a leap. And a slanderous one at that."

"How do you make your money?" Joyce asks, blowing on her tea to cool it down. "If you don't mind me being nosy?"

"Antiques," says Samantha.

"We were looking at your house on Google," says Joyce. "There must be an awful lot of money in hat stands."

"I shall be doing some Googling of my own when you leave," says Samantha.

"Any sidelines?" asks Ibrahim.

"I teach line dancing at the Seniors' Club," says Samantha. "Unpaid though."

"Anyway," says Joyce, her tea finally cool enough to take a sip. "Heroin."

The shop door opens, and a large man in a padded jacket and woolly hat fills the open doorway and then stoops inside.

"Garth, darling," says Samantha. "This is Joyce and Ibrahim."

"And Alan," says Joyce.

Garth looks at Joyce and Ibrahim, expressionless, then looks back at Samantha, and shrugs. Alan makes a beeline for this exciting new man, but if Garth even notices Alan jumping up at him he doesn't show it.

"We hear this is your Battenberg," says Joyce, cake fork in hand. "It really is delicious."

"Stone-ground flour," says Garth.

"Garth, dearest," says Samantha. "Joyce here was just wondering who might buy a hundred thousand pounds' worth of heroin?"

Garth looks directly at Joyce. "You're selling heroin?"

"No," giggles Joyce. "A friend of ours. Though give it a couple of years and I wouldn't put it past us."

"Someone got himself killed," says Samantha. "Some deal or other gone wrong. The heroin went missing, and we're being canvassed for our expert opinion."

"Don't know nuthin' about it," says Garth. "Funny question for a Thursday."

"Isn't it?" says Samantha.

Alan is absolutely infuriated that Garth won't pay him attention. He's bringing out every trick he has, but Garth won't even look at him. Garth is thinking, like a mighty supercomputer blinking into life. He fixes Joyce with a stare.

"You know where the heroin is now, old lady?"

"Joyce," says Joyce. "But no. Floating around somewhere. I suppose someone must have it. Someone must, mustn't they? Wouldn't you say, Garth?"

"It'll be somewhere, for sure," says Garth. "You got any idea? You got an inkling?"

"Who would you call, Garth?" asks Joyce. "If you suddenly had a box full of heroin in your drawer?"

"I would call the police," says Garth, then nods to Samantha. "Wouldn't I, honey?"

"Anything illegal," agrees Samantha. "Straight to the police. Trust them with our lives." Joyce sips her tea.

"Do you suppose you're close to finding the heroin?" asks Samantha. "Another cup of tea, Joyce?"

"I don't have the bladder for two cups of tea these days," says Joyce. "I used to be a camel in that respect."

"We will find it," says Ibrahim. "I remain confident of that. If you want my considered opinion—"

Garth, still being leaped at by Alan, turns away from Ibrahim and addresses Joyce. "This dog is a million bucks, by the way."

"You can stroke him if you'd like?" says Joyce. "He's called Alan."

Garth shakes his head. "You gotta play hard to get with dogs. They gotta earn it off you."

"Absolutely," says Ibrahim, surreptitiously putting a Polo mint back into his pocket.

"Ibrahim, I have a question," says Samantha. "The man who brought the heroin to the shop? You wouldn't happen to know who that was?"

"We do," says Ibrahim. "In fact, we've met him. He seemed agreeable enough, if prone to mood swings. Though I suppose that's the nature of the business, isn't it? Selling drugs is not like selling shoes, is it? Or selling antiques. It must attract a certain sort of—"

Garth holds up a hand to stop Ibrahim. "I need you to talk less. I have a low boredom threshold. I was born with it, the doctors can't do nothing."

"Understood," says Ibrahim. "A low boredom threshold can often mean—"

Garth holds up his hand again. Ibrahim, with some difficulty, restrains himself. Annoying, because he had an interesting point to make. So often people will cut him off when he is merely in the foothills of an observation. It is very frustrating. What a lot the world misses out on by not giving Ibrahim enough time to really get into high gear. There is certainly an attention deficit in today's society. The overwhelming stimuli of the modern world have all but been destroyed . . . Ibrahim realizes that someone has just asked a question.

"I'm sorry?" he says.

"I was asking, what is the gentleman's name?" Samantha is cutting another slice of Garth's Battenberg.

"Mr. Dominic Holt," says Ibrahim. "Of Liverpool."

"Have you heard of him, perhaps?" asks Joyce.

"Dominic Holt?" Samantha looks to Garth. Garth shakes his head.

"We haven't," says Samantha. "Sorry."

But Ibrahim, gladly accepting a second slice of Battenberg, would bet his Petworth parking space that they are both lying.

30.

Elizabeth has asked me to speak with you, Stephen," says Viktor. "Whisky?"

"I shouldn't, I'm driving, and you know how they are these days," says Stephen.

Stephen and Viktor sit on a wide, white semicircular sofa in Viktor's huge penthouse apartment. London is laid out before them through the panoramic windows. Elizabeth and Bogdan have moved outside, and are sitting on Viktor's terrace, wrapped up against the cold.

"Stephen, you have dementia," says Viktor. "I think you know?"

"I, uh, there's been talk of that, hasn't there? I'm not completely out of it. Still got some juice in the battery."

"Elizabeth gives you this letter each morning?" Viktor holds Stephen's letter out to him. Stephen takes it, casts his eye over it.

"Yes, I know this letter."

"You believe it?"

"I think, yes, I think that's my only option."

"It is a very brave letter," says Viktor. "Very wise. Very sad. Elizabeth says you are not sure what to do, the two of you?"

"Remind me who you are again?"

"Viktor."

"Yes, I know you are Viktor, it was 'Viktor this' and 'Viktor that' on the way up here. Who *are* you though? Why are we here?"

"I was a high-ranking KGB official," says Viktor. "Now I am, I suppose, a kind of referee for international criminals. I solve disputes."

"And you know my wife how?"

"I met Elizabeth when she was in MI6, Stephen."

Stephen looks out onto the balcony. Looks at his wife. "Dark horse, that one."

Viktor nods. "Very dark."

"Do you know, when I was a boy," says Stephen, "there was a bus, a trolleybus. You know trolleybus?"

"Is it like a bus?"

"Like a bus, certainly. Not quite a bus but like a bus. Overhead lines. They went all over Birmingham, that's where I was from. Wouldn't know I was from Birmingham, would you?"

"No," says Viktor. "I wouldn't know that."

"No, they beat it out of me at school. There was a trolleybus from town that went past the end of our road—we lived off a steep hill, saved you walking. You could take it right from the center of town. We wouldn't get the trolleybus on the way into town, because, you know . . ."

"Downhill," says Viktor.

"Downhill," confirms Stephen. "But here's the thing, chief, here's the thing. Do you know the number of that bus?"

"No," says Viktor. "But you do."

"The 42," says Stephen. "And on Saturdays it was the 42a, and on Sundays it didn't run."

Viktor nods again.

"And I can remember that, as clear as day. It sparkles in my mind. But I didn't know my wife had worked for MI6. I'm guessing she told me?"

"She did," says Viktor.

"How is it," says Stephen, "for Elizabeth? Living with me?"

"It is very difficult," says Viktor.

"She didn't sign up for it, eh?" says Stephen.

"No, but she signed up for love," says Viktor. "And she loves you very much. You are lucky there."

"Lucky, is it? You got a little thing for her yourself?"

"Doesn't everyone?"

"Not really, chief," says Stephen. "Just you and me, as far as I'm aware."

The two men both smile.

"She trusts you," says Stephen.

"She does," says Viktor. "So tell me a little about how you feel."

Stephen breathes deeply.

"Viktor, inside my head, while I can still explain . . . Things are not moving forward. The world, *that* keeps moving forward, I understand that, I sense that. It won't *stop* moving forward. But my brain is doubling back on itself. Even now, back I go. It feels like a bathtub, when someone pulls out the plug. Circles, circles, circles, and, every time around, something new, something not understood, and there's me trying to scramble up the sides. And this is me at my best, this is when I still have a grasp."

"I can see that," says Viktor. "You make it plain."

"The 42 bus, Viktor, that's where I remain. Everything else is noises from above, words I'm not hearing."

"Stephen, I am here to help, I hope," says Viktor. "To listen, and to see how much pain you are in. That is what Elizabeth wants to know. And she knows you won't tell her the truth if she asks. So she needs me to ask."

Stephen understands.

"I think I know the answer to this question already," says Viktor. "I think your face tells me. But are you in a great deal of pain?"

Stephen smiles, then looks to the floor. Then out to Elizabeth and Bogdan on the terrace, and finally back to Viktor again. He leans across and puts a steadying hand on Viktor's knee.

"That's it, chief, that's it. Pain I couldn't begin to tell you."

31.

Joyce

I just made some Battenberg with stone-ground flour, and Garth was quite right. It's still not as good as his, so I suspect he's holding something back. If we meet again, I shall ask what it is.

And I do have the feeling that we will meet again, don't you?

I think Ibrahim and I could both tell that Samantha Barnes and Garth were lying. About what though? They certainly know more than they're telling.

Either way, he can bake.

It was such a treat to go to Petworth yesterday. After visiting Samantha and Garth we went round a few shops. I bought a horseshoe, because I thought Gerry would approve, and Ibrahim, for reasons known only to himself, bought an old London street sign: "Earls Court Road." He said he bought it because it sounded very regal, but I wasn't entirely convinced. He'll have a reason, Ibrahim always does. I asked him what was going on with Ron and Pauline, but he said he was going to ask me the same thing, so I think it might all be over. That would be a shame. It's always tempting to interfere when you know someone is making a mistake, isn't it?

As soon as we got home, I popped over to Elizabeth's to give her a full debrief, but she wasn't back. So wherever she was going with Stephen and Bogdan, it wasn't a flying visit.

Visiting a home, do you think? For Stephen? I don't really want to talk about it for now. We shall find out in due course. The Battenberg is for her anyway, if she wants it.

I decided in the end that I wouldn't bake scones for Connie Johnson. Ron was quite right there. And, besides, Ibrahim says that Connie gets a regular delivery from Gail's Bakery at the prison, so they would probably be surplus to requirements. They have a branch of Gail's in Fairhaven now and, while I still prefer the vegan café near the front, Donna told me to try one of Gail's sausage rolls, and I confess I'm hooked. What I tend to do is have a tea and a muffin at Anything with a Pulse, and then buy a sausage roll on my way back to the minibus, to take home and heat up later with an episode of *Bergerac*.

One time, when I arrived home, I forgot it was in my handbag, and I came back into the living room to find my lipsticks and purse on the floor and Alan pretending to look innocent with crumbs around his mouth.

I still can't find a thing online about that new man who is moving in soon, Edwin Mayhem, which only makes him more mysterious and exciting to me. If he doesn't ride in on a motorbike, I shall be very disappointed.

It is Saturday tomorrow, and nothing ever seems to happen on a Saturday, does it? Unless you like sport, then everything happens on a Saturday. I hope I'll be able to report back to Elizabeth, but she does seem to have other things on her mind.

This is completely understandable, but we're still no nearer finding the murderer or the heroin, so perhaps it's time I took charge a little bit?

Joyce in charge. I don't know. I don't really like taking charge; I prefer taking orders. But I like to be listened to, so perhaps I should be brave.

Because if Elizabeth is absent, then who will take charge?

Ibrahim?

Ron?

I've made myself laugh there. Anyway, so long as nothing major happens before Elizabeth surfaces again, it will all be fine. And, as I say, nothing ever really happens on a Saturday.

Sweet dreams one and all.

32.

Sometimes Donna wishes she was in the Thursday Murder Club rather than in the police. The Thursday Murder Club don't have to wear uniforms, or salute buffoons, or worry about the Police and the Criminal Evidence Act, do they? They get results, and Donna reasons that if she were allowed to plant drugs, point guns, fake deaths and poison suspects, she would probably get results too.

Today is her first attempt at finding out.

Strictly speaking she shouldn't be doing it, of course she shouldn't. But Donna had felt goaded by SIO Regan. Chris is made of sterner stuff, but Donna really wants to get one over on Regan and the NCA. And perhaps she wants to prove to Elizabeth that she could break a few rules too. So she is going to find out a thing or two about Dominic Holt today. What harm can it do?

Besides, she's never been to a football match before, and she gets to spend a couple of hours with Bogdan and still call it work.

The corporate box is beginning to fill up for the Saturday lunchtime game. There's a buffet and a bar in the warm, and, outside, currently behind sliding doors, twenty seats, all overlooking the halfway point of the pitch. The pitch looks gorgeous, like an emerald amphitheater. Shame to spoil it with a game of football, but there we are.

Donna has never been undercover before. Not that she's officially undercover now. Chris would kill her if he knew what she was doing. This is strictly off the books. Chris is currently in the garden center with her mum, because she is worried that his flat lacks oxygen.

Donna had thought that she might stick out, but, so far, everyone who has walked into the box has struggled so endearingly with the dress code—ties, jackets, no jeans, no trainers—that they all look like undercover cops. Bogdan brings her an English sparkling wine. It's from a local vineyard; they do tours. Bogdan is drinking still water because sparkling water is bad for your tooth enamel.

"He is not here yet?" Bogdan asks, looking around.

Donna shakes her head. The box belongs to Musgrave Car Dealership, which, as far as the Home Office computer can tell, is a genuine and legitimate business. Statistically there must still be a few legitimate businesses dotted around.

Donna helps herself to a vegan sausage roll. At every home game Dave Musgrave invites friends and clients to come and watch the match, have a few drinks, maybe do a bit of business. Goodness knows what this whole setup costs him, but Donna guesses it must be worth it. You don't have to sell many Range Rovers and Aston Martins to pay for a few sausage rolls.

Donna sees Dave Musgrave walking toward them.

"Can you do banter?" Donna quickly asks Bogdan.

"Banter? Of course," says Bogdan.

"Are you sure? I've never heard you do banter?"

"Is easy," says Bogdan. "I've lived here a long time. You say something about golf."

Dave Musgrave is upon them, and he holds out a hand to Bogdan. He doesn't look at or acknowledge Donna. That's fine. If given the choice between men who pay women no attention and men who pay them too much attention, Donna will always take the former. Besides, she is happy to stay as low profile as possible. She keeps worrying that someone she's arrested will walk through the door next and recognize her. After all, it is the football.

"You're Barry?" Dave Musgrave asks Bogdan.

"I am Barry," agrees Bogdan.

"Nicko says you're a bloody legend."

"Nicko" is a friend of Bogdan's. Nicholas Lethbridge-Constance. He invented a type of portable wind turbine and retired on the proceeds at fifty. Bogdan has done some work for him. Just building work, Donna hopes—she never likes to pry too closely. Nicko had been glad to make the introductions, not even blinking at the fake name Bogdan had asked him to use. Bogdan really is a very good builder.

"Nicko said, 'Dave is a good guy,'" says Bogdan. "He says, good cars, good prices, but bad at golf."

Dave lets out a roar and slaps Bogdan on the back.

"Oh, you I like, Barry! You I like!"

"You like me, I like beer!" says Bogdan, slapping Dave's back in return. Dave roars again.

"Beer, he says! We've got a live one here."

So Bogdan can do banter. Why had she ever doubted it? Donna browses the buffet table again and lets the boys talk. There is a plate of prawns, but Donna has never had the confidence to know which bits to eat and which bits to leave, so she has a chicken goujon instead.

"What do you reckon to the score, Bazza?" Dave asks Bogdan. Uh-oh. Bogdan is an expert in many things, but football is not one of them.

"I think three–one," says Bogdan. "This Everton defense too shaky, letting in too many goals, too many old legs now. Welbeck and Mitoma too much for them. And if Estupiñán starts, then game over."

So *that's* what he was doing on his phone last night while she was watching *Die Hard*.

"Hope you're right, Bazza," says Dave. "Would love to have one over on the Scousers. Ah, talk of the devil."

Dave Musgrave has turned to face the door. Donna follows his gaze. In walks Dom Holt, swishing expensively. Finally, someone who does not look like an undercover cop. Dave leaves Bogdan, to stalk this new, richer prey.

Will they discover anything they don't already know? A fatal slip from a man enjoying the football, lips loosened with drink? A little nugget she can take back to Chris? Let's hope so. One way or another Dom Holt is up to his cashmere-scarfed neck in the murder of Kuldesh Sharma. And if she has to sit through ninety minutes of football to prove it, it'll be worth it. She has brought a book just in case, and wonders if she will be allowed to read it.

She thinks of Chris, her boss, pushing a trolley through the shrubs at the garden center, his arm interlinked with her mum's. Forgive me, Chris, someone has to be a maverick sometimes, and it's never going to be you.

33.

hris downs his second English sparkling wine. Two glasses come free with the tour. After that you have to pay.

Strictly speaking Chris shouldn't be here, but he'd love to get one over on SIO Regan. He really shouldn't be so petty. Shouldn't have risen to it, should have been strong, like Donna, but here he finds himself. Couple of glasses of bubbly, an afternoon with Patrice, and, at some point, a suitable lull, when he can make himself scarce and have a little nosy around the warehouse of Sussex Logistics just across the car park. Donna would kill him if she knew he was here; he's supposed to be at the garden center. Donna and Bogdan have gone to see an art exhibition in Hastings. You wouldn't wish it on anyone.

Although the woman at the Brighton café had identified Dom Holt—as had the Thursday Murder Club—believe it or not, her evidence would not hold up in court. There was no way they could get a warrant to search Sussex Logistics, not in a million years, so Chris thought perhaps he might take matters into his own hands.

Not like him, really, but he is beginning to tire of seeing Elizabeth and her merry band cutting corners that he is not allowed to cut. It isn't fair. Chris is determined to solve this case before SIO Regan, and, if he is being entirely honest with himself, before the Thursday Murder Club too. He'd love to see the look on Elizabeth's face if he finds the heroin, and finds Kuldesh's killer. And, wherever the Thursday Murder Club are today, perhaps starting a gunfight in a hollowed-out volcano, he knows they won't be breaking into Sussex Logistics.

Dom Holt also won't be there today, Chris is fairly sure of that. Brighton are playing Everton just along the coast. A man like Dom Holt will be in a corporate box somewhere. Chris has always wanted to go into a corporate box at the football. He's seen them sometimes, at Crystal Palace: booze and food, and comfy seats and warmth and men shaking hands with other men. Maybe one day. Policing must have been so much easier in the seventies, when you could just openly take bribes. He remembers an old DI of his from his early days on the force who'd got Wimbledon Royal Box seats just for losing a vital piece of evidence.

Perhaps no one at all will be at Sussex Logistics? Unmanned for the weekend? Chris has been hearing all about Dom Holt's boss, Mitch Maxwell, who paid the Thursday Murder Club a visit the other day, but he lives up in Hertfordshire somewhere and is rarely at the sharp end of things.

Perhaps a window will be left open somewhere? A fire door ajar? There will be alarms for sure, but Chris has disabled enough of them in his time. And if the police are called out, Chris has brought his radio, so he can be first on the scene to investigate the break-in.

The wine tasting has ended, and there is a suggestion that people might like to use the bathroom before the tour of the winery begins. Chris thought they were going to see a vineyard, but vineyards and wineries are different things. What a lot he is learning today.

He looks at Patrice and nods in the direction of the door. She nods back. She couldn't have been more enthusiastic when he'd outlined his plan ("I'm going to be an *actual lookout*? Finally a proper date"). Slipping out unnoticed, into the chill air, he takes her hand and kisses it.

"Ready to break some laws, m'lady?"

"For you, sir, always," says Patrice. "Donna would kill us, wouldn't she?"

"She's at an art exhibition in Hastings," says Chris. "She'll kill herself first."

34.

Bogdan has managed to sit in the seat next to Dom Holt. He'd had to very slightly nudge a child out of his way to do it, but he wasn't about to let Donna down. He lowers his muscular frame into a seat barely adequate for the job. He and Dom Holt nod to each other, like strangers on a train. Bogdan takes an Everton scarf out of his jacket and drapes it over his enormous shoulders. This gets Dom's attention.

"You Everton?" he asks.

"Yes, Everton," says Bogdan. "I think I'm the only one."

"That's what I thought," says Dom, holding out a hand to shake. "So now there're two of us. I'm Dom."

Bogdan shakes Dom's hand. Good grip, not that it matters. Some of the worst people Bogdan has ever met have the firmest handshakes. "I'm Barry, is not my real name. My real name is Polish."

"Fine by me," says Dom. "How's a Polish geezer end up an Everton fan? You poor sod."

"My grandfather shared a cell with a murderer from England. He was a big Everton fan. Then he killed a guard and they shot him, so my grandfather didn't see him no more, but we are an Everton family ever since."

Dom nods. "Fair enough, Bazza. Don't fancy our chances against this lot. You?"

"I don't know why I do this every week," says Bogdan. "This game will kill me."

Bogdan can sense Donna in the seat directly behind Dom Holt. Listening in. Bogdan had said that it wouldn't be necessary, and that he would remember everything, but Donna is an independent woman.

"How do you know Davey Musgrave?" Dom asks.

"I know a guy who knows him," says Bogdan. "I did him a favor."

"What's your line of work?"

"This and that," says Bogdan.

"Something else we have in common," says Dom. "That's my line of work too."

The match kicks off, and Bogdan confines himself to talking to Dom Holt about the on-field action. "Iwobi keeps looking for runners. Where are they?"

"Too right, mate, too right."

He wants to make Donna proud. Christmas had been a dream, waking up late, watching Australian reality TV shows, losing at board games. Bogdan has not wanted to make anyone proud since his mother died. He likes it.

Everton concede a goal in the tenth minute, and the two men sulk together. A further Brighton goal arrives in the twenty-fifth minute, and their attention begins to wander from the game.

"You based around here?" Dom asks.

"Fairhaven," says Bogdan. "But, you know, I travel. All around. If there's a job, there's Barry."

"You were pretty eager to sit next to me?" says Dominic Holt. He's scrolling through his phone, not looking at Bogdan.

"Huh?" says Bogdan.

"Made quite the beeline for me," says Dom.

"Is a good seat," says Bogdan. "And you have a nice coat."

Dom is still scrolling through his phone. "I think your name is Bogdan Jankowski."

"I cannot lie," says Bogdan. "I wish I could. Your Polish pronunciation is very good."

"And PC Donna De Freitas is sitting right behind us too." Dominic twists in his seat and offers his hand to Donna.

"Dom Holt," says Dom, as Donna takes his hand. "You already know that."

Bogdan has blown it.

"Funny setup, this," says Dom. "You and your boyfriend? Is that normal practice for Kent police? Or are you off the books?"

"Just watching the football," says Donna. "No law against it."

"Can you name one of the Everton players?"

"God, no," says Donna. Bogdan had been training her last night, just in case. But, really, who has time for that? "Can you name one of the Sugababes?"

"I'm going to call it a day," says Dom Holt, standing. "This time I'll let it slide, I get it. But if I see either of you following me again, I'll be making a complaint. Does that sound fair enough?"

"Where's the heroin, Dom?" Donna asks him quietly. "You looking for it? Or did you steal it yourself?"

Dom replies, just as quietly, "No wonder they took the case off you and gave it to the NCA. Amateur."

Brighton score a third goal, and Dom deflates as the crowd erupts around him. Bogdan cups his hand to Dom's ear.

"Donna is being polite. I knew Kuldesh Sharma. If you killed him, I will kill you. You understand?"

Dom Holt stands back and takes Bogdan in. The crowd is settling into their seats. He looks between Bogdan and Donna.

"Enjoy the game."

35

Anthony, as a rule, doesn't do house visits. But some rules are made to be broken.

Elizabeth has made him a cup of tea and is sitting on the sofa, watching as Anthony cuts Stephen's hair. She should really have had it done before the visit to Viktor, but Viktor is not the type to worry about such things.

"How did Elizabeth pull you?" says Anthony to Stephen. "The mind boggles. You've got a right Clooney on your hands here, Elizabeth."

"Clooney?" says Stephen.

"What's she like to live with, Stephen?"

Stephen looks at Anthony in the mirror. "I'm sorry, you have me at a disadvantage—"

"Anthony," says Anthony, clipping hair from around Stephen's ears. "What's it like living with Elizabeth?"

"With Elizabeth?"

"I mean, we all like a strong woman, don't we?" says Anthony. "But surely there's a limit? I mean, we all like Cher, don't we, but would you live with her? Couple of weeks maybe, dancing around the kitchen, but you'd need a night off eventually."

Stephen smiles, and nods. "Yes, sounds about right."

"Anthony always cuts your hair, Stephen," says Elizabeth. The journey home from Viktor's on Thursday had been quiet. Stephen slept, and Elizabeth and Bogdan knew there was nothing further to discuss now.

"That so?" says Stephen. "Rings a bell. Can't place you, that's probably me though. Not always on the ball."

"Got one of those faces, haven't I?" Anthony says, combing through the front of Stephen's hair, looking for the exact angle of attack. "Blend into the crowd. Useful if you're avoiding the police, nightmare on Grindr."

"I'm very gray," says Stephen, examining himself.

"Nonsense," says Anthony. "Elizabeth's gray, you're 'Burnished Platinum.'"

"You do such a lovely job, Anthony," says Elizabeth. "Doesn't he look handsome?"

"He's a looker, this one," agrees Anthony. "Look at those cheekbones. You wouldn't last a minute at Brighton Pride with those, Stevie-boy. Someone'd whisk you off to their Airbnb and have their wicked way."

"You're from Brighton?"

"Portslade," says Anthony. "Same thing, isn't it?"

"You might know my friend, Kuldesh?"

"I'll look out for him," says Anthony.

"Bald as a coot," says Stephen, and starts laughing.

Anthony catches Stephen's eye in the mirror and starts giggling too. "No good to me, then, is he?"

Stephen nods. "What's your line of work, Anthony?"

"Me, hairstylist," says Anthony, fingers on Stephen's temples, tilting him this way and that. "How about you?"

"Well," says Stephen, "I potter about. Bit of gardening. Allotment."

"I'd kill for an allotment," says Anthony. "I grow cannabis under my sunbed, but that's it. This haircut for a special occasion? Going dancing?"

"Just felt it needed doing," says Elizabeth.

"If you see Kuldesh, you tell him Stephen says hello," says Stephen. "Tell him he's an old rascal."

"I like a rascal," says Anthony.

"Me too," says Stephen.

Stephen remembers so few of his friends now. School friends mainly. Elizabeth hears the same stories, and laughs in the same places, because Stephen is one of those people who can tell you the same story a hundred times and still make you laugh. Language trips from him with such grace and joy. Most of the time now he struggles with words, but those old stories stay note perfect, and the smile on his face as he tells them stays true. He remembers Kuldesh because that was his last adventure. Out and about with Bogdan and Donna. It must have made him feel alive.

"I used to have my hair cut in Edgbaston," says Stephen. "Do you know it?"

"I've never heard of anywhere," says Anthony. "I thought Dubai was in Spain. I couldn't believe how long the flight was."

"A barber called Freddie. Freddie the Frog, they called him, I don't know why."

"Long tongue?" guesses Anthony.

"You might have it there," laughs Stephen. "An old boy he was. Probably dead now, wouldn't you say?"

"When was this?" asks Anthony.

"Gosh, 1955? Something like that."

"Probably dead, then," says Anthony. "Perhaps he croaked?"

Stephen laughs, his shoulders shaking under his gown. Elizabeth lives to see these moments. How many more will there be? It's nice to sit here with him. To not think about the case, and let the others get on with it for once. Wherever the heroin is, it can wait a while longer. Joyce probably knows something is up. Joyce always knows when something is up. Elizabeth will have to speak to her at some point.

Anthony is finishing, and Elizabeth dips into her handbag for her purse. A little heavier than before their visit to Viktor.

"Don't you dare," says Anthony. "The handsome ones are free."

Elizabeth smiles at Stephen in the mirror and he smiles back. Love can be so very easy sometimes. She decides she will switch off her phone. They can cope without her for a day. She would like to know how Joyce and Ibrahim got on with Samantha Barnes, but she would rather give her full attention to Stephen. Work isn't everything.

Anthony takes his final look at Stephen in the mirror. "There, that should last you."

Stephen admires himself. "You ever come across a chap called Freddie the Frog?"

"Freddie from Edgbaston?" asks Anthony.

"That's the one," says Stephen. "He still knocking about?"

"Still going strong," says Anthony.

"Freddie the Frog, fit as a fiddle," says Stephen.

Anthony puts his hands on Stephen's shoulders and kisses the top of his head.

36.

reaking into buildings with a warrant can be a lot of fun. A dawn raid the most fun of all. You get to have a bacon sandwich in the back of a van and arrest a drug dealer in his boxers before the world has even woken. Sometimes they'd make a run out of the back of the house and you'd get to see them rugby-tackled by an out-of-breath sergeant.

Other times they would hide in the loft and you'd have to play cards on the landing until they needed the loo.

But breaking into a building without a warrant is a different matter entirely. Patrice is perched on a parking bollard, with a perfect view of the wine warehouse, Sussex Logistics and the entrance to the business park. Chris waits awhile, until an old lady in a red coat disappears from view. To his surprise, he finds that the window has already been forced open. Who knows how long ago, but it would take a brave, or a very foolish, person to break into this particular warehouse. Chris chooses not to reflect on which of those he might be. The window leads him into a small storage room filled with cleaning products. No alarms so far.

Slowly opening the door of the room, Chris finds himself in a large, open hangar, stacked with boxes along the far wall. Filled with what? There are three raggedy sofas arranged in a horseshoe shape around a television so old it isn't even flat screen. Whoever uses these sofas is not here now. His footsteps echo on the concrete floor, and his breath steams in the cold air.

At one end of the hangar, metal stairs lead up to a wooden Portakabin office, forming a mezzanine level. Chris can see a padlock on the door. Finally, some security.

Chris decides to leave the boxes for now and head up to the office. What is he expecting to find? Phone numbers? Anything, really. Anything Elizabeth doesn't have, he realizes. Has it really come to this? Compelled to outmaneuver a pensioner for the sake of professional pride?

Perhaps the heroin will just be sitting there? Won't he be a hero then?

No one is in the building, but he treads lightly up the latticed metal stairs regardless. On a small semi-landing he sees cigarette butts, and on the door of the office he sees what looks like dried blood. Old though— hopefully there's not a fresh corpse behind the flimsy door.

Chris might have to force the lock. Will that finally raise an alarm? There's been nothing so far, which seems odd. Chris feels the padlock and, as he does so, it opens in his hand. The door is unlocked.

Chris stands, motionless, for a long moment, just listening. No sound from inside the office. From the hangar, just the erratic, metallic clang of the winter wind against the closed loading-bay doors. He presses down on the door handle and kicks the door open, very gently, with the side of his right foot.

Still no alarm.

Chris sees filing cabinets, as he was hoping, and the corner of a wooden desk.

Walking into the office, he sees the whole of the desk. And, behind the desk, in a high-backed ergonomically friendly office chair, is Dom Holt.

With a bullet hole in his forehead.

37.

So I can't phone this in, you see," says Chris. "Because I shouldn't have been here."

"Gotcha," says Ron, as he and Joyce scrutinize the corpse of Dominic Holt, with the detached air of people pretending to be professionals. "And we were the first people you rang?"

"Of course," says Chris.

"The very first?"

"Elizabeth wasn't picking up," says Chris.

"I can't believe Patrice was your lookout," says Joyce, returning to sit with Patrice on a small sofa.

"It was pitched to me as a date. I was all for it," says Patrice.

"It's a bit like an escape room," says Joyce. "Joanna did one with work, but she panicked and they had to let her out. She once got stuck in a lift in Torremolinos and it's stayed with her."

"I was only going to be in here for five minutes," says Chris. "Have a riffle through the files, see if I could find any numbers, any contacts."

"That's illegal, Chris," says Joyce. "Did you find anything?"

"Do you know, Joyce," says Chris, "after I found the corpse, I thought better of it."

"Amateur," says Ron. "What are we doing here though?"

"I need a favor," says Chris. "I need someone to pretend that they heard a gunshot, and then rang me. To explain why I'm here. You can say you were doing the wine tour and popped out for a breath of fresh air?"

"Lying to the police," says Ron. "Yeah, Elizabeth would have been good at that."

"We'll be good at it too," says Joyce. "We don't always need Elizabeth."

"Where is she, by the way?" Patrice asks.

"Usually best not to ask," says Ron.

"So is someone on their way?" Joyce asks.

"Now that you're safely here, I'm going to ring the SIO from the NCA," says Chris. "Jill Regan. I'll tell her I got a call from a distressed member of the public and I broke in and found the body."

"How long might they be?" asks Joyce. "Do you think?"

"They're all in Fairhaven," says Chris. "Twenty-five minutes?"

Joyce looks at her watch, then looks at the filing cabinets. "That will do us just fine. Let's get started on these files."

"We can't touch those files now," says Chris.

Joyce rolls her eyes and pulls on her gloves. "What would Elizabeth do?"

"If I let you look at the files, you'll play along with the plan?" asks Chris.

"You're not going to *let* us do anything, Chris," says Joyce. "You're not really in a position to be handing out permission."

"You're even speaking like Elizabeth now," says Patrice.

"Palpable nonsense, dear," says Joyce, and they giggle together.

"We love a plan," says Ron. "Half an hour ago I had my feet up, watching the curling, and now look at me. Warehouse, corpse, the lot."

"Make sure you sound breathless when you call your SIO, Chris," says Joyce. "Remember, you've just found a corpse."

"Rather than finding it after breaking in and ringing two pensioners to come and bail you out," adds Ron.

Chris steps out of the office and onto the metal stairs to call Jill Regan. Joyce tests the top drawer of the nearest filing cabinet. It won't budge.

"Ron, pop on a pair of gloves and see if you can find any keys."

"Find them where?" asks Ron.

"In his pockets," says Joyce, pointing to the corpse of Dom Holt. "Honestly, Ron, use your head."

Ron reluctantly pulls a pair of driving gloves from his jacket.

Joyce goes along each of the filing cabinets in turn, trying the drawers. She looks over to see Ron gingerly trying to get into Dominic Holt's pockets.

"You know, I could do that?" says Patrice. "If it's making you uncomfortable?"

"Oh, nonsense," says Joyce. "He enjoys it. He'll be showing off to Ibrahim the second we get home."

Ron gives a triumphant "Got the buggers!" and presents a large ring of keys to Joyce. He then says a quiet "Sorry, mate" to Dominic Holt for disturbing him.

Joyce starts trying a row of small, skinny keys as Chris comes back in through the door.

"Unit on their way," says Chris.

A drawer pops open, then another, then another. Joyce starts pulling files from the cabinets. She places them on the desk, being careful to avoid the bloodstains, and issues her orders.

"Patrice, do you have a phone?"

"Believe it or not, I do," says Patrice.

"I don't wish to hurry you, but could you photograph as many pages as you can? Chris, take Ron outside. Ron, you need to look paler, more shocked, like a defenseless old man."

"I'm not sure I like the new you," says Ron. "Can we have Joyce back?"

Joyce works quickly. It feels like being a nurse again, on one of those nights when you don't stop, but everything still has to be perfect. Once Patrice has photographed the contents of each file, Joyce replaces it in the exact same spot, in the exact same order, as it was found. The two women work in tandem, under the dead stare of Dom Holt.

The last cabinet emptied and refilled, Joyce slips the keys back into Dom

Holt's pocket, whispering, "Thank you," and motions for Patrice to follow her out.

Before descending the metal stairs, Joyce has a long think about what else Elizabeth might do. Is there anything she has forgotten? Something that will make Elizabeth roll her eyes at her on their return? A flash of inspiration hits her, and she pulls Patrice back in and asks her to take photos of the corpse from every angle. Good idea.

38.

Garth is walking around Joyce's flat, followed dutifully by Alan. You can find out where anyone lives if you know where to look. And Garth knows where to look.

From time to time Alan barks at his new friend and Garth replies, "You got that right," or "I don't disagree with you there, buddy."

He had hoped that Joyce might be in, but, in her absence, it will do no harm to have a look around. He smells baking in the air. Smells a lot like his very own Battenberg but without the cinnamon.

She keeps it nice—that doesn't surprise Garth a jot. Joyce is a neat lady. Garth likes the way she dresses, likes the way she speaks and, looking around, he likes the way she lives. Garth's own grandmother, his favorite grandmother, ran an art-theft ring in Toronto. That was what had got Garth interested in the business in the first place. She stole art and she loved art, and passed both of these advantages on to Garth. His other grandmother read the weather on TV in Manitoba.

There are still Christmas decorations up. That's bad luck, Joyce. Garth asks Alan if Joyce knew this was bad luck. Alan barks. Joyce knows: she just likes them too much.

Garth is tempted to take them down, protect Joyce from herself, but he doesn't want her to know he's been here. Doesn't want to scare her, or intrude on her privacy. Joyce has a lot of Christmas cards, a lot of friends, no surprise there. Garth wishes he had more friends, but he's never found the knack. Always moved around too much until he met Samantha.

Garth opens the fridge. Almond milk. Joyce moves with the times.

He and Samantha have just been to visit a woman named Connie Johnson. She sells cocaine, and they knew her by reputation. They had a proposition for her. Seemed like there was some kind of opportunity in the heroin business, and they wondered if she'd like to team up? Her connections, their money, might be worth everyone's while.

Connie had said she would think about it, but Garth didn't buy that. He figures they'll just have to do it themselves—how hard can it be?

Garth has turned his hand to all sorts of things in his life. Went to art college, once stole a herd of bison, played a little bass guitar. He also committed Canada's largest ever bank robbery. Though not by himself—his cousin Paul helped. And his grandmother laundered a lot of the money.

Garth had worked in corporate espionage for a while too, and had broken into all sorts of places without anyone knowing. Because he was so big, he had grown up careful. He's big as a bear but quiet as a mouse. If Garth disturbs something, then Garth puts it back.

What is he looking for in Joyce's flat? No idea. What would he have asked Joyce about if she'd been here? No idea either. But if anything has kept Garth alive over the years, it's caution, and he has to make sure that Joyce isn't trying to do a number on them. No one ever died from doing too much research.

He'd been to take a look at Elizabeth's flat, but she had a hairdresser there, and she also had an alarm system he's never seen outside of a maximum-security prison.

There's nothing here, Garth is sure of it. He is about to leave when he hears Joyce's friend Ibrahim knock on the door, and then start a conversation with Alan through the letter box. Garth quietly makes himself a cup of tea while he waits for the conversation to finish. It takes quite some time.

Once Ibrahim has gone, Garth will wash and dry up, and then have a little wander around Coopers Chase. See what he can see.

There is opportunity in this place, Garth can smell it. There are secrets here too, but what?

And he needs to think about Connie Johnson.

39.

own the stairs and out into the yard of the business park, Joyce and Patrice rejoin Chris and Ron. Chris looks nervous, but there's no need: it's all under control.

Ron, Joyce is delighted to see, looks like a terrified, defenseless old man. Joyce realizes that they sometimes take Ron for granted. All the things this man has achieved in his life. He likes to play the fool, but he's far from it.

The first squad car screeches through the gates. Quite why the need for screeching, Joyce doesn't know. It's a corpse.

Two plainclothed officers run from the car. Again, why the running? Chris takes one of them by the arm. "In here, I'll show you."

The other officer stays with Ron, Joyce and Patrice. He has questions.

"OK, ladies, sir, I need you to stay calm for me. Can you do that?"

Ron bursts into tears, and Joyce goes to comfort him, as the young officer looks embarrassed.

"Just take your time, and let me know what happened."

"We were, my friend and I—this is Ron, and I'm Joyce. We were going to a tour at the Bramber Sparkling Wine Company, it's just over there."

"It was a present from my son," cries Ron. "A voucher."

All right, Ron, don't build your part. Then Joyce realizes that, as she has become Elizabeth, Ron is having to become her. She would definitely have said something about vouchers. Everybody is stepping up today—carry on, Ron.

"We were so looking forward to it," says Joyce. "But we arrived late—we got lost."

Another squad car has pulled up, and the officer waves the new officers into the hangar.

"We'd just got out of the car, literally seconds it must have been," says Joyce, "when we heard a gunshot."

"You're certain it was a gunshot?" asks the officer.

"Yes," says Joyce.

"It's just," says the officer, "lots of things can sound like gunshots, if you don't have much experience with them."

"I have some," says Joyce. "It seemed to come from the building off to our left, and that was this building, Sussex Logistics."

"I see," says the officer. "And so you—"

"Well, Ron had the number of a police officer we'd dealt with before."

"DCI Hudson?"

"Good lad," says Ron, regaining his composure. He is loving this.

"Also very handsome," says Joyce.

"So I ring Chris," says Ron.

"DCI Hudson," says Joyce.

"And I'm all, 'There's been a gunshot, mate.' He's all, 'Are you sure?' and I'm all, 'I'm sure, I'm sure, get your skates on, could be a madman on the loose,' whatever, and he's a brave lad and he rushes over, eager to keep us safe. They're not all bad, are they, coppers?"

The officer now addresses Patrice. "And you, madam?"

"I'm Chris's partner," says Patrice. "We were on our way to the garden center when they called."

"OK," says the officer. "The SIO will have more questions for you later."

On cue, SIO Jill Regan arrives in a big Lexus with a discreet blue light.

"Nice motor," says Ron to Joyce.

"You're doing ever so well, Ron," says Joyce, and they squeeze each other's hand.

"The body's in the hangar, ma'am," says the young officer. "These two heard the gunshot and called DCI Hudson."

Jill studies Joyce and Ron in turn. "And how did you happen to have DCI Hudson's personal number?"

As Joyce searches for a good answer, Ron bursts into tears again, and buries his head on Joyce's shoulder. Joyce mouths, "Sorry," to Jill, who shakes her head, and walks into the building without another word.

"Do you think we'll be here much longer?" Joyce asks the officer.

"No, no," says the officer. "We'll be back in touch with you, but you must be keen to get home."

Keener than you know, thinks Joyce. They have an awful lot of photos to look at.

40.

Ibrahim had wanted to speak to Elizabeth about the trip to meet Samantha Barnes, but Elizabeth's phone was off. So he then thought that perhaps he might take Alan for a walk, but Joyce was not in. Ibrahim could hear Alan bark, so they chatted through the letter box for a while, but, without a key, that was the limit of Ibrahim's fun. At least Ron would be in, he'd thought, and they could watch a film. But, no, Ron was not at home either. Where on earth was he? Perhaps he and Pauline had made up?

Trudging home, thinking about Samantha Barnes, thinking about Garth, thinking about how their eyes had lit up when they spoke about the heroin, Ibrahim suddenly remembered he had a new friend, and another project. He didn't always need the Thursday Murder Club!

And so Ibrahim and Bob Whittaker are now drinking mint tea and having fun. There is a serious point to what they're doing, but there's no harm in enjoying yourself while you're at it. Ibrahim is reading through their latest exchange—as Mervyn—with Tatiana, while Bob sips at his tea and looks happy to be out of the house.

MERVYN: My love is open, like the petals of a flower, long closed under Spring's frost, scared of the sunlight that brings it life. My love is open, like a wound, delicate and vulnerable and trusting to be tended. My love is open, like a door, in a cottage, in a wood, waiting for your footsteps.

> TATIANA: The money still didn't clear. Can you try one more time,
> my darling?
>
> MERVYN: What is money in all this? A single primrose in a meadow.
> A teardrop in a waterfall.
>
> TATIANA: The bank has not received the money. I need to buy plane
> tickets.
>
> MERVYN: Fly to me, Tatiana. Let the breath of love carry you into
> my arms. I will meet you at Gatwick, there is very good
> parking in the North Terminal, although the pricing
> structure leaves a little to be desired.

"I agree with you there," says Bob. "Fifteen pounds fifty, and I was there
for only an hour."

> TATIANA: I love you, Mervyn. I must have money in next six hours
> or my heart will break.
>
> MERVYN: I will speak to the bank again. But it's a Saturday, and
> they keep asking me what the money is for. I tell them it's
> for love, and then they say they need to do further checks.
>
> TATIANA: Tell them is for a car. Don't mention love.
>
> MERVYN: How can I not mention love, my dear? When every heart-
> beat sings your name?
>
> TATIANA: Tell them is for a car. And, please, hurry. I must be
> with you.
>
> MERVYN: I could get the money in cash?

"And this is setting the bait?" asks Bob.
"It certainly is," says Ibrahim. "Donna's idea."

> TATIANA: Then you send cash?

MERVYN: Send it? Not with the postal strikes we've been having. The Royal Mail has been systematically underfunded for many years. Is it any wonder that loyal workers are taking industrial action? What other option do they have? It is the malaise of late capitalism.

TATIANA: I could ask a friend to collect the cash? A friend from London?

MERVYN: A friend? What a wonderful idea. To meet a friend of yours would be a dream in itself. We will talk of you late into the night.

TATIANA: He will not be able to talk for long. He has an important job in London. He is not to be bothered.

MERVYN: Whatever you wish, my love. I will withdraw the cash over the next few days, and will await instructions. And then the dream begins.

TATIANA: £2,800

MERVYN: That still seems very expensive for a plane ticket.

TATIANA: There are taxes.

MERVYN: Ah, it was Franklin, I believe, who said that nothing is certain in life but death and taxes. People often misattribute it to Oscar Wilde, don't they?

TATIANA: Don't speak of death, my beautiful Mervyn.

MERVYN: That is sage advice, Tatiana.

TATIANA: I must go to work now. My friend will be in touch, and then we will be together forever. That is my dream.

MERVYN: Of course, something Oscar Wilde did say was that there are only two tragedies in life. One is not getting what one wants, and the other is getting it.

TATIANA: Your friend sounds very wise. I send you many kisses.

MERVYN: And I you, sweet Tatiana.

"So now we wait," says Bob.

"Now we wait," agrees Ibrahim.

Bob looks over to Ibrahim. "You write very beautifully."

Ibrahim shrugs. "In my business you hear a thing or two about love. I find it easy to replicate. It is largely a willing abandonment of logic."

Bob nods. "You see no truth in it?"

"In love?" Ibrahim thinks. "Bob, you and I are cut from the same cloth."

"Which cloth is that?" asks Bob.

"The world of systems, and patterns, of zeroes and ones. The binary instructions that make sense of life. We may be able to see the advantages and disadvantages of love, but to regard it as an objective entity, that is for the poets."

"And you are not a poet?" Bob asks.

There is an urgent knocking on Ibrahim's door.

Ibrahim goes to open it and walks back in with Joyce and Ron. Joyce looks excited.

"You'll never guess?" says Joyce.

Ron looks at Bob and Ibrahim. "You boys doing Tatiana without me?"

"You weren't in," says Ibrahim. "I called for you."

Joyce notices Bob for the first time. "Hello, Computer Bob!"

"It's just Bob," says Computer Bob.

"But I thought we were doing this together?" says Ron.

"Bob and I are friends too," says Ibrahim. "So what's this news?"

"Dominic Holt is dead," says Ron. Ibrahim gives a low whistle.

"And on a Saturday!" says Joyce, with wonder.

"Dominic Holt?" says Bob.

"Drug dealer," says Ron, with a wave of his hand.

"You'll know this," says Joyce to Bob. "If we have photos on a mobile phone, can we show them on a television screen? I'm sure Joanna did that when she came back from Chile."

"Oh, certainly," says Bob. "Couldn't be simpler. You screenshare them from your phone. Is it an iPhone or an Android?"

"I don't know," says Joyce. "It's in a yellow case?"

"No matter," says Bob. "For an iPhone, go into 'Settings,' then 'Control Center.' You'll see an option called 'Screen Mirroring.' Now, I'm going to also assume you have Apple TV. If so, then select it from the list, which should—"

"Do you think you could come and do it for us?" Joyce asks. "Are you terribly busy?"

"No, I'm sure I could help, if you don't mind a stranger tagging along?"

"You're not a stranger," says Joyce. "You're Computer Bob."

"Come on, Bobby boy," says Ron. "You'll fit right in."

"Lead the way," says Bob.

"Before we go though," says Joyce, "most of the pictures are just of files, but how are you with looking at pictures of a corpse?"

"Umm," says Bob. "I honestly don't know. It's never come up before."

"You get used to it," says Ibrahim, pulling on his coat.

41.

Snow is starting to fall, and Coopers Chase is bathed in a silver, electric glow. The troops have been gathered, even Elizabeth has been raised, via an urgent knocking on her door, and the promise of crime-scene photos. "Can't I have a single day off?" she had sighed.

The Television Room is almost always empty on a Saturday evening, but on this particular occasion a woman named Audrey, whose husband was a light-fingered grocer, is sitting front and center, insisting that she wants to watch *The Masked Singer* on the big-screen TV. There is a short, fruitless negotiation. Money is offered. Though, in retrospect, not enough money, given how much Audrey's husband had embezzled from Tesco before he was asked to take early retirement. Ibrahim tries to appeal to Audrey's better nature, but is unable to locate it. At one point Audrey threatens to call the police, to which Chris replies, "I am the police," only to be given a withering stare by Audrey and told, "In a T-shirt? I don't think so."

In one hand Audrey is holding the remote control like she was holding her mother's hand at a traffic light, and in the other a vodka and tonic. She is not for moving.

There is a further delay as Joyce tries to explain the format of *The Masked Singer* to a horrified Elizabeth, and then more time is wasted as Ibrahim wants to see if the singer dressed as a dustbin is Elaine Paige. "I can just sense it," he says, before being dragged away.

And so, although Joyce's flat is far too small for them, it is here that they have all gathered. Joyce, Elizabeth, Ron, Ibrahim—still muttering about

Elaine Paige—Chris and Patrice, Donna and Bogdan, and, still looking in thrall to the novelty of the thing, Computer Bob. Bogdan had popped into Ron's to get extra chairs.

Alan is doing the rounds, making sure he gets all the attention he warrants. Computer Bob is new to him, and Alan spends a little extra time with him, just to ensure he's onside.

On Joyce's television screen is a photograph, front-facing, of Dom Holt, slumped back in his chair with a bullet hole in his forehead.

"You told me you were going to the garden center," says Donna to her mum. "Then this."

"I was just keeping lookout," says Patrice. "Don't get your knickers in a twist."

"As you can see," says Joyce, "another death, another professional hit. A single bullet through the skull."

Bob tentatively raises a hand.

"Yes, Bob," says Joyce.

"*Another* death?"

"Our friend Kuldesh was shot by drug dealers," says Ibrahim. "Alan, would you please leave Bob in peace? They shot him in a country lane because he stole some heroin from them."

"Any other questions, Bob?" asks Elizabeth. "Or can we get on?"

Bob fans his hands as if to say, "No, please, don't mind me."

"So," says Joyce, "who killed him, and why?"

"Must have been Mitch Maxwell," says Ron. "Dom loses the heroin, however that's happened, and Mitch can't have that so fires one into his nut."

"And Mitch would know where to find Dom, I suppose," says Joyce.

"One problem with that," says Chris. "When I broke in . . ."

Donna rolls her eyes.

". . . the ground-floor window had already been forced open. Mitch Maxwell could have walked through the front door."

"Perhaps he didn't want to be seen," says Donna. "By the way, no way you'd have fit through that window before you lost weight. See the trouble it's caused you."

"If I might venture an opinion?" says Joyce. "When Ibrahim and I went to visit Samantha Barnes, in Petworth—Bob, have you ever been to Petworth?"

"Uh, no," says Bob.

"You must," says Joyce. "It's very pretty, and not too busy on weekdays, we had the run of the place. And, if you do go, there's a lovely café just by—"

"You were venturing an opinion, Joyce?" says Elizabeth.

"Oh, yes," says Joyce. "For goodness' sake, Alan, you've seen shoes before, sorry, Bob. Yes, when we mentioned the name Dom Holt to Samantha Barnes, and to her husband . . ."

"Garth," says Ibrahim. "Almost certainly Canadian."

". . . they both swore they'd never heard it before, but they were lying, weren't they, Ibrahim?"

"They were," agrees Ibrahim.

"How can you tell for sure?" asks Donna.

"I just can," says Joyce. "Just like I know you and Bogdan didn't come here from an art exhibition. But we can discuss that later."

"Where did you come from?" asks Chris.

"We went to the football," says Bogdan.

"The Everton match?" Chris asks.

"I didn't pay attention to the teams," says Donna. "Maybe."

"Meet anyone interesting there?"

"So Mitch Maxwell, and Samantha Barnes and her Canadian, might have killed him," interrupts Elizabeth. "Anyone else?"

"Whoever Mitch Maxwell was selling the heroin to," says Donna. "That's an even bigger motive, surely?"

Joyce nods. "That's why we took the photos of the files. I hope I did the right thing, Elizabeth?"

"You did the right thing, Joyce," says Elizabeth.

Joyce rises an inch in height. "So, Bob, could you scroll through to the photographs we took of the files? You'll have to go through quite a few close-ups of the bullet wound, I'm afraid."

Bob scrolls through at speed, until the first file appears.

"And somewhere in here I'm betting we can find out exactly who he sells to," says Elizabeth. "Thanks to Joyce."

"I helped too," says Ron.

"He did," says Joyce. "He wept."

"Well done, Ron," says Elizabeth, and Ron also rises an inch in height.

"Shall I make some tea, perhaps?" suggests Joyce. "We have a long evening ahead of us."

"Let me make it," says Ibrahim. "It seems everyone else has a job."

"The files appear to be written in code, Ibrahim," says Elizabeth. "You will be invaluable in cracking it. I'll make the tea."

Ron and Joyce share a look. This is certainly a first.

"I'm not sure I have nine mugs though," says Joyce.

"I don't have to stay," volunteers Bob, but is met with cries of "Stay, stay," and Alan, curled up at his feet, seals the deal.

"I'll get mugs from Elizabeth's," says Bogdan. "And say hi to Stephen when I'm there."

Elizabeth squeezes Bogdan's hand before heading to the kitchen.

42.

Bogdan doesn't much like snow. In his long experience, only two types of people do like snow. People who don't see much of it, like the British, or people who live near mountains. In Poland he saw an awful lot of snow, but nobody was skiing. So what was in it for him?

He lets himself into Elizabeth and Stephen's flat. The sitting room light is on, so Bogdan enters. Stephen is standing at the window, staring out into the snowy darkness.

"Stephen," says Bogdan, "is me."

"Old chap," says Stephen. "Something queer is afoot."

"OK," says Bogdan. "You want a cup of tea? You want a whisky? Watch TV?"

"I know you," says Stephen. "We've spoken."

"I am your friend," says Bogdan. "You are my friend. We went for a drive the other day."

"Thought as much," says Stephen. "If I tell you something, you won't think I'm off my rocker?"

"Off your rocker?" This is a new one on Bogdan.

"Off my rocker," says Stephen, suddenly irritated. He has never been irritated with Bogdan before. "Doolally, round the twist, for goodness' sake."

"You are on your rocker," says Bogdan, hoping that's an expression.

"Only," says Stephen, "there's a fox, who comes to see me."

"Snowy?"

"Snowy, yes," says Stephen. "You know him? Chap with the ears?"

"I know him," says Bogdan. "He is a fine fox."

"He hasn't been this evening," says Stephen.

"Is the snow," says Bogdan. "He's keeping warm somewhere."

"Nonsense," says Stephen. "A fox doesn't mind a bit of snow. A fox doesn't mind a bit of anything. Don't you know anything about foxes?"

"Not really," says Bogdan.

"Well, take the word of a man who does. Where is he?"

"Did you miss him maybe?" Bogdan asks.

"I never miss him," says Stephen. "You ask my wife, she's knocking about somewhere. I never miss him. We never miss each other."

"You want I should go and look?"

"I think we should look together," says Stephen. "I don't mind telling you I'm worried. You have a torch?"

"Yes," says Bogdan.

"And we're pals? Good pals?"

Bogdan nods.

"Was I short with you?" Stephen asks. "I feel like I was quite short, and I didn't mean to be. I wasn't expecting you, you see, and we don't have anything in."

Bogdan shakes his head. "No, you weren't short with me. Let's get you dressed. Is cold out there."

"There was a big chap with a beard and hat around earlier too," says Stephen. "There's been all sorts going on."

43.

As they scroll through the files and let Ibrahim do his work, Elizabeth hears their progress from the kitchen. Elizabeth had thought of calling a woman she used to work with, Kasia. Kasia was possibly the greatest cryptographer in the history of MI6, and now works for Elon Musk. But as soon as she heard Ibrahim explaining to Joyce, "You see A = 1, B = 2, and so on," she realized this particular code might not need Kasia's full attention.

God bless Joyce. What a good job she has done. Elizabeth will need a little more time off soon, so it bodes well.

Elizabeth looks down at the cups of tea she has made. Joyce was right: there were only eight mugs; but, even so, Elizabeth has had to boil the kettle three times. And then she forgot to take the first tea bags out, so some of the cups are much stronger than the others. And then she accidentally used almond milk because it hadn't occurred to her that that's what Joyce would have in her fridge. And, finally, she turned the sugar up the wrong way and it spilled all over the floor. She had cleaned it up immediately because she remembers Joyce once telling her that sugar attracts ants. Twice Joyce had called through, "Do you need any help in there?" and twice Elizabeth had called back that she was perfectly capable of making a cup of tea, thank you, Joyce.

The things Elizabeth could do, and the things she couldn't.

Carrying the mugs through on a tray, Elizabeth hopes they will be OK for everybody. They will all make encouraging noises, she knows that, but she will concentrate on Joyce's eyes, because they never lie.

Ibrahim has provided them with a name, hidden in the inexpertly coded files.

"Luca Buttaci, Elizabeth," says Joyce. "If that's how you pronounce it."

"I pronounce it Buttaci," says Ron.

"That's not helpful, Ron," says Joyce.

"I'm doing some Googling," says Bob. "Just to be useful, and nothing is coming up. Or nothing drug-related. Various Italian mayors and garden contractors, and a schoolboy from Southwest London, but no police records, no arrests, nothing criminal."

"Probably an alias," says Joyce.

"Probably an alias," agrees Elizabeth. Oh, God, now she's repeating Joyce? Enough! Time to take charge again. She claps her hands. "OK, so this Luca Buttaci becomes a new suspect in the murder of Kuldesh, and also in the murder of Dominic Holt."

"So what's next?" asks Donna, looking around. "I got spotted at the football, and then Chris found a corpse. I don't think we're as good at breaking the law as you are."

"Very few people are," says Elizabeth. "What we need is a summit."

"Oh, a summit, Alan!" says Joyce. Elizabeth notices Joyce hasn't yet drunk any of her tea.

"We need to get everyone together in a room and see their cards," says Elizabeth. "At the moment it feels like everyone is lying to us. Mitch Maxwell is lying to us, Samantha Barnes and her husband are lying to us. Chris and Donna, the National Crime Agency are lying to you. Dom Holt was lying to us and, given the bullet in his skull, perhaps he was lying to somebody else too?"

"That's what you get for smashing up my Daihatsu," says Ron.

"Lovely cup of tea, Elizabeth," says Joyce.

"Not you as well, Joyce, goodness me," says Elizabeth. "So let's find Luca Buttaci. Ibrahim, I imagine your friend might be able to help there?"

"Bob?" asks Ibrahim.

"Connie Johnson," says Elizabeth, "but that was a touching response. Ask her where we can find Buttaci, and then we'll invite him, Mitch, Samantha and Garth over for Sunday lunch next week. See what we can see."

"Best cup of tea I've had in yonks," says Ron, raising his mug to her. Which gives her a surprising thrill.

"I do like it when it's all of us together," says Joyce.

"And, Joyce," says Elizabeth, "I would like it if we could find Kuldesh's lock-up before the summit? Monday perhaps?"

"You're actually around, are you?" Joyce asks. "That makes a nice change."

Joyce isn't being mean, Elizabeth knows that. She just knows something is wrong, and is worried about her. Elizabeth has never been good at dealing with people caring about her.

The summit is a good idea. It will give everyone something to work on. And, when it's over, Elizabeth can move on to the real business at hand.

Thinking of which, Elizabeth is beginning to wonder where Bogdan might be. If there was a problem, he would ring, she knows that. Perhaps he and Stephen are playing chess? That's a comforting thought. But doubtful now. Perhaps they are sitting and talking? Stephen doesn't always know who Bogdan is these days, but he likes his calmness. He fell asleep on Bogdan's shoulder the other day, and Bogdan missed a weightlifting session because he refused to disturb him.

44.

The two men trudge through the freshly settled snow, silhouettes in a world of black and white, and hazy sodium light. Snow underfoot, snow overhead. Stephen is in a long overcoat Bogdan found at the back of his cupboard, a woollen hat, gloves, two scarves and a pair of hiking boots. Bogdan himself is, in a rare display of weakness, wearing a long-sleeved T-shirt.

The paths are slippery, so Bogdan holds Stephen's hand. His torch plays across the white grass, looking for Snowy. Looking for the swish of a tail, the glint in the eyes, the tips of those ears.

Stephen stops and looks over to his right. They are probably forty or so yards from the flat now. In front of the flowerbed is a small mound, just a bump really, nothing to it. But Stephen lets go of Bogdan's hand and clambers up the slope toward it. Bogdan swings the torch to illuminate the ground in front of Stephen. Stephen kneels and places his hand on the top of the mound. Bogdan catches up to him, and sees what Stephen sees. The fox in the snow, silent and lifeless. The tips of his snowy ears sunk into the whiteness.

Stephen looks at Bogdan and nods. "Dead. Heart gave out, I'd guess; he looks peaceful."

"Poor Snowy," says Bogdan, and kneels beside Stephen. Stephen is brushing freshly fallen crystals from Snowy's fur.

Stephen looks back toward his own window. "On his way to see me, I suppose. On his way to say goodbye, and didn't make it."

"We don't always get to say goodbye," says Bogdan.

"No," says Stephen. "It's pure luck when you do. Sorry, Snowy old pal."

Bogdan nods, stroking Snowy's fur. "Are you sad?"

Stephen is playing with Snowy's ear. "We would look at each other, through the window, and both know we weren't long for this world. That's what drew us together. I'm not well, did you know that?"

"You're OK," says Bogdan. "Will Elizabeth be sad?"

"Remind me, again?"

"Your wife. Will she be sad?"

"I expect so," says Stephen. "Do you know her? Is she the type to get sad?"

"Not really," says Bogdan. "But this will make her sad, I think."

Stephen stands, brushes the snow from the knees of his trousers. "What do you think? Funeral with full military honors?"

Bogdan nods again.

Stephen tests the ground with the tip of his boot. "You much of a digger? You look like you might be."

"I have dug a few holes, yes," says Bogdan.

"This soil's a bugger in winter though," says Stephen. "Like breaking tarmac."

"Where will we keep him till morning?"

"He'll be safe here," says Stephen. "No predators out in this weather. But turn him to face my window, so I know he can see me."

Bogdan gently moves Snowy's body. He rests Snowy's head on his paws, facing in the direction of Stephen and Elizabeth's flat.

Stephen bends, and pats Snowy's head. "Safe now, old chum. Out of the cold soon, and no more sleeping with one eye open. It was lovely knowing you."

Bogdan puts his hand on Stephen's shoulder and gently squeezes.

45.

hris and Donna had asked if they could chat to Jason. Asked very politely, fair's fair, and Ron hadn't thought it was a terrible idea. Ron asked Jason, Jason didn't see why not, and so here they all are, bright and early on a Monday morning.

Ron loves coming to his son's house. The whole basement is a den. He's got a pool table, a jukebox, a bar, his gym stuff. It makes Ron proud.

The big money had come from boxing, and Jason had been no fool. Hadn't spent it all like some of them. Even so, there had been a few years when Ron could see his boy was beginning to struggle. No more pay days, no work. But he'd buckled down, built a lovely career for himself on the reality shows, bit of punditry, even the odd bit of acting, and the money started coming back in. Jason was a grafter, and nothing made Ron more proud than that. Seems to be settling down too.

Ron is currently sitting on a jet-black sofa with Chris and Donna. Right at this moment they are all watching Jason shadowboxing on a rug in the middle of the room. He has asked them to be silent for a couple of minutes, so that is what they are doing. Ron hates being silent. Jason is keeping up a running commentary as he boxes.

"Jason Ritchie with the jab, trying to rattle Tony Weir, but it's not getting through. Tony Weir, this resilient man, forty-five years of age, has come out of nowhere to fight for the Middleweight Championship of the World. And what a fight he's putting up. Weir throws a big right hand at Jason

Ritchie. Ritchie dips out of the way, what a fight between these two great boxers. And there's the bell . . ."

Jason stops boxing, drapes a towel around his shoulders and bends down over a laptop set up on his bar. He looks straight into the laptop camera.

"Hi, Tony, mate, it's Jason Ritchie here. Happy birthday to you, Big Man, great fight. Your wife, Gabby, tells me you're forty-five years young today, and says she loves you like crazy. So keep ducking and diving, brother, and when you get knocked down, you just get straight back up again. Gabby and the kids, Noah and Saskia, wanted me to wish you the very best, so have a great day, don't eat too much cake, and back in the gym tomorrow. Have a knockout day, mate, peace and love from Jason."

Jason gives his trademark cheeky wink, then presses stop on the screen, and turns his attention to his guests.

"Who's Tony Weir?" asks Ron.

"Some geezer," says Jason. "Don't know."

"Nice of you to wish him happy birthday," says Ron. "Nice touch. Good lad."

This last comment is directed at Chris and Donna. Ron knows Jason has connections that aren't always aboveboard, but, equally, he wants to remind Chris and Donna that he's a decent kid. Decent fifty-year-old kid.

"They pay me, Pops," says Jason. "It's called Cameo. You get a celeb to send you a message. Happy birthday, whatever, happy wedding, I just did a divorce one for someone."

"They pay you?" says Chris.

"Forty-nine quid a message," says Jason. "All the celebs do it, and I can record them in my boxers if I want to."

"Don't let me stop you," says Donna.

Ron is shaking his head in bemusement. "How many do you get asked to do?"

"Ten a day," says Jason. "Something like that. Lot of boxing fans out there."

"You're getting five hundred quid a day for saying 'Keep ducking and div-ing' and giving a little wink?" asks Donna.

"I used to get paid for being punched in the head," says Jason. "I think I've earned it."

"Does David Attenborough do them?" Ron asks.

"I don't think he does, Dad, no," says Jason. "He's probably got more money than me."

"You seem to be doing all right for yourself," says Chris, looking around at the bar and pool table in Jason's basement. "Talking of which, there's a couple of things you might be able to help us with."

"They keep saying you're dodgy, Jase," says Ron. "With no evidence to back it up."

"We're not saying he's dodgy," says Donna. "We're just saying that pretty much every single person he knows is dodgy."

"Things do get lively from time to time," agrees Jason. "What are you after?"

"You heard anything about any heroin?" asks Ron. "Recently like?"

"How come?" Jason asks.

"Load of it gone missing," says Ron. "And it might lead us to someone who killed a friend of ours. You know a geezer called Dom Holt?"

"Scouser?" says Jason. "Got his head blown off after the Everton game?"

"That's him," says Donna.

"I heard a couple of things," says Jason.

Jason's partner, Karen, pokes her head around the door. "I'm getting beet-root and papaya, hello, Ron, hello, guys, do we need anything else?"

"Hello, darling," says Ron. Chris and Donna raise a hand.

"I used the last of the quinoa," says Jason.

"All right, gorgeous," says Karen. "I'll be back in twenty. Love you."

"Love you, babe," says Jason, as Karen disappears again.

"She moved in?" asks Ron.

"Pretty much," says Jason.

"Nice," says Ron. Then, again, to Chris and Donna, "Good lad. He's a good lad."

"I think we were talking about heroin?" says Chris. "What do you know?"

"There's one main gang down here," says Jason. "One main route in. Geezer called Maxwell. Word got out he was in trouble, and that's got the sharks circling."

"Which sharks?" Chris asks.

"Your mate for one, Dad," says Jason. "Connie Johnson. She's been sniffing around."

"How did Connie Johnson find out Maxwell was in trouble?" asks Donna.

"There's some old guy visits her at the prison," says Jason. "He was there a few weeks ago, and after he went she was action stations. The whole of the South Coast's gone mad. No one knows who the guy is though, so don't ask."

"We know who the guy is," says Chris.

"Ibrahim," says Ron.

"Jesus, Dad," says Jason, laughing. "Of course it'd be Ibrahim. You and your mates are starting drug wars now. I used to prefer it when you wrote letters to the council complaining about the bins."

"It should be once a week, Jase," says Ron. "I pay my council tax."

"When you say 'action stations,'" says Chris, "what do you mean?"

"Just she was making moves," says Jason. "Talking to Maxwell's people, seeing if they wanted to jump ship and join her."

"Control the heroin trade as well as the cocaine trade?" Chris asks.

"Well, Amazon don't just sell books, do they?" says Jason.

"Did she speak to Dom Holt?" asks Donna.

"No idea," says Jason. "This is all just pub gossip."

"Luca Buttaci?" asks Chris. "She spoken to him?"

"Don't know the guy," says Jason. "I think I've probably done my bit now. I keep forgetting you two are police."

"I keep forgetting too," says Chris. "I blame your dad."

"If Connie wanted someone killed?" Donna asks. "That's something she'd be able to arrange from her cell?"

"Easy," says Jason. "Simplest thing in the world."

This is food for thought for everyone. Ibrahim is with Connie right now. But Ron has something else on his mind.

"Can I ask you a question too?"

"Course, Dad," says Jason.

Ron leans forward.

"When did you and Karen open presents on Christmas Day?"

"Straight after breakfast," says Jason. "When else would you open them?"

"I bloody knew it," says Ron.

Ron looks at Chris, and looks at Donna. Vindicated. Chris waits a moment or two, then continues his previous conversation.

"Who would Connie use, Jason?" asks Chris. "If she wanted someone killed?"

"Good question," says Jason, back on his feet, getting ready to record another video. "Ibrahim's not been her only mystery visitor in the last couple of weeks. Woman in her forties, maybe late thirties, been a couple of times. No one knows her, but she's got a dangerous air. And that's coming from prisoners."

"No name?" asks Chris.

"Nothing," says Jason. "Suddenly started turning up a couple of weeks ago. Not long after your murder, eh?"

46.

Ibrahim thought that Mondays in prison might feel a little different, but they seem identical to every other day. He supposes that's the point of prison.

Although he is a psychiatrist, and he has a professional duty, Ibrahim needs something from Connie today. Elizabeth has given him a task, and he will endeavor to provide satisfaction.

Connie is leaning back in her chair. She is wearing an expensive new watch.

"Have you ever heard of a man named Luca Buttaci, I wonder?" he asks.

Connie considers this while she breaks off a finger of her Kit Kat and dunks it in her flat white. "Ibrahim, do you sometimes think you're not a very good psychiatrist?"

"I think, objectively, I am skilled," says Ibrahim. "Do I have self-doubt? Yes. Do I believe I have helped many people? Also yes. Have I helped you?"

Connie is now working on the second finger of her Kit Kat. She gestures to Ibrahim with it. "Let me tell you a story."

"May I make notes?"

"Will the police ever see the notes?"

"No."

"Then you can make notes," says Connie, and settles into her tale. "A girl pushed in front of me in the lunch queue today—"

"Oh dear," says Ibrahim.

"Mmm, oh dear. I suppose she didn't know who I was. Sometimes the younger ones don't. Anyway, she elbows her way in, so I tap her on the shoulder and say, I'm terribly sorry, you appear to have taken my place."

"Were those your exact words?"

"They were not," says Connie. "So she turns to me and says, Apologies, but I don't queue, and if you've got a problem with that, then you've got a problem with me—again, not exact words. And then she pushed me."

"Oh dear," says Ibrahim again. "Does she have a name, this young woman?"

Connie thinks for a moment. "Stacey, I think the paramedics called her. So there's silence all around, of course there is. Everyone looking. You can start to see she realizes maybe she's pushed the wrong person—"

"How would she have realized that?"

"One of the warders was coming over to intervene, and when I sent him away he just nodded and mouthed, 'Sorry,' to her. I think that's when the penny dropped. So I take a swing and she drops to the floor."

"OK," says Ibrahim. "Is there a point to this story? I don't really like it."

"The point is what happens next," says Connie. "I see her there, sprawled on the lino, and I'm just rolling up my sleeves and getting ready to really teach her the error of her ways, when I hear your voice in my head."

"Goodness," says Ibrahim. "Saying what?"

"You were telling me to count down from five. Do you feel in control? In this moment do you feel at peace with yourself? Who is in charge, you or your anger? What is the rational course of action?"

"I see," says Ibrahim. "And what answer did you find?"

"I couldn't see what would be achieved by kneeling on her chest and continuing to pummel her. Like, that one punch was enough, and my point had been made. Anything extra would just be for my ego."

"And you are not your ego," says Ibrahim. "Or not solely your ego, at least."

"And this girl," says Connie. "I have to hand it to her: it takes guts to jump a queue in prison, so she must have something about her. Her lesson's learned, I can see that, so I simply stepped over her, got my lunch and got on with my day. And I felt proud of myself, and I thought, 'I bet Ibrahim will be proud of me too.'"

"And the girl?" asks Ibrahim. "How is she now?"

Connie shrugs. "Who cares? So are you proud of me?"

"Up to a point, yes," says Ibrahim. "It is a progress of sorts, isn't it?"

"I knew you would be," says Connie, beaming.

"I wonder if one day," says Ibrahim, "you might even reconsider the initial punch?"

"She pushed in, Ibrahim," says Connie.

"I remember," says Ibrahim. "And, without thinking, without hesitating, your reaction was swift and immediate violence."

"Thank you," says Connie. "It was pretty quick. Now let me help you down from your high horse, because I think you wanted to ask me about Luca Buttaci?"

"Well . . ." says Ibrahim.

"Here's me," says Connie. "The bird with the broken wing, paying you to heal me, to lead me from the path of violence and ego, to find some meaning in a life lived in chaos—these are all direct quotes, by the way—"

"I know," says Ibrahim, touched.

"But every session you drag me back in. How would you kill someone, Connie? Can you steal something from a cell, Connie? And now, do you know one of the South Coast's biggest heroin dealers?"

"It's unorthodox, I will grant you that," says Ibrahim. "I'm sorry."

Connie waves this away. "Doesn't worry me—stops you being too sanctimonious. I just want you to take a look in the mirror once in a while. You come in here, asking a vulnerable patient about a lowlife criminal and that's OK. I tell you a story of how I hit someone only once, instead of thirteen or fourteen times, and, I'll be honest with you, Ibrahim, you didn't look *that* impressed."

"I accept my flaws," says Ibrahim. "And if I wasn't sufficiently impressed by your punching a young woman so hard she had to receive medical attention, then I apologize."

"Thank you," says Connie. "Yes, I know Luca Buttaci. Know who he is."

"And would you have a way of getting in contact with him?"

"I would," says Connie. "Why do you ask?"

"We have a lunch invitation for him," says Ibrahim.

"I think he only eats what he kills," says Connie.

"It's a carvery on a Sunday," says Ibrahim. "It's very good. You must come, if they ever release you. And if you promise not to kill Ron. Do you think I might get Luca Buttaci's number?"

"Remind me how this is therapy?" says Connie. "You do remember I'm paying you?"

"Therapy is always a dance," says Ibrahim. "We must move to the music."

"You are so full of it," says Connie. "It's lucky I like you. I can't give you his number, but I can pass on a message. His brother-in-law works here."

"In the Prison Service?"

"I know, they seem so squeaky clean around here, don't they?"

Ibrahim looks down at his notes. Time to change the subject.

"Elizabeth wondered if you might have a view about the murder on Saturday?"

Connie breaks off a third finger of Kit Kat. Out of character—she normally eats two in the session and takes two back to her cell with her. It is Ibrahim's job to notice things like this.

"Who was murdered?" Connie asks.

"Dominic Holt," says Ibrahim. "One of the men you told us about. Are you enjoying that Kit Kat?"

"Huh," says Connie. "Comes to us all, I suppose."

There is a buzz on Ibrahim's phone. It is common practice to confiscate the phones of all visitors to Darwell Prison, but if you mention Connie's name they let you keep it. He checks his message. Donna.

"You have another regular visitor?" Ibrahim asks.

"I've got a few," says Connie. "Sports masseur, tarot reader, Spanish tutor."

"Woman in her early forties," says Ibrahim. "Started appearing a few weeks ago?"

Connie shrugs. "There's a florist who comes in from time to time. Cells can get very drab."

"I don't think she's a florist," says Ibrahim.

"It's a mystery, then," says Connie. "Now anything else you need from me, or can we get on with some actual therapy?"

"You are telling me everything, Connie?" Ibrahim asks. "Everything you know?"

"You're the expert," says Connie. "You tell me."

47.

Joyce

Well, we found Kuldesh's lock-up without a great deal of bother. Don't get too excited though.

Elizabeth wanted to find it before our "summit." She also wants to pay a visit to SIO Regan tomorrow, I don't know why, but I shall look forward to finding out.

I say "we" found it. Elizabeth had the bright idea of pretending to be Kuldesh's widow and turning up at the Fairhaven Council offices.

She gave them the works. Grieving widow, lost the number of the lock-up. Full of family photos and mementos. It took a good five minutes or so, she was really getting into it. Every now and again the woman from Fairhaven Council—she was called Lesley—would nod sympathetically. Elizabeth finished with a flourish, throwing herself on the mercy of Lesley, and of Fairhaven Council, and of the gods themselves.

At which point Lesley nodded sympathetically for a final time, then told her they weren't allowed to let her know where the lock-up was because of the Data Protection Act.

I had told Elizabeth that would be the case. All the way down in the minibus I'd said, You're wasting your time, you won't get anything out of the council. She said, Well, I got Russian nuclear secrets out of the KGB, I think I can probably handle Fairhaven Council. I knew she was wrong, however, and it was nice to see it proved. I even gave Elizabeth my "I told you so" look, which always infuriates her.

So she then pulled my usual party trick of breaking down in tears. More convincing than usual, I'll give her that, but I could have told her that was useless too. Lesley from Fairhaven Council remained unmoved. At one point she suggested that Elizabeth might like a glass of water, but that is as far as she would bend.

And so I stepped in.

As Elizabeth was slumped, sobbing, in her plastic chair, I mentioned to Lesley that, as Kuldesh was dead, and his accounts had been frozen, he wouldn't have paid his rent for this month. This got her attention. If there is one thing local councils like more than the Data Protection Act, it is money.

I told her that I would gladly pay what was owed. Felt, in fact, that it was my duty. Minutes later I had a printed invoice in my hand: £37.60 for rental of council storage garage number 1772, Pevensey Road, Fairhaven.

I told Lesley that payment would be forthcoming, thanked her for her efficiency and led Elizabeth out of the double doors to freedom.

Elizabeth was very complimentary, and we agreed in future to leave the KGB to her, and local councils to me. Everyone has to have a specialty. For example, I asked Elizabeth how we were going to get into the lock-up without a key, and she laughed.

I suggested that if we were going to have a poke around, we should call Nina Mishra. If we don't find the heroin, we might find something else that would lead us to it, and Nina would have a better idea of what to look for. Elizabeth accused me of having a "girl-crush" on Nina, which is probably true. I like strong women. Not bodybuilders, but you know what I mean. Anyway, Nina agreed to come and meet us after her morning lectures.

We wandered down to Pevensey Road; it's just off the front. I asked Elizabeth if she thought we'd be invited to the wedding if Donna and Bogdan ever got married, and she said, "Can't you concentrate on heroin for two seconds?"

There were two rows of garages, facing each other. Bright green doors, security notices fixed to each one. Two or three of them had their doors open, and from within you could hear banging and sawing. We walked down the middle of the garages, stepping aside occasionally to let the seagulls walk past, until we found number 1772.

Elizabeth took something from her bag, I didn't see exactly what, but it was a thin piece of metal. She placed it in the garage lock and gave it a sharp nudge with the palm of her hand, then pulled the garage door up and open.

I don't know what I was expecting. Some sort of treasure trove, I suppose. The sort of thing you'd see in a Disney cartoon, gold and jewels and doubloons. But really there were just old cardboard boxes stored against the walls, each with a number scribbled on it. We were taking the lid off the first few boxes when Nina arrived in a taxi and joined us.

She was wearing a very beautiful pin in her hair.

We didn't find the heroin, of course. If we'd found it before now, I would have said, I promise. If I had a hundred thousand pounds' worth of heroin on my dining-room table, I wouldn't be going on about hairpins and bodybuilders.

There were all sorts of things in the boxes. Old watches, jewelry, even a couple of Picasso prints. Elizabeth asked if Nina could find a good home for any of it, but Nina was of the view that a lot of it was probably stolen, and that the first stop ought to be the local police station, and I said we were going there tomorrow. Elizabeth asked if the Picasso prints were valuable, but Nina took one look at them and said they were fairly obvious forgeries, so Elizabeth and I should take one each, which we did. Mine is a sketch of a dove and is currently propped up on the mantelpiece. There is a man in Haywards Heath who does very good framing, so I will take it there next time I'm visiting. I will pretend it is real, of course. I suppose that's how people get away with forging things? It suits everybody to pretend it's real.

By the way, earlier I might have given the impression that, while I like strong women, I don't like bodybuilders. I didn't mean that at all. Bodybuilding is not for me, but I see why you would enjoy it. It's healthy fun, which is the second-best sort of fun there is.

Now you might think that the afternoon was a disappointment, but far from it. Elizabeth says that this garage is our trump card. All we have to do is hint that it exists during the lunch on Sunday and keep it under surveillance afterward. They will all have the capacity to find it, and they will all want to take a look.

And, of course, if someone doesn't take a look, we can assume they already have the heroin.

That's Elizabeth's thinking, and she has asked Nina to come to the lunch to help her drop the hint. Nina seemed terrified and thrilled in equal measure. Which, I suppose, is also how I've felt nonstop since I met Elizabeth.

So tomorrow we are going to see SIO Regan. The more information we have before the Sunday lunch, the happier Elizabeth will be. Not that she seems especially happy at the moment. There was a funeral today, an unusual one. I will tell you more about it when I have worked out what I think.

I asked Elizabeth if we had an appointment with SIO Regan tomorrow, and she said that of course we didn't, and not to worry myself about it. I also reminded her that the minibus doesn't run on a Tuesday, but she says Ron is going to drive us in, because he was feeling left out of things, and his Daihatsu is back from the garage.

I sense this is the big week for finding out who murdered Kuldesh. Maybe even for finding the heroin. Elizabeth seems to be putting all of her pieces in place. Does she know something?

Alan is in a mood because I was out all day. You can't explain heroin and murder to a dog. Well, a sniffer dog, perhaps. He's sulking in the spare bedroom, sighing every few minutes just so I know he's there. I know he won't be able to keep it up for long though. Let me call him.

And in he comes, tail wagging. All is forgiven.

48.

"SIO Regan, please," says Elizabeth to the desk sergeant at Fairhaven police station.

"Who might I say wants her?" asks the desk sergeant, a woman in her early fifties.

"You might say it is Elizabeth and Joyce," says Elizabeth. "Concerning the murder of Dominic Holt."

"You confessing?" asks the sergeant, as she dials upstairs. "I have an Elizabeth and a Joyce for SIO Regan. Information about Dominic Holt."

There is a brief wait, then the sergeant nods and says, "Thanks, Jim."

"She's out, I'm afraid," says the sergeant, turning to them. "Perhaps you could leave your number?"

"She's out?" asks Elizabeth.

"Afraid so," says the sergeant. "That confession will have to wait."

"Well, that's very peculiar, isn't it, Joyce?" Elizabeth motions to Joyce. "This is Joyce."

"It is very peculiar," says Joyce. "We watched her come in at"—Joyce flips open a notebook—"ten twenty-three a.m., and we've been watching the front door ever since, and she hasn't come out."

"They have cars," says the sergeant. "And you shouldn't be watching police stations."

"Oh, we were on public property," says Elizabeth. "On a little bench in the park."

"I brought a flask," says Joyce.

"And only two cars have left the station since then, and she was in neither," says Elizabeth. "It's—what time do we have now, Joyce?"

"Eleven oh four," says Joyce.

"It's eleven oh four now—"

"Eleven oh five now," says Joyce.

"And we thought that would probably give SIO Regan plenty of time to have settled in, had her morning briefing. She's probably having a coffee now, reading her emails."

"So we thought what better time?" adds Joyce.

"What better time?" says Elizabeth. "So if you could ring up again, and make sure there hasn't been a mistake? We would very much like to talk to her. The minibus returns to Coopers Chase at three p.m., and we have other chores today."

The desk sergeant stands and rests her palms on her counter.

"Ladies, fun though this is, SIO Regan is not here. There is more than one exit from this building—"

"Yes, Ron was at the back exit," says Elizabeth. "She hasn't left."

"And I'm telling you she has," says the sergeant. "So if you'll leave me a phone number, I'll make sure it is passed on to her. And, in the meantime, I would strongly advise against keeping watch on a police station, unless you want to get arrested."

Elizabeth takes out her phone and takes a photograph of the desk sergeant.

"Photograph taken, eleven oh seven," says Joyce.

"You take another photograph," says the desk sergeant, staring at Elizabeth, "and you're under arrest."

Elizabeth looks at Joyce, with one eyebrow raised. Joyce looks at her watch, considers for a moment, then gives the gentlest of nods.

Elizabeth takes another photograph.

49.

Sayed looks down across the mountains. Everything on the valley floor is his, and everything on the northern slopes too. The slopes to the south are Pakistan. Who owns them, Sayed doesn't know, but they have never been any trouble. That's all you can ask. There is trouble enough these days.

He hasn't heard back from Hanif since Wednesday. He was in Moldova, asking questions, and said he was heading to England, so he must have found something out. Sayed won't feel completely happy until it is sorted. Of course he won't. Shouldn't even be up in this helicopter—could be bad luck, and it takes only one stray bullet to bring it down. But the alternative was a six-hour trip by Jeep and horse.

This is not a position he has been in before, and it needs fixing quickly. He will give Hanif another week or so. He knows he'll be on the trail of the shipment. It's not like he can just ring him and have a chat.

Hanif will speak to Mitch Maxwell, and Mitch Maxwell will speak to Luca Buttaci. Politely at first, and then less politely if he doesn't get what he wants. Sayed does not like to be fooled or cheated. That way lies death.

Hanif will have to be punished too, of course, if they fail to find it between them. So he'll be motivated at least.

From the open door of the helicopter, Sayed sees the fields where poppies will soon be blooming, and that cheers him a little. Because everybody knows that fields of red poppies in full bloom can signify just one thing.

Profit.

50.

SIO Jill Regan is distinctly unimpressed.

"And you," she points to Joyce. "You were at the warehouse where Dominic Holt was shot."

"I was," says Joyce. "That's very good, people often forget my face. Or they don't remember where they know me from. I'd have patients years later come up to me in Sainsbury's and say—"

"Please," says Jill. "Spare me, I'm supposed to be leading a murder investigation."

"Not very well," says Elizabeth. "If you don't mind my saying?"

"I do mind," says Jill. "Either of you ever caught a murderer?"

"Yes," says Elizabeth.

"More than one," agrees Joyce.

"You have five minutes," says Jill. "What information do you have for me? Make it very good."

"Might I ask first," says Elizabeth, "what it is you are doing here?"

"Sitting in an interview room with the Golden Girls?" says Jill. "No idea."

"No," says Elizabeth. "You know full well what I mean. Why were the National Crime Agency drafted in to investigate the murder of Kuldesh Sharma?"

"How is that your business?"

"We're taxpayers," says Elizabeth. "But also interested observers."

"You know DCI Hudson?" Jill asks Joyce.

"Yes," says Joyce. "And his girlfriend, that's Patrice, do you know her?"

"He's asked you to come in, has he?"

Elizabeth laughs. "Goodness me, no. I imagine he'd be horrified if he knew we were here."

"He can join the club," says Jill.

"I will give you my theory at least," says Elizabeth. "I don't think you have any particular interest in Kuldesh, or the National Crime Agency don't, at least. I think you have a professional interest in the heroin."

"Not everything has to be cloak and dagger," says Jill. "This isn't Netflix."

"Oh, I've lived a life that would make Netflix blush," says Elizabeth. "I think the heroin was part of a major NCA operation. You planned to track it and let it into the country before swooping and arresting everyone. Am I right?"

"If this is all you have, I should get back to my desk," says Jill.

"But the heroin goes missing," continues Elizabeth. "Heroin that you allowed into the country. That you waved through at Newhaven. So your operation is ruined, and the reputation of the NCA is in great danger. Not for the first time, let's be honest. What's more, an innocent man is shot dead, well, I say 'innocent,' a friend of ours at least. I'm willing to believe you had never heard of Kuldesh Sharma, and hadn't realized he would be involved. So, while I'm sure you would like to solve his murder, I think above all else you need to find that heroin."

"OK," says Jill. "That's time up, I think."

"And then Dom Holt is murdered too," says Elizabeth. "I wonder if perhaps he was your man on the inside? And somebody found that out?"

"Who are you?" says Jill.

"Finally, an intelligent question," says Elizabeth. "I'm somebody who could help you."

"Help me how?"

"We could help you to find the heroin," says Elizabeth. "Couldn't we, Joyce?"

"We've done it before with diamonds," confirms Joyce.

"If you know where this heroin is, and you don't—"

Elizabeth hushes Jill. "We don't have it, SIO Regan, of course we don't. But I would be willing to bet we are a great deal nearer than you are. And, because I want to find out who murdered our friend, what I would really like to know from you is: who is working for you? Who are you protecting on the inside? Was it Dom Holt?"

"I'm not protecting anyone," says Jill.

"Mmm," says Elizabeth. "So you planned the operation without any inside help? It's possible. We did that in Budapest in '68, but I don't buy it, I'm afraid."

"What happened in Buda—"

"So Joyce is going to say four names to you," says Elizabeth. "One of them is, or was, working for you, and we'll be able to tell which one by your reaction. The slightest muscle twitch is all we'll need."

"Enough," says Jill. "This is a circus."

"Mitch Maxwell," says Joyce.

Jill gets up to leave. "Sorry, ladies."

"Luca Buttaci," says Joyce.

"Is that how you pronounce it, Jill?" Elizabeth asks.

"Samantha Barnes," says Joyce.

"I'll get one of the constables to come and collect you," says Jill.

"Dominic Holt," says Joyce.

Jill stops by the door. "If I ever see either of you again, it had better be because you have found my heroin."

"*The* heroin, surely," says Elizabeth, as Jill shuts the door behind her.

She turns to Joyce. "She's good."

"She didn't flinch," says Joyce.

"Which means one of two things," says Elizabeth. "Either she's a psychopath—"

"Ooh," says Joyce.

"Which I don't believe," says Elizabeth. "She put on fresh lipstick before she came down to see us. She wanted to make a good impression."

"I think psychopaths wear lipstick too," says Joyce.

"The other alternative, Joyce," says Elizabeth, "is that she didn't flinch, because no one in the gang is working for the NCA."

"Then why would they be here?"

"Because perhaps someone in the NCA is working for the gang?"

51.

The restaurant at Coopers Chase has seen many things over these last few years. It has seen a former High Court judge die while waiting for a banoffee pie. It has seen a row so blazing that a woman of eighty-nine eventually divorced her husband of sixty-eight years, and it has even seen a public marriage proposal, which was greeted with much fanfare at the time, and then quietly forgotten about when the man involved turned out to be already married. It has seen celebrations, wakes, new love, the parading of children, grandchildren and great-grandchildren, and even a hundredth birthday, which ended in the police being called due to an incident involving a male stripper.

But it has never seen the sort of gathering currently sitting around the private table in the conservatory. Two of Britain's most prolific drug smugglers, a multimillionaire antiques dealer and her enormous Canadian husband, a professor of historical archaeology at Kent University, a heavily tattooed Polish builder and, at the head of the table, the proud hosts, a former nurse, a former spy, a former trades union official and an occasionally still-practicing psychiatrist.

The subject of conversation is where they might all find a consignment of heroin. Introductions have been made. The conversation is interrupted from time to time by waiting staff bringing food, and it is agreed that at these points they are to pretend they are an organizing committee discussing a charity summer fête.

"Now we each have our own reasons," says Elizabeth, "for being here.

Mitch, you have had your heroin stolen, and your second-in-command shot dead. Though of course you might have shot Dom Holt yourself—"

"I didn't," says Mitch Maxwell.

"Someone did," says Luca Buttaci.

"Well, that's why we're here," says Ibrahim. "To discuss these questions frankly."

"Luca," says Elizabeth, "you have also lost out financially though, again, you would be a suspect both in the disappearance of the heroin and in the death by gunshot of—"

"And a bouncy castle for the children," says Joyce, as three young waitresses bring in their starters. "They're very reasonable to hire. We could charge fifty pence a turn."

"Two pounds a turn," says Samantha Barnes.

"One fifty," says Mitch Maxwell. "Come on. *Two quid?*"

"Don't talk to my wife like that," says Garth, nodding his thanks to the waitress.

"The absolute key will be no shoes on the bouncy castle," says Ibrahim. "Even with insurance we must—"

"And the death by gunshot of Dom Holt," continues Elizabeth, as the last waitress departs.

"I didn't shoot no one," says Luca.

"That's a double-negative," says Ibrahim. "It might be better to—"

Ron puts his hand on Ibrahim's arm. "Not now, mate, he's a heroin dealer."

Ibrahim nods, and tucks into his buffalo mozzarella.

"Samantha and Garth," says Elizabeth. "You are here for a number of reasons. First, your expertise in this area. And, secondly, because you lied to Joyce and Ibrahim, when you said you'd never heard of Dominic Holt."

"We're lying, are we?" says Samantha. "Says who?"

"Says Joyce and Ibrahim, and that's good enough for me."

"You were definitely lying, I'm sorry," says Joyce. "I wish I'd had the prawns now, yours look very good."

"And, most importantly, you have a Code 777 block on your phone, which is exceedingly rare, so we suspect that Kuldesh called you on the afternoon before his murder."

"I bet Mitch and Luca do too," says Samantha.

The two men shake their heads. "We just throw our phones away," says Mitch.

"So that's why we wanted you here, Samantha," says Elizabeth. "Though I do wonder why you accepted the invitation? What's in this little meeting for you?"

"Such a good question," says Samantha. "We're all being honest?"

"As much as a table of liars and cheats can be, yes," Elizabeth replies.

"There's a hundred thousand pounds' worth of heroin out there, and I'm betting . . ." says Samantha, ". . . that we could have stalls selling jams and chutneys."

"And there could even be a competition for the best one," says Joyce. "Judged by a local celebrity. We know Mike Waghorn, the newsreader."

The waitress has placed a new jug of water on the table and left.

"And I'm betting that someone here is going to find that heroin," says Samantha. "And Garth and I wanted to sit and listen and see if we can pick up any clues as to where it is."

"And then steal it for ourselves," says Garth. "Just a bit of fun—it ain't much money to us. But I figure we're the smartest people around this table, so I like the odds."

"I once took an IQ test," says Ibrahim, "as a schoolboy, and I was—"

Ron puts his hand on his friend's arm once again. "Let him think he's the smartest, Ib. Plays into our hands."

"But I am the smartest," says Garth.

Ibrahim goes to speak, but Ron flashes him a look.

"Nina is here because she is the last person we definitely know spoke to Kuldesh, and so is, naturally, a suspect; it can be proved, so sorry, dear."

"Not at all," says Nina. "I'd feel patronized if you left me out."

"And Bogdan is here in case any of you try to kill us," says Elizabeth. "I do have a gun, but there are rather a lot of you, so better to be safe than sorry."

"Also I was hungry," says Bogdan. "And I knew Kuldesh."

"And how about the four of you?" says Samantha Barnes. "Why are you here? What's in it for you?"

"What's in it for us," says Elizabeth, "is that someone murdered my husband's friend, and I would lay fairly good money that it's someone around this table."

"So we're just going to sit and listen," says Joyce. "And have a nice lunch, and see if anyone gives themselves away."

"However bright they may be," says Ibrahim, looking at no one in particular.

"If you find the heroin," says Elizabeth, "it's all yours, we couldn't give two hoots. So shall we start at the beginning? Ibrahim?"

Ibrahim takes out a file. "Mr. Maxwell, we'll start with you. The heroin originates where? Afghanistan?"

"And a beer tent," says Ron. "Local beers, see if we can get a discount."

The main courses have arrived.

52.

Hanif is staying at a hotel called Claridge's. It's in the very heart of London, and he has a room on the top floor. And there is only one room on the top floor. It has a private butler, a swimming pool and a grand piano. Hanif can neither swim nor play piano, but they look great on his Instagram.

It is his favorite hotel, for many, many reasons. The location can't be bettered, close to the shops of Bond Street and Savile Row, and the art galleries of Cork Street. The bar and restaurant are quintessential London, relaxed yet elegant and robustly expensive. But best of all is the absolute discretion of the staff. Hanif, who is forgetful at the best of times, had left a revolver and eighty thousand pounds in cash on his bed when he'd gone downstairs for breakfast, and had come back up to discover that the cleaner had neatly tidied both into a bedside drawer. You just didn't get that sort of service at the chain hotels.

He has made contact with Mitch Maxwell and presented him with the ultimatum. Find the shipment by the end of the month, or be executed. And he has made sure that the same message has been passed on to Luca Buttaci. The deadline should be sooner, but Hanif is eager to enjoy a couple of weeks in London; he hasn't been here since university, and also he really wants to see Coldplay at Wembley. If he kills Mitch and Luca, he'll have to leave straight away, and it won't do them any harm to have a bit of extra time. Hanif has never met Luca Buttaci, but he and Mitch had met in a FIFA corporate box at the Qatar World Cup and got along famously. Mitch assures him that all is under control, however, so Hanif is optimistic that he won't have to kill him.

This whole thing, the shipment, was Hanif's idea, and Sayed is very unhappy with how it is going. If the shipment isn't found, then, sure, Hanif will kill Mitch and Luca, but on his return to Afghanistan there is no guarantee that Sayed won't kill him. That's the game though, that's why he gets paid. He is going to have a massage this afternoon and try to forget about it for an hour or so.

Tonight there is a party in Mayfair. A Sunday evening soirée. One of his old friends from Eton is throwing it, and was delighted to see on Instagram that Hanif was in London, if a little surprised to see him playing the piano.

It will be nice to see a few old friends, hear what they are up to, lie about what he's up to, see if anyone fancies a swim.

Hanif rolls his shoulders—there's a knot he can't get rid of. He hopes the masseur will work some magic.

He really wants this plan to succeed. Hanif really doesn't want to have to kill anyone else. And certainly doesn't want to be killed. He has until the end of the month.

All in all it would be welcome news if someone could just find that box.

It would be nice to be able to enjoy the Coldplay gig without having to bury any bodies beforehand.

53.

The case has been discussed and dissected over the main course and dessert. While coffees were being served, there was a debate over whether they should hire a marquee, or trust in the August English weather.

"I didn't know who Kuldesh was until he was dead," says Mitch Maxwell.

"Same," says Luca Buttaci. "He was just a guy with a shop."

"You've got rivals though?" says Ron. "You can't be the only people selling heroin on the South Coast?"

"Honest answer," says Mitch. "If anyone else around here suddenly had heroin to sell, we'd hear about it. You can check that with your mate Connie Johnson."

"She's not my mate," says Ron.

Elizabeth asks, "And you still deny that Kuldesh contacted you, Samantha? Garth?"

"I wish he had," says Samantha. "That would have been a nice easy deal. And I wouldn't have killed him."

"Garth?"

"I probably would have killed him. Just to keep things neat. But I didn't."

"I have a thought," says Samantha. "If it might be helpful?"

"Please," says Elizabeth.

"What does the box the heroin was smuggled in look like?" asks Samantha. "I don't imagine that the heroin stayed in it for very long, so it's probably somewhere. Perhaps the box will show up one day in someone's shop? And there's your killer?"

"That's a very long shot," says Nina.

Mitch laughs. "You're telling me. I'll show you it, wait a minute. I don't think anyone's going to be selling it in an antiques shop."

Ibrahim takes the reins. "We still haven't addressed the murder of Dominic Holt. The who and the why."

Mitch has scrolled through his phone and found the photo he's looking for. He slides it across to Samantha. She takes off her glasses and holds the screen up close. "You really put a hundred thousand pounds' worth of heroin in a thing like that? No class."

She passes it to Garth, who pulls a face. "Junk shop maybe. But good idea, babe. Keep an eye out for it." He slides the phone back to Mitch.

"It certainly wasn't in his lock-up," says Nina. This is a line that Elizabeth has dictated to her.

"In his what?" says Mitch.

"That's just what he called the back of his shop," says Elizabeth. "We had a root around."

"No one calls that a lock-up," says Luca. "You're saying Kuldesh had a lock-up?"

"Sorry," says Nina to Elizabeth. Again, note perfect.

"All right," says Elizabeth. "Yes, Kuldesh had a council lock-up, no, I'm not going to tell you where it is—"

Garth raises his hand.

"No, Garth, not even if you threaten to kill me."

No one looks happy with this situation. Which is perfect.

"All in all though," says Elizabeth, "I would like to find this heroin before SIO Ronson finds it."

"Regan," says Luca.

"My mistake," says Elizabeth. "It goes without saying that if everyone here is telling the truth, there will be no problems. Because we all have a common goal. We can join forces to find the heroin and the person, or people, behind the murders."

"But if everyone here isn't telling the truth—" starts Ibrahim.

"Then, sooner or later, there's going to be a bloodbath," says Ron. "And maybe donkey rides, can you still do donkey rides or are they banned?"

The waitresses have come in to clear away the coffee cups, and lunch draws to a close.

Off they all go to their plots and their schemes—Elizabeth would put good money on that—and, as Nina Mishra gets up to leave, she asks, "What now?"

"Now we see who survives the week," says Elizabeth.

54.

Joyce

We had a lunch yesterday with some very unsavory characters, and it was a lot of fun. We hired the private room, and you could tell that put some people's noses out of joint. I heard someone whisper, "Who does she think she is?" as I went to the loo.

There was Mitch Maxwell, the heroin dealer, Luca Buttaci, also a heroin dealer, who sounds like he should be Italian but isn't. Then Samantha and Garth, who we met in Petworth. Samantha gave me a peck on the cheek, but Garth just said, "Where's Alan?" and then "That's not what I had hoped for," when I told him he was snoozing in front of one of my radiators. Nina Mishra came too and cooed over Coopers Chase. The winter sun was out, and I have to admit the whole place did look rather lovely. She is already planning to move in in thirty-five years' time.

We learned nothing, but learning nothing was the whole point of the lunch. Elizabeth just wanted to get everybody together, to shake the tree.

Give them enough rope, was what we used to say, but "Let's see who kills whom next," was how Elizabeth actually put it.

It felt to me like everyone there knew a part of the picture, but no one knew all of it, and I suppose that is what Elizabeth is banking on.

So now we wait. Let them tear each other apart, and see what secrets fall out of their pockets while they do it.

Afterward Elizabeth told me she is going to be out of circulation for a couple of days. Uncontactable. She says she has business to attend to, and perhaps she does.

Her business is not my business, and of course we all need a bit of privacy from time to time. Especially round here. We can sometimes be in each other's pockets a little, which I know is not everyone's cup of tea. I like it. I like to be around people. I like to chat, and I don't really mind about what.

But Elizabeth is different, and I have learned to respect that. To give her a bit of space, and resist the temptation to spy. That said, I saw out of my window that Anthony the hairdresser was heading into her block the other day, and, as he always makes a point of telling us, he never makes house calls, so something must be going on. I might take the scenic route when I walk to the shop later, just to see if her curtains are drawn. That will tell its own story.

Why was Anthony going into Elizabeth's? Knowing her, she's probably off to the Palace. Meeting the King, getting a medal. They do that for spies all the time. Not so much for nurses. I swear though, if she meets King Charles without telling me first, I will have something to say about it. A friend of Gerry's was once invited to a garden party at Buckingham Palace. He was head of the Rotary Club or something, and they'd raised some money for a hospice. Anyway, he didn't go, because he was playing golf. Can you imagine?

I think the Queen and I would have got on. She reminded me a lot of Elizabeth. A bit more approachable maybe.

But with Elizabeth out of reach, I find myself at a loose end, and I'm not always great with being at a loose end. I can potter around the house for a bit, watch a *Bargain Hunt* with Alan. But sooner or later I need something to do, and someone to do it with. With Gerry it was easy: I could help him with the crossword, or tell him what I thought about something or other. I often tell Alan what I'm thinking about something or other, and it works very nicely until you catch yourself doing it.

Perhaps I could work with the boys on their romance-fraud plan for a couple of days? I could offer them a woman's eye. Though, according to Ron, Ibrahim is very capable of writing messages that would make "a docker blush."

They'll know that Elizabeth is out of bounds too, so they won't be surprised to see me. I'll bake them something.

Perhaps I should go to see Mervyn too? I wonder how he is? We've slightly been avoiding each other, staggering our dog walks. Sometimes Alan sees Rosie out of the window and he loses his mind. Starts rolling around and showing his belly. He really reminds me of myself sometimes.

I'm looking out of the window right now, over to where I saw Anthony's car parked. One of the guest bays. And I do know what you're thinking—I promise, I'm not a fool. I know why he was really there.

We buried Snowy the other day—I haven't mentioned it, what with everything. He's the fox with the white-tipped ears who rules the roost around here when we all go to sleep. Bogdan had dug Snowy a grave, "nice and deep, so no one can touch him." Not the first grave Bogdan has dug recently, so he knows a thing or two about them. Watching Bogdan dig a grave is one of the few things that could change my mind about wanting to be cremated when I die.

Bogdan and Stephen had found Snowy last weekend. Now he's in a biodegradable wicker basket, which people laid white flowers on.

There was a surprisingly big turn-out. I think we all thought he was our own special secret, but, once the details were put on the noticeboard, half the village turned out to pay their respects. They all knew him by different names, "Lucky," "Tippy," "Moonlight," all sorts of things.

The name "Snowy" had come from Stephen. I always used to call him "Mr. Fox," so perhaps I lack imagination. Joanna always says that I do.

A recently widowed woman from Ruskin Court called him "Harold," and she was one of many people in tears as we sang a hymn and laid him to rest.

Anyway, to my point, among the mourners, out in public for the first time since goodness knows when, was Stephen.

He and Elizabeth walked up to the allotment, arm in arm, and Stephen said his hellos to the congregation. Everyone was "old chum," "old friend," "chief." Ibrahim gave him a hug, and Stephen smiled with joy and called him Kuldesh.

Ron rather formally shook his hand; he finds hugs hard. Stephen took one look at Ron's tattoos and said, "West Ham man, eh? Better watch out for you," and then Ron gave him a hug too. When he met me he said, "It's Joyce. There she is."

Anyway, it felt like Elizabeth was allowing us to say our goodbyes. Certainly when I hugged him, I didn't want to let go.

And, of course, Stephen's hair was immaculate.

So, yes, I am not entirely a fool. I know in my heart that Anthony was there to see Stephen. And that Elizabeth is "out of circulation" for the next few days because they are off to take Stephen to a home where he might be looked after properly. She is finally going to let him go. She should have done it months ago, and she knows that, but, while you have something to cling on to, you cling on. I wonder what has made her change her mind? Are they able to discuss it?

Anthony had done a lovely job. Elizabeth just wants Stephen looking at his best. Wherever he is going, Elizabeth will want him to make a good impression, make people understand how special he is, and how loved he is.

I don't know how they will cope apart. Stephen will enter a new world, of course, but his walls closed in long ago now. Elizabeth loves him so utterly, and is loved by him so utterly, and that is being stolen from her.

I hope she finds him somewhere nearby, where she can visit often. The two of them will have talked it through, as much as they are able. Love always finds a language. Elizabeth hasn't come to ask me for help or advice, and I understand that completely. I know from experience that grief rides alone.

I cannot begin to imagine what Elizabeth is going through. Perhaps she feels that Stephen has already left. Perhaps that is where they are. It's between the two of them, and all I know is that I will be there for her. That's all I have to give.

They say that time softens the pain, but that's a fairy tale. Who would ever love again if anyone actually told the truth? I'm afraid there are some days when I could still rip out my own heart and weep myself hollow for Gerry. Some days? Every day. That's the journey my best friend has just begun.

So forgive me if, for just a while longer, I choose to imagine that Elizabeth is going to the Palace to see the King.

55.

Ron was expecting the ring on his doorbell. Could have timed it almost to the second.

Elizabeth is away for a couple of days, so Ron knows it must be Joyce. At a loose end, certainly, and, hopefully, with cake. He leaves Ibrahim and Computer Bob to their work, and buzzes her in.

"It will be Joyce, and she will have cake, Bob," says Ibrahim. "I am sure of it."

"Where is Elizabeth anyway?" Ron asks them, door held open for Joyce's arrival.

Ibrahim shrugs. "Shooting someone?"

Joyce appears at the top of the stairs, with a Tupperware box. Alan trots behind her, sniffing for adventure.

"Coconut and raspberry," she says, lifting the box in offering. "Hello, boys."

Bob stands as she walks into the flat.

"Sit down, Bob, don't mind me," says Joyce.

"Cup of tea?" Ron asks.

"Do you have milk?"

"No," admits Ron.

"Do you have tea?"

Ron thinks. "No, out of tea too. I've got lager?"

"I'll get myself a glass of water," says Joyce. She wanders into Ron's kitchen, then calls over her shoulder, "So where are we with Tatiana?"

"We've followed Donna's advice to the letter," says Ibrahim.

"She didn't say write a fifteen-verse love poem," says Ron.

"I have added my own touches," admits Ibrahim. "But the bait is laid, and the trap, we hope, is about to be sprung."

Joyce walks back in, pulls a dining chair over to Ron's desk and sits down next to Bob and Ibrahim. "Are you enjoying it, Bob?"

Bob thinks for a moment. "I suppose I am, yes. I'm only here as tech support, really, Ibrahim does the hard work, the poetry and so on. But occasionally the wi-fi goes off and I can be useful. So I find that fun."

"And we talk about the world," says Ron.

"And, yes, we talk about the world," agrees Bob.

"Tell me one thing Bob thinks about the world, Ron?" asks Joyce. "From all your conversations?"

Ron thinks. "He likes computers."

Joyce turns to the screen. Ibrahim has started typing. "So where are we?"

"We've agreed to pay them a further £2,800," says Ibrahim. "But we've told Tatiana that our bank won't allow us to transfer it to her. That they've flagged it as a suspicious payment."

"They did that with my payment when I bought my sofa," says Joyce. "They had me jumping through hoops."

"So we've asked if they know anyone in England who could come and collect the money from us and take it to her."

"An accomplice?" says Joyce.

"We arrange the meet," says Ron. "A real person shows up, we hand over the money, and Donna and her pals swoop in and arrest them."

"So a friend of Tatiana's, rather than Tatiana," says Joyce.

"There is no Tatiana," says Ibrahim.

"Oh, yes," says Joyce.

"I am communicating with this friend of Tatiana's," says Ibrahim. "He is called Jeremmy. With two *m*'s."

Joyce reads what's on screen as the conversation continues.

JEREMMY: You have the money?

MERVYN: Tell me more about Tatiana? How long have you known her? Are her eyes as clear and blue as they seem? Do you simply fall into them?

JEREMMY: I am free Wednesday.

MERVYN: None of us are truly free, Jeremmy, all of us have our chains. You have a very unusual name? Is there a story of how it came about?

JEREMMY: Are you free Wednesday also?

MERVYN: Will you deliver the money to Tatiana yourself? If so, I envy you. I must wait over a week to see her face, to breathe her in.

JEREMMY: London is best. London and Wednesday.

MERVYN: No can do, I'm afraid, Jeremmy. I have limited mobility, and I find London very difficult. Also noisy, don't you think? How do you bear it, Jeremmy? I suppose you are a younger man, and the excitement of a city drives the pulse? You will have to come here.

No reply is forthcoming for the moment.

"That will be fun," says Joyce. "If he comes to Coopers Chase and gets arrested. One for the newsletter."

"I would like Mervyn to meet him," says Ibrahim. "Might provide some closure. How is he?"

"Haven't seen him," says Joyce.

"Alan must miss Rosie terribly?"

Alan, hearing both his name and Rosie's, falls to the floor and exposes his belly. Ron does the honors.

"What did you make of yesterday?" Ron asks Joyce.

"I don't trust Mitch, I don't trust Luca, I don't trust Samantha, and I don't trust Garth," says Joyce. "Although he is very rugged."

"I saw you had the private room," says Bob. "It was the talk of the restaurant."

"But I also think this," says Joyce. "If any of them had the heroin, or knew where it was, then they wouldn't have come to lunch. I think they were all fishing for clues."

"And Kuldesh?"

"I think someone around that table killed him," says Joyce. "At least one of them."

"And what about the man I saw?" says Bob. "Dominic, with the bullet through his head?"

"Could have been any of them," says Ron. "Villains shoot villains. Who cares?"

"Thank you, Ron," says Ibrahim. "Really helping with the load while Elizabeth is not with us."

"Where is she anyway, Joycey?"

"You know as well as I do where she is," says Joyce. "I saw you hug Stephen."

"Yeah," says Ron, and looks at the label on his lager instead of at Joyce. "Should we be helping?"

"Nothing to be done," says Ibrahim. "She knows we're here."

A new message appears on the computer screen.

JEREMMY: OK, I come to you. You sure you have money?

MERVYN: Oh, that's very kind of you, Jeremmy, thank you for going out of your way. People often fail to make allowances for those older than them. I sense your kindness and sensitivity. Will you stay for dinner? I would love to get to know you a little better. Perhaps we will be firm friends once Tatiana arrives!

"Have they not noticed you don't sound like Mervyn any more?" Joyce asks.

"They are so close to the money, they just want to believe," says Ibrahim. "It's the same trick they play. Dangle the thing you want most just out of reach. Mervyn wants love; they want Mervyn's money."

JEREMMY: I cannot have dinner. I have to leave. You have the money in cash?

MERVYN: I do. The whole £2,800. Money well spent.

JEREMMY: £5,000 now. For expenses.

MERVYN: I don't have £5,000.

JEREMMY: Just ask. Otherwise I can't come and Tatiana will be angry with us both.

MERVYN: Well, we can't have that. When can you come?

JEREMMY: Tomorrow.

"No," says Joyce. "Wait until Elizabeth is back. It'll be something nice for her. An arrest."

MERVYN: Next week. I have an operation on my testes this week.

Ibrahim looks at Joyce. "If I say 'testes' that's the end of any argument. No man wants to negotiate."

JEREMMY: OK, next Wednesday. We have your address.

MERVYN: Smashing. Looking forward to meeting you, Jeremmy.

Joyce claps her hands, waking Alan. "Lovely! What shall we do next?"

"We were going to drink whisky and watch the snooker," says Ron. "It's the only sport we both like."

"Though I'm coming around to darts," says Ibrahim.

"The darts," corrects Ron.

"Perhaps I'll stay?" says Joyce. "We can have a good old natter?"

"If we're watching the snooker," says Ibrahim, "then the only good old natter is about the snooker. How many points Mark Selby might be ahead, for instance. Or whether Shaun Murphy is likely to pull off a particularly tricky safety shot. There will be no general conversation."

"Perhaps I will take Alan for a walk," says Joyce. "Bob, would you care to join me?"

"I, uh . . ." There is something Bob doesn't want to say.

"You a snooker man, Bob?" Ron asks.

"I am, yes," says Bob. "I was about to head off and watch it."

"Fancy watching it with two mates?"

"Well, I, yes, that would, that would be very enjoyable," says Bob, looking like a boy invited to a friend's house after school.

"No conversation not about snooker though," says Ron.

"Perfect," says Bob.

Joyce stands. Alan is chasing his tail on Ron's rug.

"You'll never catch it, Alan," says Ron.

"That's just it, isn't it?" says Joyce, pulling on her coat. "There's always something just out of reach. Love, money. Alan's tail. The heroin. Everyone chasing the thing they don't have. Going mad until they get it."

"Mmm," says Ron, turning the snooker on.

"It's like that every night. I dream of Gerry. I know I can't have him, but I never give up trying."

Ibrahim and Ron both look at Joyce, and then at each other. Ibrahim gives a slight nod, and Ron rolls his eyes.

"All right, you can stay and chat about whatever you want."

"Only if you're sure," says Joyce, coat already halfway off again.

56.

Nina Mishra doesn't really like her job. Doesn't like the pay, certainly. She really felt it yesterday, sitting around that table with the drug dealers and the art forgers, while she was being careful not to spill anything on her dress so she could fold it up and send it back to ASOS the next day.

Actually, that's not fair. There are bits of the job she *does* like. She likes the reading, curling up in an armchair, delving into the sexual politics of Mesopotamia, that bit is fun. And she likes the travel, Turkey, Jordan, Iraq, she's been all over. She's quite happy sleeping with colleagues at conferences too. What she really doesn't like, pay aside, is the teaching. And, more specifically, the students.

There's one with her now, an identikit boy of around twenty, a first year, certainly. He's called Tom or Sam, or maybe Josh. The boy is wearing a Nirvana T-shirt, despite being born many years after Kurt Cobain died.

They are discussing an essay he hasn't written. "Roman Art and the Manipulation of Historical Memory."

"Did you enjoy the reading at least?" Nina asks.

"No," says the boy.

"I see," says Nina. "Anything else to add? Reasons you didn't enjoy it?"

"Just boring," says the boy. "Not my area."

"And yet your course is titled 'Classics, Archaeology and Ancient Civilizations'? What would you say your area is?"

"I'm just saying I don't pay nine thousand pounds a year to read a bunch of left-wing academics rewriting Roman history."

"I imagine it's your mum and dad paying the nine thousand pounds, isn't it?"

"Don't privilege-shame me," says Tom or Sam or Josh. "I can report you."

"Mmm," says Nina. "Am I to take it that you're not planning on finishing the essay anytime soon?"

"Read my file," says the boy. "I don't have to do essays."

"OK," says Nina. "What do you imagine you are doing here? What and how do you hope to learn?"

"You learn through experience," says the boy, with the world-weary air of a wise man tired of having to explain things to fools. "You learn from interacting with the real world. Books are for lose—"

There is a knock at Nina's door, despite the SUPERVISION IN PROGRESS note stuck on it. Nina is about to send the unseen caller away when the door opens, and who should walk in but Garth, the colossal Canadian she had met at Sunday lunch.

"Sorry, this is a private session," says Nina. "Garth, isn't it?"

"I need something," says Garth. "And I need it right now. You're lucky I even knocked."

"I'm teaching," says Nina, then looks at the boy. "Up to a point."

Garth shrugs.

"So you'll have to wait. We're trying to discuss Roman art."

"I don't wait," says Garth. "I get impatient."

"Probably ADHD," says the boy, clearly glad there is now a man in the room.

Garth looks at the boy, as if noticing him for the first time. "You're wearing a Nirvana T-shirt?"

The boy nods, sagely. "Yeah, that's my vibe."

"What's your favorite song?"

"'Smells Like—'"

"And if you say 'Smells Like Teen Spirit' I will throw you out of that window."

The boy now looks decidedly less happy that there is a man in the room.

"Garth, I'm teaching," says Nina.

"Me too," says Garth.

"Uh . . ." says the boy.

"Easy question," says Garth. "Nirvana is the fourth-greatest band of all time. Name their best song."

"'The Man Who . . . ,' uh."

"If you're about to say 'The Man Who Sold the World,' think again," says Garth. "That's a Bowie cover. We can have a different discussion about Bowie when we're through with this."

"Leave him alone, Garth," says Nina. "He's a child. And a child in my care."

"I'm not a child," says the boy.

"You want me to help or not?" says Nina. "Why don't we call it a day anyway? If you haven't done the essay, there's no point."

"My pleasure," says the boy, getting up as fast as he can.

"Wait, you didn't do your essay?" Garth asks.

"Leave him alone, Garth," says Nina.

"What was it about? The essay?"

"Roman art or something," says the boy.

"And you didn't do it? Couldn't be bothered?"

"I just . . . didn't . . . just wasn't . . . interested."

Garth roars and beats his chest. The boy instinctively ducks toward Nina, and she puts a protective arm around him.

"You weren't interested? In Roman art? You are out of your *mind*. You're in this beautiful room with this intelligent woman, and you get to talk about Roman art, and you're not interested. You're not interested? You've got three years till you actually have to go and get a job! You know what jobs are like? Terrible. You think you get to discuss Roman art when you've got a job? You think you get to *read*? What are you interested in?"

"I have a TikTok channel," says the boy.

"Go on," says Garth. "I'm interested in TikTok. I was thinking of dabbling. What do you do?"

"We do . . . fast-food reviews," says the boy.

"Oh, I like that," says Garth. "Fast-food reviews. Best burger in Canterbury?"

"The Yak House," says the boy.

"Noted," says Garth. "I'll check you out. Now I need a word with Miss Mishra here, so I'm going to ask you to skedaddle."

The boy doesn't need asking twice, and shoots for the door. Garth puts out a massive arm to stop him. "Three things before you go though. One, if that essay isn't done by next week, I'll kill you. I mean that. Not like 'Your mom will kill you if you don't tidy your room.' Actually kill you. You believe me?"

The boy nods.

"Good, stop wasting this opportunity, brother, I swear. Two, if you tell anyone I threatened you, I will also kill you. OK? Not a word."

"OK," says the boy.

"It better be OK. God cries every time someone lies to a Canadian. And three, the best Nirvana song is 'Sliver' or 'Heart-Shaped Box.' Understand?"

"Understand," agrees the boy.

"I played bass for a band called Mudhoney for two tour shows once. You heard of them?" says Garth.

"I think so," pretends the boy.

"Great, you check them out, and I'll check out your TikToks. Off you go, champ."

Garth ruffles the boy's hair and watches him run out. He turns back to Nina.

"Nice kid. Where's the lock-up garage, Nina?"

"You terrified him, Garth," says Nina. "A child."

"I don't care," says Garth. "Again, not like 'I don't care what film we see,' I literally do not care, I can't overemphasize that. Where's the lock-up?"

"I don't know," says Nina.

"Come on," says Garth. "We going to do this quickly or slowly? I promise quickly is best."

Nina has to think fast. She has one primary concern. They want to figure out who killed Kuldesh—so how to play this situation? Is this man going to help or hinder them? This is exactly what Elizabeth had wanted. To set the whole lot of them on a false trail. See what dust was kicked up. She makes up her mind.

"Let's say I tell you?" she begins.

"Let's say that," agrees Garth.

"What's in it for me?"

Garth laughs. "That's pretty obvious. I don't throw you out that window."

"Garth, you keep threatening to throw people out of windows," says Nina. "I'm guessing you've never done that in real life."

"Guess again, miss," says Garth. "Where's the lock-up?"

"I want ten percent, if you find it," says Nina.

"You want ten percent of the heroin?"

"I don't want to go anywhere near heroin," says Nina. "But I want ten percent of the profits when you sell it."

"Huh," says Garth, thinking about this. "But you already searched the lock-up, I bet. I'm guessing it's not there?"

"I didn't know what I was looking for," says Nina. "You might have more luck."

"Ain't no luck involved," says Garth. "You just gotta keep grinding."

"And they trust me, Elizabeth and the gang. Whatever they tell me, I can tell you."

"Why don't you do this deal with them?"

"They're not going to sell the heroin, are they?" says Nina. "There's no profit."

"Yeah, those cutie-pies would give it straight to the cops. OK, deal," says Garth. "Where's the lock-up? Then I'm going to pay a visit to the Yak House. Why'd you think they didn't call it 'The Yak Shack'?"

It is apparent that Garth is actually looking for an answer. She stops writing for a moment.

"I don't know, I'm afraid. You'd have to ask them."

"I will," says Garth. "You'd better believe I will."

Nina hands him the address. Is this a very good idea, or a very bad idea? She is sure it will turn out to be one or the other.

57.

Donna sips her coffee and reads out the text.

> Not urgent, but if you were ever to get married, do you think
> it would be a big wedding? What sort of numbers would you
> be thinking about? I saw a police officer in a film yesterday
> shoot someone in a car park, and I thought of you.

"From Joyce?" Chris asks.

Donna nods. Elizabeth has asked them to keep an eye on the lock-up after a lunch they'd had yesterday. "See what you can see," she had asked.

"What did you say?"

"I said I'm not getting married, and they still don't let me have a gun," says Donna. "And she said that's a shame, you'd suit both."

Chris holds binoculars up to his eyes for a moment, then puts them down. "False alarm. So you wouldn't get married?"

"Things to do first," says Donna. "Never been to India, never jumped out of a plane. Never really punched anyone."

"Yeah, get those out of the way," says Chris. "Wouldn't want to get married with those hanging over you."

"You must have a bucket list?" says Donna.

Chris thinks. "Well, I've never watched *Titanic*. And I'd like to go to Bruges. But I could probably do both of those with your mum."

"She's a lucky woman," says Donna. She takes the binoculars now and does a quick scan.

"Nothing," she says. "You reckon this is a waste of time? Sitting on a hill waiting for heroin dealers?"

"Elizabeth says they'll be here," says Chris. "So they'll be here."

"She really has you under her spell, doesn't she?"

"Yes," says Chris. "I choose to embrace it."

Donna and Chris are parked high on a hill above the row of lock-up garages by Fairhaven seafront. They have been in this exact spot before, carrying out surveillance on Connie Johnson's office. Connie now has her office in a cell at Darwell Prison, though word on the street says she's as busy as ever.

In their absence the Benenden horse-theft case is ongoing, and thefts have recently spread as far afield as Peasmarsh. No horse is safe, and people are up in arms.

Chris and Donna already have a fairly good idea who is carrying out the thefts, however: a man named Angus Gooch who runs a livery stable near Battle, and has a string of previous convictions to his name. He is stealing horses to order, and then transporting them across the country. He has an Audi TT, so presumably it's good business.

It took them about a day to solve, and they certainly have enough evidence to arrest him. But they are biding their time in order to look busy while they're working on finding the heroin with the Thursday Murder Club. He's not killing the horses, so they can afford to let him nick a few more, safe in the knowledge that they'll be back with their rightful owners soon enough.

If SIO Regan knew what they were up to, there would be immediate disciplinary action, but Chris and Donna are now being as good as gold around the station, giving her plenty of space, and no trouble. So she, in turn, is leaving them alone. Whatever SIO Regan's problem is, it is now not Chris and Donna. Which gives them a certain freedom.

If she were ever to ask why they are staking out this particular lock-up, which she won't, as she is very incurious for a police officer, they will say they are investigating a tip-off about a Fairhaven local who has suddenly come into possession of a number of saddles.

"Here we go," says Donna, binoculars up again. She hands them to Chris, so he can see what she has just seen.

Mitch Maxwell, glancing this way and that, is walking between the garages, holding a piece of paper in his hand. He reaches number 1772 and tries the door. It doesn't budge. He takes a piece of metal from his coat, jams it in the lock and pushes. The faint clang carries up the hillside. But the door doesn't open. He tries again.

"There's a knack," says Donna.

On the fifth attempt the lock springs, and Mitch opens the garage door.

"So we tick Mitch Maxwell off the list," says Chris. "If he knew where the heroin was, he wouldn't be searching here. I'll text the boss."

"The boss?" says Donna.

"Elizabeth," says Chris.

"Silly me," says Donna. "How's the sea-swimming going?"

"I went once," says Chris. "It was freezing. I mean, I figured it would be cold, but come on. So I'm going to learn the trumpet instead."

Mitch is clearly busy in the lock-up garage. Searching for the heroin, which Chris and Donna could already tell him isn't there.

"Have you found out anything about Samantha Barnes?" Donna asks.

"I put in a call to Chichester CID," says Chris. "Told them we were looking into the horse thefts and her name came up. They said she's very polite, and never puts a foot wrong."

"Any previous connection to drugs?"

"Connections to everything, they said. Though the DI said that horse theft was a new one to add to the list."

Chris looks through the binoculars again. "Poor Mitch, no one to trust."

"It's a real shame," says Donna, "when even heroin dealers lose faith. Has Elizabeth replied?"

Chris checks his phone. "Hasn't even been received. What's she up to?"

"And how about you?" says Donna. "You thinking of getting married to anyone?"

"I promise you'll be the second to know," says Chris.

A black Range Rover cruises slowly down the lane between the garages, and pulls up outside lock-up number 1772.

58.

Mitch is too clever for Elizabeth, and, on this clear Monday afternoon, he is already inside the lock-up, searching through cardboard boxes. Mitch had seen the look on Elizabeth's face when Nina Mishra had mentioned the lock-up. There was *something* here for sure.

A Fairhaven Council data clerk with a heroin problem had been only too happy to help with the address. Though he was slightly miffed afterward when Mitch had told him that, due to unforeseen circumstances, just at the moment he had no heroin.

Hanif has landed and given Mitch until the end of the month to find the heroin. Mitch has assured him he will have it back by then.

If Dom really was the weak link in his organization, his death should iron things out a bit. Perhaps Hanif will understand even if Mitch can't find the drugs? But he *will* find them, he knows it.

Mitch picks out a vintage TAG Heuer watch from one of the boxes and slips it into his pocket. Waste not, want not.

The garage door opens with a metallic roar and Mitch pulls his gun. The figure of Luca Buttaci ducks into the garage, and Mitch tucks the gun back into his waistband.

"Wondered how long you'd be, lad," says Mitch. "How'd you find it?"

"Tracker on your car," says Luca. "You find anything?"

"Some nice watches," says Mitch. "No heroin."

"Anyone else been in here? The Canadian?"

"If he's been here, he left it neat and tidy," says Mitch. "And he doesn't seem the neat and tidy type."

Luca sits on a pile of boxes and lights a cigarette. "Where the hell is it?"

"You haven't heard a peep? I still don't trust Connie Johnson."

"It's just"—Luca makes a "puff of smoke" motion with his fingers—"gone, pffff. You know at some point I've got to find someone else to supply me with heroin, Mitch? If you keep having these problems?"

"I know," says Mitch. "Can I ask you a question? And you tell me the truth?"

"Depends on the question," says Luca. "Try me."

"OK, I'm asking John-Luke Butterworth now, my old mate," says Mitch. "Not Luca Buttaci. Have you been in touch with the Afghans?"

Luca shakes his head. "I don't know the Afghans. Don't want to know them—that's your job."

"OK," says Mitch. "You're sure?"

"I'm certain," says Luca. "I don't need that sort of trouble. Why you asking?"

"One of them has come over," says Mitch.

"Over here?"

"Yep."

"But they never come over here?"

"I know," says Mitch. "They want to meet us."

"RIP, us," says Luca. "What do they want?"

"We'll find out, I guess," says Mitch. "But it'll be easier if we find the heroin before they show up. And it's not in this lock-up."

"How much do we know about this Garth guy? The Canadian?"

"Not enough," says Mitch. "We know about the wife. She's enough all by herself."

Mitch feels the weight of the watch in his pocket. That'll make a nice welcome present for Hanif. If he's going to be killed, he's going to be killed, but the watch won't do any harm.

And, besides, perhaps there's a perfectly innocent explanation for Hanif flying thousands of miles to meet him.

Mitch follows Luca out of the garage, and into the wintry, seaside air.

The two men both give a merry wave to the police officers watching them from high up on the hill.

59.

Samantha Barnes is giving a lecture to the Petworth Women's Institute next week. Fakes and forgeries, and how to spot when you are being conned. It's all too easy these days.

She has lots of good facts lined up.

The key thing, if you are buying a piece by Banksy, for example, is that it needs a certificate of authenticity from an organization named the Pest Control Office. The certificate of authenticity will have one half of a ten-pound note stapled to it. That organization keeps the other half of the ten-pound note. If your piece does not have this, it's a fake. Do not, under any circumstances, buy it.

It is a clever system of authentication, and Samantha herself has spent this afternoon cutting up fake tenners and stapling them to fake headed paper to replicate it for the Banksys she prints in the loft. If her buyers really, truly wanted to look into it, they would discover the fakery, but who, having just spent ten thousand pounds on a signed Banksy with a legitimate authentication certificate, would want to look into it any more deeply? Just get it framed and up in your living room, where your friends can see it and coo. And when it comes to reselling, hopefully the next owner won't look too closely either. It was ever thus. If anyone complained, she would give them their money back, but, thus far, having sold many thousands of Banksys, Picassos, Lowrys, Hirsts and Emins, not a single complaint has arisen, other than the time a delivery man threw a Kandinsky over someone's garden wall. Full refund.

It's a victimless crime. As is the one that she and Garth are about to commit.

She is waiting for Garth to return, and for their plan to fall into place. The lunch at Coopers Chase had changed everything. Everything.

To think they almost didn't go. That she'd had to persuade Garth that it might be worthwhile. "Lunch? With nearly dead people?" But she'd persuaded him and they were both glad she had. In the car on the way home Garth had said, "When you're right, you're right, babe."

Samantha understands that, from the outside, their relationship might look peculiar. The very proper English lady, and the silent, hirsute, Canadian mountain, twenty years her junior. But from the moment he had pointed his gun at her they both knew it was love. What a path of fire they have walked ever since. Samantha with her wit and skill, Garth with his brains and menace. Sometimes she looks at their bank accounts and laughs out loud. Charities in the surrounding area have done very well out of them, though Samantha knows that's a sticking plaster. It's not like she pays any tax, so it's the least she can do. Whenever she sends another donation to another local cause, Garth rolls his eyes and calls her a sentimentalist. Garth gives money to Battersea Dogs and Cats Home, and nothing else. Last year he gave them seven hundred thousand pounds.

Samantha is thinking of her next move.

She hadn't thought much of Mitch Maxwell and Luca Buttaci. They must be good at what they do, she supposes, drug smuggling being a very competitive business, but she doesn't trust them to find the heroin. Elizabeth. She'll be the one. She and her merry band. And when they find it, Samantha and Garth will be waiting. Nina had already let slip about the lock-up garage. That's where they'll start. Garth is out looking today. Elizabeth Best knows where it is, the professor from the university knows where it is, and it won't take Garth too long to find out either. The box may not be there, but she bets something will be, some clue to follow, something that the old lady had missed. Had Mitch and Luca picked up on the lock-up? If so they'll be on the trail too, and, once they find it, they'll be tearing it apart to find their heroin. Garth will make sure they win this particular game. Garth never lets her down.

They'll drive to the lock-up tomorrow, maybe listen to a true-crime podcast on the way. They're listening to one at the moment about an ice-hockey player who dies in an airplane toilet. It is fourteen episodes long.

Samantha starts to read an article about Grayson Perry, the artist they put on television sometimes. His work is very valuable now but, looking at it, fairly hard to forge. She could find someone to do it, she's sure, but really she prefers it when she can forge them herself. More profit, fewer moving parts. Damien Hirst is her absolute favorite, both for how beautiful she finds his work, and for how easy she finds it to forge.

The downstairs door creaks. Garth must be back, so she will call it a day. She stands and stretches, hearing him moving about downstairs, a little quieter than usual. Is he losing weight? She hopes not. His bulk is what keeps her on the ground. Keeps her from floating up to be with William again.

Climbing down the narrow stairs from the very top of the house, Samantha reaches the grand staircase. A hundred and fifty thousand, the staircase had cost, marble and cherry wood, and just a pinch of ivory, but please don't tell anyone. She calls out, "Garthy, I'm upstairs."

But if Garth answers, Samantha doesn't hear him, as a blow to the back of her head sends her tumbling down the staircase. The thousand lights of the chandelier are the last thing she sees. She has always dreamed that one day she would float up to see William again, but the final sensation she feels before she dies is that she is falling. Down, down and down.

60.

The curtains are drawn, the heating is on, and Dvořák plays on the gramophone. Just as they had agreed.

The deed is done. Deed? That surely can't be the word? Either way, there is no going back. They had both been sure.

They have been talking for hours. They have laughed, they've cried, both understanding that laughter and tears are the same thing now. He looks beautiful, in his suit. Bogdan took a photograph of them before he left. Before he hugged Stephen and told him he loved him. Stephen told Bogdan not to be such a silly old fool. Bogdan hugged her too as he left, asking her if she was certain.

Certain? Of course not. She will never be certain about anything again. Certainty is for the young and for spies, and she is no longer either.

But they had agreed. Stephen had injected the drug himself. Had insisted. Elizabeth would also have done it herself if she'd had to.

"We've got time all wrong, you see," says Stephen, his head in Elizabeth's lap. "Don't you see?"

"It wouldn't surprise me," says Elizabeth. "We get most things wrong, don't we?"

"Quite so," agrees Stephen, his voice quiet. "Nail hit well and truly on the head there, old girl. We think time travels forward, marches on in a straight line, and so we hurry alongside it to keep up. Hurry, hurry, mustn't fall behind. But it doesn't, you see. Time just swirls around us. Everything is always present. The things we've done, the people we've loved, the people we've hurt, they're all still here."

Elizabeth strokes his hair.

"That's what I've come to understand," says Stephen. "My memories are like emeralds, clear and bright and true, but every new day crumbles like sand, and I can't get hold of it at all."

It had been fiddly, the injection. Not traumatic, not peaceful, not devastating, just fiddly. Just another everyday task in a lifetime of everyday tasks.

"It has shown me the lie of the thing," says Stephen. "The lie of time. Everything I've done and everything I've been is present in the same place. But we still think the thing that has just happened, or is about to happen, we think that's the most important thing. My memories aren't memories, my present isn't present, it's all the same thing, Elizabeth. That man?"

"Which man?" Elizabeth asks.

"The Polish man?"

"Bogdan," says Elizabeth.

"Yes, just the chap," says Stephen. "He's not, forgive me if this seems obvious, or we've been over it. He's not my son, is he?"

"No."

"I thought not, he's Polish," says Stephen. "But not everything adds up, does it? In life?"

Elizabeth has to agree. "Not everything adds up."

"I wanted to ask him, but whether he was or he wasn't, I'd have felt ridiculous. Do you have friends?"

"I do," says Elizabeth. "I didn't use to, but now I do."

"Good ones?" asks Stephen. "Good in a crisis?"

"I would say so."

"Is this a crisis? Would you say?"

"Hmm," says Elizabeth. "Life is a crisis, isn't it?"

"Quite so," says Stephen. "Why should death be any different? Do they know what we're doing? Your friends?"

"They don't," says Elizabeth. "This is between us."

"Will they understand?"

"Perhaps," says Elizabeth. "They might not agree, but I think they will understand."

"Imagine if we hadn't met," says Stephen. "Imagine that."

"But we did," says Elizabeth, picking some fluff from the shoulder of his suit.

"Just imagine what I would have missed," says Stephen. "Will you make sure the allotment is OK?"

"You don't have an allotment," says Elizabeth.

"With the radishes," says Stephen.

They walk past it every day and Stephen looks at the radishes and says, "Dig 'em up. Grow roses, for goodness' sake."

"I'll look after it for you," says Elizabeth.

"I know you will," says Stephen. "There's a museum in Baghdad, you know. Have we been together?"

"No, my dear," says Elizabeth. The places they won't go together now.

"I've written down the name for you," says Stephen. "On my desk. It has pieces from six thousand years ago, can you imagine? And on these pieces you can see fingerprints, you can see scratches where someone's child has come in and distracted them. You understand that these people are still alive? Everyone who dies is alive. We call people 'dead' because we need a word for it, but 'dead' just means that time has stopped moving forward for that person? You understand? No one dies, not really."

Elizabeth kisses the top of his head. Tries to inhale him.

"I understand this," says Elizabeth. "For all the words in the world, when I go to sleep tonight, my hand won't be in yours. That's all I understand."

"You have me there," says Stephen. "I have no answer for that."

"Grief doesn't need an answer, any more than love does," says Elizabeth. "It isn't a question."

"Did you get milk?" says Stephen. "People will want tea."

"Let me worry about milk," says Elizabeth.

"I don't know why we're on this earth," says Stephen. "Truly I don't. But if I wanted to find the answer, I would begin with how much I love you. The answer will be in there somewhere, I'm sure. I'm sure. There's still half a pint in the fridge, but it won't be enough. I forget I love you sometimes, did you know that?"

"Of course," says Elizabeth.

"I am glad I remember now," says Stephen. "And I'm glad that I shall never forget again."

Stephen's eyelids are beginning to droop. Just as Viktor has said they would. Just as she and Stephen had discussed. As best they could. The last time they read the letter together.

"Are you sleepy?" Elizabeth asks.

"A little," says Stephen. "It's been a busy day, hasn't it?"

"It has, Stephen, it has."

"Busy, but happy," says Stephen. "I adore you, Elizabeth. I'm so sorry about all this. You saw the best of me though? It hasn't always been like this?"

"It's been a dream," says Elizabeth. Stephen, in clear moments, had been very certain. His race was run.

"And they'll look after you? Your friends?"

"They will do what they can," says Elizabeth. They will all think about the choice that they would make in Stephen's position. What choice would Elizabeth make? She doesn't know. But Stephen was sure.

"Joyce," says Stephen. "Joyce is your friend."

"She is."

"And tell Kuldesh I will see him soon. Weekend if he's around."

"I'll tell him, my darling."

"I might shut my eyes for a moment," says Stephen.

"You do that," says Elizabeth. "I think you've earned a rest."

Stephen's eyes close. He sounds drowsy.

"Tell me the story of when we first met," says Stephen. "That's my favorite story."

It is Elizabeth's favorite story too.

"I once saw a handsome man," says Elizabeth. "And I knew I was in love. So I dropped my glove outside a bookshop, and he picked it up and presented it to me, and my life changed forever."

"Handsome was he?"

"So handsome," says Elizabeth, tears now streaming. "Like you wouldn't believe. And, you know, my life didn't change that day, Stephen. My life began."

"He sounds a lucky bugger," says Stephen, half asleep. "Will you think of me in your dreams?"

"I will. And you think of me in yours," says Elizabeth.

"Thank you," sighs Stephen. "Thank you for letting me sleep. It's just what I need."

"I know, darling," says Elizabeth, and strokes his hair until his breathing stops altogether.

61.

Joyce

Well, I don't know what to say or do. So will you just let me write? Let me think out loud?

The ambulance arrived at about five p.m. No sirens, which usually tells its own story. No hurry.

You always wonder where the ambulance is going, that's only natural. One day it will come for you, and other people will look, and other people will talk. That's the way of things. The undertakers use a long white van, and that is no stranger to Coopers Chase either.

Stephen has died. Elizabeth went with him in the ambulance. I rushed down as soon as I had worked out what was going on. I got there in time to see his body being taken away. Elizabeth was climbing into the back of the ambulance. She caught my eye, and she nodded. She looked like a ghost, or an entirely new person. I held out my hand and she took it.

I told her I would tidy the place up a bit while she was gone, and she thanked me, and said she would like that. I asked if it was peaceful, and she said that for Stephen it was.

I saw Ron hurrying toward us, knee and hip both hobbling him. He looked so old. Elizabeth pulled the door of the ambulance closed before he could reach us.

Ron held me as the ambulance drove away. I should have known, shouldn't I? Should have known what Elizabeth and Stephen were up to. What would I have said if I'd known? What would you have said?

There is nothing to be said, and yet I want to say something.

It is not a choice I would have made, I know that. If I had been Elizabeth, and Gerry had been Stephen, I would have clung on to him for dear life. Found him a nice place in a nice home, visited every day, as he went from knowing me, to recognizing me, to not recognizing me, to never having heard of me. I would have seen it out, right to the end. My love wouldn't have allowed another outcome. I know plenty of people with partners in homes, dying slowly, and you wouldn't wish it on your worst enemy. But to end it all? To end it before the finish? That's not a decision I could take. While love is alive, I could never choose to kill it.

But I suppose I am talking about *my* love, aren't I? What if my love were alive and Gerry's wasn't? What if I am simply thinking of the joy that looking at him and holding him would bring me? A joy that would last far longer than his? And all the while knowing that every night and every morning he would sleep and wake alone, frightened and confused?

I really don't know at all. Dementia doesn't rob everyone of joy and love, even though it does its damnedest. There are smiles and laughs, but, yes, there are cries of pain. We had a debate at Coopers Chase, two years ago or so, about euthanasia. It was impassioned, and reasoned, and thoughtful, and kind, and moving, on both sides. I don't remember if Elizabeth spoke. I said a few words, just about my experience with end-of-life care in the hospitals. And about the times we had upped a medication to hasten things along right at the very end, just to stop the cruelty of the pain.

But Stephen wasn't at the very end, was he? Perhaps people define "the end" differently?

The two of them must have made a very deliberate decision. Imagine the conversations. Normally people visit Switzerland; they go to

Dignitas—we've had two or three here. But that decision often has to be taken much earlier than one would like. You have to be capable, in mind and body, of giving your consent. Of being able to travel. So you are not able to wait until the last minute, which is another cruelty. I have looked into all this, of course I have. Anyone my age who says they haven't at least taken a peek is lying.

Elizabeth and Stephen wouldn't have needed Dignitas of course. Elizabeth has access to anything she needs. As the ambulance arrived, a GP was leaving, and he wasn't a GP I've ever seen around here before.

I often joke about how emotionless Elizabeth is, and sometimes she can be, it's true. But not this. She will speak about it when she's ready, I'm sure, but this must have been Stephen, mustn't it? He was always a very strong man, a very certain man. I don't think he could bear what was happening to him. The life he was losing. And he was still just about in a place where he could do something about it.

I should have seen it. Elizabeth taking a few days out. Anthony coming to visit. I should have known Elizabeth and Stephen weren't about to separate, Stephen wasn't about to let Elizabeth care for him as wave after wave of dementia crashed over his brain. Wasn't about to let her see him go through all of that. Some people live by different rules. I have always been too frightened to.

I understand, I do. If Gerry had begged me, I would have said yes too. I don't like to admit that to myself, but I would. Love can mean so many different things, can't it? And just because it's precious doesn't mean it can't be tough.

When I saw Elizabeth in the ambulance, and held her hand, that was love. And when I saw Ron trying to run to her, that was love. And Ibrahim has taken Alan out for me, just for half an hour, and that's love too.

I am cooking a shepherd's pie, and I will leave it in Elizabeth's fridge when I go over. I know Elizabeth well enough to know the place will be spotless, but it won't do any harm to run the Hoover round, and maybe light a candle.

I will miss Stephen, but then I missed him already. Perhaps that's how Elizabeth felt too. And, most importantly, that's how Stephen must have felt. He must have missed himself every day.

Would I wish that on either of them? No.

Would I want someone to do the same for me? No.

I will cling, kicking and screaming, to every second life has in store for me. I want the full picture, for good or for ill.

I know that Ron and Ibrahim will be together this evening, and I know I would be very welcome, but I need time to think. About Gerry and Stephen, and Elizabeth and love.

I will think back to Stephen saying goodbye to us the other day. The proud husband, looking so handsome, his smile working its usual magic. That's how Stephen wanted to be remembered, and surely he is allowed that?

And it is how I'll remember him. Stephen's final message to the world, "Hello, chief," "Hello, old boy." In the winter sunshine, birds up above, and love all around.

62.

High up on the hill there is construction noise, down in the village, people go about their business. Dogs chase dogs, delivery vans unload. Letters are posted.

The cold sun simply can't compete though. Coopers Chase is wearing death like chain mail.

It is Thursday at eleven a.m., but nobody is in the Jigsaw Room.

The Art History class have stacked their chairs away, as always, and that is where the chairs will remain until Conversatioal French comes in at noon. Motes of dust float in the air and settle. The Thursday Murder Club is nowhere to be seen today. Their absence echoes.

Ron is texting Pauline, hoping beyond hope that she finally replies. Joyce has done some shopping for Elizabeth and dropped it outside her door. She rang, but no reply. Ibrahim sits in his flat, staring at a picture of a boat on his wall.

Elizabeth? Well, she is no longer present in a time and a space for now. She isn't anywhere or anything. Bogdan has his eye on her.

Joyce switches off her television—it has nothing for her. Alan lies at her feet and watches her cry. Ibrahim thinks that perhaps he should take a walk, but, instead, he keeps looking at the picture on the wall. Ron receives a text, but it is from his electricity provider.

There is a murder still to be solved, but it won't be solved today. The timelines and the photographs and the theories and the plans will have to wait. Perhaps it will never be solved? Perhaps death has defeated them all with this latest trick? Who now has the heart for the battle?

They still have each other, but not today. There will be laughing and teasing and arguing and loving again, but not today. Not this Thursday.

As the waves of the world crash around them, this Thursday is for Stephen.

63.

Joyce

The cremation was in Tunbridge Wells. We all made our way there in a little procession. There was the hearse, then Elizabeth, and Bogdan and I followed in a funeral car. Then Ron's mended Daihatsu, with Ron, Pauline and Ibrahim. It was a nice surprise to see Pauline. Finally, Chris, Donna and Patrice in Chris's new car. I'm not sure of the make, but it is silver, so it fit in.

I thought there might be a bit of a crowd at the crematorium, but, as we pulled up, there were only four people, three men and one woman, all looking as old as us. They each hugged Elizabeth and introduced themselves to me. There was a Marianne and a very handsome Wilfried, but I didn't catch the other names properly. Wilfried must have been Polish, because he spoke to Bogdan for a while. He knew Stephen from the Middle East somewhere—I didn't get all the details. Marianne knew Stephen from university. You could just tell they had been lovers.

So this was all that was left of Stephen's gang. Or all that Elizabeth felt she needed to invite. I don't suppose she cast the net any further than she absolutely had to.

The crematorium was very pleasant, as far as these things go. The sky was blue, the sun shone. Bogdan, Donna and Chris got into position to carry the coffin, with one of the undertakers. At the last moment, Ron tapped the undertaker on the shoulder and took his place.

We filed in first, my arm through Elizabeth's. It was neither the time nor the place, but I told her she suited black, which she does. It washes me out, I'm afraid. I wore a nice brooch, a sun, which I thought Stephen would like, and that gave me a bit of sparkle. I saw Wilfried eye it up.

These places do their best to feel gentle and calm, to feel like a place where the world can't get in, a cocoon. But then you'll see a FIRE EXIT sign above a door, and the real world crowds back in. Someone had left an old pen without a lid on one of the pews.

When the coffin was in place, Bogdan came and sat on the other side of Elizabeth. He was crying; she wasn't. Donna sat in the row behind and, every now and again, she would reach out and squeeze his shoulder. Just letting him know she was there. I did the same for Elizabeth, but no one was there to do it for me.

A very nice young woman conducted the ceremony. She had stories about Stephen—Ibrahim had gathered them together—and she read a couple of passages from the Bible, which I know is the done thing. I've been to many funerals now, and an awful lot of people have walked through the valley of the shadow of death. I might have something a bit more upbeat at my funeral. I find being solemn very difficult, but I suppose it is necessary. The only time I stopped crying during Gerry's service was when the vicar was telling us how kind and forgiving God was.

I tried to imagine how Elizabeth was feeling. Knowing the part she played in Stephen's death. But I hope she was thinking more about the part she played in his life. There was a hymn I didn't know, and then the coffin slowly disappeared as some classical music played. I didn't recognize it—nothing from an advert or anything, Stephen was very into his music. This was when Elizabeth started weeping. Bogdan's arm was around her shoulders, and my arm was around her waist, but I could tell she felt neither of them.

I sneaked a peek, and Ron and Pauline were both in floods. Ibrahim was head down, eyes closed. Further back, I noticed that Marianne had gone.

We had agreed to have drinks and nibbles back at mine—no need to hire a hall and put Elizabeth on display. Stephen's friends didn't come back with us; they said their goodbyes at the crematorium. Marianne hadn't, in fact, left: she was outside, crying on one of the benches. Wilfried went over to comfort her. Everyone has a story, don't they? If you'd followed Marianne or Wilfried home, what might you have found?

I had a picture of Stephen on my dining-room table. He was smoking a cigar, clearly telling a joke. I lit some candles, and Bogdan had set up a chessboard. The pieces were in the position of the last game Stephen ever won. He tried to explain it to me, but I told him I was better off sticking to candles.

We had some English sparkling wine that Chris had brought with him. Patrice bought it, even after Dominic Holt had been murdered, "because it was thirty percent off if you'd been on the tour." She is a woman after my own heart.

The nibbles were mainly Aldi, but with a sprinkling of Waitrose for effect.

I put Classic FM on the radio, which worked a treat, except for the adverts.

It was important that we showed Elizabeth that we were all there for her. That she had a gang. Not just the Thursday Murder Club anymore, but also the band of waifs and strays we seem to have picked up along the way. Bogdan, of course, and Donna. Chris and Patrice. Pauline now looking like a permanent fixture. Even Computer Bob came over to pay his respects. No Mervyn, even though I told him he'd be welcome. "Didn't know the man," was his response.

Chris had an announcement to make, but you could tell he wasn't sure about it. Briefly I thought he was about to propose, which I do think might have been a bit much in the circumstances, but instead he told us, in the strictest confidence, that Samantha Barnes had been murdered. He said it wasn't a discussion for today, but he felt we would like to know sooner rather than later.

Elizabeth chose that moment to make her exit. She will not be investigating anything for a while. Bogdan walked her home, and didn't come back for an hour or so.

We talked about Stephen, we talked a little about Samantha Barnes, but without much conviction, because without Elizabeth is there any point continuing? Donna spoke to the boys about Mervyn and Tatiana. They are having fun. Life continues, whatever you do. It's a bulldozer like that.

Everybody left at about nine-ish, and I did the washing-up. And now there are long nights ahead for us all.

I think I will call Joanna. I know it's quite late, but I don't think we really keep the same hours. I once rang her at nine a.m. on a Saturday and she gave me a lecture. I had been up for three hours already. I hope she will pick up, I just want to hear about her day, just normal things. Perhaps talk about her dad for a while.

Alan knows I am sad. He is lying by my chair, his paws on my feet, making sure I come to no further harm.

64.

Ron has his arm around Pauline.

He missed her, so he texted her. She missed him, but she didn't text back. He missed her, so he texted her again, this time a joke about a horse playing cricket. She missed him, she laughed at the message, but she didn't text back. He missed her, so he rang her even though he knew he shouldn't. She missed him, but she didn't pick up.

He missed her, so he texted her about the funeral. Told her how he felt, told her he loved her and missed her. And so she took a sick day from work, dressed in black, drove to Coopers Chase, knocked on his door, kissed him, told him he couldn't wear a West Ham tie to Stephen's funeral, then relented when he said he had no other ties. He told her how much he fancied her in black, she told him that was inappropriate, then she took his hand and hasn't let go since.

"Do you think anyone's asleep?" Ron asks.

"No," says Pauline. "Elizabeth will be crying, Joyce will be baking, Ibrahim will be out walking, pretending to think about something else."

"You think they did the right thing? Stephen and Elizabeth?"

"There is no right thing, Ronnie," says Pauline. "No right thing, no wrong thing. If it's what they wanted. They've harmed no one but themselves, and you're allowed to harm yourself."

"Like texting your ex when you shouldn't?" says Ron.

"Assisting in the suicide of your partner and texting your ex are maybe not the same thing," says Pauline. "And, besides, I'm not your ex."

"Are you not?" asks Ron.

"Nah," says Pauline. "We're both ridiculous people, Ronnie. But perhaps that's OK?"

"I'm not ridiculous," says Ron. "You'll go a long way before you find someone le—"

Pauline puts a finger to his mouth. "Shh! You're ridiculous. That's why they all love you, Ronnie. Your mates. You're a lovely, big, strong, ridiculous man."

"Well, you're not ridiculous," says Ron.

"I'm in bed with you, aren't I? And I didn't walk past a queue of sensible women to get here," says Pauline.

Ron smiles, then feels guilty about smiling. "What are we going to do with Elizabeth?"

"Just give her time," says Pauline. "Just be there, and give her time. She'll need a couple of weeks of—"

Ron's phone starts to ring. He looks at Pauline, who nods to him to answer it. The display says LIZZIE.

65.

brahim can't sleep. He knew this would be the case. He knew he'd be up all night, and he knew what he would be thinking about.

Marius.

He has gone for a walk around the village. There is a soft light on in Ron's window. Pauline will be there, and Ibrahim is very thankful for that. That's what Ron needs this evening. Ron pretends he needs nothing and no one. Who does that remind Ibrahim of?

There is a light on at Joyce's too. She has Alan with her. He will be excited to be up in the middle of the night. She will be watching repeats of something on the television and thinking about Gerry. Maybe she will have spoken to Joanna this evening. He hopes Joanna will have understood why her mother might have wanted to speak to her.

Days of death are days when we weigh our relationship with love in our bare hands. Days when we remember what has gone, and fear what is to come. The joy love brings, and the price we pay. When we give thanks but also pray for mercy. That is why Joyce is thinking of Gerry, why Ron and Pauline are in each other's arms, and why a lonely, old Egyptian man is walking through Coopers Chase thinking about Marius. Thinking about another lifetime.

One day perhaps he will speak about him, but, also, perhaps, he may not. It is a box that, once opened, can never be closed, and Ibrahim wonders if his heart is strong enough to take it. Who would he speak to anyway? Elizabeth? Well, she would understand now. Ron? And get an awkward hug?

Joyce? What if he saw pity in her eyes? Ibrahim is not sure he could bear that.

There is another light on, of course. Elizabeth's. That light will be on for many nights now. She has all the darkness she needs.

Ibrahim thinks about the boxes. The box with the heroin inside, which has caused so much trouble. The "box" with Marius inside, which contains so much pain. He supposes they will abandon the search for the heroin now. Who has it? Who knows? Who murdered Kuldesh? Whoever it is, they will get away with it.

But the box containing Marius. Dare he open it? Dare he tell *that* story?

A day of death is a day of love. Ibrahim knows plenty about both. Perhaps it's time to—

His phone rings.

66.

It is three a.m. and Bogdan is crying in Donna's arms.

Crying for what he did, and crying for who he has lost.

He has been brave and strong for Elizabeth. No crying in front of her, except at the funeral. Just listening, and helping.

He and Stephen had had their final game of chess a week ago. Not a game as such. Bogdan had offered to teach Stephen to play, and Stephen had accepted. "Always fancied giving this a go."

Bogdan had hoped the game might come back to Stephen as he showed him the moves, but Stephen just shook his head. "Not getting it, compadre." But they were sat either side of the board, and they chatted, and Bogdan could pretend. Stephen always knew that he was safe with Bogdan, even when he was unsure of exactly who he was. And Bogdan always felt safe with Stephen.

Stephen told him the plan. Elizabeth had already told him, but Bogdan was pleased he heard it from Stephen too. Heard the certainty. Stephen had no interest in fading out, in spinning away into space. He wanted to be in control, and Bogdan would not have denied him that right.

At the funeral Bogdan had sat with Elizabeth, and he was very glad of that. Donna had sat behind him, connected to him, and he was very glad of that too.

Donna is kissing his tears.

"Tell me about something else," says Bogdan, letting his voice stop his tears. "Sing me a lullaby."

Donna buries her head in his neck, and whispers, "Samantha Barnes was struck with a blunt object. But died from the fall down the stairs."

"Thank you," says Bogdan, lids closing.

"Garth is nowhere to be seen," she continues. "So either he did it himself, or maybe he's on the run from the person that did."

"But why kill her?" says Bogdan. "Unless she had the heroin? You think she did?"

"Who knows?" says Donna. "Mitch Maxwell and Luca Buttaci have both been to the lock-up and come away empty-handed, so perhaps they paid her a visit? And Garth hasn't been to the lock-up, so maybe he has it?"

"Mmm," says Bogdan. "I don't think Elizabeth will have the heart to carry on looking."

"She needs a lot of time," says Donna. "Do you think she had anything to do with Stephen's death? Do you think she . . . you know?"

"No," says Bogdan. "Is illegal."

"But come on," says Donna. "It's Elizabeth, and I'm not blaming her, you'd understand if she had. Illegal would mean nothing to her."

"It would be illegal for her to help Stephen," says Bogdan. "And it would be illegal for anybody else to know she had helped. Would be illegal for me to know, would be illegal for you to know."

"I'm with you," says Donna. "Hypothetically, though, would you have helped her?"

"I would have helped Elizabeth, and I would have helped Stephen," says Bogdan.

"I know you would," says Donna.

"So you think maybe Garth has the heroin? He's found it somehow, you think?"

"I think it's worth looking at," says Donna. "I think you're right, Elizabeth is done for now. So wouldn't it be nice to wrap this up by ourselves? Our little gift to her?"

"Is an unusual gift," says Bogdan.

"She's an unusual woman," says Donna.

"You really think you can f—"

Bogdan's phone starts vibrating on the bedside table. It is three fifteen in the morning. He looks at Donna, who nods at him to take the call. His phone screen tells him it is Elizabeth.

"Elizabeth," says Bogdan. "You OK? You need me?"

"I need you," says Elizabeth. "Is Donna with you?"

"She is," says Bogdan.

"Bring her too," says Elizabeth. "I know where the heroin is."

67.

Will she ever sleep again? Elizabeth lies on the bed and wonders how a broken heart can beat so fast.

It is five to three in the morning. Anyone who has ever worked nights or been kept awake night after night will tell you that three a.m. to four a.m. is always the longest hour. The hour when brutal loneliness takes total control. Where every tick of the clock is agony.

It had needed to be done, she has to keep telling herself that. Stephen had given his orders, and Elizabeth knows how to follow orders. It had been right, it had been painless, Stephen had been in charge and in control, and that gave a final dignity to a man who had prized it and deserved it.

After Viktor had spoken to Stephen, he had reported back. We are agreed. Stephen knows what he wants.

Viktor had given her a little box of tricks. Where he had got them from she hadn't cared to ask. All she had wanted to know is that it would be quick, and painless. And, yes, undetectable. That was the one final practicality. Stephen wouldn't want her in prison and, truth be told, most of the law courts in the land wouldn't want her in prison either, but they would have no choice. To stand by and do nothing makes you an accomplice. Thou shalt not kill.

The GP was an old friend from the Service. She had given him a time and a place, and there he was. His credentials were impeccable, should anyone care to look. They might, you never know. Time of death, cause of death, a hug and words of reassurance for the widow, and he was on his way. No need for a visit to Switzerland, no need to take Stephen away from his home.

So Stephen's pain is over. He is no longer trapped in the static of his mind. Tormented by stabs of clarity, like a drowning man surfacing above the waves before being engulfed again. There will be no further decline. From here on the decline will be all hers. The pain all hers. She is glad of it, deserves to endure it. It feels like penance.

Penance for helping to kill Stephen? Is that right? No. Elizabeth doesn't feel guilt at the act. She knows in her heart that it was an act of love. Joyce will know it was an act of love. Why does she worry what Joyce will think?

It is penance for everything else she has done in her life. Everything that she did in her long career, without question. Everything she signed off, everything she nodded through. She is paying a tax on her sins. Stephen was sent to her, and then taken away, as a punishment. She will speak to Viktor about it; he will feel the same. However noble the causes of her career were, they weren't noble enough to excuse the disregard for life. Day after day, mission after mission, ridding the world of evil? Waiting for the last devil to die? What a joke. New devils will always spring up, like daffodils in springtime.

So what was it all for? All that blood?

Stephen was too good for her tainted soul, and the world knew it, so the world took him away.

But Stephen had known her, hadn't he? Had seen her for what she was and who she was? And Stephen had still chosen her? Stephen had made her, that was the truth. Had glued her together.

And here she lies. Unmade. Unglued.

How will life go on now? How is that possible? She hears a car on a distant road. Why on earth is anybody driving? Where is there to go now? Why is the clock in the hall still ticking? Doesn't it know it stopped days ago?

On the way to the funeral, Joyce had sat with her in the car. They didn't speak because there was too much to say. Elizabeth looked out of the window of the car at one point, and saw a mother pick up a soft toy her child had dropped out of its pram. Elizabeth almost burst into laughter, that life was daring to continue. Didn't they *know*? Hadn't they *heard*? Everything has changed, everything. And yet nothing has changed. Nothing. The day carries on as it would. An old man at a traffic light takes off his hat as the hearse passes, but, other than that, the high street is the same. How can these two realities possibly coexist?

Perhaps Stephen was right about time? Outside the car window, it moved forward, marching, marching, never missing a step. But inside the car, time was already moving backward, already folding in.

The life she had with Stephen will always mean more to her than the life she will now have going forward. She will spend more time there, in that past, she knows that. And, as the world races forward, she will fall further and further back. There comes a point when you look at your photograph albums more often than you watch the news. When you opt out of time, and let it carry on doing its thing while you get on with yours. You simply stop dancing to the beat of the drum.

She sees it in Joyce. For all her bustle, for all her spark, there is a part of her, the most important part, locked away. There's a part of Joyce that will always be in a tidy living room, Gerry with his feet up, and a young Joanna, face beaming as she opens presents.

Living in the past. Elizabeth had never understood it, but, with intense clarity, she understands it now. Elizabeth's past was always too dark, too unhappy. Family, school, the dangerous, compromising work, the divorces. But, as of three days ago, Stephen is her past, and that is where she will choose to live.

There weren't many friends at the funeral, though she'd been able to gather a few together. She wonders if Kuldesh would have come if things had been different? Stephen spoke so much about him in the final weeks.

Elizabeth turns the bedside light on again. She won't sleep. Perhaps she will go for a walk? While there is no one to see her, no one to give her their condolences. She is just thinking that she might come across Snowy doing his rounds, when she remembers. Poor Snowy. Elizabeth starts to weep. For Snowy, and Kuldesh. She will keep her tears for Stephen back for now. They will be of a different order entirely.

The poor fox. Buried up by the allotment, by the radishes that Stephen had become obsessed with in his final days. He was never a gardener, his brain just playing another trick on him.

She can just imagine him, wa—

Elizabeth has never known where moments of inspiration truly come from. The sudden thought that explains things, that shines a light where there once was darkness. The closest she can come to describing it is that inspiration strikes when two completely different thoughts come together, and they suddenly make sense of each other.

Stephen speaking so much about Kuldesh in his final days. "Saw him recently." Stephen talking about the allotment, and the radishes. "Promise you'll take care of the allotment."

Oh, you clever man, thinks Elizabeth. Even in the fog you were shining a light for me.

Ever since Elizabeth left the Service, she has had certain protections. Panic buttons, hotlines, in case her past were ever to catch up with her. And, she realizes now, she herself almost certainly has an untraceable number. A Code 777.

She is a fool. The second call Kuldesh had made that afternoon was to her own home phone. To her beautiful Stephen.

Stephen is Elizabeth's past now, and perhaps one day she might find a way to make that bearable. But perhaps, for a few days longer, Stephen can be her future too.

Elizabeth wonders if it is too late to ring Bogdan. And then she remembers that time has stopped altogether, and that Bogdan won't be able to sleep any more than she can, and so she decides that she will.

First though she slips on some shoes and a coat, and walks up the hill, just to make absolutely certain. She picks the lock on the allotment shed and, all credit to Ron, there awaits a brand-new spade.

PART THREE

There's No Place Like Home

68.

Joyce received the call around twenty minutes ago, and is already up on the hillside, engulfed by her winter coat. Elizabeth and Bogdan were there to meet her, and down below she sees Ibrahim, Ron and Pauline making their way up.

"I hope I didn't wake you," says Elizabeth.

"You know you didn't," says Joyce. "I was watching *Antiques Road Trip* and crying. Bogdan, you really should be wearing a jacket."

"Bogdan considers a jacket a sign of weakness," says Elizabeth.

"Yes," agrees Bogdan.

"I would have brought a flask if I'd known," says Joyce as Ibrahim, Ron and Pauline reach them. "I could pop back?"

"Nice morning for it," says Ron, and gives Elizabeth a hug. Elizabeth accepts it reluctantly.

"Let's not make a habit of that," says Elizabeth, detaching herself. "Thank you all for coming."

"I thought we'd be giving up on the heroin," says Joyce. "After what you said."

"As did I," says Elizabeth. "But I was awake, as you'd imagine. Thinking about Stephen."

"Of course you were," says Joyce. "I was too. Well, Stephen and Gerry."

"I was thinking about all sorts of things, punishing myself with the happiness of it all. And then I starting to think about Kuldesh," says Elizabeth.

"How nice it would have been to have him there. How much Stephen spoke about him lately."

Joyce sees Ron, after taking a look at Bogdan, start to slip his jacket off. He will not be out-machoed.

Elizabeth continues. "But then my mind was off in all sorts of directions. Why was Stephen speaking about him quite so much? He said he'd seen Kuldesh recently, and we all assumed he was talking about his visit to the shop, with Bogdan and Donna."

"He wasn't?" Bogdan asks.

"It just struck me," says Elizabeth. "Perhaps I had missed something. What if Stephen had seen Kuldesh more recently than that?"

"Meaning?" asks Ron, pretending not to shiver.

"What if he saw Kuldesh after Christmas?"

"After Kuldesh disappeared?" says Joyce.

"Well, we know Kuldesh was in trouble," says Elizabeth. "He rang Nina and told her so. And if Nina couldn't help, who might Kuldesh ring next?"

"Stephen," says Ibrahim.

"Kuldesh was in a dilemma," says Elizabeth. "Had stumbled across some Class A drugs and decided, in his wisdom, to steal them."

"And needed someone he could trust?" says Donna.

"Precisely," says Elizabeth. "An old partner in crime. Someone he had seen recently. Someone he could trust completely. Someone who lived somewhere remote."

"But Stephen would have turned him down flat," says Joyce.

"Maybe he would," says Elizabeth. "But I don't think so. I think Kuldesh came over on the twenty-seventh, while we were with Donna and Mervyn. Two old men, a fortune in drugs and trouble on their tail. Where safer to hide the box than Coopers Chase?"

"When we found Snowy," says Bogdan, "Stephen said this ground was rock-hard to dig. I didn't even think of it."

"And he told me to take care of an allotment he has never had," says

Elizabeth. "Over and over. Kuldesh and the allotment. Kuldesh and the allotment."

"So it's buried here?" says Donna. "That's the theory?"

"We're about to find out," says Elizabeth. "Bogdan, could you do the honors?"

Bogdan lifts the new spade and starts to dig, as near to the radishes as he can.

"You need a hand, Bogdan?" asks Ron.

"I'm OK, Ron," says Bogdan. "Thank you."

As Bogdan continues digging, and metal scrapes against the ungiving earth, Ibrahim raises his hand like a schoolboy.

"Forgive me," says Ibrahim. "I may be being a fool, but why would Stephen help Kuldesh?"

"Mates, ain't they?" says Ron. "I'd help you."

"If I were burying heroin, you would help me?" asks Ibrahim. "You wouldn't say, Don't bury heroin, Ibrahim? Take it to the police, Ibrahim? Give it back to the gangsters before they kill you, Ibrahim?"

"Well, I wouldn't say take it to the police," says Ron.

"Good boy," says Pauline.

"But I take your point," says Ron. "Why would he do it, Lizzie? Messing about with drugs. That ain't Stephen."

"Possibly friendship, Ron," says Elizabeth, "possibly foolhardiness. But most likely he didn't fully understand what he was being asked to do."

This quietens the group a little, and the only sound out on the dark hillside is Bogdan shoveling soil, and Ron putting his coat back on.

Bogdan strikes something solid.

"Here we go," he says, shifting the loose earth around whatever the object is. He eventually kneels and tugs a small, squat, ugly box from the hole. He places it on the ground.

"Stephen, you old bugger," says Ron.

The lid of the box has a slight lip. They all stare at it for a moment.

Joyce decides it is too cold to wait. She kneels next to the box and looks at the others. "Shall I be mother?"

Receiving nods, Joyce gently puts her fingers under the lip of the box, and it starts to give. She is sure it is going to be empty. She doesn't know why, but she is sure. She lifts.

The box is not empty. The box is packed with white powder.

"Are we sure it's heroin?" says Ron. "Could be washing powder?"

Pauline bends over the box, takes out her keys and cuts into the plastic packaging. She wets the tip of her finger, dips it into the powder and then tastes it.

"It's heroin," she says.

"Good to have you on board, Pauline," says Elizabeth.

"A hundred grand's worth of heroin," says Ron.

"That has already killed many people," says Ibrahim, looking around, as if for snipers in the trees.

Joyce shuts the lid of the box and tucks it under her arm. "May I say something? For the record?"

The others indicate that she has the floor. Joyce isn't certain exactly how to put what it is that she wants to say. But here goes.

"This is the sort of moment when Elizabeth would normally take charge. But I'm not allowing it. Elizabeth has more important things on her hands. So I am going to take charge again, forgive me, Elizabeth, and this is my position . . . Bogdan, would you *please* put on a jacket . . . We now have what everybody is looking for. And what everybody is killing for. This little box. Kuldesh, Dominic Holt, Samantha Barnes, goodness knows who else. And nobody knows we have it, which puts us in a strong position."

"This is very good," says Ibrahim. "Very Elizabeth."

"Thank you," says Joyce. "So what I suggest is this. Elizabeth, you do as much or as little as you choose, we are here for you. As for the rest of us, those of us who are able to get some sleep, get some sleep. And soon, we let it be known that we have found the heroin. Not where we found it, not where it is, but that we have it in our possession. And then we wait."

"Wait for them to kill us too?" says Ron. "Very Elizabeth indeed."

"Precisely that," says Joyce. "We wait and see who comes to kill us. We will use the heroin as a trap and see if it leads us to whomever murdered Kuldesh. You never know, do you? You have to make things happen."

She gives the gang her very best stern look. She is not to be disagreed with.

"That's our gift to Stephen. OK, Elizabeth?"

Elizabeth nods to her friend. "It's *whoever* murdered Kuldesh, but, other than that, yes."

69.

He has never had a dinner party before. Is this a dinner party? Vegetable curry on a Sunday lunchtime?

"Turn the heat down," Patrice says to Chris, before pouring a glass of wine for Joyce.

Chris supposes it is a dinner party. Of sorts. Donna and Bogdan. Joyce and Ibrahim. Chris and Patrice. The heroin has been found, well of course it has, why did Chris ever doubt it, and now all they need to do is use it to catch a murderer. Simple.

"I have created a WhatsApp group entitled 'Who Killed Kuldesh?,'" says Ibrahim. "You are, naturally, all included in the group. I am sending you through a spreadsheet, now I am paper-free."

"You know they mine cobalt to make these phones?" says Patrice.

"Please," says Ibrahim. "One fight at a time."

Various phones ping in different tones.

"Ron and Elizabeth are both in the group too," says Ibrahim. "But I think we shouldn't expect too much from Elizabeth right now. Do you think, Bogdan?"

"I think," says Bogdan. "Yes."

"And Ron is stubbornly refusing to understand how WhatsApp works," Ibrahim adds.

Donna has opened the attachment on her phone and reads. "'Who is dead?' That's a bold start."

"Thank you," says Ibrahim. "Who is dead? Kuldesh is dead. Dominic

Holt is dead. Samantha Barnes is dead. According to Donna, the man named Lenny is dead."

"Worked for Mitch," says Donna. "Killed in Amsterdam. I picked that up by the coffee machine yesterday. One of the NCA team was trying to show off to me."

"You give me his name," says Bogdan.

"It was a she," says Donna. "Stop being so binary."

"Let me add him in," says Ibrahim. "That curry smells delicious, Chris."

"Are you sure there's nothing I can help with?" says Joyce.

"Everything chopped, everything peeled, everything simmering," says Chris, from the hob. "You just drink your wine, and talk about drug-related murders, and Donna being chatted up."

"OK, I have added Lenny to 'Who is dead?,'" says Ibrahim.

"So who is still alive?" reads Bogdan from his screen.

"Mitch Maxwell is still alive," says Ibrahim. "Luca Buttaci, and, probably, Garth, though he hasn't been seen since his wife was murdered. I would suggest that one of the names on our 'Who is alive?' list will turn out to be the killer of at least some of the names on our 'Who is dead?' list. We must also add Nina Mishra and Jonjo Mellor to 'Who is alive?,' as they were involved right at the beginning. Joyce, why aren't you looking at your phone?"

"I couldn't make the spreadsheet work," says Joyce. "But I promise I'm following it all. Nina Mishra would make a very glamorous murderer. Jonjo Mellor might be a bit wet though? Can we still say 'wet'?"

"Can we add the middle-aged woman who keeps visiting Connie Johnson in prison?" suggests Donna.

"Grub's up," says Chris, carrying a steaming pot of curry to the table. The table that, for so many years, sat unloved, covered in takeaway menus, old newspapers and, occasionally, crime-scene photographs. And now look at it. People sitting around with knives and forks, ladling rice onto their plates. What a long way he has come. He does note, however, that there is a large photo of the dead body of Samantha Barnes right next to the okra, so some things don't change.

"This is very good, for vegetables," says Donna.

"It really is," says Joyce. "Ron would hate it."

"Where is he today?" Patrice asks.

"He's gone to aromatherapy with Pauline," says Ibrahim.

"So it's back on?" says Patrice. "It's like *Love Island* with those two."

"In Poland, *Love Island* is called *Love Mountain*," says Bogdan. "And one time someone froze to death."

"Help yourself to more," says Chris. He's always wanted to say something like that. The conversation is flowing, and the food really isn't at all bad. Donna was right: you honestly wouldn't know it was aubergines.

"How are you getting on with the horse thefts?" asks Joyce.

"Our toughest case yet," says Donna. "We've been all over. No horses."

"Where's the heroin now? Out of interest?" says Chris.

"Somewhere safe," says Joyce.

"That usually means your kettle, Joyce," says Donna.

"There was too much for the kettle," says Joyce. "So it's in my microwave."

"Not still in that box?" says Bogdan. "Was filthy."

"No, I gave the box a good scrub, and it's perfect for all the bits and bobs I keep under my sink."

"Waste not, want not," says Ibrahim. "Chris, did you know that the aubergine is actually a fruit, and the Americans call it eggplant, because early varieties were white in color and oval in shape?"

"I didn't know that, no," says Chris.

"I'll send you an article," says Ibrahim. "Donna, I need to update you on our Tatiana scheme too. I believe we have had a breakthrough."

Again, various phones ping. A group message. Chris takes a look. It is from Ron, and it is, for no discernible reason, a picture of a panda wearing a hat. They see Ibrahim composing a reply, and it pings through. *Thank you, Ron.*

"How are you going to let them all know you have the heroin? How do you set the trap?" asks Patrice.

Everyone really seems to be getting along, thinks Chris, conversation really flowing now. Could this be described as a success? He thinks it could.

"It's very simple," says Ibrahim. "Tomorrow I'm visiting Connie Johnson again. I will tell her that we have found the drugs, and I will tell her that she mustn't tell a soul."

"And then we wait for her to tell everyone," says Joyce. "I wouldn't say no to another drop of that wine, Patrice. We wait, and we see if anyone tries to kill us."

70.

This time Ibrahim has been a little more professional. He's finished his hour with Connie, and given her full value for money. They have been talking about pain. The shapes we twist into when we try to avoid it.

As he leaves, Ibrahim drops the bombshell.

"You just dug it up?" Connie asks. "A hundred grand's worth?"

"I am told it's worth a hundred thousand, yes," says Ibrahim. "I'm not as up on the market rate as I should be."

"What did it weigh?" asks Connie.

"One point two kilos," says Ibrahim. "According to Joyce's kitchen scales."

"One point two kilos, straight from Afghanistan," says Connie, doing a mental calculation. "A hundred and ten thousand pounds or so. Is it uncut?"

"I don't know," says Ibrahim. "I could ask Pauline."

"How white is it?" Connie asks.

"Very white," says Ibrahim.

"Probably pure, then," says Connie. "Might be worth about four hundred grand by the time they're done with it."

"I thought you only knew about cocaine," says Ibrahim.

"A fisherman needs to know the price of chips," says Connie. "What are you going to do with it?"

"We don't know," says Ibrahim. "What would you do?"

"I'd sell it, Ibrahim," says Connie. "I'm a drug dealer."

"Well, yes," agrees Ibrahim. "But if you were us, what would you do?"

"Ibrahim, the simplest thing to do is take it to the cops," says Connie. "But when have you lot ever done the simple thing?"

Ibrahim nods. "Yes, I think if we felt it would lead us to finding out who murdered Kuldesh, we would take it to the authorities. But I don't believe Joyce and Elizabeth have a great deal of trust in SIO Regan, and they believe that we might be better placed to find that out."

"You any nearer to working it out?" Connie asks.

"Well, Mitch Maxwell and Luca Buttaci are still looking for the heroin," says Ibrahim. "They seem very keen."

"That's heroin for you," says Connie.

"And then Samantha Barnes has also been murdered. But her husband, Garth, is at large. Or possibly dead. Though he doesn't seem the type to die, so probably at large."

"Do they know you have the heroin now?"

"We haven't told a soul," says Ibrahim. "We are plotting our next move."

"Well, they won't hear it from me," says Connie.

"I'm banking on that, Connie," says Ibrahim. "I think we trust each other."

"Can I make an observation though?" asks Connie. "In my professional capacity?"

"Please," says Ibrahim. "You know I encourage a frank exchange of views."

"One point two kilos is not an awful lot of heroin," says Connie. "In the grand scheme of things."

"It looks a lot when you see it in Joyce's microwave," says Ibrahim.

"I'm just letting you know," says Connie. "Mitch and Luca wouldn't be killing anyone over one point two kilos of heroin."

"And yet a lot of people are dying?" says Ibrahim.

"Too many," says Connie. "Everyone's chasing ghosts, and one of the Afghans has come over. This is about something bigger. Or someone bigger, you mark my words."

"But none of it solves the question of who killed Kuldesh?"

"Well, that's your job, not mine. I'm quite busy, you know," says Connie. "But Kuldesh stole from two of the biggest drug dealers in the South of England. A day later he's shot dead. This isn't rocket science."

"So you think either Luca or Mitch killed Kuldesh? Lured him into that country lane and shot him?"

"It's what I would have done," says Connie. "All due respect to your mate."

"But which one of them?" says Ibrahim.

Connie walks to the door, and opens it for Ibrahim. "I'd say the last one to die probably did it. Wouldn't you?"

"They're both still alive, Connie," says Ibrahim.

"Well, let's see how long *that* lasts, shall we?"

"Will you walk out with me?" Ibrahim asks.

"Staying here," says Connie. "Another appointment."

Connie touches Ibrahim's arm as he leaves. She has never done that before. It is a very intimate moment, very unlike Connie. Signifying what? I trust you? I'm concerned for you? I appreciate you? Each would be progress in its own way.

Ibrahim steps out into the free world; he will think about it on the drive home.

As he gets into his car, he spots a middle-aged woman walking into the prison.

71.

The view from the top of the multi-story car park is to die for. The English Channel stretching off to infinity. You could turn this place into flats, Mitch is thinking, as he spots the cars up ahead. Property development, that's the game to be in. Bribe a few local councilors, no one tries to kill you, you get to choose color schemes. Maybe he'll have a think about it when this is all over. If he survives.

Mitch parks his black Range Rover next to Luca's black Range Rover. Next to Luca's car is a small, yellow Fiat Uno, from which Garth is currently unfolding himself. He looks like he's been sleeping rough.

"You been sleeping rough, mate?" asks Mitch.

"Yes," says Garth, stretching his arms above his head. "Thank you both for coming."

"You sent me a message with my address and said you'd firebomb my family if I didn't," says Mitch, brushing some sausage-roll crumbs from his jacket.

"And you threw a brick through my front window," says Luca.

"Well, you're here," says Garth. "That's the main thing."

The wind is bitterly cold, high above the streets of Fairhaven. What does Garth want with them? Does he have the same information as they do?

"I'm sorry about your wife," says Luca.

What's this about Garth's wife? Garth also looks puzzled.

"Excuse me?" he says.

"I'm sorry about your wife," repeats Luca.

"What happened to his wife?" asks Mitch.

"Someone killed her," says Garth.

"Jesus," says Mitch. How many more people are going to die? Hopefully none. Or at least hopefully not him. "Sorry, mate."

"Did you kill her?" Garth asks him.

"No," says Mitch.

"Then why are you sorry? Now I hear the heroin is at the old people's village. You hear that too?"

"Yup," says Luca.

Mitch nods. He heard it from one of Connie Johnson's people last night.

"So how do we get it without killing them?" asks Garth.

"We could ask politely?" suggests Luca.

"Or make a deal," says Mitch. Imagine, walking into the meeting with Hanif with the drugs in his hand? Or in a bag, sure, but imagine. If he has to pay off four pensioners, so be it. He'd rather be out of pocket than dead. Give Hanif the drugs, handshake and apologies, get out of the game for good. Straight into property development. Or sparkling wine.

"I don't make deals," says Luca.

"How's that working out for you?" asks Garth. "Here's what I suggest. You two get two hundred grand together. We go down to Coopers Chase again with guns and a suitcase of cash. They give us the heroin, you give them a hundred grand, we get out."

"And the other hundred grand?" says Luca.

"You give to me," says Garth. "For my help, and for my emotional anguish."

"I'll tell you what," says Luca. "Why don't Mitch and I go down there, wave our guns around and walk out with the heroin? Nothing for them, nothing for you. What about that?"

"I wouldn't advise it," says Garth.

Luca laughs. "Garth, we're drug dealers. You're some antiques guy in over his head. So run along home, bury your wife and sell a few clocks."

Mitch is not at all sure about this. Garth seems like he might be many things, but he's not a simple antiques dealer. And Mitch has dealt with the old people at the village before too. And they don't seem scared or stupid.

"Garth," says Mitch. "We give you fifty thousand, we give them fifty thousand. No guns."

Luca shakes his head. "Come on, Mitch. Let's kill him and go."

"No more killing," says Mitch. "Please."

They hear a siren from the streets far below. Each man stops like a meer-kat until it fades into the distance, then they resume their conversation.

"Last one, I promise," says Luca, reaching for a gun tucked into the back of his trousers and pointing it at Garth.

There was a rugby union player, Jonah Lomu, a New Zealand Māori, who rewrote the rules of the game, because of his size and speed. No one had seen anything like him before. This hulk, this oversized tank, who moved with such grace and pace. It is Jonah Lomu that is going through Mitch's mind as Garth runs at Luca, grabs him around the waist and hurls him over the parapet of the car park. There is a long, astonished silence, followed by a loud, distant crunch, and the wail of a car alarm. Mitch stares at Garth. Garth is combing his hair.

"How did he know my wife had died?" Garth asks.

"Huh?" says Mitch. He had meant to say more, but that's all that came out.

"How did he know my wife had died?" Garth repeats. "Only the cops and the killer knew."

"So, he—" says Mitch.

"He killed her, and I loved her," says Garth. "I know I don't look like the sensitive type. But I am."

"I see that," says Mitch, trying to regain a little composure. "So what now?"

"I figure we've got about seven minutes to get out of here," says Garth. "Let's take your car."

"Where are we going?" Mitch asks.

"To Coopers Chase," say Garth. "See if we can't get your heroin back."

"No killing," says Mitch. "I'm serious now. Enough."

"Can't promise anything," says Garth. "But if they play ball, they'll be just fine."

Mitch hears the screams of the public down below, and feels sick to his core. Why is everyone dying? What is he missing?

Please make this end soon. And please let him get out alive.

72.

Ibrahim knows that it is just a waiting game now. Somebody is sure to visit Coopers Chase, looking for the heroin. Every new car through the gates could be bringing death.

So, just for today, it is quite nice to have something to take their minds off it all.

Tatiana's friend "Jeremmy" is coming this evening to pick up his money. Or so he thinks. Truth be told, he may be in for a rude shock. Joyce, as is increasingly her wont, has a plan for him.

They are all meeting at Joyce's flat at six p.m. Donna is there now, enjoying Joyce's hospitality. So if anyone tries to steal the heroin today, at least they have some strength in numbers to fight them off.

Ibrahim has invited Bob over a little earlier than necessary, he's not sure why. Actually, perhaps he *is* sure why. Time will tell.

"What must you make of us, Bob?" Ibrahim asks, pouring two cups of mint tea.

"I've never really felt it's my business to make anything out of anyone," says Bob. "I've never been good with people. Almost everyone is a mystery to me."

"Every true soul is unknowable," says Ibrahim.

"Who says that?" Bob asks.

"Me, Freud, Jung, some others," says Ibrahim. "That's why I enjoy my job. You can only ever know so much. We remain out of reach to each other."

"We certainly do," agrees Bob.

"I know a woman," says Ibrahim. "A cocaine dealer, who can kill people with the click of a finger. Yet, on Monday, she laid her hand on my arm like a lover."

"I don't think that makes up for killing people," says Bob. "Unless I have that wrong?"

"No, goodness, no," says Ibrahim. "And today she sent me a beautiful bunch of flowers. They are in the sink."

"I do like flowers," says Bob. "But I never think to buy them for myself. It makes me feel foolish. I bought some orchids once, this is a few years ago, and as I was paying I told the man they were for my wife. I don't know why. Anyway, I left them on the train."

"I've enjoyed working with you though, Bob," says Ibrahim. "These last few weeks."

"I don't know that I've been much help," says Bob. "After the initial stages."

"You've had fun though?"

"Do you know, I have," says Bob, taking a first sip of his tea. "Often I just do online quizzes, or read up about things, or wait for lunch, and this has given me something else to do. I think I spend too much time alone."

Ibrahim nods. "It's nice to have the choice, isn't it?"

"And to watch the snooker," says Bob. "I enjoyed that. I even enjoyed answering Joyce's questions."

This feels like a good time? Does it? Ibrahim supposes there will never be a good time.

"Do you know, Bob, when I was twenty I was a medical student."

"I didn't know that," says Bob. "I was an engineer in the factory my dad worked in."

"Oh, I can see that," says Ibrahim. "Tell me a little more?"

"No, no," says Bob. "You tell me more, Ibrahim."

"Are you sure?"

"We have half an hour or so," says Bob.

"So we do," says Ibrahim, and settles back into his chair. He chooses not to look at Bob directly. Instead he looks at the painting of the boat on the wall, the painting he has carried around with him from office to office over many years. "I lived in Earls Court, do you know it?"

"Yes, it's in London," says Bob.

"That's it," says Ibrahim. "I had very little money, but I had a scholarship that saw me through the worst of it. I would study all day, and come home at night to this tiny bedsit. Nineteen sixty-three, I would say."

"The Beatles," says Bob.

"The Beatles," agrees Ibrahim. "My English was good; I had learned it at school. I got along with my fellow students well enough, I liked to eat out in cafés, and sometimes I would go to hear jazz. If it was free."

"That sounds enjoyable," says Bob. "Might I help myself to a biscuit?"

"Please," says Ibrahim, motioning to the plate. "One evening I met a man named Marius."

"I see," says Bob, through a chocolate digestive.

"He liked jazz. Not as much as I liked jazz, but he was happy enough with it, and I met him in a pub just off Cromwell Road. It was called the Cherries."

"Mmm hmm," says Bob.

"It's not there anymore," says Ibrahim. "It's a Tesco Metro now."

"Isn't everything?" says Bob.

"I would always sit by myself," says Ibrahim. "I'd take the newspaper with me, although I would have read it already, but just so I felt less embarrassed to be on my own. And Marius was at the next table, also with the newspaper. Do you think we ought to think about heading over to Joyce's?"

Bob looks at his watch. "We have plenty of time."

Ibrahim nods. "Yes, I suppose so, Bob. He was German, Marius, I discovered. You wouldn't know it, didn't look it. Looked Finnish, if anything, and he said to me, his first words to me were 'You have already read that newspaper, I think,' and my first words to him, 'I'm afraid I don't remember,' but he bought me a drink. I didn't really drink back then, but I asked for a pint, because it's nice to fit in, isn't it?"

"It is," says Bob. "People like it when you fit in."

"It took me a long time to drink," says Ibrahim. "He drank very quickly. Or normally quickly, I suppose, just, you know."

"Just in comparison," says Bob.

"Yes," says Ibrahim. "And we spoke, and he told me he was studying chemistry at Imperial College, that is also in London."

"I know it," says Bob, reaching down for another biscuit. "You can never have just one, can you?"

"It is the combination of sugar and fat," says Ibrahim. "It drives us quite mad. The jazz band started to play then, they were a quartet, very gentle, but they knew their business, so I started listening, and Marius started listening, and before you knew it we were listening together."

"That sounds pleasant," says Bob.

"It was very pleasant," says Ibrahim. "That's the word. I don't know that I had done anything *together* in my life before then. When Marius went to use the facilities, the bathroom, I tipped away the rest of my pint, and, by the time he returned, I had bought two more pints for us, and he said thank you and asked if I had eaten at the Italian restaurant next to Earls Court tube. I hadn't, but I said that I had, because I wasn't sure of the right answer to give, and he suggested we have dinner once the quartet had finished, and I said I had other plans, and he said cancel them."

"Did you have other plans?"

"I never had other plans back then," says Ibrahim. "So I had spaghetti vongole, and Marius said he would have the same."

"And what happened next?" asks Bob.

"That's a very good question," says Ibrahim. "Every story must have a

'What happens next.' He walked me back home, we said goodnight, and he said that if it were of interest, he would be in the same pub at the same time the next week."

"And was it of interest?"

"It was," says Ibrahim. "So I went back, still with a newspaper, you know, just in case?"

Bob nods. "Mmm."

"And this time I asked for a glass of wine," says Ibrahim. "Because I felt I could be honest. And it was the same quartet, and we went to the same restaurant, and we talked about Germany, and we talked about Egypt, and we talked about why we found ourselves so far from home, and I spoke a little about my father, which I hadn't done before, and I haven't done since, and, underneath the table, his hand found my hand. You had to be careful, of course."

"Of course," says Bob.

"We moved in together, after a month or so, into a two-bedroom flat," says Ibrahim. "In Hammersmith. Do you know it?"

"I know of it," says Bob.

"And Marius got some work as a cycle courier for one of the newspapers, and I got some work in a shop selling umbrellas, just so we could afford it. And I continued my studies, and he continued his. He had a job waiting for him. Bayer—they were a chemical company, perhaps they still are. He was so strong and so vulnerable, and I became myself, which I hadn't thought possible. And I talk a lot of nonsense about love sometimes, Bob, but we were in love. I don't think I've ever said that out loud before."

"No," says Bob. "No."

"His course was about to come to an end," says Ibrahim, staring at the boat on the wall, "and his job would take him to Manchester. So a decision was going to have to be made. Make or break. I couldn't quite see what the future might hold for us. It wasn't like today. That's not complaining—you are born when you are born. I looked into changing my course, to a university in the North, and I was told it wouldn't be a problem. I had good grades. So I thought, you know?"

"Give it a go," says Bob. "Hang the consequences."

"Hang the consequences," agrees Ibrahim. "I had always acted from fear before. But I took the leap, and decided to act from love. First time for everything."

"Yes," says Bob.

"And then came a knock at the door," says Ibrahim. "This would have been around nine thirty. May, getting dark. I had beefsteak cooking in red wine. And it was a police officer and he informed me that my flatmate had been knocked from his bicycle and killed, just off the Strand, and did I have details of his parents?"

"I'm with you," says Bob.

"And I didn't have their details, they never spoke to Marius, but I said that I would contact them, and you could see the police officer was glad to have the burden taken from him. And so I was able to make the arrangements, under the cover of acting for them, and we had a cremation in St. Pancras, and I offered to take the ashes."

"Where are they?" asks Bob.

"There is a safe," says Ibrahim. "Behind the picture of a boat."

Bob looks up at the picture. "You don't choose to have Marius on display?"

"Old habits die hard, I suppose," says Ibrahim. "I keep my love locked away. And no one has ever reached for my hand under the table since."

Bob nods.

"I think that perhaps our time is up?" says Ibrahim. "You have been very kind to listen."

Bob looks at his watch. "Yes, we should make a move."

The two men stand together.

"Thank you, Bob," says Ibrahim.

"Not at all," says Bob. "I look forward to hearing the rest of your story."

"You've already heard it all," says Ibrahim.

"Well, yes," says Bob. "Except, what happens next?"

73.

Garth drives like he lives. With an absolute, calm certainty that the rules don't apply to him.

That is not to say he is reckless, far from it. Yes, he drives through red lights, but he checks both ways before he does. Yes, he will drive on the verge or the pavement to avoid a line of traffic, but if there is anyone walking on the pavement, Garth will wind down a window and apologize for disturbing them. He even gave a woman waiting at a bus stop, whom he had narrowly avoided hitting, a lift to a local village.

It is pitch black, but he only uses his lights when absolutely necessary. "Too much light pollution in this country, Mitch," he says. "In Canada you can still see the stars."

Mitch would describe his own feelings in this moment as conflicted. He has just watched one of his oldest friends being thrown off the fifth story of a car park. But he is on his way to pick up his heroin, and save his own life. The swings and roundabouts of a businessman's life.

"You think it's definitely there?" he asks Garth again.

"The heroin? Sure," says Garth. "Don't sweat it."

"Don't sweat it?" says Mitch. "You know I die this week if I don't get it back?"

"You reckon?" says Garth.

"Reckon? I know," says Mitch.

"You don't think it's weird?" says Garth, now driving on the wrong side of the road for no reason Mitch can discern.

"I think it's all weird," says Mitch. "Why are you driving on the wrong side of the road?"

"When nothing's coming, I drive where I like," says Garth. "But you don't think it's weird, all this excitement over a hundred grand?"

"I've seen everything in this business," says Mitch.

"Are you a clever man, Mitch?" asks Garth. "Do you think?"

That was a fair question. Mitch used to think he was clever. Before all of this. Before the shipments started getting stopped, and people started getting killed. What if he'd just been lucky though? Ruthless and lucky would take you a long way. Mitch realizes he has lost a bit of confidence. His father-in-law had told him once that the first three things to go are the knees, the eyesight and the confidence. Mitch looks over at Garth once again—this man mountain who seems to care and not care in equal and enormous measure.

"I really am sorry about your wife," says Mitch.

"Thank you, buddy," says Garth. "I don't get cut up about much, but I'm pretty cut up about it."

"You want to talk about it?"

"Nope," says Garth. "Least not to you."

"You really think Luca killed her?" asks Mitch. "It feels like maybe—"

"I said not to you," says Garth, shutting down the conversation.

Mitch is aware, as they drive toward Coopers Chase, that Garth is in charge. It might be Mitch's heroin, but Garth's wife has just been murdered, he's just thrown Luca Buttaci off the top story of a car park, and he probably has a much bigger gun. So Mitch will gladly play the junior partner for now. But he supposes they both know that once they have the heroin, all bets are off.

74.

There are five people in Joyce's flat now. Joyce, Elizabeth, Ron and Ibrahim all present and correct, and their new friend Computer Bob. Ibrahim can see that Bob feels like the fifth Beatle. Ibrahim is glad he is happy, and is glad that he has finally told somebody about Marius.

There had been six people until a moment ago, but Joyce has just sent Donna outside to hide behind a bush.

Joyce has had the whole thing planned, from the moment they dug up the heroin. Ibrahim is very proud to know her.

The laptop has been set up, the tea poured and extra chairs borrowed from around Joyce's dining table, when the door buzzes for what they know is the final time that night. By this stage of the evening, Alan has sat through three door buzzes and is absolutely beside himself with joy.

Joyce opens the door to a young man, who clearly isn't expecting such a welcoming committee.

"Come in," says Joyce. "You must be Jeremmy."

"Where's the money?" Jeremmy asks.

"Jeremmy": supposedly the "emissary" from "Tatiana." Unfortunately, he is not as clever as he seems. Computer Bob discovered that "Tatiana" and "Jeremmy" both send messages from the exact same IP address.

So Jeremmy is not working for the romance fraudster, he is not doing a favor for the romance fraudster, Jeremmy *is* the romance fraudster. The man who has stolen five thousand pounds from Mervyn and is here to steal another five thousand.

He may, however, be out of luck.

"Goodness, no rush, dear," says Joyce, and gives him no option other than to follow her into the flat.

Jeremmy looks around. "Who's Mervyn?"

"He couldn't make it," says Ibrahim. "Sit down for a moment—we have a proposition for you."

"I have to be back," says Jeremmy.

"Nonsense," says Ron. "Night's young. Sit down and have a listen."

"You'll have to make do with a dining-room chair," says Joyce. "It was first come first served."

Jeremmy takes his seat, eyes on everyone at once. Arms around his holdall.

"First things first," says Ibrahim. "You won't be getting any money, I'm afraid."

Jeremmy shakes his head slowly. "Five thousand," he says, "in this bag. Or someone gets shot."

Ibrahim looks to Elizabeth, out of habit.

"Don't look at me," says Elizabeth. "This one's all Joyce's."

"Gun in the bag, is it?" says Ron.

Jeremmy nods.

"You came down on the train, as a favor for a mate, to meet an old man, and you brought a gun with you?"

"I'm careful like that," says Jeremmy.

"I don't buy it, but OK," says Ron. "OK, OK. Let's play 'Hands up if you've got a gun in your bag.'"

The man puts up his hand, and then sees Elizabeth do the same. Ron looks pleasantly surprised.

"Wasn't certain you'd have one today, Lizzie."

"I'm grieving, Ron," says Elizabeth. "I'm not dead."

Ron nods and turns back to the man. "So even if you do have a gun, which you don't, we've got one too, so shut up and listen, and we'll get you out of here as quickly as we can."

Ibrahim sees Joyce nodding happily.

75.

hris is having the sweet-potato fries. He is convincing himself that they are just as good as chips, but of course they're not. But we have to convince ourselves of all sorts of things just to get through the day, don't we? Patrice is watching him push them around his plate.

"I know, love," she says. "I'm having the steamed fish, I feel your pain."

Le Pont Noir is busy, not bad for a Wednesday evening. Chris once arrested one of the co-owners of this place. Drunk driving on the A272. Nice Porsche, as he remembers it, so there's clearly money in samphire and chorizo.

Chris spots SIO Jill Regan as soon as she walks in. Jill is scanning the room, looking for someone.

"Pretend we're talking," he says to Patrice.

"I thought we were talking," says Patrice.

"Jill Regan just walked in," says Chris. "Pretend I said something funny."

Patrice bangs on the table three times and pretends to wipe her eyes.

"I just meant laugh," says Chris. To his horror, he sees the noise has attracted the attention of SIO Regan. To his further horror, she spots him, and, then, the final kicker, it becomes apparent that Chris is the person she has come looking for, and she walks over.

"She's coming over," says Chris. "Don't forget, horse thefts."

Jill drags a chair from a nearby table, and tucks in between Chris and Patrice. She smiles at Patrice. "You must be Patrice; I'm Jill Regan."

They shake hands.

"I'm sorry to disturb you both," says Jill. "I need some help, and everyone I work with hates me."

"You know we work in the same building?" says Chris. "You don't have to find me in a restaurant?"

Jill waves this away. "What have you learned from tailing Mitch Maxwell and Luca Buttaci?"

"I haven't been tailing them," says Chris, skewering a sweet-potato fry. "I've been investigating horse thefts."

"I don't have time, Chris," says Jill. "Luca Buttaci is dead."

"That's a shame," says Chris.

"It is a shame," says Jill. "Because he was working for us."

"I thought he was a heroin dealer?" says Patrice. "I know the NCA get up to all sorts of things, but even so."

"He was a heroin dealer," says Jill. "Until we nicked him at Claridge's with a bag of coke, a couple of hookers and his wife's sister. And since then he's worked for me."

"Who killed him?" asks Chris.

"And how?" asks Patrice. "Help yourself to some broccoli."

"Do you know a man called Garth, Chris?"

"No," says Chris.

"Haven't stumbled across him while you've been tracking down those horses?"

Chris shakes his head.

"Seriously though," says Patrice, "how did he kill him?"

"Threw him off the top of a car park," says Jill.

"Oh," says Patrice, nodding respectfully. "Which one?"

"Cards on table," says Chris. "Imagine I know who you're talking about. Why are you here?"

A woman at the piano has just started playing "Tiny Dancer" softly in the corner of the restaurant.

"'Tiny Dancer,'" says Patrice.

"I'm in trouble," says Jill. "And everyone in the NCA is delighted about it."

"You're not popular?" Chris asks.

"Come on, you've met me," says Jill.

Chris smiles and nods. "You seem OK to me. I didn't like being thrown out of my office, but you seem like a proper copper."

"Jesus, why don't you just marry her," says Patrice.

"I ran Luca Buttaci, you see," says Jill. "He was mine. This whole operation was mine. The heroin."

"A sting?" asks Chris.

Jill nods. "We'd been disrupting Mitch Maxwell's operations for a few months. Stopped a lot of heroin, arrested a few foot soldiers, tested Luca's loyalty and tested his information."

"And this was the big one?"

Jill nods again. "I couldn't have one of your chips, could I?"

"They're sweet-potato fries, I'm afraid," says Chris.

"Oh, not to worry, then," says Jill. "We'd got the go-ahead to let this shipment through customs, and to follow it every step of the way."

"Catch Maxwell in the act?" says Chris.

"Exactly," says Jill. "Follow every move, photographs, videos, the lot, and when the heroin was safely in Luca's hands, therefore safely in my hands, we were supposed to swoop in and arrest Maxwell."

"Only it never reached Luca's hands? Or your hands."

"My worst nightmare," says Jill. "The go-between, Sharma."

"Kuldesh," says Chris.

"Drove off in the middle of the night, gets himself murdered, and the heroin disappears."

"A hundred grand's worth of heroin out on the streets, and you with no evidence it ever even existed?"

"Could have been washing powder in that box," says Jill. "Until we could test it, and prove it was our heroin."

"So they bring you all down from London," says Chris, "to investigate the murder, but really to find out where the heroin is?"

"Well, we could have done both," says Jill. "But yes. Now Luca thought he was on the trail. He had new information, and was going to confirm it today."

"Until he got thrown off a car park," says Patrice. She is then distracted by the pianist. "'Careless Whisper'!"

"So I'm facing disaster, and an inquiry," says Jill. "And I'm working in a room full of people I don't trust, all of whom know it's my neck on the line, and that my job is up for grabs."

"What a mess," says Chris.

"What a mess," agrees Jill. "And it's all mine. Which is why I'm asking you, officer to officer, can you help? Do you have the same information that Luca had?"

Chris thinks. "Let's say Donna and I had been looking into it?"

"Chris, I know you have," says Jill. "I've let you both do it."

Chris raises his eyebrows. "I thought the NCA didn't trust us?"

"They don't," says Jill. "But I don't trust the NCA, so I took the chance."

"And if I help you with this?" says Chris.

"Then, oh, I don't know," says Jill. "Then, off the top of my head, I never show anyone the surveillance videos of you breaking into the hangar on the day Dom Holt was murdered?"

Chris looks down at his sweet-potato fries, gives a little nod, then looks back at Jill.

"You knew I'd broken in?"

"I knew you'd broken in, I knew Donna had gone to the football." Jill starts counting things off on her fingers. "I know a man called Ibrahim Arif visits Connie Johnson in prison once a week. I know he also went to visit a woman called Samantha Barnes with a woman named Joyce, who, by coincidence, was outside the hangar when you found Dom Holt's body. I know she took photos of his files while he lay dead. I also know that she was helped by a man named Ron Ritchie, father of Jason Ritchie, whom you went to visit two weeks ago."

"OK," says Chris, but Jill hasn't finished.

"I know Samantha Barnes, Luca Buttaci and Mitch Maxwell went to visit a retirement village ten days ago and now two of them are dead. I know Donna found Kuldesh Sharma's phone, but I have no way of proving it, so I hope you've been putting it to good use. But, most of all, I knew the more you hated me, the more you would investigate, just to spite me, and I knew that you, and Donna, and this group you seem to hang about with were my best chance of saving my job."

"Huh," says Chris. "I did say you were a good copper."

"So have you found it?" asks Jill.

"The heroin?" asks Chris. "Yes, we've found it."

"Can I have it?" says Jill. "Do you think?"

"Depends. Could you help us find out who killed Kuldesh?" asks Chris. "Do you think?"

"Huh," says Jill Regan. "Well, I can tell you a few people who definitely *didn't* kill him. Would that help?"

"It would certainly be a start," says Chris.

76.

Jeremmy just needs to check he has heard Ibrahim correctly.

"Heroin?" he asks.

"You see, we don't know what to do with it," says Joyce. "But we thought, what luck, you seem to be a criminal, and you're coming to see us."

"Where did you get it?" Jeremmy asks.

"We dug it up by the allotment," says Elizabeth. "Believe it or not. Heaven knows what it was doing there."

"So we thought," says Ibrahim, "rather than hand it in to the police . . ."

"A lot of admin," says Joyce.

". . . perhaps we might branch out and make ourselves a bit of money," continues Ibrahim.

"Pensioners don't have a lot of cash, old son," says Ron.

"So what do you say?" says Elizabeth. "We give you this bag of heroin, you sell it, and we split the proceeds?"

Jeremmy has been given pause for thought. But he's not convinced. "I don't like it, I don't know you. Just give me my five grand and I'll be on my way."

"He's playing hardball," says Joyce. "You see it all the time on *Bargain Hunt*. All right, Jeremmy, we've been on Google and looked up how much heroin costs, and it's *a lot*."

Elizabeth offers the heroin to Jeremmy, who wets his finger and dips it in.

"We are no fools," says Joyce. "Even though we might look it, and we've worked out that we have about twenty-five thousand pounds' worth of heroin here."

Ibrahim sees Jeremmy twitch. He knows there is an awful lot more than twenty-five thousand pounds' worth of heroin in the bag. Greed will always get you.

"That's worth fifteen grand, tops," says Jeremmy.

"I just told you we're not fools," says Joyce.

"What do you say, son?" says Ron. "Help a gang of old fogeys live a little?"

"Say, you give us five thousand, and you can keep the other twenty for yourself?" suggests Ibrahim.

Jeremmy takes them all in one more time. This master criminal. "Five grand for this bag of heroin?"

"If you're agreeable?" says Ibrahim.

Jeremmy is agreeable. Ibrahim is not surprised. He came here for five grand, and he's going to walk away with ninety-five grand in profit.

"And, not that we don't trust you, dear," says Joyce. "But could you send us the five thousand by bank transfer before we let you go? Just so we're sure."

Jeremmy is packing the hundred thousand pounds' worth of heroin into his holdall, clearly delighted to have pulled off the scam of the century. Bob hands him an account number, and Jeremmy opens his banking app.

Joyce zips up the bag for him. "Can I give you some Battenberg for the train home? The buffet at the station isn't always open."

"No, thanks," says Jeremmy, and completes his transaction.

"Your loss." Joyce looks over at Bob, who is looking at his computer screen.

Ibrahim has to hand it to Joyce. She had asked Donna's permission, of course. While the heroin was in her flat, could she put it to work? "I know you'll want it eventually," Joyce had said, "but would you mind terribly if we borrowed it for a bit?"

"All there," confirms Bob, shutting his laptop.

Meaning that Jeremmy has just transferred five thousand pounds, every penny he has stolen from Mervyn, straight back into Mervyn's bank account.

"Off you pop," says Ron. Jeremmy doesn't need asking twice, and is straight out of the door with his huge stash of heroin.

Joyce picks up her phone and rings Donna. "He's on his way. Yes, the whole lot is in his holdall. Hope you're not too cold behind that bush."

77.

"You have a beautiful home," Garth says to Joyce, his gun pointing straight at her. He's been here before of course.

They should have got here much earlier, but, as they'd arrived, there had been a long argument with a woman who said she was from the Coopers Chase Parking Committee and Garth, knowing when he had finally met his match, had had to park back out on the main road.

"Thank you," says Joyce. "I have a cleaner for two hours on a Tuesday morning. I resisted for such a long t—"

"Where is it?" says Mitch Maxwell, gun also pointed at Joyce.

"Could one of you point his gun at someone else?" says Joyce. "Don't point it at Elizabeth—she's just lost her husband. Point it at Ron perhaps?"

"I just lost my wife," says Garth to Elizabeth. "My condolences."

Joyce turns back to Mitch. "I'm afraid you're a bit late, Mr. Maxwell. Half an hour ago it was here."

"What?" says Mitch. He starts to visibly shake. "Who has it?"

"You don't look at all well," says Ibrahim. "If you don't mind my saying?"

"For the love of God," says Mitch. "Just tell me where it is."

"The police have got it," says Ron. "Taken in evidence."

Mitch puts down his gun. "You gave it to the police? My heroin?"

"I'm afraid so," says Ibrahim.

"I'm dead, you understand?" says Mitch. "You've killed me."

Garth starts to laugh. He has an infectious guffaw, and soon Joyce is laughing with him, despite his gun still being pointed at her. He calms himself down and turns to a furious Mitch.

"You still haven't worked it out, Mitch? All this time, and you don't have a clue what's happening here?"

78.

The young man they have just interviewed is called Thomas Murdoch. He said "no comment" to every question except when Jill asked who had sold him the heroin and he said "five pensioners," but even his solicitor looked dubious.

Thomas Murdoch can "no comment" all he likes; he has an extensive criminal record and a bag full of heroin, and he will be going to prison for a long time.

As for the five pensioners, Jill doesn't imagine Thomas Murdoch will be volunteering that information in court.

Jill, out of professional duty, had asked Donna what the real story was, and Donna had told her that Thomas Murdoch was a romance fraudster who stole money from lonely old people, and that was a good-enough answer to ensure that Jill had no further questions.

She has her heroin back; her job is saved. She also has her coat and gloves on, because she is sharing a bottle of wine with Chris and Donna in the freezing Portakabin.

"It wasn't Mitch Maxwell or Dom Holt," she says. "They were both being followed throughout. Including the night of Kuldesh's murder."

"Luca Buttaci?" Donna asks.

"It wasn't Luca Buttaci," Jill replies, knocking back her wine.

"You're sure about that?"

"Certain," says Jill. "He was at my place."

"Jesus," says Donna.

"Jesus," says Jill.

"I can sort of see it though," says Donna, and Jill manages a small smile.

"So you've broken into a warehouse," says Jill, gesturing with her wine glass in gloved hand. "You've aided and abetted tampering with a crime scene and withheld evidence in a criminal investigation, and I've been shagging a key witness, which makes us all about even, I'd say."

"How do you feel about him being thrown off a car park?" asks Donna.

"I suspect I'll move on," says Jill. "Thank you both for saving my job."

"Ma'am," says Donna with a tiny salute.

"And you'll help us?" says Chris.

"I think that's fair," says Jill.

"You must have looked into rival dealers?" says Chris. "Someone who'd like to get their hands on the drugs?"

"Mitch and Luca have got no rivals down here," says Jill. "Not for heroin anyway."

"Someone new trying to muscle in?" says Chris.

"I just don't know who else would have been aware of the shipment," says Jill.

"And the Afghans are on the hunt too?" says Donna.

"Honestly no idea why," says Jill. "Maybe worried the police are onto them?"

"It's been responsible for a lot of deaths," says Chris. "Kuldesh, Dom Holt. Luca thrown off the car park, Samantha Barnes pushed downstairs. Someone killed them all. And all for that little bag of heroin. Ridiculous."

79.

It is fair to say that Garth has the attention of the room. He puts down his gun and takes a seat.

"Sit down, Mitch," he says. "Let me ask all of you a question."

Mitch takes a seat.

"I asked Mitch earlier," says Garth, "did no one think it was odd? That everyone was running around after this heroin?"

"Don't people run around after heroin?" asks Joyce.

"A hundred grand though," says Garth. "That's worth all this effort, all these deaths?"

"I needed—" starts Mitch.

"I know why *you* needed to find it," says Garth. "Your whole enterprise was crumbling, and an Afghan is going to kill you. Of course you wanted it back. But me? Why did I want it so bad? My wife? The Afghan guy you're trying to avoid? Why were we all chasing a hundred grand so hard? We're rich people."

"I just figured . . . greed? I don't know," says Mitch. "I didn't really think about it."

"So why were you chasing it?" asks Ron. "Like blue-arsed flies, the lot of you."

"Can anyone guess?" Garth asks, looking around the room.

Elizabeth looks up. "I can guess."

"Go on," says Garth.

"There was one big thing I honestly couldn't understand," says Elizabeth.

"Why on earth did Stephen agree to help Kuldesh? To sell heroin? Kuldesh wouldn't ask, and Stephen wouldn't agree. And when did Kuldesh suddenly decide he knew how to organize a drug deal? That was another thing that bothered me."

"I bet it did," says Garth.

"That little box of heroin, coming into the country," says Elizabeth, "destroyed everything and everyone in its path. People were so desperate to find it, and Kuldesh was so desperate to hide it, and I can see only one reason. It wasn't about the heroin at all."

Garth nods, and lets her finish.

"It was about the box."

"By George, I think she's got it," says Garth.

"The box?" asks Ron.

"You must have seen it at our lunch, Garth," says Elizabeth. "On Mitch's phone?"

"We nearly didn't come to the lunch," says Garth, "but Samantha had a feeling about you all, and she was kinda interested in heroin. But the second we saw that box, we forgot all about the heroin. It's the most beautiful thing I ever saw. I'm glad Samantha saw it before she died. Six thousand years old, can you believe that? Made from bone, not terra-cotta. And carved with the eye of the devil."

"I did notice some markings," says Joyce. "Now you mention it."

"Pull the other one, Joyce," says Ron.

"These things were looted," says Garth. "Hundreds of years ago. From Egypt—"

"Ooh," says Ibrahim.

"Iraq, Iran, Syria. They'd loot temples, archaeologists some of them, robbers all of them. Smuggle them out. I've seen stuff come up from time to time, stuff that shouldn't be for sale, stuff you'd do serious time for. But I never saw nothing like this. Hoo boy, not never. Those clever Afghan boys were smuggling a box worth tens of millions into the country, Mitch, and they never even told you. That's why everyone's killing everyone. No one cares about your hundred grand."

Mitch points his gun at Joyce now. "Give me the box. Now!"

Garth points his gun at Mitch. "No, Joyce, give me the box now."

"No one else needs to get hurt," says Mitch. "This is my box, fair's fair. I'll take it, I'll give it back to Hanif, no more guns, and no more trouble."

"Dude, my wife died," says Garth, gun still trained. "I'm having the box."

Mitch swings around to point his gun at Garth.

"Perhaps there's one more death to come?"

"Perhaps there is," says Garth.

Mitch unlocks the safety on his gun. Garth unlocks the safety on his.

"Boys," says Joyce. "I don't mean to spoil your fun, but I don't have the box anymore."

"No, no," says Mitch. "Not when I'm this close."

"It was under my sink for a few days, but it started to smell quite musty. Alan didn't like it one bit, so I put it out for the binmen yesterday," says Joyce. "It'll be at the Tunbridge Wells tip by now."

80.

Joyce

What a day we've had of it. Alan and I are both pooped. He is face down on the rug with his tongue out, and I'm just going to get everything down on paper before bed. I'm going to do it as a list, in the order of everything that happened today, as I'm very sleepy.

1. They have had almond milk in the shop for some while now, but I had never paid it much attention until my row with Joanna. I was pretending to browse there earlier and I saw two people pick it up and put it back down again. You can just feel it's going to catch on. I sent Joanna a photograph of me next to it with a thumbs-up, but no reply yet. I think she is in Denmark for work, so perhaps the message hasn't got through.

2. Alan was chased by a squirrel. Honestly, I wish he would defend himself sometimes. He ended up hiding behind my legs as the squirrel stopped about five yards in front of me and stared.

3. There is a new afternoon quiz show on ITV called *But What's the Question?* I didn't understand it at all, but guess who the host is? Mike Waghorn! Hasn't he done well for himself? A woman from Aberdeen won a barbecue set, and I will be watching again tomorrow.

4. The man calling himself Jeremmy came down from London to visit us, with a large holdall, hoping someone was going to give him five thousand pounds. As so often when people think they are going to be able to get things from us, he left disappointed. Tea, biscuits, a good gossip? Yes, we will provide you with those. Money, heroin, diamonds? No. Anyway, we used the heroin we dug up the other day, and, long story short, Mervyn has his money back and Jeremmy is going to prison.

5. There was something different about Ibrahim. Don't ask me what, but I will find out when there aren't quite so many distractions.

6. Mitch Maxwell and Garth (I'm sorry, I realize I don't know his last name) came in with guns to get (so we thought) the heroin. We told them the police had it, and you could tell that Mitch was devastated (I'm not sure how much he enjoys his job) but Garth laughed, and we soon found out why.

7. The heroin wasn't the issue at all. It was the box. It's six thousand years old, and it protects you from evil or something along those lines. Though it is doing a fairly bad job of that, I would say. Elizabeth said she had already worked it out, but, honestly, I think she just worked it out in that second, because she had said nothing to us about it. But it was nice to see her on the front foot again, so I didn't say any of that, I just said, "Well done."

8. I told them I had put the box out for the binmen and Mitch Maxwell went as white as a ghost—you could see clean through him. He ran. For his life, I suppose. Garth took it in good part and said, "Them's the breaks," which is a fun expression, and then we all had a cup of tea. He said how well he thought we had handled everything, and if we ever needed a job to come and talk to him. Then he and Elizabeth spoke for a while and I left them to it.

9. As Garth was leaving, he spotted the "Picasso" I'd picked up from Kuldesh's lock-up. As he was looking at it, I told him I knew it was a fake, but I liked it anyway, and he shook his head and told me it was real. Apparently his wife produced most of the fakes in the UK. "This is Picasso, not my wife," were his exact words. So I own a Picasso. I texted this to Joanna too, but, again, I think maybe the internet is slow in Denmark. They definitely *have* it there though, because I Googled it.

10. And one final thing, before I turn in. Elizabeth congratulated me afterward for my quick thinking, which put a big smile on my face. I think that, since I've stepped up a bit after Stephen's death, I've been surprised at what I'm able to do. Elizabeth rubs off on me in a very good way. I hope I rub off on her in a good way too. She was very impressed anyway. "A very calm reaction in a situation of great pressure, if you don't mind my saying?" I told her I didn't mind her saying that one bit. Because when Garth had revealed to us the secret of the box—the fact that the box I'd been keeping under my sink was highly illegal and worth millions and millions of pounds—it's true, I did make my mind up quickly. To tell them I had left it out for the binmen.

Because I hadn't left it out for the binmen, you see. The box is still under my sink. Though I have taken the bottle of drain unblocker out of it.

Elizabeth says she now has a good idea who murdered Kuldesh, and the box will help to prove it. And she also has one other plan for it.

81.

I was wondering if it might be Mesopotamian," says Elizabeth, as Jonjo examines the box on his desk.

Jonjo Mellor's office is exactly what you might hope. Two walls lined floor to ceiling with books, a wall of mullioned windows overlooking the University of Kent campus, and every surface covered in vases, skulls, pipes and a "World's Greatest Uncle" mug.

To make room to inspect the box, he has cleared as much of his writing desk as he can. There are now piles of papers on the chairs and on the floor. His computer is on the windowsill, next to a bronze cow.

"If that's a guess, it's a good one," says Jonjo. He is brushing specks of dirt from the box with a fine brush. "I'd say you're spot on."

"Stephen spoke about a museum in Baghdad," says Elizabeth. "He rarely wasted words, even when they were easier to come by. He and Kuldesh must have identified it between them."

"It's an extraordinary find; I will have to report it," says Jonjo. "But might we sit with it? Just for an hour or two? I have never seen a piece like it."

"Stephen talked about pieces on which you could see fingerprints and scuff marks," says Elizabeth.

"Well, he was talking about this," says Jonjo. "All present and correct. And it was smuggled in by heroin dealers?"

"Unwittingly, I think," says Elizabeth. "They thought they were just importing the heroin. So it will have come from Afghanistan."

"Makes sense," says Jonjo. "Wherever there is turmoil, people try to protect their assets. Or sell them."

"And it was religious?" Elizabeth asks.

"This long ago, everything was religious," says Jonjo. "All the gods and devils were loose. This, I would say, was a sin box. It would have been outside an important tomb, to ward off the spirits. It will have been looted many years ago. The Iraqis will know for sure."

"So what's the next step?" asks Elizabeth.

"I inform the Foreign Office of what we have," says Jonjo. "They come and collect it, authenticate it, liaise with the Iraqis, and it'll be in Baghdad within the year. We might ask them if we could display it for a while though."

"I won't wait a year," says Elizabeth.

"I'm sorry?" says Jonjo.

"I won't wait," says Elizabeth. "I must level with you, Jonjo. I have a proposition, and I won't take no for an answer."

"Goodness," says Jonjo.

"I want the box to go to Baghdad," says Elizabeth. "And I want Stephen's ashes in it."

"His ashes?"

"He as much as asked me," says Elizabeth. "I realize that now. So, once we are done here, I will be taking the box back with me, and I will be keeping it until those arrangements are made and are acceptable to both parties."

"I don't think you should take the b—"

"I don't much mind what you think," says Elizabeth. "And I hope you know that doesn't come from disrespect. But that is how things are going to be done. Do you think you might be able to swing it?"

"I suppose I can try," says Jonjo, not sounding convinced.

"Excellent," says Elizabeth. "That's all I ask. That you try. The only reason we have this box is because Kuldesh and Stephen chose to protect it. Kuldesh, don't forget, lost his life trying to protect it."

"Still no nearer to finding out how?" says Jonjo.

"I'm hoping that the box has one final story to tell," says Elizabeth. "One final evil spirit in its sights."

"Very cryptic," says Jonjo.

"Might there be a back channel we could explore?" Elizabeth asks. "To get the box to Baghdad sooner?"

"Well . . . it wouldn't be correct procedure," says Jonjo.

"The right thing to do so rarely is," says Elizabeth.

"But I'm sure there are ways," says Jonjo. "Would you be happy to leave that with me for a few days? And the box?"

"Of course," says Elizabeth. "I know it's in safe han—"

The insistent, shrill pulse of a fire alarm fills the air.

"Blast it," says Jonjo. "Sometimes it stops after a few seconds."

They wait a few seconds, but the alarm does not stop. Jonjo looks at the box and looks outside.

"Come on," he says. "The box will be safe here. If it's a real fire, we'll rush back in and save it."

Jonjo pats the box; Elizabeth takes a final look out of the window. She sees Joyce making a quiet exit off the campus. Elizabeth pats the box too and follows Jonjo from the room.

"You make your way down to the quad," says Jonjo. "I'll go and check what's what."

"As you wish," says Elizabeth, and descends a spiral stone staircase. It opens out onto the large, lawned quad, currently dominated by students delighted with the excitement and the brief moment of freedom the fire alarm has gifted them.

How young they all are, though many of them will feel old. How beautiful they are, though how ugly some of them will feel. Elizabeth remembers lying on the grass in quads like these, almost sixty years ago now. Though, of course, not sixty years ago, because she is still there, can still smell the grass and the cigarettes, and the rough tweed arms brushing against hers. She can taste the wine and the kisses, neither of which she had yet developed a liking for. She can hear the cries of boys looking for attention. She can breathe in the air. How young and beautiful she was, how old and ugly she felt. She feels young and beautiful now—Stephen made sure of that. Made sure she understood who she was. Whether today, or sixty years ago, Stephen was right, as he so often was: our memories are no less real than whatever moment in which we happen to be living. The big clock to the left of the quad has a job to do, of course. But it doesn't tell the whole story.

Two girls kiss to her left. To one of them, kissing is new, and this moment will live forever. Things that happen do not unhappen. Stephen's death will not unhappen. Elizabeth's childhood will not unhappen, but the wine and the kisses and the love and the helpless laughter will not unhappen either. The glances at dinner parties, that final crossword clue, the music, the sunsets, the walks, none of it will unhappen.

None of it will unhappen until everything unhappens.

And Joyce, Ron and Ibrahim? They will not be unhappening anytime soon. Elizabeth knows she is utterly alone, but knows, also, that she is not. She will be existing in this state for some while, she thinks. The experienced girl props herself up on one elbow, while the inexperienced girl looks up at the sky and wonders if this is her life now.

Elizabeth lies back and looks up at the sky too. At the clouds. Stephen isn't up there, but he is somewhere, and it's as good a place as any to find him. To find his smile, and his arms, and his friendship and his bravery. Elizabeth starts to cry, and, through the tears, gives her first small smile since that awful day.

The fire alarm stops, and students reluctantly start returning to lecture halls and libraries. Elizabeth pushes herself up, and brushes grass and earth from her skirt.

As she heads back to Jonjo's staircase, she meets the man himself coming out of a nearby door.

"False alarm," says Jonjo. "Hope you weren't too bored."

"Not at all," says Elizabeth. "Time of my life."

They reach Jonjo's landing, he opens the door, and she follows him in.

Two walls, lined with books. One wall, overlooking the quad. Tables of vases, and skulls and pipes, and a mug saying "World's Greatest Uncle."

But the box is gone.

As Elizabeth had known it would be.

Because the box still has a story to tell.

It has one final devil to catch.

82.

The British motorway service station in the gray January rain. Not where anyone would choose to be. Which makes it perfect really.

And, on this occasion, there are compensations.

The box is, what, six thousand years old? Just sitting there in the car boot. Worth millions of course, to the right person. And there were plenty of right people if you knew what you were doing. One of them will be popping along in just a moment. A quick coffee, a handover and then what? Out of the country, certainly. Lebanon perhaps?

Six thousand years old. And people still thought they were important.

Looking about. A man with a briefcase and a sad face plays an arcade machine. A young mum with red eyes pushes a stroller back and forth, trying to kill the day. A teenaged girl can't believe what she is being told on her phone, and an old man in an overcoat hunches over a plastic table, an undrunk cup of coffee in front of him.

It makes you think.

We are all tiny insignificant blinks in history, in a world that couldn't care a hoot if we live or die. You think whoever made this box six thousand years ago cares if we do Pilates and eat our five-a-day? We complain about life so endlessly and so bitterly, and yet we cling to it so dearly? Surely that makes no sense?

There is a covered walkway that traverses the road. It must have looked so glamorous, so sleek and futuristic in the 1960s. It must have looked like the future. Well, guess what? The future's right here, and it's as gray and tired as the past. Whatever they were hoping to achieve with their walkway, whatever their grand vision was, they failed. Everything fails, everyone fails.

At that moment, the unmistakable bulk of Garth appears through the windows of the bridge. Here he comes. Someone else who gets it.

The butterflies begin in earnest.

Mankind finds futility very hard to stomach. People find all sorts of things to give their brief lives meaning. Religion, football, astrology, social media. Valiant efforts all, but everyone knows, deep, deep down, that life is both a random occurrence and a losing battle. None of us will be remembered. These days will all be covered, in time, by the sands. Even the five million pounds Garth is going to pay for the box will be dust. Enjoy it while you can.

These are not original thoughts, sure, but they are soothing ones. Because, once you really accept the hollowness of everything, it makes it an awful lot easier to kill someone.

To kill Kuldesh.

83.

Ron rarely ventures North, but, whenever he does, he enjoys it. The nights out he had with the Yorkshire miners in 1984. The steel workers in County Durham. They could all drink the cockneys under the table. Three coppers once broke his ribs in a Nottingham police station. One rib each. Does Nottingham count as North? It does to Ron. They are currently heading to a motorway service station near Warwick, and even that counts as North. As a precaution he is wearing a thick jumper over his West Ham shirt. Pauline has recently been buying him clothes, because, as she says, "I have to be seen with you, darling, don't I?"

"You can't rely on the food," says Joyce, unpacking a Tupperware box of chocolate hazelnut brownies. She, Elizabeth and Ibrahim are squished together in the backseat. Bogdan is driving. A steady 95 mph so far.

Is Elizabeth asleep? She has her eyes closed, but Ron doubts it.

Donna and Chris are heading up separately. With SIO Regan. Apparently they are all friends now. You just never knew with coppers. Law unto themselves.

Elizabeth has told the police to be there by three p.m. But the deal will be done at two p.m., and Elizabeth will accept the consequences when the police find out she has lied.

Ron starts to think, "There never seem to be any consequences for Elizabeth," and then remembers himself. Grief scares him, Elizabeth's grief particularly. To see her laid so low. To see that there was an iceberg finally able to sink her. You have to be so careful with love, that's Ron's take on the thing. One minute they're buying you jumpers and smoking pot with you on the bowls lawn, the next minute you care, and your heart is not your own. He looks down at his jumper and smiles. He wouldn't have chosen it himself in a million years, but what are you going to do?

"Brownie, Ron?" Joyce asks from the backseat.

"Not for me," says Ron. He is saving himself for a full fry-up at the service station. He hopes there will be time.

"Is it true that Pauline puts marijuana in her brownies?" asks Joyce.

"She does," says Ron. "Marijuana and coconut."

"I wonder if I should try marijuana," Joyce says.

"It makes you very talkative," says Ibrahim.

"Oh, perhaps I shouldn't, then," says Joyce. "You barely get a word in as it is."

Up ahead, Ron spies the long, covered walkway that spans the motorway. Grimy windows, and long-faded primary stripes. Bogdan leaves the fast lane for the first time in ninety miles, and arrows the car toward the service-station slip road.

"We're here!" says Joyce.

Elizabeth opens her eyes. "What's the time?" she asks.

"One fifty-two," says Bogdan. "Like I told you it would be."

Bogdan aims the car for a parking spot far enough from the exit to be discreet, and with a view of the covered walkway. Ron can smell the fry-up. He is aware that they are here for other reasons, but you're allowed to have what Pauline calls a "side hustle." Pauline's "side hustle" is selling used Iron Maiden drumsticks on eBay. She buys them in boxes of fifty from the music shop in Fairhaven.

Meanwhile, talking of boxes, the unmistakable figure of Garth appears through the grimy walkway windows.

"Here we go," says Ron.

"Good luck, everybody," says Bogdan.

84.

Garth can feel the walkway shake as he strides across. It is rusting and unloved. He likes it. He has already pressed record on his phone. He knows the deal.

Since he threw Luca Buttaci from the roof of the car park, the police have been searching for him. Garth can see their point. They won't catch him, not in this life, but they wouldn't be doing their jobs if they didn't at least try. He reaches the steps at the end of the walkway. He smells cheap, fried food and urine. The downside of never complaining is that the British really do put up with a lot. Imagine this in Canada. Or Italy.

Italy might be where Garth goes next. A good place to lick your wounds, and Garth has wounds for the first time since he was a kid. He was all set to go last night, before Elizabeth found him at the house deep in the woods.

How on earth had Elizabeth found him? Garth has no idea, but he is glad that she did. She told him what she knew, and she told him what she wanted. Told him who had killed his wife, and told him how to get his revenge.

Garth walks past the toilets, past a man with a sad face and a briefcase playing an arcade machine, past a red-eyed woman pushing a stroller. He places a hand on her shoulder and says, "It'll get easier, you're doing a great job," and walks on. An old man sits hunched over a cardboard cup of coffee. Garth dips into his own pocket and gives the man a ten-pound note. "Get yourself some food, pops," he says. Garth finds kindness interesting. It's not really his thing, but Samantha would have spoken to the mum, and would have given the old man money for food, so that's the sort of thing Garth will do from now on.

And then Garth sees his wife's killer. He sits down opposite her.

"Hey, Nina," he says.

"Garth," says Nina. "Thank you for meeting me."

"You have something I want," says Garth. "Let's get this done quickly. I have to be out of the country and I'm guessing you do too?"

"I don't have to go anywhere," says Nina. "No one knows I have the box, except you. No one saw me steal it. And you don't seem the type to tell. So I'm in the clear."

Elizabeth told Garth about the theft. As soon as she'd known about the box, she'd had only two suspects: Nina, and her boss, a professor. A friend of Elizabeth's had set off a fire alarm, another friend, a computer guy, had rigged up a little camera, and Nina had walked straight into her trap. A guy from the KGB has been tailing Nina ever since. They knew she had the box, but they had no evidence to prove that she'd killed Kuldesh to get it. Which is why Garth is here.

He'd rung Nina last night, told her he couldn't find the box for love nor money, but, if she ever stumbled across it, he had a client who would pay handsomely for it. Which is actually true, but Garth knows he is not getting the box. Elizabeth wants it, and when she told him why, he happily agreed. Garth's reward is seeing his wife's killer go to jail. Ideally he would like to kill her, but Elizabeth is a bit too canny to let him get away with that. You have to know when you've met your match.

"You have it?" Garth asks.

Nina opens a bright blue IKEA bag at her feet. In the bag is the box.

"Can I touch it?" Garth asks.

"Sure," says Nina. "But try anything and it leaves with me."

Garth can't help but laugh. He touches the box. It's kind of a buzz.

Samantha would have loved it, he knows that. They're crazy, all of them, Samantha, Nina, Kuldesh. Childish, getting so excited about a box. Garth got excited about how much the box was worth, sure, but not about the box itself. So someone made it a long time ago? Get over yourself. So it has the eye of the devil? Ain't no such thing, Garth knows that. The devils walk among us.

But Kuldesh had laid down his life for it, and Nina had killed for it. Samantha probably would have killed for it too, Garth has to accept that, but Nina got to her first. As soon as Nina worked out that Garth knew what the box was, she'd signed Samantha's death warrant right then and there. And he'd gone off to eat a burger while she'd done it.

Though, now he thinks about it, how *had* Nina worked that out? Garth worries that perhaps he has some kind of "tell." It would be very unlike him to have a weakness. And, besides, if Nina hadn't killed Samantha, then who had?

He expects that Nina would have killed him too if she could, but Garth isn't easy to kill. Many have tried.

"You set up the company like I told you?" Garth asks, taking out his phone.

Nina nods.

"Then you'll get an alert the second the five million hits your account," says Garth. "After that, it's up to you. They'll never trace that account, but how you get the money into regular accounts is your business. You can look this up online."

"I've been doing little else," says Nina.

"Why'd you have to kill him?" says Garth. "That's the only bit I wouldn't have done."

"I didn't kill anyone," says Nina.

"Nina," says Garth. "I don't think like other people, you get that?"

"I get that," says Nina.

"Then don't lie to me," says Garth. "You don't need to. I respect what you've done. You saw an opportunity, you're making five million, while everyone's chasing their tails."

"Thank you," says Nina.

"But I still don't get why you killed him? Why not just scare the guy and take it?"

"He was eighty, Garth," says Nina.

"OK," says Garth.

"This box was six thousand years old," says Nina. "Can you even begin to comprehend that? None of us matters, Garth. We pretend that we do, we pretend that we have a purpose, but this planet existed without us for millions of years, and it will exist for millions of years more without us. Every breath we take is a dying breath. Human life isn't sacred."

"That's all very convenient for you," says Garth. "At least just say you were greedy and you didn't care a single damn. You could have simply stolen the thing."

"He was asking me to take it to a museum. He trusted me," says Nina. "Trusted that I would take it to the right people. He'd known me since I was a kid, known my parents. You think he would have kept quiet when I sold it?"

"Throw him a million?" Garth says. "That might have bought his silence."

"He would have said no," says Nina. "But look at it this way. He was old, he'd had fun, a full life, whatever people mean by that. He rings me, he trusts me, he tells me what he has. I tell him not to be frightened, that we can find our way through this, that I'll help. I'm calm, and that makes him calm. We arrange to meet—"

"In the woods?" says Garth.

"As far away from prying eyes as we can," says Nina. "I could tell, by the time we'd finished talking, that even he was getting a little excited."

"It is pretty exciting," says Garth.

"He drives to Kent, drives down the lane, meeting someone he trusts. Up I walk, one shot. He doesn't see it, doesn't feel it, has no moment of fear. His life ended quickly, which is all you can ask for, isn't it? A long life and a quick death, that's the dream. I did him a favor."

"A painless death for him, and five million for you?"

"Everybody wins," says Nina. "It's everything my parents never would have done. I don't intend to ever be poor again."

"You're a pretty good shot," says Garth. "Hard to kill a guy through a window with one bullet. Believe me, I know."

"YouTube videos," says Nina. "I'm a quick learner. I wanted it to be painless, so I watched videos of vets killing horses."

"Jesus," says Garth. "And they call me a psychopath."

"I'm not a psychopath," says Nina. "I had no money, I have debts, I have a job I hate. My parents are gone. Suddenly the chance to never work again fell from the heavens."

"This box doesn't come from the heavens," says Garth. "It comes straight from hell."

"It's just a box," says Nina.

Garth shakes his head.

"So I did the rational thing," says Nina. "That's all I did."

Garth thinks about this. He finds philosophy interesting. But, whichever way he cuts it, he can't agree with her. Kill people, sure, if they've done something wrong. If they deserve it. But for profit? No. He only realized when Elizabeth explained it to him that Luca Buttaci hadn't killed Samantha. Luca knew she was dead because he was working with the cops. Which is almost as bad.

But Luca had killed plenty of other people. And if you kill plenty of people, you've got to expect someone's going to throw you off a car park one day. One day someone will throw Garth off a car park, or run him down with a truck, and Garth won't have any complaints. But Kuldesh didn't deserve to die.

"You could have not killed him?" says Garth. "You could have buckled down at work, you know? Got on with your life, paid off your debts and taken some responsibility for your own problems."

Nina nods. "I suppose so, but this was so much easier."

"You have a bad attitude," says Garth.

"My whole life I've had a good attitude and been poor," says Nina. "Now I have a bad attitude, and suddenly I'm rich."

"And killing my wife was the rational thing too?"

"Your wife?" says Nina. "Samantha? I didn't kill her."

"Don't lie to me," says Garth.

"I killed Kuldesh," says Nina. "And he didn't feel a thing. I didn't kill your wife. Why would you give me five million pounds if you thought I'd killed your wife?"

"You killed her," says Garth. "There is no five million. The deal was just that I get you to confess, and they'd let me disappear."

"Who would let you disappear?" says Nina.

"Who do you think?" says Joyce, as she, Elizabeth and Bogdan sit at the table.

"No, this is . . . What are you d—" Nina cannot get her words out.

"Walk with us please," says Elizabeth. "No struggling, no fuss. Garth, you have twenty minutes to disappear."

"Obliged to you," says Garth, and hands his phone to Elizabeth. "It's all on there."

"You can't do this," says Nina.

"And yet here we are, dear," says Elizabeth.

She turns to Garth. "And where will you go now?"

"Spain," says Garth. "I love the tapas. You be careful with your grief now, take your time with it."

"I will," says Elizabeth. "And you stop killing people."

"Only bad guys, ma'am, I promise," says Garth. He turns, and they watch him leave, followed by his massive shadow.

"You're just going to let him go?" says Nina, now being shepherded toward the car park by Bogdan, as Elizabeth and Joyce walk behind.

"That was the deal, yes," says Elizabeth.

"We could make a deal?" suggests Nina.

"No, dear," says Joyce.

Nina looks around her. "What if I start screaming?"

"Then I'll start screaming too," says Elizabeth. "And, believe me, I may never stop."

85.

It is somewhere below freezing, a sheeting rain is falling, and Mitch Maxwell is clambering up an enormous pile of waste at the Tunbridge Wells tip. A mountain of metal and slime, the smell clinging to him as he slips and slides his way up and across. Unable to wipe the appalling sweat from his brow, because of the unspeakable smears on his gloves. All the while searching, burrowing into the depths, looking for the box that will save his life. He is, in this moment, a frightened animal, scavenging for survival. He thinks about his yacht, moored in Poole Harbour. He'd once had Jamie Redknapp the footballer on board for a barbecue. He thinks of the stables at his house, his daughter's horse, the ski trip they have planned for the half-term holidays. He thinks of touch-screen TVs and cashmere sweaters, and premium vodka in gold bottles and front-row seats at the boxing. He thinks of first class on British Airways, of dinner at Scott's, of being measured for suits at Oliver Brown on Sloane Street. Of castles with heli-pads and nightcaps. He thinks of ease and comfort and quiet, expensive luxury.

He thinks of his children and their schools, and their friends with pools. A shard of metal slices through his jacket and cuts his arm. He swears, and slips, and falls. Blood starts to seep through as he makes his way back up the pile. The stinking mass of everyone else's lives. Somewhere in this pile is the box. Somewhere in this pile, his salvation.

He is seeing Hanif at two, at an airport hotel next to Gatwick. Hanif has asked him to bring the box, and has said that if Mitch isn't there, he will find him and kill him.

But Mitch is not going to die today. Not after everything he has been through. After the life he has made for himself—from the home he grew up in, to the home his children enjoy. He wishes it hadn't been heroin that had brought him such success, but he wasn't from a place that gave him a great deal of choice. It was what he grew up with, what he was good at.

But, after this, if he finds the box, *when* he finds the box, that's it. Luca is dead, and the Afghans won't trust him anymore. Time to diversify. He's been talking to the English sparkling wine people. There's a plot of land in Sussex, in Ditchling, south-facing slope, chalky soil, the works. Mitch will buy it, they'll run it, a real business.

And if he doesn't find the box? Well, then, a change of plan. He will still go to Gatwick, but instead of heading to the piano bar at the Radisson he will head straight to check-in and he'll be on the three p.m. flight to Paraguay before you know it. He knows people out there.

His wife and kids flew out this morning. Kellie has been around long enough to know that if Mitch tells her to pack a suitcase and get the kids out of the country, he'll have a good reason. She texted him as they were about to take off. The Afghans won't catch him in Paraguay, that's for sure. They'd have to get through the Colombians, and they won't have the heart for it.

Mitch continues to clamber up the slope of rubbish, arm bleeding, clothes soaking, legs bruised and aching. He'd gone straight to the tip after leaving Joyce's flat, but they don't let you climb the rubbish piles. So a couple of calls and a contact in Kent County Council have bought him ninety minutes in which to search today. A group of men in hi-vis jackets are sheltering in a Portakabin with tea-steamed windows, wondering what the Scouser in the padded jacket is up to. One of the more enterprising ones even offered to help, but Mitch wants to do this alone. None of them recalled seeing a small terra-cotta box coming in on a Kent refuse truck.

Mitch steps on a doll that says "Love me" in the deep, slow voice of a toy with low batteries. The wind blows a KFC box into his face. He bats it aside and keeps climbing. He is nearly at the top now, the wind howling around him, carrying the smells of everything that has been left behind, everything that has been discarded. Still no box. Mitch knows he is not going to find it. He knows he is going to have to flee. To take his wife from her job, his kids from their friends, to start anew, somewhere unfamiliar. He breathes in the stench and welcomes it. For a moment his heart skips as he sees a box. He digs down, through nappies and toasters, clearing a line of sight. He imagines, for a bright moment, some kind of glory, but, as he dislodges a spaghetti of coat hangers, he sees that this box is simply an old orange crate. Of course it is. Mitch starts to laugh.

Up and up he climbs, no longer really looking, just anxious to reach the top. Why? Who knows? We all want to reach the top, don't we?

Mitch crawls onto a fridge freezer, green with slime. This is it. The very top, nowhere left to climb. Gingerly he pushes himself up to standing. A broken, bleeding, soaking man at the top of the world. He looks out at the view. Nothing. Just gray cloud, gray rain and gray mist.

It will be sunnier in Paraguay, and he will find work. Build a business. Something wholesome. Fruit or something. If any of the Colombians want to come and say hello, then that's fine. He'll tell them he's out of the game. They can keep their cocaine, and he'll keep his bananas. If they grow bananas in Paraguay.

Mitch wipes a brown smear from his Rolex. One p.m. Time to head to Gatwick. He rests his hands on his knees for a moment, recovering from the exertions of his climb, and preparing for his descent. With decent traffic he can—

A pain shoots through Mitch Maxwell's left arm. He clutches it. He feels the rain pouring down his face, before realizing that it is no longer raining. Mitch slumps onto his knees, then his knees slip from under him on the slime of the freezer. There he lies for a few moments longer, before Mitch Maxwell, at the top of the pile, heart on fire, gasping in pain, filth and grayness all around him, shuts his eyes for the final time.

86.

Ibrahim leans his elbow on the roof of the squad car, and listens to the traffic thunder by in the distance.

Chris and Donna arrived with SIO Jill Regan about fifteen minutes after Joyce and Elizabeth left. Ron just had time to sneak in his full English breakfast, and Ibrahim has rarely seen him look so happy. He is currently on the other side of the car, contentedly patting his stomach through his new jumper, which is actually a wonderful color on him.

"What are we calling that? Cerise?" says Ibrahim.

"Red," says Ron.

The three officers are listening to the recording in the back of their squad car. One by one they emerge. Jill holds up the phone.

"The other voice on this recording?" Jill begins. "It's Garth?"

"It's unmistakable," says Ibrahim.

"Where is he?" Chris asks.

"He got away," says Ron. "Couldn't stop him, big lad."

"You told us to be here at three," says Jill. "And this phone starts recording at just before two."

"Not my area," says Ibrahim. "You'd need to talk to Elizabeth."

"And where is Elizabeth?" asks Chris.

"Back at Coopers Chase," says Ibrahim. "As far as I know. We're trying to give her a bit of space at the moment."

Elizabeth and Joyce are currently being driven home by Mark from Robertsbridge Taxis. It was explained to Mark that the job was fairly time sensitive, and he wouldn't be able to join Ron for the full English breakfast. He had looked crestfallen, but, at heart, he is a professional.

"So you and Ron organized this whole thing yourselves?" says Chris.

"We are capable men," says Ibrahim, as Ron lets out a small belch, and apologizes.

"To be clear," says Jill. "You told us to be here at three p.m., and that you'd deliver Nina Mishra, Garth and the box to us. I see Mishra, but I don't see Garth or the box? You told us to trust you?"

"I would say this," says Ibrahim. "In our defense. We have already delivered the heroin to you. And we are now delivering the murderer of Kuldesh Sharma and Samantha Barnes."

"Murderess," says Ron.

"It's just 'murderer' these days, Ron," says Ibrahim.

"But the man who probably murdered Luca Buttaci has mysteriously vanished. Maybe murdered Dom Holt too," says Jill. "And where is the box?"

Ron shrugs.

"I promise you it's quicker just to accept it, ma'am," says Donna. "It honestly saves so much time."

"The box will surface, I'm sure," says Ibrahim. "And, as for Garth, justice will catch up with him one day. But I suspect your superiors will be delighted that two murders have been cleared up and their heroin has been recovered. I suppose you have tested it by now?"

"Absolutely pure," says Chris.

"And so you will be able to arrest Mitch Maxwell also," says Ibrahim.

"I'd say that's a result," says Ron. He motions over to the Daihatsu, and Bogdan emerges to bring Nina to them.

Jill meets them halfway, reads Nina her rights, cuffs her and leads her to the squad car.

Chris looks at Bogdan. "This lot lying to us, I understand. But you must have known you were due here at two?"

"One fifty-two," says Bogdan.

"But you lied to us anyway?" Chris continues. "You lied to Donna?"

Bogdan looks at Donna.

"He didn't lie to me," says Donna. "I knew too. Garth was the only one Nina would confess to. And without the confession we had nothing. I would have done anything to get her. Kuldesh was the first person who knew Bogdan was in love with me."

"I told a guy at the gym too," says Bogdan.

"Don't spoil it, baby," says Donna.

Chris looks at the motley crew in front of him. Ron and Ibrahim, Donna and Bogdan. He shakes his head.

"And where's the box?" he asks.

"Elizabeth needs it," says Ibrahim. "I hope that's enough for you to forgive us?"

87.

Hanif looks at his watch, and finishes his coffee. Mitch Maxwell isn't coming. He's not suddenly going to walk into the Gatwick Radisson holding the box.

So be it. Hanif had come up with the whole scheme. Sayed had had an offer for the box, from a Swedish guy who lived in Staffordshire with ten million burning a hole in his pocket. Rather than going to the trouble of finding some elaborate new route to smuggle it in, why not just send it through their regular chain? If they'd told Mitch and Luca what it was, they'd have asked for a cut. He actually should have cut them in; in retrospect, they might have taken a bit more care. Although Hanif is starting to hear that they'd been having trouble with shipments, so, really, he shouldn't have trusted them at all.

A young cousin of Hanif's had been tasked with following the box every step of the way, and retrieving it from Luca Buttaci. Hanif had even bought his cousin a motorbike for his troubles. But then the box went missing, and his cousin was only following ghosts.

Hanif had messed up, that was the long and short of it. Thought he was being clever, but didn't do his homework. Everybody lost money, everybody died, and it was all because of him.

Still, you can't go around apologizing for every little mistake, can you? That way lies madness. The chaos that follows in your wake is not your responsibility.

If he flies back to Afghanistan, he will be killed too, and so, on reflection,

Hanif will stay in London, out of Sayed's reach. The heroin trade has been a steep learning curve, not to mention very, very lucrative, but perhaps it is now time to take what he has learned and do something new? Fresh start, clean sheet, no regrets.

A friend from university has offered him a job at a hedge fund, and someone he met at the party suggested he go into politics and offered to make a few introductions.

Nice to have options.

88.

Caroline kills people for Connie, always has done. If you need her, you call the number for a launderette in Southwick and ask for a service wash. She's quick, she's reliable, and she's a breath of fresh air in a traditionally male-dominated industry.

Connie is emailing her with a bit of good news. Somebody else has murdered Luca Buttaci for them. Connie's emails are all encrypted by a highly sophisticated piece of software that is illegal in every single country in the world except Venezuela. Naturally Caroline will keep the 50 percent engagement fee for the job, as per their usual agreement.

Connie and Caroline have been very busy recently.

You have to spot opportunity when it falls into your lap. That's how Connie has got where she is today. Not in prison, that part was unfortunate, but the leading cocaine dealer on the South Coast of England.

And now, as she reads another email from Sayed in Afghanistan, the leading heroin dealer too.

But Connie feels guilty. And she is struggling to work out why. She feels guilty, and she recognizes that this is a new emotion for her. She doesn't like it one bit, but, for once, she will not hide from it. Do what Ibrahim says, let it all in. Sit with it, even if it's painful for you. And the guilt is painful for her.

It all started when Ibrahim told her about Kuldesh.

Connie is very glad they caught the woman who killed Kuldesh, she really is. He wasn't in the business, was he? If you're in the business, you expect someone's going to shoot you at some point. Comes with the territory.

But Kuldesh just got involved in something he shouldn't have. Connie prides herself on knowing everything, but even she hadn't known who shot Kuldesh. No one in the drugs world seemed to have a clue about it, and now she understands why. It wasn't anything to do with drugs.

But from the moment Ibrahim told her about Kuldesh, she had started planning. Mitch and Dom were in trouble already, and this had unbalanced them still further. Connie had sensed their weakness, sensed the opportunity to take their business, and gone on the attack. She had decided to kill Dom Holt the moment Ibrahim told her the story. Two hours later she was on the phone to that launderette in Southwick.

She remembers she and Ibrahim had had a discussion about whether killing someone and paying someone else to kill someone were the same thing. They had agreed to differ, but perhaps Ibrahim had been right.

Caroline had killed Dom Holt for her; she had subcontracted the killing of Maxwell's third-in-command, Lenny Bright; and Luca Buttaci had been next on the list.

Samantha Barnes had come to visit her. With the same idea as Connie. She had suggested a partnership. Connie had listened, recognized some of the benefits that Samantha and Garth could bring to the business, and promised Samantha she would think about it. They shook hands, and minutes later Connie was on the phone to the launderette again. Word is the police actually think that Nina Mishra killed Samantha too. Poor Nina. Though, in Connie's experience, when you start killing people you do tend to get stereotyped. Comes with the job.

When Caroline killed Samantha, she had intended to kill Garth at the same time, but he hadn't come into the house. Must have been spooked by something. Fair enough, the Canadian fella clearly has a survival instinct. Now he was out of the country, so he's a loose end that might need tidying up someday.

But why is she feeling guilty?

Everyone Caroline killed was in the business, so that's not what Connie feels guilty about. They would all have killed her if the situation had been reversed.

The contracts with Sayed are signed, and she is now a major heroin importer, but that's not what she feels guilty about either. Someone is going to import heroin, so why not her?

In truth she knows. Of course she knows. She has lied to Ibrahim. Worse than that, she has used him. She had wanted to say sorry when he left the other day, but she doesn't yet have the words. Connie is not sure she has ever said sorry and meant it. Her florist had organized flowers for him, but that's not saying sorry either.

Connie shuts her eyes. She tries to think about Garth, running loose. He'll find out at some point that Connie ordered his wife's death, and he'll come looking for her. That's fine—Connie enjoys thinking about that sort of thing. Garth vs. Connie, that'll be a battle worth watching.

But the images of Garth keep getting replaced by images of Ibrahim, his kind eyes and his gentle soul. His belief in her. She tries to concentrate on guns, and drugs, and chaos, but Ibrahim's kindness is stronger.

Connie will find a way to say sorry one day.

89.

Joyce

The box, that simple little box, which once held the spirits of the devils, then held a big bag of heroin, then contained my drain unblocker, multi-surface polish and bin bags, now contains Stephen's ashes. Jonjo flew over to Iraq with it. It's on his Instagram. I didn't know professors were allowed Instagram.

It is in its rightful place in Baghdad, and we have an open invitation to visit if we are ever in the area. The Foreign Office got involved at one point, but Elizabeth made a phone call.

Elizabeth is going to fly over there next month. She promised Stephen they would visit together one day. She is going to Dubai with Viktor soon, to follow up some leads on the Bethany Waites case, and apparently the flight from Dubai to Baghdad is not too arduous.

Quite what we will do with her when she gets back is anyone's guess. Bogdan is going to redecorate while she is away. Not too much though. You mustn't paint over everything.

Coopers Chase is full of widows and widowers. Falling asleep with ghosts, and waking up alone. You have to soldier on, and Elizabeth will do that. Of course not everyone here assisted in the death of their partner, but, between you, me and the gatepost, there are more than you'd think. Love has its own laws.

They told us that Mitch Maxwell died looking for the box at the tip. You live by the sword, you die by the sword. Ron's hip is still giving him gyp.

You'd think that the closer you get to death, the more it would matter, but I'm finding the opposite to be true. I don't fear it. I fear pain, but I don't fear death. Which I suppose is the choice that Stephen was faced with.

What else can I tell you? Joanna bought me an air fryer. I'm just experimenting with it at the moment—a spaghetti Bolognese and some sausage rolls—but so far so good. I realize I've had a kettle full of diamonds and a microwave full of heroin recently, so you never know what it might come in handy for one day.

Mervyn was delighted to get his five thousand pounds back, but is otherwise heartbroken. I would say that at least it was a lesson learned, but the last I heard Mervyn was planning to invest the whole lot with a broker who had emailed him out of the blue about buying into a secret fund "the experts don't want you to know about." Donna had to pop round and have another word with him.

Ron and Pauline have just got back from a weekend in Copenhagen. I asked Ron what it was like and he said it was like everywhere else abroad. When Ron dies, I don't think we will be taking his ashes to Baghdad.

Also, and I swear this is the truth, he was wearing a lilac polo shirt. It really brought out his eyes.

Ibrahim has been quiet. I think he finds being around sadness very difficult. I think he takes it all very personally, loads it onto his own shoulders. I get sad when others are sad, of course I do, but life will give you enough sadness of your own to be getting on with, so you must be careful. Sometimes you just have to slip your big coat off, don't you?

I saw he was having lunch with Computer Bob on Saturday. That made me happy. Ibrahim relies too much on Ron for company sometimes, and I think he and Bob have a lot in common.

The daffodils are out very early this year. I've seen the daffodils bloom for nearly eighty years now, and they are still a miracle to me. To still be here, to see the flowers that so many other people won't see. Every year, poking their heads up to see who's still around to enjoy the show. Though they are out *very* early this year, which I know is probably global warming, and everyone will end up dying. You can still appreciate a flower though, can't you? Gives you hope, despite the apocalypse.

Alan has been to the vet after a cat scratched his nose. Ron was very mean, saying he can't believe Alan lost a fight with a cat, but Alan is a lover, not a fighter. The vet said Alan was in fine shape, and that I was obviously looking after him well. I said that Alan was looking after me well too.

I think we're due a period of peace and quiet now, aren't we? A few months without murders, and corpses, without diamonds and spies, without guns and drugs and people threatening to kill us. Some time for Elizabeth to find her new feet.

I'll tell you what I'd like instead. A few weddings. I don't mind who. Donna and Bogdan, Chris and Patrice, Ron and Pauline, maybe Joanna and the football chairman. That's what happens when you get older. Too many funerals, not enough weddings. And I love a wedding. Bring them on. Bring on love.

There's something I forgot to mention. Do you remember, a few weeks ago now, before all this kerfuffle, I'd spoken about a man named Edwin Mayhem? A new resident, about to move in?

I'd got excited because of his name and had imagined so many wonderful things about him. A motorcycle stunt rider or TV wrestler.

Well, it turns out that it was just a typo, and his real name is Edwin Mayhew, which actually makes an awful lot more sense. When I went to see him he was just wearing a jumper and an old pair of cords. He is from Carshalton and used to be a quantity surveyor. His wife died about four years ago—a decent-enough interval, I think—and his daughter, who is Joanna's age and also lives in London, persuaded him to move in here. I asked if his daughter still drinks proper milk, and he said that she doesn't. He said that last week she had made him a turmeric latte, and it had disagreed with him.

Anyway, Edwin's daughter, Emma—lovely name, I would like to have been an Emma—thought that Coopers Chase might give him a new lease on life. I know that it will, but you could see that he has his doubts. No offense, he said, but I worry the pace of life might be a bit slow for me here. As if Carshalton was Las Vegas.

He was very grateful for my lemon meringue though, and he said if I ever needed anything fixed, that's where his talents lay. Taps, shelves, you name it, he said. I said I had a Picasso that needed hanging, and he laughed.

He made us a pot of tea, then walked in with the tea cozy on his head and pretended he couldn't find it. Alan was beside himself. I've promised to show him around, and to introduce him to a few people. He will fit right in, you can tell straight away. One day I will tell him that I thought he was called Edwin Mayhem. Not today but one day.

That's the thing about Coopers Chase. You'd imagine it was quiet and sedate, like a village pond on a summer's day. But in truth it never stops moving, it's always in motion. And that motion is aging, and death, and love, and grief, and final snatched moments and opportunities grasped. The urgency of old age. There's nothing that makes you feel more alive than the certainty of death. Which reminds me.

Gerry, I know you'll never really read this, but then perhaps you will? Perhaps you're reading over my shoulder right now. If you are, then that silver gravy boat you bought at the car-boot sale is very fashionable now. So you were right and I was wrong. Also, if you are reading this, I love you.

I didn't mean to sound morbid, by the way, I just feel tired, like I need a holiday, a nice little break somewhere. Joanna is buying a cottage in the Cotswolds, so maybe that will fit the bill. I really am very proud of everything she has achieved. She eventually replied to my message about the almond milk and told me I was now officially a hipster. I told Ron, and he said he was going to be an artificial hipster one of these days.

I am going to make a pavlova later. But with mangoes. I bet that has surprised you? I saw them do it on *Saturday Kitchen*. There will be plenty for Ibrahim, Ron and Elizabeth. And maybe, just maybe, there will be some left over for Edwin Mayhew.

By the way, when I went to see Edwin, he asked me if I was a member of any of the clubs at Coopers Chase.

Am I a member of any clubs at Coopers Chase?

I think that's probably a conversation for another day, don't you?

Time for me to turn in now. I know it sounds silly, but I feel less alone when I write. So thank you for keeping me company, whoever you might be.

ACKNOWLEDGMENTS

I have so many people to thank for the part they have played in *The Last Devil to Die*, but I would like to start with you, the reader. I would simply like to echo Joyce's final words in the book. Thank you for keeping me company. This relationship we have makes me very happy. May it all continue for many years to come.

This was the fourth Thursday Murder Club book, and I promise it won't be the last. But I will be making you wait for a little while, as I'm going to write something new next, about a father-in-law/daughter in-law detective duo. I promise you'll like them, but, as I say, rest assured that Joyce, Elizabeth, Ibrahim and Ron will also be sticking around for a long time to come.

Here come the acknowledgments and, as anyone who has ever had to wrangle a book into existence will know, they are heartfelt.

Thank you to my wonderful agent, Juliet Mushens, and welcome to the world, Seth Patrick-Mushens. You have an incredible mother, Seth, you lucky boy.

Juliet's team are the very, very best, and look after me with skill and grace and great humor. Thank you, Liza DeBlock, Rachel Neely, Kiya Evans, Catriona Fida, and the whole Mushens Entertainment team, it is a great pleasure to work with you. Huge thanks too to my US agent, Jenny Bent.

Thank you to my amazing UK editor, Harriet Bourton, for, among many other things, convincing me that *The Little Box of Death* was not a good name for a book. Thank you also to the incredible Thursday Murder Club team at Viking: Amy Davies, Georgia Taylor, Olivia Mead, Rosie

Safaty and Lydia Fried. Thank you to the forensic Sam Fanaken and her outstanding sales team in the UK, and to Linda Viberg and the wonderful international sales crew. And a huge vote of thanks to the amazing Penguin audio team, who always give the audiobook such care. Donna Poppy did her usual exemplary job on the copy edit too, she is the very best in the business, and Natalie Wall and Annie Underwood saw the novel through its production seamlessly. Richard Bravery produced yet another cracking front cover (featuring Snowy, if you hadn't spotted the details on the ears!). Thank you to Karen Harrison-Dening for her thoughtfulness and insight. And thank you to Tom Weldon for the continued support and wisdom.

My US publishing team are equally brilliant, and you're able to email them later in the day because of the time difference. Thank you to my legendary editor Pamela Dorman, and her soon-to-be legendary right-hand woman Jeramie Orton. (I wonder if I subconsciously introduced an unusually spelled Jeremmy into the book in your honor?) Further thanks to the indispensable Brian Tart, Kate Stark, Marie Michels, Kristina Fazzalaro, Mary Stone, Alex Cruz-Jimenez, and to the rest of the team at Pamela Dorman Books and Viking Penguin. By the way, "Viking Penguin" is a terrific idea for a kids' book. Let's talk numbers.

Three special mentions for this particular book. Firstly I want to thank Raj Bisram for his sage advice on the world of antiques and forgery. Raj certainly has some amazing stories to tell (although none, I should point out, about murder). Thank you to the real-life Luca Buttaci for lending me your name, and apologies to your mum, Kay, for making you such a bad guy. She promised me it was OK. Finally, the character of Computer Bob is entirely fictional, but I would like to extend a huge vote of admiration to John, who lives in my mum's retirement village, and who really did set up his computers and treat everyone to a New Year's Eve three hours in advance. John, it won't surprise you to learn, is too modest to have his whole name mentioned.

To my family, my eternal thanks. To my children Ruby and Sonny, who continue to humble and delight me. To my mum, Brenda, and her undimmed curiosity about the world. To my brother, Mat, and his awesome wife, Anissa, and to my Aunty Jan, who has had a tough time of it this year, and faced it with a great deal of bravery.

But also to my sparkling new family of in-laws. I am immensely lucky to have been welcomed into the world of Richard, Salomé, Jo, Matt and Nicola, and, especially, my new nieces and nephew, Mika, Leo and Neni.

And of course the reason for this new family of in-laws is my beautiful wife, Ingrid. Ingrid, thank you for the most wonderful year. Thank you for your love, your wisdom, your brilliance *and* for always knowing how to make the book better. And thank you for everything you have brought into my life, not least the incomparable Liesl the cat. I love you both.

One great sadness is that I was never able to meet Ingrid's father, Wilfried, so I gave him a cameo in this book as my way of introducing myself to him, and of saying thank you. I hope he approves of me.

Finally, I want to make a further, special acknowledgment in this book to everyone who has lost loved ones through dementia, or is living with loved ones experiencing dementia. This book is dedicated to my beloved grandparents, Fred and Jessie Wright, who both found their sharp, brave and funny minds submerged, in different ways, toward the end of their lives. They were in my thoughts as I wrote about Stephen, as were many other people, especially Hazel Buck, mother of the wonderful Lucy Buck, who smiled throughout our Sussex lunch as I was writing *The Last Devil to Die*. To Fred, to Jessie, to Hazel, to Lucy and Didi, and to the millions more, however you are experiencing it, and however you are coping with it, I send you love and strength.

Surprise . . . Bonus Pages

How to Complain, by Joyce Meadowcroft

I always think it pays to have friends with different skills.

I was recently having a spot of bother and I thought you might be interested in how it was all resolved.

A few years ago now, my daughter, Joanna, bought me a subscription to a wine of the month club, which she had no doubt read about somewhere. For a few months it was a very pleasant surprise to receive three bottles of wine—one white, one red and one rosé—each month, but soon they started to stack up. So I began giving them away, and then three more would come, and three more, and three more, until I had to start storing them with my vacuum cleaner.

So, once my vacuum cleaner was fully hemmed in by walls of wine, something had to be done, and I decided to cancel my subscription. This is the story of how that went and, as you will see, it is also a story about how different people use their different skills to get different results. We will begin with my email. The company is called the Wentworth Scott Wine of the Month Club.

Dear Mr. Wentworth or Mr. Scott,

My name is Joyce Meadowcroft and I am a subscriber to your Wine of the
Month club, or, at the least, my daughter subscribed on my behalf, which was
very thoughtful of her. I don't know if you have daughters, but you know how
they can be at times? Though don't get the wrong idea, I do realize I'm very
lucky. A lady here has a daughter who works on a boat in the Caribbean, and
she barely hears from her. I don't think working on a boat would suit me, but
I bet the sunshine is nice.

First, I want to thank you for all the wine, I do appreciate it. I remember
we had a lovely white a few months ago (September?), and I was recently
very pleasantly surprised by a Lebanese. However, and here I'm afraid I
have some bad news, the volume of wine is beginning to prove a little much
for me. It is not that I am not grateful, believe me I am, it's just that there's
only so much my cupboard can take. I know what you will say—Joyce, you
should drink more or Joyce, you should use the wine as gifts—but, believe
me, I have tried both, and the stockpile continues to grow. More than
anything I feel guilty that perhaps there are other people out there who
might enjoy your service more than I do. Which is not to say I don't enjoy
it, I think you do a terrific job, and I don't want you to worry that you are
doing something wrong. It is very much "me," not "you." You should hold
your heads high, not only for the quality of the wine but for the politeness of
your delivery drivers. There was one recently called Malcolm who I would
particularly like to commend. He not only carried the wine into my flat,
but he also fixed my dripping tap when he was here. He had, it turned out,
previously worked in the engineering department at British Telecom before
being made redundant and taking a job in deliveries. And, wouldn't you
know it, he also has a daughter, so we had a good old gossip. Anyway, that's
Malcolm if you know him.

Now here's the difficult part. I'm afraid I have come to the conclusion
that I must cancel my subscription. I hope that won't be a shock after the
paragraph above. I have been on your website, which is very jaunty, but I
was unable to find a way of cancelling. Therefore I am emailing you directly
with the bad news. This is where we find ourselves.

Again, to reiterate, I remain an admirer of Wentworth Scott Wine of the

Month Club, and I know that it must work a treat for many people, but I'm afraid my race is run and I would like to give notice of the cancellation of my subscription. Also, if there is any way we can do this without my daughter, Joanna, finding out, it would be greatly appreciated.

Yours faithfully,
Joyce Meadowcroft (Mrs.)

I was very nervous about sending it, because the last thing I wanted to do was to upset anyone, but sometimes needs must. It was with a great deal of anxiety, then, that I opened their reply, which was sent seconds later.

Dear Joyce Meadowcroft (Mrs.),

Thank you for taking the time to get in touch, and for your support of Wentworth Scott Wine of the Month Club. We love hearing from our customers!

   If there is anything else we can help you with, please don't hesitate to get in touch!

Sincerely,
Callum Davies
Customer Relations

So they seemed to have taken it well, or Callum Davies had, at least, and I presumed the message would be passed upstairs. However, the following Monday I received six bottles of wine rather than my usual three. I suspected it might be Wentworth Scott's thoughtful parting gift, "no hard feelings," but the following month there were six more. So there I was, not even back to square one, but further back than where I'd started. I showed the email above to Elizabeth, Ron and Ibrahim, and each of them took issue with it, so I said I'd like to see you do any better, and Ibrahim said, "Challenge accepted." And so I next sent the following email to Wentworth Scott, this time written by Ibrahim.

Dear sir or madam,

There is a gap, is there not, between those things we need and those things we want? And how readily we mix up the two? We need water, we need shelter, we need, in my view, love, but do we need satellite television? Do we need the latest pop record? And, to get straight to the point of this letter, do we need three—or now seemingly six—bottles of wine delivered to us each month?

We might want them, that I concede. But do we need them?

In my professional opinion (qualifications available on request), we do not. It is thus with a heavy heart that I must cancel my subscription to your Wine of the Month club. I wish you safe travels, and good fortune in all that you do.

Yours sincerely,
Ibrahim Arif
(on behalf of Joyce Meadowcroft [Mrs.])

I didn't have the highest hopes, but Ibrahim was very proud of it and kept saying, "But don't you see, Joyce?" I told him I saw very well. I sent it anyway, and back came the following reply.

Dear Ibrahim Arif (on behalf of Joyce Meadowcroft [Mrs.]),

Thank you for taking the time to get in touch, and for your support of Wentworth Scott Wine of the Month Club. We love hearing from our customers!

If there is anything else we can help you with, please don't hesitate to get in touch!

We are currently running a special promotion for new customers. Please enter the code WINE50 on our order page to receive 50 percent off your wine subscription for the first year.

Sincerely,
Callum Davies
Customer Relations

And so, you'll be ahead of me here, I'm sure—not only have I not been un-subscribed, but Ibrahim has now signed up to the Wentworth Scott Wine of the Month Club too. "The offer is for a limited time only, Joyce," he said.

At this point Ron felt he should take matters in hand. So this next email was from him.

Callum,

Enough is enough, old son. Joycey is a good mate of mine, and you're taking liberties.

Callum, this ain't worth it, boy. Don't do the bosses' dirty work for them. I'll bet good money that Wentworth and Scott are on the golf course, or sunning themselves in Spain, while you're at a desk answering emails on minimum wage. Is that right, Callum? Is that fair? They're profiting from your labor, and the sooner you recognize that, the sooner you can do something about it. Organize, unionize, agitate, tell Wentworth and Scott they can shove their job where the sun don't shine until they start to pay you a living wage.

Don't let the buggers grind you down. If you let them, the bosses will crush you like grapes and get drunk on the wine. Fight, Callum! Fight!

In solidarity,
Ron Ritchie

Now, I don't know about you, but I felt that Ron had been somewhat diverted from the matter of my subscription. Ron was having none of it, however, and in-sisted that "some things are bigger than subscriptions."

Perhaps he is right, but this is the reply that was sent back.

Dear Ron Ritchie,

I'm afraid that your email has been rejected by our system for containing "language not acceptable to the Wentworth Scott group of companies."

Sincerely,
Callum Davies
Customer Relations

Which left only Elizabeth. She had honestly just been waiting to be asked. This email was sent this morning.

Dear Mr. Jonathan Shaw,

I note from Companies House that you are a director of the Aurora BlueJay hedge fund, which is the majority shareholder in Johnson Liberty Subscriptions, which is the owner of a company named Silversmith Jeffrey Holdings, which trades to consumers as the Wentworth Scott Wine Company.

You have seven days to cancel the subscription of Joyce Meadowcroft (Mrs.) to the Wentworth Scott Wine of the Month Club. Beyond that date, legal proceedings will begin. I don't know which consumer law you are breaking by making unsubscription so difficult, but I would place good money that a lawyer would know.

Your obedient servant,
Dame Elizabeth Best

At three this afternoon my doorbell rang, and there was Malcolm with a huge bunch of flowers from Wentworth Scott, and, on checking my bank account, I see I have been reimbursed for the last twelve months of wine purchases. I think we will crack open a bottle of wine to celebrate.

So, as I said, it really does pay to have friends with different skills.